SOMETHING BAD

RICHARD SATTERLIE

Medallion Press, Inc.
Printed in USA

DEDICATION:

For Tricia, Erin, Jake and Alison—my lifeblood.
And to my brothers, David and Bob (Ooglie
Googlie—sorry Bob, had to do it). Finally,
this is for our late parents, who live through us.

Published 2007 by Medallion Press, Inc.

The MEDALLION PRESS LOGO
is a registered tradmark of Medallion Press, Inc.

Copyright © 2007 by Richard Satterlie
Cover Illustration by James Tampa

Typeset in Adobe Caslon Pro

Printed in the United States of America

10 9 8 7 6 5 4 3 2 1
First Edition

ACKNOWLEDGEMENTS:

I thank Tricia for her patience in putting up with me through all of my late night writing fits, and for being my main reader and critic (and main everything else). I also thank Alison—my other main reader, and a devout fan of the genre. Heidi Ernst deserves special mention. It was her strange quote on the screen saver of our laboratory computer that triggered this story, and my high-dive belly-flop into fiction writing. A hearty thank-you goes to Sandy Tritt, a master at turning rough wood into smooth planks. Her tool marks are all over this story.

CHAPTER 1

Boyston, Tri–Counties, 1982

GABE LEANED FORWARD in the confessional and eased the door open a crack. Light from the church flowed into the dark chamber in a narrow slash. He squinted the altar into view. In two years of early morning visits to the All Saints Catholic Church, Father Costello had never been late.

That wasn't the only thing wrong with today. The air carried an abnormal chill for this far into the spring. Gabe had overheard his father talk about it—this growing season had more than its fair share of unexpected thunderstorms and strong, dust-laden winds. And then there were the fogs. They rarely extended more than a mile from the swamp up north, and hardly ever as far as Boyston. But this year, they were enveloping the town two or three times a week. Today's was a doozy.

Gabe squirmed in the confessional, which he jokingly called the inhouse. It was the same size as the outhouse his grandfather had built at their farm. And even though the farmhouse had indoor plumbing, his father had maintained the structure for sentimental reasons—to teach a lesson on appreciation for what one has, his father had often said.

Gabe pushed the door open a little farther, enough to open a crack on the hinge side. Enough to get a view of the massive double front doors of the church. Nothing there either. He let the door slide shut. The hard wooden seat, and the near blackness, would help him think of another sin or two.

He wasn't Catholic but he liked the idea of confessing his sins. The recurring comfort of the lifted burden and the cleansing feeling of official acknowledgement and forgiveness gave him a sense of reverent calm. As he had done so many times, he had left home early to ride his bike to town to confess his week's worth of moral hiccups to Father Costello before heading up the street to join his family at the Lutheran church service.

Their interactions didn't have the formality of the official sacrament. Father Costello was just a good friend. In the confines of the dark confessional, with a screen between him and the good father, twelve year-old Gabe could talk about anything, especially things he was uncomfortable discussing with his real father.

A door slammed and an unrecognized, high-pitched voice brought Gabe out of his search. It came from the back room, behind the altar. He pushed on the door and squinted at the business end of the church.

For an unsettlingly long time, no one appeared, but he could hear the voice, muffled, at a distance.

I could run for it, he thought. But the inhouse was closer to the altar than the front doors, and the huge latch that bolted the doors was hard to throw open in a rush. His mind was made when the door of the back room opened and Father Costello walked out, in full white robe, followed by a small man, only three-quarters of the Father's height. The small man leaned forward as he walked, apparently to counterbalance a half-full gunnysack that was slung over his right shoulder. A red stain wimpled the bottom of the sagging sack.

Gabe slid his butt back on the inhouse seat and closed the door to the narrowest crack that would allow a view of the two men. His breathing echoed in the small, dark space, so he switched to mouth breathing to avoid the occasional nose whistle that sounded an exhalation.

The small man dropped the sack on the first step of the altar and walked to the side of the church, out of Gabe's sight. He reappeared in only a few seconds, carrying a bare metal chair that he unfolded and placed at the front, center of the altar. He motioned to Father Costello, who walked to it, robot-like, and sat, feet together, hands on his thighs.

Gabe leaned closer to the gap. Father Costello's eyes seemed to follow the small man, but they were wide, unblinking, like the eyes of hypnotized people in the old black-and-white television movies.

The small man reached into the sack and pulled out a limp animal. It looked like a dog. He placed it on the top step, to Father's right, and fished his arm into the sack again. Over the next minute, he pulled two more animals from the bag. One was definitely a cat. Then, he brought the sack to the center of the altar, right in front of Father Costello, and reached in. The bottom of the sack went limp when the object was lifted.

Gabe's forehead pressed into the door as he strained to see, but his visual angle, and the railing of the first row of pews, prevented a clear view. Whatever kind of animal it was, it didn't have fur. He was sure of that. The brief glimpse he got was of an animal about the size of a small dog, but with grayish-pink, wrinkly skin. Once it was set down, all he could see through the wrought iron railing was the tip of one of its appendages. He stopped down his eyes with an exaggerated squint, but the image still blurred.

An idea struck—a trick from school that allowed a better focus at a distance. He pinched the tips of his two thumbs and two forefingers together into a square and peered through the pinhole created by the space between the tips of the four digits. The view of the altar sharpened, but it didn't help. The obstructions still prevented a full view. He pushed the door open a little more with his forehead and looked through his fingertips again. A little more came into focus. He pushed farther. When the image cleared, an involuntary breath sucked his lungs full. His back hit the rear wall of the inhouse just as the slit of light narrowed and extinguished. Knees to his chest, he strained for his next breath. He thought he saw toes.

Gabe's mind swirled, accompanied by a dizziness

that nearly turned the feeble light that seeped around the edges of the inhouse door to pitch black. When the sensation passed, he leaned forward for another peek.

This time, his vision was tuned to an acuity that was almost painful, as if vision were his only fully functional external sense. It was silent in the church, and there were no smells.

In the close quarters of the inhouse, Gabe's internal world was anything but quiet. The lub-dup of each heartbeat reverberated as if branches of his heart extended to every part of his body. And the tensile stretch of his lungs, on each inhalation, felt like the rasp of wood dragged across cement, until it gave way to a twang of elastic recoil and an exhalation. In the darkness, he was keenly aware of the position of his own body parts—every joint spoke to him of its position—and he knew if he moved one, it would scream its swing.

He inched the door outward to enlarge the crack and gasped again.

Father Costello sat perfectly still on the bare metal folding chair. All around him were animal parts and blood. The pieces were so small, and so carefully carved, it was impossible to tell what they had been in life. Gabe saw they half surrounded the priest in an arc that ran from one end of the altar to the other, and that they were being purposely arranged, as if to highlight the altar, or to degrade it.

Gabe's eyes flicked to the artist, who was engrossed in his work on the carpeted canvas. The strange looking little man didn't change his evil grin as he went about his task. Precise and efficient at his craft, no blood seemed to spill beyond where he wanted it to go. The knife he wielded appeared sharp enough to cut through bone without perceptible resistance, and it cut so swiftly blood flowed from its cuts without the slightest splatter, forming enlarging, smooth-edged pools. Everything was rounded—the pieces of flesh, the pools of blood, the semicircular arrangement of parts around the altar. Just like the features of the little man, there were no sharp edges.

Gabe was mesmerized by the developing masterpiece. And by the way the little man carefully placed each new severance and then paused to scan the altar, as if he were gaining a wide perspective on his artwork.

Gabe pinched himself. The pain was real. Blood flowed from each of the little man's cuts—it was real. This wasn't a dream.

When Gabe regained his focus, the little man was at the far side of the altar. With a stiff-necked spin, the man shuffled up to Father Costello, his evil grin unchanging, like a painted on clown face. A small voice echoed, the only sound in the cavernous church.

"You don't want to miss this part." The man's lips barely moved when he spoke. "I've saved the best for last."

Father Costello didn't react. Not even an eye blink.

"That's right, Father. You look right here. You think you've defeated me? I can assure you that I always take the game in the end."

The man lifted a gold communion chalice toward Father Costello.

"This is HER blood, shed for me because of your sins."

He extended both of his arms, so his small body formed a cross, with the chalice still gripped in his right hand. A loud "Ha" sound reverberated in Gabe's ears, and the chalice flew from the man's still hand. It impacted the Father's chest with a dull thud, spilling its crimson contents down the front of his white robe and up onto his neck and face.

Gabe's eyes widened and the scene blurred, then came back into sharp focus. Droplets of blood fell to the carpet in slow motion. One drop suspended from the priest's chin for an agonizing instant, gaining volume, before releasing, then splattering onto the lap of his satin robe.

The little man stepped forward and picked up the chalice and turned it in his grip, inspecting it from every angle. "Now, for the final touch to my masterpiece."

Gabe wanted to look away. To curl up in the corner of the inhouse and turn his mind to another time and place. But it wouldn't turn. He felt the same sense of perverse curiosity that captured him a year ago when he had witnessed a head-on collision on State Route 27. A passenger in one of the cars went through the windshield, all the way to his ankles, and his leaking, lifeless body colored the white hood with streaks of maroon, like painted-on flames of a hot rod, but going in the wrong direction. He had felt sickened then, but he couldn't look away.

Gabe's eyes flicked to the animal pieces and their

surrounding pools. The blood that spilled on the royal blue carpet drew the red and blue hues to a neutral, dull gray. But the blood that adorned the white, satin robe of the priest emitted a metallic sheen that resonated to an intensity that was hard to look at straight on. His eyes returned to the primary actor in this gruesome play.

The little man reached down and pulled Father Costello's left hand from its resting place on the father's thigh, and turned it palm up. He placed the stem of the chalice across the palm and pushed the father's fingers closed around it, then gently lowered the hand back to the thigh. When the little man stepped back, Father Costello's grip on the chalice had a slight tremor, like he was straining, strangling it.

"You're ready, now," the man said. He pivoted and ambled toward the front doors of the church. "I'd like to stay and watch the show, but my services are needed elsewhere. I hope to see you again, later rather than sooner." The church doors unlatched with a dull metallic clunk.

Gabe jumped. Nudging the inhouse door, he peered toward the front doors. Pressing his head a little closer to the hinge-side crack, so his forehead was against the door, he strained to expand his field of view.

Something hard smacked against the door and slammed it shut. Gabe screamed. His head ricocheted off the sidewall, and then the back wall of the confessional, and he slumped to the floor with a loud thud. His head spun and a stinging sensation crept up his back.

The door of the cubicle swung wide open, and the invading light lent more confusion to his sensory world. Both hands extended toward the light—he tried to shade his eyes and fend off the blurred image at the same time. He squinted between his spread fingers. A small, round head hovered above him. It was backlit with the harsh light of the church, but he made out high arching eyebrows and a strange, tight-lipped grin. And the scars. Both corners of the mouth had thick scars that turned upward, forcing the face into the wicked smile. But the rest of the face didn't smile. The eyes were black with anger. Or evil.

Gabe pulled his knees up to his chest and folded his arms over his head and face. And prayed.

A high-pitched voice came from above, with a Yankee accent. "You'll forget what you saw today if you know what's good for you."

The spin of Gabe's world accelerated and then went dark.

He didn't know how long he'd been out, but it was dark again in the inhouse. The church was still. Too still. Then, a commotion registered, muted, off in the distance, as if filtered to a cacophony of unrecognizable frequencies. He peeked through the door crack, at Father Costello, who sat paralyzed, eyes wide. This time, the scene was surreal.

The sun had broken the sills of the east windows, casting multi-colored beams across the altar through stained glass images of saints, who stood glaring in disgust. Faint noises of a gathering congregation filtered through the windows and closed doors of the church. Gabe wanted to run, but he didn't dare.

The din increased with each passing second, and he imagined the impatient group, awaiting the traditional and symbolic opening of the church doors. A doorknob turned, and a muffled voice echoed. "It's unlocked."

The doors of the church opened wide and a slow wave of horrified gasps swept into the church. Gabe shifted to the other side of the door. The morning glare from the doorway spilled a V-shaped beam across the altar, spotlighting the little man's artwork, and Father Costello's frozen body.

Back to the hinge side of the door. People flowed in, moving along the walls, avoiding direct movements toward the altar. Within minutes, the group framed the back and two sidewalls of the church.

When the influx of the now-hushed group slowed, a man's voice boomed in the cavernous room. "Father Costello?"

Gabe lunged back to the other crack just as Father Costello's paralysis lifted. The chalice fell to the floor with a muted bell ring as he stood on wobbly legs. Without saying a word, he pivoted and hurried into the back room. The back door of the church slammed.

Gabe slid back on the inhouse seat and the door bounced to a rest. A moment later, bright light flooded the inhouse again. He lifted his arms against the luminescence and flailed, trying to fend off something he vaguely remembered as threatening. He wasn't quite sure what it was. There were voices, different voices, seemingly off in the distance.

"There's someone in here." A deep one.

"It's a boy." A little higher in tone.

"Who is it?" A woman's voice?

He flailed his arms as hands touched him, pulled him from his sanctuary, lifted him up, and placed him on a hard wooden pew. He curled into a fetal position and crossed his hands over his head and face. And more voices aimed at him.

"Is he all right?"

"What happened here?"

"Did you see anything?"

"Who is it?"

In answer to his prayers, the room went black again.

<u>CHAPTER</u> 2.

GABE DIDN'T KNOW what was worse, his last hangover or going to Mac McKenna's general store in the late afternoon. It took two days to get over the first, and today, he couldn't avoid the second. He knew John Johnson would be holding court on the store porch, and he didn't relish the prospect of walking through the thick air that always formed between him and John.

Two of the three members of John's crew were there with him. Billy Smyth sat hunched in his mechanic's jumpsuit, splotched with the grease of trucks, tractors, and assorted farm machinery. In contrast, Press Cunningham's pristine overalls bore no evidence of his farm ownership. John stood over the other two, his flannel shirt rolled up to show huge forearms, the left bearing the words, "Semper Fi" in the faded blue of a Viet Nam era tatoo.

Gabe parked to the side opposite "John's" bench and tried his best to hurry into the store with a nod.

Billy Smyth leaned forward and swiveled on the bench. He flipped his head to the left sending a cascade of straight blond hair toward his ear. It fell back over his left eye. "Gabe. Where you going in such a hurry? Come and sit awhile. John was just telling us about—"

"Billy." John's booming voice vibrated the corrugated metal roof over the porch. The crimson flush of John's face extended to the top of his bald head, highlighted by the horseshoe of grey-silver hair that connected his ears.

Gabe rolled his eyes. Not another one of John's schemes.

"Come and sit," Press Cunningham said. "Maybe you can get John off his high horse."

John scowled at Press.

Gabe suppressed a chuckle. He loved to watch Press mess with John. Of John's three cohorts—Billy, Press, and Mac McKenna—Press was the only one John didn't try to bully, and Gabe enjoyed it more than Press did.

It wasn't a secret why John left Press alone. John's full name was John J. Johnson, and only one person outside of John's family knew what the "J" stood for. That was Press.

Gabe shook his head. Secrets were like a narcotic to residents of the Tri-counties. The lifespan of most was short as the locals had snooping and prying down to a science. But none was as long-lived and protected as John's middle name. John became furious whenever it was mentioned, and Press resisted all attempts to draw out the information.

Gabe thought of how he loved the way life played out in the Tri-counties. It was predictable, but with its share of local intrigue. There was order and understanding, with few surprises. It was no wonder he felt so comfortable here.

Gabe's mind came back to the porch. "I can't hang around. I only have a few minutes." He remained standing. "What's up?"

Press smoothed the bib on his overalls. They always looked like they were dry cleaned instead of washed and hung out. "You have to hear John's latest," Press said. Like John, he was in his mid-fifties, but his clothing hung on him the same as in his youth when he earned the nickname, "No-ass Cunningham."

"Shut up, Press," John said.

Gabe rolled his eyes again. He didn't want to hear John's latest, or earliest, or middle for that matter. It was bad enough he horned in on their card games, but every time Billy or Press started to tell a good story that involved John, John would shut them up.

Press blew a noisy exhalation and looked up at Gabe. "Heard you had quite a time after the game."

Gabe smiled. He didn't want to open up the conversation to John's ridicule. "Did just fine. Had a bit of a headache, though."

"You hear about Horace Murtry?" Billy said.

"Shut . . . up," John said.

Gabe bounded two steps closer. "No. What

happened?"

Billy looked at John and slumped against the bench back.

"Disappeared again, for two days," Press said. "The way I heard it, he came back smelling like whiskey and women's perfume, and I ain't talking about the store bought kind of either."

John stood up and stomped to the edge of the porch, then turned to face Press. He bobbed his head downward and clenched his fists.

Gabe's mind accelerated. What was Horace up to? Another of his schemes to frustrate his wife? He shook his head and scanned the group. "Is Miz Murtry doing anything about it?"

"No." John said. He took a step closer to the bench and positioned himself between Press and Gabe.

The roar of an engine increased in pitch at a rate that suggested an unusual speed for Main Street, and all four men turned their heads to watch a U-Haul whip by. It stirred up a small cloud of the same dust that had been stirring and settling in the town of Boyston for decades.

Billy started to say something but John held his hand up in front of Billy's face in a stop motion. "Go get Mac," John said.

No one moved.

The U-Haul turned left at the four-way without stopping, circled behind the church, and skidded to a stop in front of the rectory. All four men turned to face the truck, without a word.

The doors of the U-Haul opened to reveal two of the

most mismatched individuals imaginable, even for these parts. What should have been a cacophony of speculative "betchas" was replaced with total silence. Gabe's eyes flicked back and forth between the two men.

The driver was about the largest human Gabe had ever seen. His arms were as big as the thighs of a normal man, and they were decorated with a series of tattoos that stretched from shoulder to elbow, showing more faded blue decoration than normal skin tone. He wasn't a young man and his barrel chest gave way to a midsection that was well on its way to dominating his shadow at high noon. He arched his back and stretched his arms skyward, turning his head toward the general store. To Gabe, his nose appeared to be missing its cartilage, like he had been a sparring partner for a series of heavyweight contenders over the past couple of decades. His dirty white tank top was tucked into faded jeans that fell significantly short of the top of well-worn steel-toed work boots.

The giant lumbered to the back of the truck, bringing his passenger into unobstructed view. Only about five feet tall, Gabe thought. Probably weighs in double figures fully clothed.

The man was dressed in a dark gray, three-piece suit over a silver turtleneck that seemed to reflect the sun, even when he was standing in the shade. In contrast to the lumbering walk of the giant, the passenger took small steps that barely placed the heel of one foot ahead of the toe of the other. To Gabe, it looked like he adjusted his gait like he was consciously trying to avoid stepping on sidewalk cracks and concrete spacers.

The passenger ascended the four steps of the rectory porch, bringing both feet to each step before navigating the next. He disappeared through the double doors as the driver raised the sliding door on the back of the truck.

An ache tugged at Gabe's belly. It was weak, but it was there, and it appeared to be building, rising.

The giant man jockeyed a large wooden crate to the edge of the truck bed. The U-Haul was the smallest one available, and the box took up nearly the entire back of the truck. Its apparent weight made Gabe take a silent wager that it was highly unlikely the two men could lower the box out of the truck, much less carry it up the stairs into the rectory. As the giant inched the box to a tilting balance point part way over the edge of the truck bed, the passenger appeared from the doors of the building.

The giant grunted and strained against the box in a futile effort to lift the protruding edge, and Gabe counted the proceeds of his imaginary bet.

Billy Smyth uttered the only words that came from the general store porch over the next minute or so. "I betcha—" was interrupted by a jerky movement of the small man; his hands clenched into tiny fists, his elbows bent slightly, and his torso curled forward. The box appeared to lighten so the giant could easily lift it out of the truck. It looked like the only problem facing the giant now was the awkwardness of the box's size.

Gabe bent forward slightly as a stomach cramp shot through to his backbone.

The giant maneuvered the box like it was made

of styrofoam, first up onto the sidewalk and then up the rectory steps. The whole time, the small man remained at the top of the steps and kept his wide-eyed gaze on the ungripped end of the box. He turned his whole body rather than his neck as it was moved toward him. The little man walked backwards ahead of the box, through the rectory doors, never changing his unique posture.

"You see that?" Billy said. No one answered.

The beginnings of another contraction grumbled through Gabe's midsection, so he shifted his weight and took a deep breath. He wanted to go into the store. Tending to his business would dull the cramps, but he couldn't move. He needed to see what happened next.

John turned to say something, but he spun back around when Billy flicked his eyes back to the rectory. The two strangers emerged from the doors and stopped on the porch. The small man presented the large man with a white envelope, and the giant turned on his heels and jogged to the U-Haul. He sped away like he wanted to put a great deal of distance between him and his employer as quickly as possible.

The little man moved back toward the rectory doors, but suddenly spun around, stiff-necked, to face the general store.

Gabe felt the little man's eyes burn into his, and his stomach let loose with a powerful pain that nearly doubled him over. Hair raised on his arms. He felt like he was looking through a telescope, with a fix on the man—nothing in the periphery of his vision. His knees went weak. The little man had high-arching eyebrows and a mouth guarded by narrow lips that were straight for most of their length. The corners of his mouth appeared to turn in upward arcs, ninety degrees, giving the mouth a strange grin. But the upward turns didn't look the same as the lips. His eyes were dark, cold looking, as if there were no irises, only pupils.

A shock of panic hit Gabe from head-to-toe all at once. He wanted to drop on the ground and curl up into a ball. His heart produced an extra beat, then another, and his throat felt thick, full. Lightheadedness darkened his peripheral vision. No way this should be happening here, in his comfort zone.

As quickly as the little man made the long-distance visual acquaintance, he terminated the greeting with a pivot, again with stiff neck, and short-stepped back into the rectory.

Someone spoke, but Gabe didn't focus on it. His mind was closing down. Something in its deep recesses tried to warn him that the little man was familiar, and evil, but that was as far as it went. Gabe had no active recollection of the man, yet connections were coming, each with a wrong-number hang-up. He resisted the urge to drop to the floor, and hunched slightly to get control of his heart. The words came out of his mouth involuntarily, but loud, interrupting John in mid-sentence.

"Something bad."

"What?" Billy said.

Gabe blinked three times and focused on the three men. "Huh?"

"You said, 'Something bad,'" John said. "You know that man?"

"No, I don't think so," Gabe said. "Must have been day dreaming. I have to go now. See you later." Gabe turned and headed for his pickup.

"Thought you had to do some shopping," John said.

Gabe didn't react. A command echoed in his head, its source unknown. "You'll forget what you saw today if you know what's good for you." But who had said it? Did it have to do with the little man in the rectory? Was it a clue to his missing years? He had to find out. Even though his instinct screamed for him to run.

CHAPTER 3

Lake Oswald, Jefferson County, Two weeks later

A BRIGHT STREAM of crimson light shot through his closed eyelids and heated the pain in his head. Gabe curled tighter, into a ball. He crossed his arms over his head, bringing his hands over his eyes, but the pain wouldn't go away. It throbbed with his pulse, way too fast. He turned slightly, and the surface gave with his weight. He was in a space that was small, confined—he felt something solid with his feet and with the top of his head. He knew his left side was on some kind of soft floor, and his back against a soft wall. Then, he felt the cold. A shiver started in his back and diverged into two waves; one ran down his legs and the other up his torso. The violence of the first wave pulled his hands away from his eyes and he closed them tight to keep the light from getting through. The pulsing pain in his head crashed like cymbals with the effort. It felt like his head was expanding and contracting with each heartbeat. He turned away from the light.

His right arm hit something hard. Or, was it the left? With his arms crossed and the pain in his head, he had trouble telling. But whatever arm it was, it hit something hard. He pushed his back against the wall and pulled into a tighter ball. Both arms hit. It was solid, immovable, and right in front of his head.

He was always safe when he curled up. He could roll up his mind into a tight ball, just like his body, and let it go black. But now, the light pulled at him, unfolding his mind from its dark cocoon. And the light carried something hard, closing in on his head. He had to do something. He had to get away.

Gabe pushed his hands outward at the hard object, and his legs involuntarily kicked. The force pushed his head against the opposite wall hard, amplifying the pulsing pain. He struck, then grabbed the hard object, and twisted, trying to move it away. It turned slightly with his push.

Light flooded his eyes and his mind let it in. The blurred image showed a horizon, removed from his immediate view by a tall ledge. His focus moved from the light to the ledge, and to a large, round dial with numbers in a circle. Closer in, a large ring projected from the ledge.

Gabe's mind was slow to put the images together through the pain, but the initial sensation was of familiarity. Friendly familiarity. He shifted his eyes downward toward his feet and a bright beam of orange cut through the horizon directly into his eyes. He cringed, eyes shut, and felt the give of the wall against his head. His unfolding mind was making connections now, and his anticipation turned the pain loose again. He was . . . in his truck. He was curled up on the seat of his truck.

The connections were now outpacing the pain pulses. He was in his truck. Last night was card night. He was in the front seat of his truck sleeping off the Jack Daniel's from his bi-weekly card game. Maybe if he drank more frequently the alcohol wouldn't have such an effect. His stomach growled in agreement. Then, another sensation elbowed its way in. He had to pee.

He reached for the top of the steering wheel and pulled himself up on the seat. The long, angled gear-shift poked into his side. He looked down at the floorboard, at the rubber bellows that hid the entry of the gearshift into the floor, and smiled. The original leather casing disintegrated years ago. But two years back, when he was junking an old washing machine, he noticed the rubber bellows sealing the washer's transmission shaft against the outer water tub. It fit perfectly on the gearbox of his truck and solved his annoyance of seeing daylight through the floorboard.

His smile faded. The stretch of the bellows was severe left, down. "I left it in reverse?" Gabe said out loud. "I always leave it in first." No wonder it's poking me, he thought.

He shifted his weight so he could raise his head over the dashboard and supported himself with a straight left arm. He rubbed his right eye, then his left with his right fist, and waited until the blazing after-images faded. He squinted at the morning, forgetting about his pounding head.

"What the hell?" He fell into a fetal ball on the truck seat so fast the last word came from beneath his arms, which were crossed over his face and head. His knees bumped against the gearshift and the steering wheel brushed his right ear.

It's a lake, he thought. I'm right on the edge of a lake. He relaxed his body a little. "Which one?" he said out loud.

He pulled himself back up by the steering wheel and squinted to his left, following the bank of the lake off in the distance. His head started to pulse again. He gripped the steering wheel with both hands, so tight his knuckles went white, and flicked his gaze to the right. He followed the lakeshore into the distance. Looked left again.

"God damn it." He collapsed back into the seat, in a ball again, and his body shook with the violence of an electric shock. Eyes wide, he stared at the metallic shine of the clutch pedal. He could feel his heartbeat again, each beat a piercing streak of pain that shot through his head, and his worry came to life. An extra large beat, too soon, then a pause. He felt the tingling of sweat beading on his skin and the drifting feeling of slipping toward darkness. He was about to enter a spinning whirlpool, pulling him into its light-less vortex.

"Come on," he said out loud. The beat came back, fast. Then, another extra beat. Two, three in a row.

It felt like his heart was in his throat. Then the long pause.

"Come on, damn it."

He knew what he had to do. He wasn't having a heart attack. He just had to slow his breathing. Think about something pleasant. Take control. Focus on the clutch. It's been slipping a little lately. Maybe the cable is going.

The lake pushed the clutch aside.

"Not in the Tri-counties," he said. "But where?"

Another extra beat.

"Something bad always happens." He patted his right knee.

Gabe's mind flew back over the past twenty-five years. That was the boundary of his memory. One recollection was etched deep. It was the one time he had left the Tri-counties. In all that time. One time on a hunting trip, and what happened? Tripped on a log and put out the knee. Gun went off, right into poor old Rumford. One time out of the Tri-counties and I get a limp for life and lose my best hunting dog.

"Something bad," he said out loud.

The memory slowed his pulse and turned his mind on his predicament.

"Got to think about his. Which way back home?"

His mind began its usual spiral toward a solution. His spiral was quick. One of the quickest in the Tri-counties, he thought, although he would never say so to anyone.

"Reverse," he said, loud. "Must have gone too far. Had to put it in quick."

He sat upright in the seat and peered over the hood. His mind was in control of his heart now. He was figuring. There was no land between the hood and the water.

"Must be at the edge."

He opened the driver-side door and leaned out, but not too far. The front tire was three, maybe four feet from the water's edge, but a wheel rut led into the water. Actually, two ruts went into the water, but they were partly overlapped. He slammed the door shut. The need to pee was back. He'd have to get out to do that. An extra beat and a pause.

He turned to look out the back window. If only he could see something familiar in the distance. He could hold the pee for a little while longer.

The truck was pulled off a paved road, on a gravel and sand turnout. He had an idea. Hopefully it wasn't a well-used beach. He turned around and kneeled on the seat and put his face close to the glass of the rear window. The pulsing in his head was regular, but it was matched by a similar pulsing in his bladder. He looked left and then right, and then swung his head left. There they were. Tracks in the sand bent off to the left. He had come from the left.

He swung around in the seat and pushed his legs toward the pedals. The gearshift found his abdomen and the pulsing in his bladder turned to pain.

"Got to go now." He scanned to the right and left. The closest bushes were to the right, but a good twenty-five yards away. He slumped.

"Something bad."

An extra beat, then another left a long pause, and he felt the beginnings of light-headedness.

"Control," he said. "Got to do it."

He slid over to the passenger side, threading his legs past the gearshift, and cranked at the window lever. "Better do it on this side. Some will probably get on the running board." He opened the door and let it fly, relaxing into a regular heartbeat. It felt like he was draining fluid all the way from his shoulders.

The clutch was a stiff one. Good thing it's my good leg, he thought. He hoped the starter button would do its job. A quick push and the engine snarled at the water. It was already in reverse, but the truck had to be eased back. The lake sand was loose and deep in these parts. At least it was in the Tri-counties. He let the clutch out a little fast, but the truck responded with movement so he stayed on the gas and swung the truck around, facing his tracks. Instead of first gear, he went down to second. It was a four-speed with a close first-to-second ratio, and in snow or other loose footing it was better to start in a higher gear to keep from spinning the tires. The engine lugged a little, but the tires gripped, and he forgot to look back to the right before the front tires found pavement. Fortunately, the road was deserted.

Gabe leaned back into the seat. He was headed back. Then his mind spiraled. Headed back where? To the Tri-counties? To somewhere else? Where would the road lead?

An extra beat. And a pause.

Gabe scanned the horizon through the windshield. Nothing familiar. If he had turned even once on the way to the lake, he'd be in trouble. He tried to wring a clue from his situation. When he had been lying on the front seat back at the lake, the sun had reflected into his face in the passenger-side rear view mirror. He must have been facing west. Then he turned around and faced the sun, and turned left onto the road. Going north. Now, the direction of the sun told him he was heading northwest. To where? There weren't any familiar landmarks. He could be going away from the Tri-counties just as easily as he could be going toward them.

His heart gave an extra beat, then the pause. He tried to think of something else, but the extra beats came one after another, fast. It felt like his heart was in his throat again. His head went light. He gripped the steering wheel hard and took a huge inward breath. The thumping continued, irregular, and he was beginning to lose the light at the periphery of his vision. He slumped in his seat and sealed his mouth and nose. Valsalva's Maneuver, Doc called it. Contract the stomach muscles and hold the breath in. Just like you're taking a dump, he thought. Just like Doc said. It increased pressure in his chest, as it was supposed to, but it made him feel even more light-headed. He held it as long as he could and then released, and his heartbeat came back, fast. And regular. His vision cleared and he scanned the horizon again.

"Got to find something familiar—fast." He leaned forward until his chest was nearly against the steering wheel.

Nothing registered as familiar and he felt the pressure building in his chest again. Just need to see something from the Tri-counties and everything will be okay, he thought.

A sign grabbed his attention—"Speed Limit 55." He hated speed limit signs. Who came up with these numbers? They seldom represented what was safe. He knew what was safe, and for this road it wasn't fifty-five. Not even close. He looked down at the speedometer and the needle pointed directly where he wanted it.

He wasn't one to resort to vandalism to make a point, although he was tempted to run the speed limit signs down every time he saw them. One of his greatest joys was to see a sign peppered with buckshot. Each time, he imagined himself with the warm wooden stock of his 12-gauge pressed against his cheek and shoulder. He squeezed the trigger between breaths and grinned. Pellets flew from the barrel in slow motion, spreading as they approached the sign. The shot produced a staccato chord as the lead beads punched holes in the two fives of the sign.

He looked down again. "That's a safe speed," he said out loud. "Forty-five. No one needs to go faster than that. Not around here." His mind wasn't done, so it spun off leaving his reactions on autopilot.

A little over two minutes, he thought. If someone drives ten miles at fifty-five, he only saves a little more than two minutes over someone driving forty-five. Was two minutes worth the extra risk?

"Never," he said. "Stupid thing to do. Risk your life for two minutes."

A car whizzed past to his left. It slid back into the right lane without a signal and shrunk as it ran away from Gabe's old pickup. He shook his head. Something bad can happen when you drive that fast. The speeder would find out, sooner or later.

Gabe gave the steering wheel an affectionate pat. "You always get me there safe."

His truck qualified for an "Historic Vehicle" license plate, but he didn't want one. It wasn't a glorified relic. It was a co-worker and a good friend. It listened to his problems without judgment, and on more than one occasion it got him out of a bind. Just like today, he hoped. He patted the steering wheel again.

When he scanned the horizon, Gabe realized that the distractions had returned his heart into a regular rhythm.

"See?" he said. "Control. Just don't think about it."

His mind started to slip back into apprehension when something familiar flashed in his peripheral vision. He pulled his foot from the gas pedal and touched the brake, but he didn't apply pressure. Off in the distance, to the left side of the windshield, he saw them. His foot went back on the gas.

The two silos of Wes Worthing's farm were visible from most parts of two of the three counties that made up the Tri-counties. The silos were huge—at least twice the size of everyone else's. Some said he didn't need them that big. That he was just showing off. But Gabe knew better of his good friend. Wes had the largest farm in the area, and a huge crowd of livestock. His silos were large for a purpose. He was one of the few farmers in the area who didn't face the pressure of debt when the crop prices fell. His farm was the model of efficiency, and the silos were part of that.

"Just jealous." Gabe smiled. "They'd never say anything to Wes' face."

Wes was six-feet five, and his skin was the color of the rich soil he farmed. He was the voice of reason in an area of small minds, so he was on his fourth consecutive term as Chairman of the Corporation of the Tri-counties. Gabe was glad to have Wes as a friend since their minds usually ran in parallel. He was glad for another reason. Because of Wes, he could get shoes. They both wore size fifteen shoes, and with two customers with like needs, Mac McKenna kept at least one pair of fifteens in stock in his General Store in Boyston. Otherwise, Gabe would have to leave the Tri-counties to get shoes. No. He would do without until someone else was going. He sent a silent thank-you to Wes.

Gabe wanted to push on the gas pedal, to speed up across the county line, but his eyes locked on the "45" of the speedometer. The needle stayed right there. He eased back in his seat. It was the first time his back had rested fully on the fabric of the seat covers for miles. He knew what he needed now—what he always needed the morning after a card game. Scrambled eggs and aspirin powders. And he needed to see

Miz Murtry.

Gabe passed up the county road that looped around to his farm and stayed on State Route 27 as it approached the border of Herndon and Boyston Counties. He squinted at the Herndon's Edge Café, which straddled the line, and counted the cars in the parking lot. Two cars. A white Olds Dynamic 88, around 1965, had mud caked on the side panels giving it a two-tone appearance from a distance. The pickup was a newer model Ford, early eighties, with a badly dented tailgate.

He looked for the Volkswagen. The one that had the rear engine cover held in place with baling wire. The one in which the interior headliner was detached, hanging down across the back window to render the rear view mirror useless. It wasn't there.

He thought about going home when an abdominal growl brought his stomach and head pain back into his consciousness.

He swung the pickup between the two cars and ambled to the door, trying to decide which was worse, the pounding pain in his head or his dizziness.

When he entered, the blast of the space heater caught him off guard. The swirling in his head intensified and the churn of his stomach nearly made him retch. He bypassed his usual stool at the bar and settled at the far end of the counter, as far from the straining heater as he could get.

"Hey, Gabe. Why you sitting over there?"

Gabe looked up at Teddy Rosewald's smiling face.

"Your stool messed up or you still drunk?" Teddy

said. "You really went after it last night. I was worried about you."

Gabe forced a smile. He owed Teddy a smile. Teddy was a friend of the caliber of Wes Worthing, and the main reason Gabe still attended the card games.

"I was going to grab your keys, but you drove off before I was done taking a leak," Teddy said. "You know you can always sleep it off with us."

Gabe's smile turned timorous. For all of his harping on speed limits and safety, he didn't think twice about driving after drinking. Maybe it was the hour—all roads were nearly deserted after midnight. Maybe it was a false sense of control, or a need to prove his control in his safe universe. More likely, it was one of those inconsistencies of character that come out in extreme circumstances.

"Where'd you end up?" Teddy said. "Sleep in the truck again? You still have the same clothes on."

"Yeah. Better get me some aspirin right away. My head's about to split in two."

Teddy leaned over the half-wall that separated the counter area from the kitchen and tossed a bottle of aspirin to Gabe. "Pour your own," he said. "Scrambled?"

Gabe nodded and rounded the counter. He filled a glass with water and headed back to his seat. Movement caught his eye from the opposite end of the bar. He should have recognized the Olds, but his mind was focused on his own problems. Horace Murtry was hunched over a cup of coffee, muttering to himself. The only word Gabe could recognize was "damn." It seemed to come out every two or three words.

Gabe downed three aspirin with a huge swig of water and looked down the counter. He thought about how much he hated Horace Murtry. It wasn't the kind of hate that produced daydreams of physical harm, or worse. It was a resentful kind of hate. He resented the fact that Horace and Miz Murtry were married. Horace didn't deserve her, and she deserved much better. He resented Horace for how he treated Miz Murtry. On the best days, Horace was indifferent towards her. And he resented how Horace seemed to revel in her dedicated attempts to make their marriage work.

Teddy slid a plate onto the counter and Gabe swung his stare from Horace up to Teddy.

"Don't get worked up about him again," Teddy said. "He's not worth it."

"Where's Miz Murtry?"

Teddy stiff-armed the bar with his right hand. "Called in. Said she would be a little late." Teddy pushed off from the bar and rounded the half-wall and started working on a new batch of biscuits. "Said she had some big news to share," he said loud enough for Horace to hear.

Gabe glanced at Horace, who remained hunched over his coffee mug.

Maybe she's dumping him, Gabe thought. Maybe she's churning up the courage to tell him to get out. For the first time, the pain in his head receded a little.

He was halfway through his eggs when the door of the Edge slammed open, then shut, jingling the entry bell on each pass. He swung around on the stool and smiled. Even though her name tag said "Deena Lee," he couldn't bring himself to call her anything but Miz Murtry.

Deena Lee sauntered to the bar with exaggerated strides. When she rounded the counter, Gabe noticed her pursed smile—her raspberry lipstick had already run into the creases around her mouth.

Deena Lee grabbed her apron and tied it around her waist. "Better get this thing on while it still fits," she said, looking in Teddy's direction.

Teddy chuckled as beads of sweat formed on his forehead and threatened to add their own unique flavor to the biscuits.

Deena Lee kept the smile as she slid to the far end of the counter where Horace still stared at his mug.

"How you doing this morning, Daddy?" Her smile widened, allowing her crooked teeth to peek through.

Horace grunted, as if she had interrupted an ongoing conversation between stimulant and patron.

Gabe stared, expecting a revelation.

Deena Lee pouted a little, leaned over the counter, and craned her neck to put her face between Horace and his coffee.

"Do you love me, Horace?"

Horace rolled his eyes and sighed. "What the hell's this about, Deena Lee? Did you back your car up into the pole at the gas station again? Jesus Christ, woman, if I said it once, I—"

Deena Lee placed her hand up to Horace's mouth and shook her head.

"Darling, you're going to be a daddy."

Horace's mouth dropped open. His eyes followed Deena Lee as she turned to face the two other patrons in the Edge.

"That's right, folks. Me and Horace are going to be parents."

Gabe did a double take. He wasn't as shocked by the news as he was by the smile on Deena Lee's face. It was a genuine smile—happy, excited. He hoped it would be more devious, portending a plot to keep a troubled marriage alive. He knew a baby was seldom a cure for a sick relationship. But her smile didn't tell that story. She was giddy, beaming. He slumped on his stool. His head throbbed.

Horace stood over his stool and gave a half-smile to Deena Lee. "I best go tell all the boys at work." He grabbed his jacket and keys with one sweep of his left hand and hurried out the door.

Gabe turned on his stool and watched Horace disappear through the door and into the dense fog. He wondered when the fog had rolled in. It pressed the light down by about half, and yet he hadn't noticed it until now. Through the gray mist he heard tires throw loose gravel and then bite pavement with a screech. He spun around toward Deena Lee. She was facing away from the counter, washing glasses that were already clean. He didn't know what to say.

After a long fifteen seconds, Gabe pushed himself up from the stool and placed a couple of bills under his plate, which still held half of the eggs. He turned. You have to congratulate her, he thought. She's not the one you hate. Don't take it out on her. He turned back to the counter.

"Congratulations, Miz Murtry."

Deena Lee kept washing the glasses. "Thank you, Gabe. You get enough to eat?"

"Yes, ma'am. Not very hungry this morning."

"Me either."

Gabe closed the door to the Edge and squinted at the bright morning sun. He stopped and scanned the horizon. There was no sign of the fog that had enveloped the diner minutes earlier. Despite the warm light, he shivered. Something in his distant memory told him to beware of the fog. Two words kept coming to him—they invaded his vocabulary whenever he felt a twinge of danger. And they carried a warning from his past, although he couldn't zero in on the associated memories. It was like the words were trying to pry open the lid to his missing years—the years that didn't exist for him. He resented the feeling. He wanted to open the past, but every time he tried to get in, his mind locked up. It allowed only small snippets of recognition. Like with the fog.

"Something bad," he said. And shivered.

Halfway home, Gabe's mind was on Miz Murtry. He didn't know much about her, except that she had come to the Tri-counties a year ago. He knew she spent her cigarette breaks reading romance novels about daring damsels with flowing hair being rescued by strapping young men with names like Dmitri and Lance. He didn't know her age, but her face didn't have the luster of the teen years. Maybe months of standing over deep fryers and the steam off newly reheated country fried steaks were prematurely pushing her toward middle age.

The pickup engine lugged so Gabe downshifted and brought it back up to speed. He often thought about his attraction to Miz Murtry. There was something about her that initially escaped explanation—it was impossible to dismiss her with a quick look. The gaze was typically extended into a full-out stare, mostly due to a prolonged puzzlement as to just what feature made her seem so appealing. Gabe liked to watch the other male patrons look at Miz Murtry that way. He imagined them looking for the one outstanding feature that made them turn their heads when she walked across the floor. It was the focus on individual features that made most people miss her full appeal, and left them wondering why they felt the strange sense of attraction when she was around. Now, Gabe saw her through a special window—one that counted up more than individual external characters. One that went beyond the usual checklist of scanning points most men used to size up a woman from a distance. He wondered what Horace saw when he looked at her.

Gabe slammed on the brakes, hard. The tires slid on the gravel and he turned the steering wheel to the right to counteract the slight fishtail of the truck. A dust cloud surrounded the truck and gave him a blink of fright. But only a blink. When the truck slid to a stop, he put it in neutral and let off the clutch. He looked down at the dashboard gauges and spoke to the truck.

"Horace said he had to go tell the boys at work." Gabe let go of the steering wheel. "But Horace lost his job five months ago. Fired was more like it. Probably the last place he'd want to go."

He double-clutched, shifted into first, and re-gripped the wheel. The clutch slipped a little as he let it out but the truck rolled on the gravel.

Gabe smiled. "Got a chance."

CHAPTER 4

As soon as Gabe came in the back door, he heard the television. He walked through the kitchen to the front room, up to the couch, but Wanna didn't move. She appeared mesmerized, maybe even hypnotized by the program.

Gabe watched a few seconds and grabbed the remote. He changed channels.

"Hey. I was watching that." Wanna spun on the couch and made a wild swipe for the device.

Gabe pulled it away. "I told you not to watch any more doctor shows."

"Damn it, Gabe. They were just getting to the symptoms. Put it back on." Wanna jumped to her feet and balled her right fist.

"You know what happens when you watch doctor shows. I know how you get. You watched one on prostate problems and had trouble peeing for two days before you found out the prostate gland is a man part."

"Oh, yeah. Well . . . mind your own business."

Gabe grinned. "Nice comeback."

"I'm not the one who can't leave the Tri-counties."

Gabe stiffened. Whenever she brought up his problem, he resorted to his best defense. Silence. Besides, she seemed like she wanted to argue. Wanna loved to argue.

A smile swept Gabe's face. Whenever an argument was at stake, she swam in past the drop-off every time. The prospect of going down for the third time never derailed her enthusiasm. To her, the destination wasn't the destination. Gabe had two ways to deal with Wanna's itch. If it was a subject of interest, he would push her to the edge of her reason as fast as possible and then weather her reliance on emotion. A much more effective tack was to go silent. He knew she hated it when he wouldn't give her an argument.

Wanna stomped her foot and walked toward the kitchen. "What do you want for lunch?"

"I'm not hungry."

"You still hung over from the card game?" "I swear, you get worse every time you go. You talk about me. You're the only one I know who has a hangover for three days at a time. Let me come to the card games and I'll keep an eye on you."

"For the last time, no. You can't come to the games."

"Why not? You afraid I'll hear some man jokes and get offended?"

Gabe laughed. "No. Just the opposite. Your jokes

would probably offend the men. Some of them are downright gross. And you don't know when to stop with them."

"What a bunch of sissies." Wanna walked to the refrigerator. "How about some corn dogs?"

"I told you, I'm not hungry."

Wanna slammed the refrigerator door and walked over to Gabe. "You need a little cuddling, sissy boy?" She put her arms around him and gave a tight hug.

Gabe felt the strength of arms on his back. She was a stocky woman of average height, but her large bosom gave her an hourglass figure, although of quite buxom proportions. In contrast to the sensation from his back, he felt her softness push into the front of his body. It wasn't a three-pat hug—the kind reserved for relatives. Her body forced into him, sealing the space between them. He felt her pelvis push forward into his.

He shoved her away. "We can't do this." He took a step back.

"Why not? We're adults." Wanna put her arms out and moved forward. Her smile looked devious.

Gabe stepped back again. "We can't. No one knows the situation. No one understands."

"As far as anyone knows, we're not doing anything right now." She moved forward again.

Gabe moved to his left. "People have a way of finding out. You think they'd believe us if we told them the truth about our family? If we did anything, they'd see a brother and sister doing this and they'd turn their backs on us in an instant. Just look at the Wilcoxes. They sit in the back of the church now. You know why?"

"They diddle their relatives?" She laughed loud.

"No. A few years back, their son was caught stealing women's underwear from their neighbors' clotheslines. Before that, they sat up front, third row."

Wanna put her hands on her hips. "What's that got to do with anything?"

"They moved to the back. They needed to show everyone that their son's behavior wasn't due to poor parenting. Their son was probably running with the wrong crowd or something beyond their control. So they moved to the back, with the newcomers and visitors."

Wanna put her arms out and moved toward Gabe again. "Let's sit in the back of the church."

Gabe deflected her arms and moved to the sink. "Maybe you don't care what happens here, but our family has been working this farm for four generations. People expect certain things of me. Of us. Besides, why are you getting like this all of a sudden?"

Wanna stopped, then smiled again. "Maybe I've always felt something for you. Maybe not. Maybe I just feel sorry for you. As far as I can tell, you haven't been laid in ages."

Movement from the window over the sink caught Gabe's eye. "What the hell? When did the fogs start coming this far from the swamp?" Gabe put both hands on the sink rim and leaned, putting his head next to the window.

The fog bank receded from the house like it was drawn by a vacuum and Gabe pushed himself from the sink. He felt like he should run, but he didn't know why. A tug in his belly made two more words come to his tongue, but he didn't let them out.

Wanna was back on the couch cycling through the television channels. "Damn. It's over. Gabe, could you put three corn dogs in the microwave for me."

Gabe stared out the kitchen window. Something vague was taking form in his mind, and it went back to the very edge of his memory. Twenty-five years back. It was a bicycle. He was pedaling a bicycle. Through fog.

CHAPTER 5

John Johnson scanned Main Street and turned to Billy and Press, who were seated on the bench outside the general store. He nodded to Billy, who was trying to pick the permanent grease from his fingernails. "Go get Mac."

Billy threw open the wooden screen door of the general store and let it slam shut behind him. A minute later he walked out, followed by Mac McKenna. Both squeezed onto the bench with Press.

John paced on the porch and stopped, facing the men. The sky opened up with a soft rain and he took a deep breath to savor the smell of the freshly wet asphalt.

"Okay. So far we know his name is A. Jackson Thibideaux. He's from New Orleans. Billy found out he's renting the rectory and I found out that the electricity isn't hooked up. No water either." John looked at the wooden floor and paced in front of the bench again. He stopped and turned to face the three.

"Anyone have anything good on him? Anyone been able to find out what he's up to?" He turned to Mac and frowned. "Mac, what you got?"

Mac's hands twitched and he rocked forward and back on the bench. "I overheard him talking about some land in the north, and the swamp. He was asking if the swamp affected the weather in these parts." He looked down at his twitching hands. "But, I don't know if that's important or not." Before John could butt in, Mac looked up again. "Oh yeah. I stayed late the other night to catch up on the books, and I saw he had a fire going in the fireplace. I don't see any firewood, though." John's hands moved in jerky circles in time to his words.

John cringed. He hoped Mac wouldn't get excited. Mac's fidgety movements consisted of a series of stereotyped nervous tics, and with a little concentration, John envisioned them as a repetitive series of syncopated drum beats with occasional drum solos of totally unique twitches that quickly yielded to the original background rhythm. If Mac became really excited, John equated the symphony of movements to the seven-minute drum solo in Iron Butterfly's *In a Gadda Da Vida*. John tried to feel sorry for Mac, but he couldn't edge out the contempt he felt for anyone who had a physical disability and didn't try to hide it.

John turned away from Mac. "Press, you got anything?"

Press shrugged his shoulders and shook his head. "No. Every time I'm around, he just says 'yes' and 'no' to all the questions. I asked him if he did most of his work in the country and he said yes. I also asked if he liked being in the cities, and he said no, except for his house in the outskirts of New Orleans. Sorry I can't add more. That any help?"

John bit his lower lip and cleared his throat. He glared at Press. "We'll see. Billy, you got anything to add?"

"I found out that he gave a stack of money to the Reverend, for rent." Billy's grin was wide.

John exhaled through his lips. "That was a great job you did finding that out, but we already know that. We need to know if you got anything new to add." He rolled his eyes.

Billy's grin faded and he looked at the floor. "No. Nothing else, but I did find out about the money."

John kept his head level and raised his eyes toward the sky. His open hands were held together as if praying, with his thumbs gripping the underside of his chin and the tips of his index fingers lightly tapping his lips. When he thought his pensive expression had provided the correct amount of suspense, he spoke. "I think they're finally going to do it."

"Do what?" Press said.

"I think they're finally going to put in the freeway shunt."

Billy frowned. "What freeway shunt?"

John rubbed his temples. "You know this one. The State has been talking about putting in a shunt between the two interstates on either side of us. Been considering it for years. They nearly did it a few years back. That's when the Tri-counties joined together. It was between us and them bastards up in Rother County. Either State Route 27, or 17, up there. Remember?"

Billy chuckled, but without a smile. "I was still in high school when the counties joined up."

"Mac, Press, you remember, right?" John said.

Mac's hands began circling out of phase, and he rocked on the bench. "Yeah. I remember a lot of bad blood between us and Rother. They kept saying that 17 was the shorter route, but it ain't true. Wes and Gabe showed them up on that one." Mac blinked in time to his hand twitches. "Them bastards made fools of themselves. They thought they could bully our three little counties. But not when we stood together."

Press patted Mac on the shoulder and leaned forward. "I spent some time up in Rother, in Calhoun Township. I can tell you they're nothing special. Just because they act superior and their high school teams always whip ours, everyone here has an inferiority complex. I remember when it started. Way back when Elvis was in the early stages of his career—they got him in for a concert. They still talk about it, and we still wish it was us. I heard it described perfectly once, and I'll never forget the words, although I forgot who said them. Whoever it was said the people here hold a festering sense of envy that oozes northward like a slime mold on the march." He looked around the table. "Anybody every see a slime mold?"

"Speak for yourself," John said. "I'm not about

to let them screw up the freeway shunt like they did before."

"I'm not so sure the State was that serious about building the shunt back then," Press said. "I seem to remember it as another Rother plot to bully us and to get more highway funds from the legislature to repair State Route 17."

"They were, too, serious," John said. "And I heard they're on it again. And that's where Thibideaux comes in." He watched the three men lift their eyes at the mention of Thibideaux.

"I talked to him the other day," John said. "I asked him if his business was in land, and he just said he was into acquisitions. And I tried to find out who he works for, but he's tight-lipped on that. I did notice a slight change in his eyes when I mentioned the State, though, so I think I got him on that one."

John paused to let his words sink in. He looked toward the rectory. "He's got to be a land broker. I bet he's here to check out our route. Maybe even start buying some land."

Billy's eyes were wide. "Where would they put the shunt?"

John cocked his head back and pointed north. "Probably pretty close to Route 27. Halfway between the southern county lines and the swamp up there."

"But what about Rother?" Mac said. "As I recall, Wes and Gabe didn't show that our route was shorter. They just showed that the two routes were about the same. Are we ready for another fight with Rother?"

"Thibideaux's here, isn't he?" John said. "He isn't

up in Rother." John pushed his sleeves up on his arms, exposing his forearms. He was two inches under six feet and weighed a full two thirty-five. At a glance, it seemed that at least one-fourth of that weight resided in his forearms. His former occupation in an aluminum smelting plant required a great deal of upper body strength, but his subsequent inactivity lent a softness to his massive physique. This was accentuated by a waistline that first exceeded his inseam measurement about six inches ago.

The showers turned to hard rain and John spun to watch the water run off the roof of the porch. The sky to the west showed blue, suggesting that the storm was winding up for its finale in Boyston.

"Can you imagine what a freeway shunt would do for the Tri-counties?" John said. "If it happens, I'm going to open up a gas station that has one of them markets. I'll put it right next to one of the off-ramps with a great big sign that can be seen for miles. I'll have the missus move her diner there, too. I'll just sit back and count the money."

John turned around. "Mac, what would you do?"

Mac's hands sprung into action. "Well, when I was driving out west, I seen a group of outlet stores along a freeway—in the middle of nowhere. You know, the ones that sell stuff really cheap. I wouldn't mind opening up a couple right here in Boyston. People will burn three dollars in gas to save two in places like that. I'd still run the general store, though, for all of the local folks."

John noticed that Billy's eyes were stuck off in the

distance, apparently in a daydream. "Hey, Billy. Star Fleet Command wants you to check out that planet over there."

The laughter of the group brought Billy back to the porch.

"What? You talking to me? Sorry, John. I was just thinking."

"We were wondering what you would do if the freeway shunt came our way," John said, still chuckling.

Billy's eyes went skyward and a slight grin spread across his face. "I'd buy a new tow truck because people would be needing help. I'd like to get one of them big trucks that can tow an eighteen-wheeler, too. Other than that, I'd just keep the shop going, but I'd probably have to hire somebody, with all the extra business."

John stared at Billy. He wanted to say something to put him in his place. But he couldn't argue with Billy's plan. It made sense. He shook his head. How could someone with the IQ of a four-legger be such a brilliant mechanic. And run such a successful business. He backed off. He remembered that it was Billy who usually financed their investigations.

John considered halting the exercise without polling Press, but he decided to be polite. "Press, what would you do?"

"I don't know. I suspect that I'd keep doing what I'm doing now," Press said.

John's face went red and he balled his huge hands into fists. "God damn it, Press. Why are you in with us? You never find out anything useful, and you never do anything to help. When was the last time you had an opinion on something?"

Press smiled. "An opinion on something, or an opinion on something important?"

"Go to hell. Why don't you just go home and boss around those people you have working your farm for you?"

Press widened his smile. "Relax, John. No one here will give you mouth-to-mouth. I think you're taking all this a little too serious. I'm here because you are my friends, and I think what we do is fun. Sometimes both fun and funny. But just to let you know I'm useful to the group, I'm planning to drive to the State Capitol next week. Maybe I'll drop in on Senator Ambrose. She owes me a favor for all the work I did on her re-election campaign. I can get the inside scoop on the freeway shunt and put in a good word for both Thibideaux and the southern route. I'm going to make it a day by taking the family for a shop-a-thon and a picnic on the bank of the Big River."

John looked up at the sky. All he saw was a contradiction—a cloudless blue sky, yet a soft rain continued to fall. It was a thankless job, he thought, making sure everything went smoothly in the Tri-counties. Sure, no one asked him to watch over things, but the elected officials didn't know a thing about the day-to-day stuff that went on. And the sheriff only cared about the black-and-white of the law. He didn't see the gray areas in between. John leaned his head out from under the roof and squinted at the raindrops. He still saw only blue.

CHAPTER 6

GABE WATCHED DEENA Lee dump coffee grounds from a stained filter and replace it with a fresh load of special grind. The bell over the door signaled entry of a new patron, but Gabe kept his gaze on Deena Lee, glad to have her back after her weeklong hiatus. Time to contact the proper authorities, she had told Teddy, to find her man, who may have met with foul play of some sort. Gabe straightened on his stool. Horace had never been gone this long.

To Gabe, Deena Lee was as cheerful as ever, but he couldn't help notice that the crow's feet by her eyes had deepened and the creases around her lips were now permanent reservoirs for lipstick runoff. He hoped his presence was a comfort to her, a reassurance that all could be normal, or better, now that Horace was gone. He was encouraged. She seemed to spend more time at his end of the counter than elsewhere.

Deena Lee turned to face the opposite end of the bar and froze with her hands on her hips. The usual din in the Edge was silenced enough to hear the gurgle of the dripping coffee.

He turned to see the strange little man from the rectory settle at the counter in the spot made infamous by Horace Murtry.

Gabe swiveled on his stool and stared. Thibideaux, he was called. A big name for such a small man, but appropriate. Both were strange. And not just that. Word spread fast that he was living in the rectory even though it was abandoned some twenty-five years ago and wasn't considered habitable.

A connection stirred a clouded memory from Gabe's past. He was already apprehensive about Thibideaux. An internal voice said that there was something bad in this half-pint of a man. But now, the rectory was also coming up unsettling, adding to the feeling. He tried to make sense of it, to pull it all together, but it was a fleet sensation—there and gone in a whiff, leaving an aftertaste that made Gabe want to pull back, to watch from a distance with one foot pointed in the direction of the nearest exit.

He watched Deena Lee wait on Thibideaux. She smiled her usual smile, but there was a twitch of nervousness in her face. He knew her that well—he could sense her discomfort like it was signed in neon. He watched her lips move and imagined her formal politeness, unlike the relaxed, joking banter she saved for the regulars.

The little man's expression didn't change. His strange grin seemed painted on—his lips barely moved when he spoke, and the corners of his mouth maintained the upturned grin that Gabe found so unsettling when he first saw him on the rectory porch a couple of weeks back.

The locals weren't a group to pass up such a valuable opportunity, Gabe thought, since gossip was a form of currency in the Tri-counties, almost as valuable as money or a good crop of wheat. His prediction was quickly substantiated as a man next to Thibideaux leaned into a conversation. Thibideaux's mouth moved once, his gaze apparently riveted on his plate on the counter.

To Gabe, Thibideaux seemed to be uncomfortable in the Edge, and he ate quickly, looking down at his food. The only exception was when Deena Lee came by. He seemed to relax when she was close and his eyes followed her as far as his stiff neck would allow. Gabe nodded, acknowledging his take on her universal draw to all men, no matter how strange.

Two younger men who Gabe didn't know got up from the corner booth and approached Thibideaux, one standing on each side of him. The one to his left leaned forward and pointed at Thibideaux's face. Thibideaux didn't make eye contact, and he appeared to respond with a one-word answer. The second man leaned in, over Thibideaux's other shoulder and said something, again with a pointing gesture. Once more, Thibideaux stared straight ahead and moved his lips once. The first man moved closer and put his arm on the counter, moving his face close to Thibideaux's. Thibideaux reached into his breast pocket and withdrew a wallet. He looked up at the man and without saying a word, or touching the man in any way, appeared to push the man back a step. A look to the right had the same effect on the other inquisitor. Both remained frozen, flanking Thibideaux as he slid a few bills under his plate and pushed away from the counter. Gabe felt a chill.

Thibideaux said something to Deena Lee, who pointed past Gabe, around the curved end of the counter, toward the unisex bathroom in the rear corner. Thibideaux shuffled along the counter turning heads as he went, except for those of the two young men, who hurried back to their booth and hung their heads over their food.

Gabe didn't want to look at him when he passed, so he hunched over his plate, pretending to be looking for the choicest piece of ham for the next bite. When Thibideaux came close, Gabe felt an overwhelming need to turn and look, and at the same time, an urge to curl into a ball. He heard the shuffling walk stop to his left and the sensation of a close stare gave him a feeling of anticipation. He tried, but he couldn't resist. He swiveled on his stool and faced Thibideaux—their heads were almost on an even level. Gabe's eyes flicked from the high-arched eyebrows, to the dark eyes, and then to the grin. A sick feeling arose from his abdomen, and a nervous panic headed in the opposite direction. He wanted to say, "Can I help you?" but his lips seemed incapable of forming words. He felt dizzy,

but his heart pounded out a stable rhythm. Thibideaux moved on.

Gabe sat paralyzed. Memories flew around in his
head, but only one came to rest long enough to make
an impression. The scars. Thibideaux's thin, straight
lips weren't turned up into a grin. The upturns at the
corners of his mouth were thick scars. And not fresh
ones, either. They sounded a frightening familiarity
of experience, but without a contextual backdrop the
terror seemed suspended somewhere between reality
and a dream. The heightened uncertainty was accompanied by an extra heartbeat and Gabe had to draw in
a deep breath to push his dizziness away. He turned in
time to see Thibideaux enter the bathroom.

Gabe wanted to leave. He wanted to run out of
the Edge and not come back, but he couldn't move. He
wanted to go, but he needed to stay. He pushed his
plate away on the counter and stared in the direction of
the bathroom. He wondered what Thibideaux wanted.
Why was he here? And why did he stop to stare?

Five minutes passed and the bathroom door remained closed. Seven minutes, and a weak sensation
of having to pee caught Gabe's attention. He wondered
how many other patrons were holding their bladders
for fear of having to disturb the strange little man.

A regular from Porter County answered Gabe's
question. "God damn it, I got to go," the man said
and stomped to the back of the diner. "If the twerp
isn't finished by now, I'll have to push him out with
his pants down."

The man pounded on the door three times and

shouted at the frame, "Anyone home?"

No response.

He pounded again, harder this time. "Anyone home?"

Again no response.

He looked around the diner and shook his head. He cocked his arm back and hit the door square in the middle. The latch gave way and the door swung open, hitting the wall inside the room and bounding back, almost closing. The man stopped the door with his hand and poked his head into the opening. Gabe heard the beginnings of an apology from the man, but it was stopped mid-flow. A muffled "What the hell?" echoed from the room.

Gabe jumped to his feet and took two steps toward the bathroom, two other regulars right behind him.

The man stumbled out into the main room. "He ain't there."

Gabe pushed the door open and looked inside; the other two men crowded around his shoulders. The room was empty. There was no back door to the bathroom and the painted-over window was held closed more tightly by the multiple coats of paint than by the twelve long wood screws that anchored the window sash into the two-by-fours that framed the window. Gabe looked up. The fan was small and intact, and it operated off of the light switch.

He backed out of the bathroom and pushed on the adjacent door. It was the only other way out of the diner, aside from the front door, but Teddy kept it locked from the outside with a large padlock and hasp.

To discourage a brute-force charge to freedom, Teddy had mounted a white-on-red sign that he had stolen from a Denny's on his last vacation that read, "Emergency Exit Only. Alarm Will Sound If Opened."

Gabe looked back in the bathroom. Down along the baseboards, next to the toilet was a small opening, but it was only large enough for a small cat to use, which was why it wasn't boarded up. Gabe knew it was there for Teddy's cat, Three, who came and went as she pleased, although she was mainly in the building at night when her primary job was to keep the rodent population at zero.

He's small, but not that small, Gabe thought. He'd have to be able to snake around the toilet and compress his body to the size of his head. He was a little one, though.

Gabe returned to his stool, but he didn't sit down. Too nervous to eat, he slipped a couple of dollars under his plate and turned for the door, then stopped. He whirled around and found Deena Lee standing at midcounter, staring at the bathroom. He caught her eye and raised his eyebrows in a concerned look.

She mouthed the words, "I'm okay," and smiled.

Gabe shifted into third gear and turned his truck onto the gravel county road that ran past his farm. His mind was still trying to make connections. He pushed in the clutch, slammed the gearshift into fourth, and popped the clutch. The truck jerked a little and slowly came up to speed.

He looked down at the speedometer and backed off the gas a little. There was something strange about Thibideaux, beyond the weird stuff. Whenever he thought about the little man, he felt the aversive shove of one of those single trial learning experiences, like when aluminum foil hits a tooth filling.

He slapped his hand against the steering wheel. He couldn't figure out what tied him to Thibideaux. But there was a tether. And every time he tried to reel it in, it snapped without revealing its anchor. Did the little man hold a key to his missing years? And what was the cost of finding out?

CHAPTER 7

TEDDY SHOOK THE deck of cards in his left hand and frowned at John Johnson.

Gabe chuckled. Teddy could disappear in a crowd of two—everyone had a friend from their hometown who looked just like him.

"How many cards you want, John-John?" Teddy said.

"Goddamn it, I told you not to call me that."

Billy laughed.

John contorted his face in Billy's direction, and Billy lowered his eyes and stifled his laugh.

John gulped from his glass of Jack Daniels like he was trying to wash the topic away in a single mouthful.

Teddy brought the side of the deck down on the table with a thwack. "If you don't want us to call you that, then why don't you tell us what the J stands for? Odds on the street are for John. John John Johnson. I'm just going with the odds."

John drained his glass. "Screw your odds. It's none of your goddamn business. Why does everyone get so weird about my middle name?"

Teddy chuckled. "It's kind of like seeing a woman's bra. You see a lot more of her in a swimming suit, but you're just not supposed to see the bra. Danged if the bra don't get you more worked up."

"Wish Press was here," Gabe said. "He knows."

John glared at Gabe.

Billy's frown pinched his eyebrows together. "Why won't he say?"

"That's the mystery of the year." Gabe said. "Teddy, you remember when we got him so drunk he puked on the counter of the Edge?" Gabe turned to Billy. "We tried to get it out of him, but he just kept saying he'd tell it when the time was right."

John slammed a pair of cards down on the table. "Just give me two, goddamn it. I swear. You guys spend more time yakking than playing."

Gabe drew a long sip from his half-full glass of Jack and shivered it down.

"I know," Teddy said as he slid two cards across the table to John. "Why don't we bring Misty Ronde-lunas in on it?"

Billy looked at John and giggled. "Yeah. She'd be able to get it out of you. She'd probably do you just to solve the mystery."

John threw his cards on the table, but Teddy

wouldn't let him speak.

"What would you do if she came on to you, John-John?" Teddy laughed. "You can still find your pecker, can't you?"

"Screw you. I don't want to talk about names. And I don't want to talk about Misty. I want to play cards."

Billy leaned forward. "What's the matter, John? You got a thing for her?"

"Shut up, Billy."

"I'll take that as a yes," Teddy said.

Gabe poured another glass of Jack.

"You guys can go to hell," John said. He pushed his chair back and waddled to the bathroom.

"He's probably one of the few in the Tri-counties who hasn't had Misty," Teddy smiled at Billy. "You've had her, haven't you, Billy? You went to high school with her."

Billy blushed. "Naw. Never did. She came around a couple of times, but every time, she was going with someone else."

"That wouldn't stop her."

Billy blushed a deeper red. "I know. But I didn't feel like it was right for me to jump in."

"Jump in?" Teddy said. "You mean fall in, don't you?"

Everyone laughed except Gabe.

"She was a cheerleader wasn't she?" Teddy said.

Billy nodded and looked down at the table.

"But she don't wear no underwear, right?" Teddy looked at the ceiling and rubbed his chin. "At least that's what I heard."

Gabe finally leaned into the conversation. "I know for a fact that she don't wear underwear. You ever seen her in them white pants she wears at Doc's office? You can see right through them if the light's right. I can tell you she ain't a real blonde, unless she's dyeing the wrong end."

"If she went without when she was leading cheers, I bet it made for some special school spirit," Teddy said.

Billy frowned. "Naw. She wore underwear when she cheered. Funny thing, though. Boys would sell their Momma to sit in the front row to watch her kick her legs up and do the splits. Same boys who probably seen it all without the underwear."

Gabe took a long drink. "Just like with the bra. What's erotic leans toward the unusual, even if it's less revealing than what you see all the time."

"Gabe, you ever had any of Misty?" Teddy said. His laugh was brief.

Billy stared.

"Naw. She's too young for me. I take a long look every chance I get, and I do get the fantasies. But I'd probably keel over from heart failure if I ever got the chance. I'll leave her to the younger boys as long as she keeps giving us all a show now and again."

The laughs were terminated by the sound of the bathroom doorknob.

Gabe leaned forward, toward Billy. "Why'd you have to invite John to the games. I can't stand to be around him more than a few minutes at a time."

Billy lowered his voice. "He invited himself. What

was I supposed to say?"

"How about no?"

John walked to the table and pulled his chair back.

Teddy giggled. "Hey, John. Why's it every time we mention Misty Rondelunas, you have to go into the bathroom for a while? Can't you wait and pound it at home?"

John stood behind his chair. He didn't join the laughter.

"Look," John said. "If you're going to spend the night talking about Misty, you can deal me out."

"You know, Misty was asking about you the other day," Billy said. "Said she heard that bald guys are better in bed. I told her you'd be willing to prove it right or wrong."

"Screw you," John said. "I'm out of here." He leaned across his chair, gathered his change and headed for the door.

"Just close your eyes when you get home and pretend the missus is Misty," Teddy said. "Oh, sorry. I guess you already had yours for the night."

John slammed the door on the laughter.

"I know," Billy said. "Why don't we ask Misty to join us in the card games? We could play strip poker instead of quarters. She'd go for it, for sure."

Gabe reached for the deck. "If Wanna got wind of that, she'd want in, too. She's been bugging me about getting in the card games. You guys want her and Misty in the same room?"

Teddy put his hands up and pushed at the air. "Not unless she leaves her temper at home. Wanna's a lot of fun when she's calm, but something always seems to set her off."

"She wouldn't last long with Misty around," Billy said. Gabe took a long drink of Jack. "Don't worry. I already said no to her." He finished his shuffle and started dealing the cards.

Teddy picked up his cards and rearranged them in his hand. "Speaking of names, where'd Wanna's name come from? I heard some things, but no one knows for sure."

Gabe didn't raise his eyes from his hand. "What did you hear?"

Teddy looked at Billy and then back at Gabe. "I heard your Momma was a hippie, with a sense of humor like Wanna's. They say she had a middle name to go with Wanna that was real funny, but she chickened out at the last minute and just left it at Wanna. Others say her name was supposed to be Wanda, but it was misspelled on the birth certificate and your Momma just left it that way. Which was it?"

Gabe sipped his Jack and smiled. Even his best friends didn't know about Wanna and him. "Wanna don't want anyone to know."

"Why not?" Teddy said. "And why didn't she change it when she grew up? I would have."

"The answer is the same for both questions. She likes that it's a joke. She likes the way people giggle and whisper. You know her. She lives for jokes. The dirtier the better." Gabe looked up at Billy. "Anyway, I don't want to talk about Misty or Wanna anymore. I want to talk about John. He only plays cards with us when he's up to something. What's he got going, Billy?"

Billy looked down at his cards. He started to say something and then stopped. He took a deep breath. "Can't tell you." He leaned back in his chair.

Gabe smiled. He knew better than to pry when Billy clammed up about John. Gabe knew about Billy's father's alcohol problem and his abusive past. He knew that Billy's mother killed herself when Billy was only five, when his father turned his wrath on his only child. No one would have blamed her if she had spread the bastard all over the living room wall with a shotgun. But she hadn't. One time, when he got Billy to open up, Gabe found out that Billy loved his mother for taking the beatings for so long, but he hated her for taking the chicken way out and leaving Billy to his father. Gabe knew Billy was desperate for a mentor and father figure. Although John Johnson was the best of neither, he was a natural draw to Billy.

Gabe looked down at his hand. "Teddy, how many cards you want?"

"I'll take two. And pass me your truck keys."

CHAPTER 8

GABE SLID HIS hands into his pockets and the absence of coins reminded him he owed Billy for the card game. That was nearly a week ago. He wondered what was wrong with him. He never forgot things like that. But since the strange little man took up in the rectory, Gabe sensed a background pull of tension, like his mind wasn't totally his. Something about the man occupied mental space that was earmarked for other things.

Gabe settled in his easy chair and flipped through the absurd television shows that filled the time slot between the news and the bedtimes of most youngsters. His eyes were already heavy from the day's work.

The phone rang, startling him to an upright posture. Wanna was busy washing the dishes, so he shuffled across the room and snatched the receiver from its resting place. He started to issue his standard greeting but then stopped when Billy's frantic voice screeched in the earpiece.

"Billy. Calm down. Tell me what happened."

Gabe shifted the phone to his other ear and leaned to look in the kitchen just as Wanna rounded the corner.

"What's wrong?" Wanna said.

Gabe held his hand up and looked down at the floor.

"Where is Press now?" He looked back at Wanna and grimaced. "Calm down. I'll be right there."

Gabe hung up the phone and Wanna grabbed his arm.

"What wrong? What happened to Press?" she said.

Gabe reached out and surrounded Wanna with his arms. "It was a car accident. Press is in the hospital. I have to go right away. I think Billy said Press's family is gone. He wasn't making much sense. You stay here in case anyone else phones. I'll fill you in when I find something out."

Gabe walked through the automatic doors of the emergency room entrance and spotted Billy, John and Mac sitting against the far wall. He walked over and John immediately stood up.

Gabe turned to face Billy and Mac. "How's Press? What happened?"

"We don't know much," John said. "Just that there was a car accident. Press is in bad shape. That's about all they've told us."

Gabe took a seat next to Billy and put his arm around Billy's shoulders. "You all right, Billy?"

Billy lost his fight with tears; wet streaks ran down his cheeks and dripped from his jaw. He put his elbows on his knees and leaned forward, burying his face in his hands.

Gabe patted his back and left his right hand on Billy's nearest shoulder. He was about to say something when Sheriff Sam Merriwether rounded the corner.

John grabbed Sam by the upper arms. "Sam. What happened? Is Press going to make it?"

Sam stepped back to break John's grip. He turned to face Mac, Billy and Gabe.

"Evidently, Press and his family were driving on twenty-seven, just east of here, and a sudden thunderstorm caught them. There was a car behind them, and the driver said a lightening bolt hit a tree, splitting is right down the middle, from top to bottom. Half of it fell on Press's car and flattened it. When I got there, they had Press and one of his girls out of the wreckage. There was no need to worry about the wife and the other two girls. At least it was fast. They never knew what hit them."

"Is Press going to make it?" John said.

Sam still didn't look in John's direction. "I don't know if he'll make it or not. He's in terrible shape. The doctors have done what they can." Sam looked at the ceiling. "It's up to someone else at this point."

Gabe stood up. "You said they pulled out one of his girls. Is she okay?"

Sam nodded his head. "It's a miracle that little girl

came out of that mangled car like she did. It was his youngest. What is she, four?"

"About that," Gabe said.

"She only had a few minor scratches and a bruise or two," Sam said. "You should have seen the car. Nothing short of a miracle."

John pushed his way into Sam's peripheral vision. "Where is Press? Can we see him?"

Sam took a step back and finally looked at John. "I'll see. You wait here."

Sam disappeared in the direction he had come, and Gabe sat back down.

John centered himself in front of the others. "Geez. We just saw him day before yesterday. It just shows you that you never know what's going to happen. One day you're up and about, and the next day your family is gone and you're on your deathbed."

Billy sobbed.

Gabe glared at John. "No one said he was on his deathbed. Let's just let the doctors make the diagnosis." He rubbed Billy's shoulders.

Mac talked through a minor drum solo of movement. "He stopped at the store for some food on the way out of town. He was so excited about the trip. His world turned for his wife and the girls." Mac wiped his eyes with his shirtsleeve.

Billy rocked back and forth, repeating the same phrase. "Press can't die. Press can't die." Finally, he added to the chorus, "How are we supposed to figure out what Thibideaux is up to with just three of us?"

"Shut up, Billy!" John said. His eyes flicked to

Gabe and then to Mac. "We're all upset, so let's just be quiet and pray for Press."

Six more patients were processed and called back, and John's guffaw-like exhalations grated on Gabe's nerves.

John stopped his circular pace directly in front of Billy and stomped his right foot. "Where the hell is Sam? He went back there over an hour ago."

Gabe looked at John and then at the ground. "Maybe we should tell Press that his accident's bugging you, John. Maybe then he would cooperate a little better."

"Screw you, Gabe. Why are you here, anyway?"

Gabe moved his mouth, then took a deep breath and let it out slowly. This wasn't the time to get in a pissing match with John.

John resumed pacing, stomping with each step, and nearly ran into a nurse as she rounded the corner. She jumped out of the way and glared at him.

"Are you four waiting to see Preston Cunningham?" she said.

Billy sprang to his feet. "Is he all right? Can we see him?"

The nurse took a step back and held out her hands. "You can see him for a few minutes if you calm down. He's still critical, but he's resting right now. It's too early to say what will happen. He's in and out of consciousness, and when he's in, he just mutters. So don't be disappointed if he doesn't respond to you. And please be quiet."

Gabe slowed his walk when he entered Press' room. It was full of enough gadgetry to make an astronaut envious. Press was on his back with his head propped slightly upward. He didn't move when they surrounded the bed.

Gabe stood back a little and surveyed the bed. Tubes wove into every available hole, including places in Press' body where there were no holes to begin with. His eyes were open, but unfocused.

The four drew as near as they could considering the multitude of tubes and wires that connected Press to his monitors and his fluid reservoirs and receptacles.

John put his mouth next to Press' left ear. "How you doing, Press? You're going to make it. You know that, don't you?"

"Yeah, you're going to be all right," Billy said. "We talked to the doc." He leaned on the bed, pulling on a tube that ran into Press' nose. Mac pulled him back.

John glared at Billy. "What are you trying to do? Kill him?"

Billy looked at his shoes.

Gabe wanted to put his arm around Billy again, but he was on the wrong side of the bed. He was within striking range of John, but he thought better of starting a ruckus in Press' room. He remembered the speed limit signs and his shotgun. John's face was on the signs.

Mac's hands twitched on Press' blanket. "Hey, guys? Press is looking at me. I think he's trying to say something."

Billy looked up and moved close. "Maybe he's going to tell us what he found out about the freeway shunt."

"God dammit, Billy, shut up," John said. His booming voice made Press blink several times.

"What freeway shunt?" Gabe said, looking into John's eyes.

"Never mind. Billy's just talking nonsense." He took a half step back.

Mac's hands were at it again. "Look, guys. His mouth is moving. He's saying something. Somebody get close to his mouth. I can't do it from here."

Billy leaned his head across the bed so his ear was less than in inch from Press' lips.

John leaned over and tried to push Billy's head out of the way. "Move, Billy. Let me hear."

Billy resisted the push and kept his ear next to Press' mouth.

John straightened up and cursed under his breath. "Can you hear anything?"

Billy looked up and then put his ear back down. "Maybe if you'd be quiet I could."

Billy listened and then nodded. Then nodded again, and once more. Press' eyes closed and his breathing slowed to where his chest barely moved with each breath. Billy looked up at the others and frowned.

"Could you make it out?" Mac said. "What did he say?"

John leaned toward Billy. "If it's something that Gabe shouldn't hear, then don't say anything. We'll talk about it later."

Gabe stared at John. He imagined putting the stock of the 12-gauge to his cheek.

"I heard him say it three times, but it don't make any sense," Billy said. "Nothing that I know, anyway."

"What was it, dumb shit?" John said. "Maybe it'll make sense to people with more than half a brain."

Gabe cocked the shotgun.

Billy stepped back from the bed. "If you want to hear it, you're going to have to ask me polite. After you apologize to me for all the insults."

John's face turned crimson and he balled his hands into fists.

Gabe lowered the shotgun. He smiled at Billy and nodded his head in agreement.

"God dammit. I'm sorry. Okay? Please tell me what Press said."

"Are you going to stop saying I'm dumb?"

Gabe's smile widened.

John looked down at the bed. "Jesus Christ."

"I'm not kidding, John."

"Okay. I won't say you're dumb anymore. Now tell me what Press said."

Billy smiled. "Okay, but it don't make any sense. He just kept saying, 'Jayne.

J . . . A . . . Y . . N . . . E.' He said it three times. Just like that. What does Jayne mean?"

John huffed and turned toward the door as Gabe worked hard to suppress a loud laugh.

Mac and Billy looked at Gabe.

"Your middle name is Jayne?" Gabe said in John's direction, still struggling with a giggle.

John turned around and nearly bumped into the door. "Screw you. It's a family name, okay?" He turned and stomped into the hall.

Billy put a hand to his mouth and squeezed a laugh up through his nose. Mac's hands kept time with his silent giggles.

Gabe looked down at Press and rubbed his hand. "Thanks, Press. You got him good that time."

Press' eyes opened wide and the corners of his mouth seemed to turn upward, at least as much as the tubes would allow. He took a large inward breath but nothing came back out. His eyes gradually defocused and half-closed.

Gabe lifted Press' hand and felt his wrist. "Billy. Get a nurse. Fast."

CHAPTER 9

DEENA LEE WALKED behind the half-wall of the Herndon's Edge and turned a profile to Teddy. "What do you think? Am I losing my girly figure?"

Teddy put his hands on his hips and exaggerated an up-and-down scan. "Definitely have a critter in there. You're not trying to hide it, are you?"

"Couldn't if I wanted to. I'm having to let out all my dresses, and I'm not good at it." She pulled her apron up past her waist. "Made a mess of this one."

Teddy laughed. "Ain't no fashion show in here. As long as the mugs are topped off, no one'll notice. I could serve tables with no pants under my apron and most around here wouldn't even look twice. Besides, you have the noble excuse."

The bell over the door rang and a strong gust of wind sent the door crashing into a coat rack, nearly tipping it over. Teddy and Deena Lee peeked over the half wall and watched Thibideaux push the door closed and amble to the counter.

Deena Lee rolled her eyes and walked in his direction.

"Good morning, Ms. Murtry," Thibideaux said. "You're looking radiant today. I trust you're through the worst of the morning sickness?"

Deena Lee froze, her eyes wide and her mouth slightly open. Most words he's said in a string since he moved here, she thought. She picked up a distinct bayou drawl in the formality of his deliberate words. All she could manage to utter in return was a throaty, "Comes and goes these days."

Thibideaux put his forearms on the counter and leaned forward. His expression didn't change. "I hope you're remembering to take your prenatal vitamins. You want your child to have the best start possible, you know."

Deena Lee approached the counter and faked a smile. "Doc gave me a bunch of samples, but they're gone. They're so expensive I'm only taking them every other day." She put a mug on the counter and filled it just short of the brim. "You like it black, right?"

"Yes ma'am. Thank you for taking notice."

She slid a menu beside the cup and forced an increase in her smile.

Thibideaux pointed to the chalkboard over the coffeemaker. "I believe I'll give Teddy's special a try today."

She reached to pick up the menu. "Good choice. It'll be up in a minute." She hustled behind the half-wall and shouldered up to Teddy.

"What's with the twerp today?" she said. "All of a sudden he's talking like we're best friends or something. Gives me the creeps."

Teddy scraped the grill with the spatula blade. "Don't you dare turn him away. You notice how many people come for lunch now?"

Deena Lee elbowed Teddy in the side. "Who do you think serves them all?"

Teddy pointed past the wall with the spatula blade. "Even John Johnson and his buddies come now. Probably pisses off his missus to no end. Best I can tell, they all come to see if Thibideaux will show up, and how he'll leave. I'm glad he comes only every few days. The mystery is probably what brings them."

"But why is he so chatty today?"

"Don't know and don't care."

"As long as he packs them in, right?"

Teddy put the spatula down. "Yeah, well I noticed that he leaves plenty for your tip jar every time he's in." He smiled. "Maybe he's got something for you."

Deena Lee faked a shiver. She leaned a little to her right so she could see Thibideaux through the doorway. He had a newspaper spread on the counter.

She turned and pulled a plate from the overhead shelf and dished Teddy's special on the plate. Her mind wandered as she spooned a little extra of everything.

What was he up to? Was he coming on to her like Teddy said? Was he interested in courting her for the purpose of marriage? She heard about how some girls married men more than twice their age or so homely they stopped traffic, only because they had money and privilege. But she could honestly say that no money in the world could get her into Mr. Thibideaux's bed. Her romance novel background convinced her that an ounce of lusty passion was worth more than a hefty bank account, even if it meant a continual paycheck-to-paycheck existence. Still, she dreamed of what it would be like to go into one of those stores that sold only clothes and try on outfit after outfit, and then leave with so many boxes it would take three people to carry them.

She balanced the overloaded plate on her hand but stopped in the doorway and turned toward Teddy. "You mind if I take a break after I serve this up? My knees are sore and my ankles are swelling something awful."

Teddy chuckled. "And that's all?"

She shook her head and leaned his way, her voice a whisper. "No. He's creeping me out today."

"Fifteen minutes enough?"

Deena Lee walked around to the west side of the building so the afternoon sun would bake into her legs. A four-foot section of log rested against the wall. She had stopped smoking when she became pregnant—now she used her breaks to daydream about what it would be like to be a mother. She sat on the log, swiveled her legs up, and tilted her head back against the wall.

Her mind drifted, but a strange sensation of being watched pulled her back. A slight movement flashed in her peripheral vision. She jerked her head up and gasped.

"I'm sorry to startle you, Ms. Murtry. I hope you don't mind if I take a minute or two of your break."

Thibideaux's shadowy eyes looked even darker in direct sunlight.

He extended his arm toward her. "I was able to obtain a full bottle of vitamins from a doctor friend who owed me a favor, and I immediately thought of you. I would be grateful if you would accept them as a gift."

Deena Lee clenched her fists and gritted her teeth. "Don't you ever do that again. And why are you being so nice to me? I already got a man."

He inched closer and held out the bottle of 100 prenatal vitamins. "I just believe that all children deserve the best possible start in life. I assure you I'm not interested in a romantic relationship with you, or anyone else for that matter. But I do have some information about your Horace. I ran into him the other day when I returned to New Orleans to take care of some business. That's where I got the vitamins."

"Screw the vitamins." She jumped up and grabbed the upper part of his left arm. "What about Horace?"

"I'm not happy to tell you this, but I think you deserve to know."

"Is he coming back? Do you know if he's coming back? Have you talked to him?" Her eyes were wide. Her fingers dug deep into his arm.

His expression didn't change. "Calm yourself, Ms. Murtry. Getting all worked up isn't good for the baby.

Yes, I have talked with Horace, but I won't tell you everything he said. To be blunt, he has no intention of coming back. But believe me. You'll be better off without him. He's developed quite a drug habit, and he supports it through petty theft and the arrangement of delivery of sexual favors by his current girlfriend."

"Jesus. If you don't want to rile me, you have a funny way of showing it. Why are you telling me this?" Tears rolled on her cheeks as sobs interrupted her breathing. "Why should I believe you?"

"I'm so sorry. I've known Horace Murtry for some time, longer than you have. He's always been headed down the path of self-destruction, and I feel bad that I didn't step in to warn you before now. So I feel a little responsible for your current situation and for the well being of your child. I owe you that much."

Deena Lee wanted to hit him. She wanted to hit any man within reach—maybe even go out of her way to find men to hit. "You've done me no favors today. I need some time by myself. Would you please leave?"

"Yes, of course. I'm so sorry. I just felt you should know, sooner rather than later." He put the bottle of vitamins on the stump and rotated on the heel of one foot and the toes of the other. He rounded the corner of the building and a stiff gust of wind bent the bushes in his direction.

Deena Lee collapsed on the log. Her left hand gripped and squeezed the vitamin bottle like it was Horace's neck.

The bell above the door jingled Deena Lee's entry and Teddy looked up through a burst of smoke from the grill. "Deena Lee. What happened?" He rounded the half-wall and hand-springed the counter. "You all right?"

"I'll be fine." She faked a smile. "Can I have the rest of the day off? I need to forget a man. Shouldn't take much more than that, the bastard."

Teddy put an arm around her shoulder. "Take what you need. Just give me a call if you won't be in tomorrow morning." He gave her a hug.

Deena Lee swiveled her hips onto the seat of her Volkswagen and inched her legs under the steering wheel. She looked up into the rearview mirror, which was already bent her way, and adjusted her hair. "I wonder if there's a man out there who ain't just trying to get something from a woman," she said to the image. She looked down and patted her stomach. "If you're a boy, I'll have to teach you how to love a woman. If you're a girl, I'll have to teach you how to teach it." She turned the key and pumped the gas pedal several times until the engine caught.

Tires bit pavement and Deena Lee's thoughts went back to her baby. What should she call him? She and Horace never did get married, but she had to say they did or the locals never would have accepted them. Now, she was stuck with the story, so she had to keep the name, Murtry, and give it to her child.

She stomped the brake pedal and the car skidded to a stop on the shoulder of the road. She threw open the door, stood, and leaned against it. Looking up at the sky, she screamed as loud as she could. "Bastard." She patted her stomach. "Not you, darlin'."

CHAPTER 10

HAZEL JOHNSON TRIED to calm herself as she walked down Main Street toward the four-way stop. The night was clear and moonless, and the dim glow of a distant streetlight stretched her faint shadow into the darkness ahead. During a town meeting over a year ago, she voted in favor of turning off two of every three streetlights to save money for the town, but now she wished she hadn't.

She felt the hair on her arms elevate against a chill that wasn't related to the temperature; the evening didn't require a jacket. The clandestine nature of her mission required all of the nerve she could muster, and some that was borrowed against the future of her livelihood. She had to do something. Now.

She turned left at the four-way and slowed her steps as she passed the front of the church. The corner of the rectory came into view, then the steps, then the front doors. She hesitated before making the turn, and gasped as a fog blew around the corner between the rectory and the church and enveloped her and the buildings, removing all remnants of shadows and edges. The distant streetlight barely penetrated the mist, but seemed to point a hazy beam to the rectory doors.

Hazel inched in the direction of the rectory, feeling her way with her toes before putting down the weight of each step. Her vision was blurred, but her other senses were on guard, ready to trigger a startle and escape at the slightest stimulus. Any sudden movement or sound and I'm out of here, she thought as she tried to silence her footsteps in the gravel that led across the side lot of the church.

She felt a sense of relief when her feet found the paved road that ran between the back of the church and the rectory, yet she slowed her gait since it meant she was getting close. The fog seemed to lift a little, allowing the streetlight to illuminate her destination. The rectory was so dark it seemed to attract and devour what little light penetrated to its doorway. She was within reach. Now, she had a job to do. Since most of her courage was needed just to get this far, she deliberately turned her mind to her task.

She fished her hand into the back pocket of her jeans and pulled out the three cards. Her foot came down on the first step of the rectory porch, which groaned at the intrusion. She lifted the cards and inspected them in the dim light. The fog lifted a little more, allowing a better view. A foot on the next step and she was halfway up to the porch. She checked the writing. All neat. Another step up and her senses went back on guard. A distant noise made her freeze. Again the noise — muffled, but somewhat familiar. A dog barking? Way off in the distance. No need to worry.

With the final step onto the porch the fog retreated, leaving an ethereal mist that clung to the roofline of the rectory, as if it were trying to maintain a finger hold on the night. Hazel looked down at her hands once again to make sure everything was just right. The three-by-five cards were carefully hand lettered and the message was perfectly centered.

> To the Bearer of This Coupon
> ONE FREE LUNCH
> Johnson's Café
> Main Street, Boyston

Hazel slipped all three cards into the space between the double rectory doors and pushed until the last remnant of white disappeared from view. The tap of cardstock on the wooden floor seemed to echo in her heightened sensory world. A creaking sound came from the other side of the doors and a slight gasp escaped her lips. She hit alternate steps of the porch on her way to a full out sprint across the road and into the gravel. Her silence wasn't important to her now, and she kicked up a little gravel with each foot strike, betraying the direction and speed of her escape.

When she reached the corner of the church, she didn't bother with the formality of streets. She headed across the vacant lot and cut a diagonal path for Main Street. With each step, she came closer to the comfort of the streetlight and closer to the safe haven of her house.

As she put distance between her and the rectory, her mind was freed of immediate tension, and the residual adrenaline rush triggered a long-ago memory of the last time she ran this fast with a similar feeling of half excitement, half fright. In her flashback, she was sixteen years old and in pursuit of John Johnson, who had just stolen her bra and panties, which she had removed on a dare by her best friend, Edna Gwynn. It turned out that Edna was in cahoots with John and got a glimpse of his privates in exchange for the set-up. Hazel gritted her teeth through a half-smile. She never forgave Edna. But she got the last laugh later that year when she received a hurried marriage proposal from John after she gave him what he wanted in the first place and became pregnant with their first child.

Hazel slowed her pace as she approached the front of the café. She wondered what had happened to Edna. She recalled how Edna tried to follow her lead with the next-best eligible man, Preston Cunningham, but through two years of trying, she was unable to get pregnant. She recalled how Press tired of Edna's constant whining and how he carried out a well-orchestrated and very public break up that devastated Edna. At the time, Hazel felt a sense of vindication, but now she was sad. Poor Edna turned reclusive after the scene and slipped out of town later that year. No one had heard of her after that.

Hazel crossed in front of the café and turned into the house next door. She opened the door and slammed it shut, waking John, who was asleep on the couch.

"Where've you been? It's late."

Hazel stomped across the floor. "What do you care?"

John leaned up on his left elbow. "What's with you lately? Why are you so snippy?"

"If you don't know, then to hell with you," she said.

John followed her into the bedroom.

She turned to face him and put her hands on her hips. "You might as well get comfortable out there because you're not sleeping in here tonight."

He threw his hands in the air. "What did I do now?"

"You know what you did."

"No. I don't. If you're going to yell at me, just do it. I can't do anything about it unless I know what it is."

Hazel collapsed onto the bed, crying.

"Jesus Christ," John whispered. He crossed the room and sat on the bed next to her. "Just tell me why you're so upset and I'll try to take care of it. I'm sorry. For whatever it is." He put his hand on her shoulder.

She swatted his hand and turned her face away. She talked to the pillows. "You know the café is hurting for business ever since that little creep started eating at the Herndon's Edge. But now, you're going there for lunch, too. You and Billy and Mac. And you're eating there." She burrowed her face into the covers again.

"I'm sorry, honey, but we have business with Thibideaux. And we never know when he's going to show.

Besides, we have enough from my pension. We don't need the café."

Hazel rolled on the bed, grabbed a pillow and swung it against John's head. "You go to hell." Another swing of the pillow and she let it loose against John's raised arm. "You might as well take this out to the couch. You've seen the last of this bed."

John turned over on the couch and nearly fell off. He looked at his watch—2a.m. His mind went to the freeway shunt. Eyes closed, he pictured the gas station and mini market, both full of customers. Then he pictured Hazel in the bright new café. She stood at a podium, menus in hand, and ushered a new set of customers through the busy dining room to the only open table.

"That'll make her happy," he said to himself.

CHAPTER 11

GABE LAY BACK in bed and watched Misty Ronde-lunas dance over, above him. She smiled and started rotating her hips slowly to music that only she heard. She reached up to her neck and gripped the zipper that held her top closed. Pulling it down slowly, she exaggerated the sway of her hips. The zipper slipped past her bare cleavage, then past her navel, all the way to the bottom of the garment, and apart. She turned away and lowered the garment from her shoulders, revealing a bare back over her swaying hips.

No bra, Gabe thought.

Misty slid the top down to her waist and then let it fall to the floor. She turned her head and smiled at him.

He felt himself rise against the covers.

Misty slowly turned, exposing her still-firm breasts.

She put both hands on the fastener of her jeans, pushing her breasts together and upward with her upper arms. She smiled as she unbuttoned the jeans.

Gabe looked down at the large lump in the sheets. He was so hard it almost hurt.

Misty eased the zipper of her jeans downward and pulled the waistband apart, revealing dark wisps of hair.

No panties, Gabe thought. He interlocked the fingers of his hands behind his neck and smiled.

She peeled her jeans downward until they fell free to the floor, but she kept her right leg slightly crossed over the left, as if she wanted to conserve a small semblance of mystery. She kneeled next to the bed and ran her left hand under the covers.

Her hand touched him, and then gripped him. The hand was big, much larger than he imagined. As she moved it against him, he writhed into a sympathetic rhythm. His excitement built.

He reached for her shoulders, and moaned at the touch of his hand on her bare skin. Her shoulders were broad and muscular. He tried to pull her to him, and she moved slowly, keeping her left hand busy. His hand moved upward, behind her head, then quickly pulled away. Misty's hair was long, well beyond her shoulders, but the hair he touched was cut at shoulder length.

A stir and a snort. Gabe's eyes opened and dark images infringed upon his fantasy world. Another dream, he thought, but then he felt the hand. It was still on him, still moving rhythmically up and down, just like in his dream. In the darkness, he saw her silhouette, kneeling by the bed. He didn't want her to stop, but his confusion intruded.

Still a dream? But his eyes were open. He reached over and pulled on the lamp cord. He fell back into the bed, pushed her hand away, and yanked the covers up to his chin. "What the hell are you doing?"

Wanna sat back on her heels and grinned. "I ain't churning butter."

Gabe strained to pull air into his lungs. He felt his heart give an extra beat, then another, and he inhaled to thwart the long pause. "We can't do this. What's getting into you lately?"

Wanna giggled. "Nothing. Yet."

"I'm serious. Why are you doing this?" He swiveled to a sitting position and reached for his robe.

Wanna grabbed her pants and pulled them on. Then reached for her shirt. "I don't know. I'm just getting an itch. It comes and goes so fast and hard I can't seem to control it."

Gabe rolled off of the bed and hurried past her, into the bathroom. "Can't you find some other man to scratch the itch?"

"It ain't for any old man. That's the strange part."

Gabe splashed water on his face and reached for the towel under the window. He noticed movement outside so he leaned close. In the darkness he thought he saw the stringy mist of fog retracting into the night.

He successfully inhaled away another extra heartbeat and slumped on the lid of the toilet. He pounded his chest with his right fist. "And why is this happening here?" he said to himself.

Wanna leaned around the corner of the bathroom doorway. "Why is what happening here? You getting weird here at home, now?"

"I'm okay," he said. "We need to talk about this. Maybe tomorrow." He leaned forward and covered his face with his hands. There was no way he could tell Wanna that he felt the attraction, too. There always had been a slight draw to her, but this was more than that. It wasn't all the time. Just some times. And it was strong—hard to resist. His mind turned to reason. Either he would have to resist his urges or he would have to tell everyone in the Tri-counties about him and Wanna. "Second one won't work." He mouthed the words. "Have to try the first."

His heart gave an extra beat. Then another.

CHAPTER 12

THIBIDEAUX SAT UPRIGHT, his eyes open wide. He was in the rectory, sitting in the single piece of furniture that had been delivered when he moved in. It was a large chair with a high back and arms that were ornately carved to imitate the damned in Michaelangelo's *Last Judgment*. The chair was made of the darkest mahogany and was polished to a bright shine. Due to its great size, Thibideaux's legs dangled from the seat, short of the floor, in front of the single pedestal base, which allowed the chair to freely swivel through three hundred and sixty degrees.

Thibideaux's eyes half-closed, and he and the chair assumed a sympathetic motion, vibrating and jerking in smallish spastic movements, beginning in his midsection, then spreading upward. As the rhythmic contractions reached his shoulders, they spread to his right arm and produced an undulating motion that belied the presence of bones.

With a dull whir, the chair swung around so it faced to the northeast. The undulations of Thibideaux's arm intensified and moved to his wrist and hand. He slowly lowered the arm until it pointed at the ground. His arm became still. Now, the floorboards in front of the chair began to creak and groan, taking up a slight undulation that moved across the room to the near wall, still holding the bearing to the northeast. The walls shook, causing the roof joists to emit a guttural growl. The room fell silent and still.

Thibideaux slumped into the high back of the chair and closed his eyes. A slight grin parted his lips—enough to expose a gap of shiny silver that reflected the dancing flames of the fireplace.

"It's begun," he said.

The farmhouse was built in the early 1900's and was added to several times, most recently in 1954. A 500-foot driveway that led to a circle of trees surrounding the compound separated it from the gravel county road. The house was on the left, perched on top of a small knoll that overlooked equipment sheds to the right, the barn and silo to the rear, and a large slough to the left.

The first shudder came at nine thirty in the evening. All but one member of the family was asleep following the "early to bed, early to rise" life of the farm family.

The man paused over his daughter's bed and admired how the nightlight enhanced the angelic look slumber always caressed onto her face. He bent down and kissed her forehead. "Daddy's girl," he whispered.

He was half way down the stairs when the low frequency vibrations started with barely perceptible movements of open doors, small furniture, dishes and glasses. They immediately placed a strain on the beams and joists of the older part of the structure. As he entered the bedroom, the intensity of the vibrations increased, and trinkets and other displayed objects fell off shelves and within cupboards. The aged wood of the old house began to separate and crack.

The earthquake spanned the resonant frequency of the house frame, so the shaking of the old house increased quickly to the verge of structural collapse. The man stood still. Before the turbidity of fatigue allowed a reaction, the second story of the old house collapsed onto the first, dragging the upper floor of the addition down and forward into a pile. The raking action of the upper floor ripped the sidewalls of the first floor addition, causing a sudden oblique shear of the outermost part of the wing, down through the lower level until the house was leveled. The one exception was the farthest, short wall of the rectangular addition, both stories of which remained perfectly erect. It stood guard over the crumpled remains of the house like a headstone marking the site of a family burial.

The entire collapse took just thirty seconds and the temblor was gone. It was barely felt in any of the surrounding farms. If not for the tremendous sound of the collapse and the late night habits of one of the neighbors, the catastrophe would have gone undetected until the following day.

CHAPTER 13

GABE COMPLETED HIS required three calls for the emergency network and headed out to the site. He was one of the first on the scene and he immediately began digging through the wreckage looking for survivors. The devastation of what appeared to be the master bedroom was so severe, he left it alone. Instead he concentrated on the compressed wreckage of the upper floor of the new wing.

As others randomly removed debris from the pile, Gabe searched for items of bedding and parts of beds. With his more orderly strategy, he quickly found the lifeless bodies of two of the children. His heart pounded out the cadence for an increased fervor of his search. He knew the family had four children. Surely they couldn't all be gone. He put the thought out of his mind—he needed his head clear, focused. He needed to control his emotions, for now.

A partially buried bed sheet and comforter glowed through the otherwise colorless wreckage, about six feet away. Gabe picked his way through the debris and shoved broken wood and wallboard from the site. He stopped. A faint sound leaked from a pile of newer wood about ten feet away. He homed in on the sound, heaving shattered wood fragments as fast as he could, trying to find the source of the muffled cries.

His heart pounded in his chest well beyond its speed limit as the cries came to him, louder. He pushed aside a smashed chest-of-drawers and uncovered a small tent-like pocket formed by the slanting fall of two opposite walls. A young girl was wedged in the tent, curled in a fetal position, hugging a doll to her chest with her arms and knees. She didn't respond to Gabe's shout, but continued the sobbing that attracted his attention in first place.

Gabe pulled her from the wooden shards and cradled her in his arms. He looked for signs of trauma and was surprised to see that she was virtually unscathed. There was no blood, no mangled or misaligned limbs, only the dust of a hundred year-old building staining her clothing.

He pulled the little girl to his chest and trudged through the rubble toward the emergency vehicles. The family had just one girl, the youngest, around three or four. He spotted the sheriff. "Sam. Over here. She's alive."

Then he stopped short. He turned the girl in his arms and faced her away from the circle of trucks. On the ground were spread five white sheets, each mounded in the middle. Two were stained red. His heart jumped to his throat and he worked hard to suppress his tears. He hugged the little girl and kissed her forehead. She relaxed in his arms.

Gabe didn't sleep. His thoughts kept running to the little girl, now without a shred of family. He watched the clock approach and pass each numeral until the roosters celebrated another day free from the chopping block.

No snooze button on the farm, he thought as he shuffled to the bathroom. He wanted to get to his chores right away, then head back out to the accident site. He liked to help Sam sort out the details of those infrequent events in the Tri-counties that carried some mystery.

Gabe found Sam standing on the knoll, near the remains of the house.

"Look at that, Gabe. The barn and silo are fine. I've been through them. The barn was as old as the house. And all of the other buildings. Not a hint of damage."

Gabe turned a circle. "Any damage in the surrounding farms?"

"None at all."

"What do you make of it?" He pushed a broken board with his foot.

Sam shook his head. "Maybe an explosion. From a gas leak. That's about all I can figure."

Gabe walked down the far side of the knoll. "Sam. You might want to look here."

Sam jogged to Gabe's side.

"What do you make of this?" Gabe said.

Several land slippages around the knoll suggested that some sort of earth movement had taken place.

"Think an explosion would cause these?"

Sam shook his head. "Not likely. I've never seen anything like this."

"How you going to write it up?"

"For now, I'll call it an accidental collapse of elderly structure."

Just like the death of an elderly person is ascribed to "old age" when the cause of death is not overtly evident, Gabe thought.

Tendrils of mist blew in and Gabe zippered his jacket and raised the collar. His mind tried to make a connection, and one flickered for a moment, then took on life.

He was a young boy, on his bike, riding through a morning fog. He had always enjoyed riding through the earth-bound clouds. On this trip, he wished he lived three or four miles from town instead of only two. He pedaled his bike through the mist, counting on memory to avoid the chuckholes and washboard ruts of the gravel road that led from his house to the county road. Everything was quiet and gray, and the cool mist that flowed past him as he cut through the thick air felt good on his face, like he was plowing through serenity on his way to inner peace. He liked the fog because it was wet, and yet it wasn't wet. Like a wetness that didn't stick. The mental contradiction added to his feeling of freedom. Pumping his pedals backward, he joined them in clicking their pleasure at the release from responsibility.

As he pedaled up to speed, he let his breathing fall into rhythm: in . . . two . . . out . . . two . . . in . . . two . . . out . . . two. Mind works best in the backdrop of that kind of order. He'd need it. He had to formulate his list of sins and it wasn't a banner week. He hadn't cussed. He hadn't been mean to anyone in his family. But he did covet Mac McKenna's new ballpoint pen. The one that had three different colors in ink, with three different plungers to push the tips of the ink cartridges through the clear plastic barrel. Covet was a good word for it. He would never think of stealing the pen, but he sure did want it. He didn't want one like it. He wanted it. It wouldn't do any good to have a duplicate—he would have to be the only one with such a marvelous pen. Covet was the perfect word.

The fog thickened as he coasted around the corner of the rectory and up to the back door of the church. The thicker fog carried a chill so he hurried to the door and gave the knob a twist. It was locked, as was any additional wisp of his memory.

Gabe shook his head back to the present as a fog surrounded him. "Something bad."

CHAPTER 14

IT WAS A slow day in the Herndon's Edge and the tone fit Gabe's mood. Still devastated by the limited success of the rescue operation, he watched Deena Lee pay a visit to the two other customers and then come his way. He sat up straight.

Deena Lee slid up to the counter and centered herself directly in front of Gabe's broad shoulders. She leaned over, placed both elbows on the counter, rested her chin on both palms, and looked directly into his eyes.

He slowly swept his eyes upward from his food and returned her stare. Instead of a smile, he furrowed his brow. He could have sworn the top button of her blouse was fastened just a few minutes ago.

Deena Lee's smile faded a little. "What's the matter? Did I startle you?"

Gabe put on his best "great to see you" smile. "No.

I was just trying to figure something out."

Deena Lee's full smile returned. "You're pretty good at figuring, I hear. Any ideas on how we can both get rich and run away together to some island in the ocean?"

Her flirtation caught him off guard. His face felt hot. Usually one to watch a situation until he was familiar with its boundaries, and only then jump in, he decided to leap at this one.

"We could buy some tickets to the Lotto. If that don't work, I have a decent sum saved up. It won't get us a long stay at an island, but it would get us a bit of fun for awhile." He looked in her eyes again, to see her response as well as to hear it.

"A good bit of fun is what I'm needing. It's been a long time since any's come knocking on my door."

"I'm surprised that men aren't lined up at your door—to have some fun, I mean." His face returned to hot. "Uhhh—to want to take you out for dinner or something."

Deena Lee stood up straight and laughed. She turned and gave Teddy a wink. "I've been wondering. You live alone with Wanna. She's your sister, right?"

Of all people, Gabe wanted to be truthful with Deena Lee. But would she understand? Worse yet, if she knew, would that turn her away? Today was a major event for him. She was flirting. No doubt about that. Now wasn't the time to introduce such a complication.

"Yeah. When my Daddy died, we just decided to keep the farm going ourselves. I was nearly on my own a few years back when Wanna was sweet on the Robertson boy, but that didn't work out, so here we are."

Deena Lee leaned back on the counter. "And what about you? Any hot romancing come your way?" She didn't smile.

"Had my flings, but none seemed like the settling down type."

His mind caught a snag. On more than one occasion, Wanna had told him that he was too slow in his relationships. "Your romancing is like your driving — at least ten miles per hour below the speed limit," she had said. Evidently, in this part of the country, once courting was initiated, it quickly filed through all of the local formalities leading to matrimony. Anything less than an accelerating succession of requisite events in the relationship was viewed as a lack of significant interest.

Before he could say anything else, Deena Lee's attention was swiped by a request from one of the other customers. As she busied herself to satisfy the patron's needs, she opened a long-range conversation with Teddy.

"Teddy, I'm needing a partner for the couple's bowling tournament on the twelfth. You know anybody who can knock down a pin or two?" She shifted her eyes in Gabe's direction.

Gabe knew there were two kinds of conversation in the Herndon's Edge. If one was initiated loud enough for all to hear, it was an invitation for full out participation by the entire congregation of diners. On the other hand, if the conversation was meant to be private, it was necessary to speak in hushed tones, either in a booth, at the ends of the counter, or in Deena Lee and Teddy's case, behind the half-wall of the kitchen. This subject was now officially open to all in the diner.

Deena Lee took two steps in Gabe's direction, raised her eyebrows, and smiled. "Gabe, you do any bowling?"

Gabe frowned. "Naw. Tried it once, but my fingers were too big for the holes in the balls they have there. I couldn't find one that fit so I had to hold the ball in both hands and roll it at the pins. I kept putting them in the gutters. Got blisters on two of my fingers, so I haven't been back to it since."

Deena Lee lost some of her smile. "You can have a ball specially made. One with the holes drilled to fit your fingers."

"That's what I call too big a chance. I could do that, sure, but what if I didn't like it, or didn't do well? If I spent the money to buy a special ball, I'd feel like I had to get my money's worth. Then I'd be doing something just because I spent the money, not because I liked to do it. That'd make me a fool." He looked at Deena Lee, then lowered his gaze. Her eyes seemed to be watering.

Gabe's stomach churned. *Maybe I should have lied and told her I hadn't tried bowling, but I'd like to,* he thought. *Then we could have gone out together, just the two of us, somewhere other than the café. Or I could have told her that I did try it and I'd like to try it again.* He rejected both alternatives since she might lose respect for him if she found out he was lying just to go out with her. He didn't want to take that risk.

Gabe finished his meal, put a handsome tip under his plate, and stood at the counter. He curled his index finger in a "come here" motion to Deena Lee. When she came close, he leaned so his mouth was near her left ear. As Teddy and the diner patrons tried to home in on the words, Gabe whispered, "Maybe we can go out sometime."

He didn't wait for a response since it was once again blistering hot in the Edge. He thought he heard a soft "okay" as he turned to leave. There's plenty of time to confirm the response, he thought. Don't want to rush her.

Gabe drove home the long way and mulled over whether he should make an investment in a bowling ball. He decided against it since Deena Lee might interpret that as being too forward. He wanted to take special care to consider her feelings at every step. He was already feeling hungry for lunch the next day.

CHAPTER 15

A TAP ON the shoulder brought Thibideaux out of a deep sleep, but he didn't jump. If the chair didn't react, it had to be someone familiar. He settled into the hardwood and opened his eyes to the light.

He didn't know who to expect. In the last five years alone, he had been visited by six different councillors. Each, it seemed, was younger than the previous one. The last one probably shaved once a week. Are these the people who are making the mid-level decisions in the Organization? A sad state of affairs, he thought.

Once in command of his senses, he turned his head to meet his visitor. He was surprised to see a man in his late twenties with a dark mask of unrelenting facial hair belying the morning shave. Still young, Thibideaux thought, but not one of the teens they've paraded through recently.

"Sorry to wake you," the councillor said. "My business will be brief."

Thibideaux leaned forward. "What is it this time? Don't you people have anything better to do than bother me when I'm working?"

"You know why I'm here."

"And do you know why I'm here? Do you know how I work? Have you ever even been in the field?"

The councillor shuffled his feet and frowned. "We all know your accomplishments. And your reputation."

"Then why do you keep bothering me?" Thibideaux slid forward on the seat and brought his face close to the councillor's. "If my techniques produce results, why are you people constantly butting in?"

The councillor held his ground. "You know why."

"Oh yeah. The rules." He leaned back a little. "I knew the rules inside and out before you took your first breath. The Organization hasn't had a problem with my methods before."

"Yes. They have. I've read your file."

Thibideaux rolled his eyes. "Okay. Have your say, then, and let me get back to my work."

The councillor squared himself in front of the chair and moved his feet apart a little. He pulled a folded piece of paper from his inside coat pocket and opened it. "Your case has now gone up to the Provost level. This is their memo."

Thibideaux rolled his eyes again. "Shall I hold out my wrists so you can slap them?"

"I don't think you want to be so flippant this time. This is serious."

Thibideaux leaned forward and tightened his lips against his teeth. His voice was shrill. "Just have your say."

The councillor cleared his throat and looked down at the paper. "The provosts say you are to be given no more latitude. They acknowledge your long, dedicated service and your contributions, but they are tired of your continual breach of organizational statutes. They fear you're becoming a liability to the Organization. They send this warning. If you don't alter your path, you'll be pulled from the field and terminated."

"And what has them so upset this time?"

"You know what you've done."

Thibideaux slid off the chair directly in front of the councillor, who took two steps backward. "Acquisitions in rural areas are complex these days. If you'd ever done one, you'd know that. They take preparation. There has to be a set-up. People have to be primed. That's all I've done on this job. This is legitimate set-up work."

"And the lives of citizens are fair game?"

"I'll explain my actions to you once, and only once. So don't ask again. The first one was going to compromise my set-up plan. He had to be neutralized. The second case is the hook for the plan. If you'll have a little patience, you'll see how it plays out. Maybe you'll learn the difference between theory and actual practice. Maybe the provosts will learn the difference. Besides, I do follow the rules. In both cases, the little ones weren't harmed."

"You need to follow all of the rules," the councillor said.

Thibideaux exhaled. "You're new at this so I'll do you a favor today. How carefully have you studied the Organization? The statutes may seem clear to you, but once you've worked with them for awhile, you begin to see flexibility in the wording."

The councillor frowned and shook his head. "The wording is as unambiguous as it can get. There is no room for personal interpretation. You know the Organization forbids it."

"The statutes would be fine if all of the targets were robots, or computers, but we're dealing with people here."

The councillor balled his hands into fists and scowled. "The others don't have any problem following them."

Thibideaux took a step forward. His voice climbed up in tone to match his volume. "Compare my success rate to the others. Don't you suppose there's a reason? Working in the country isn't like working in the cities. If you want success out here, then stand back and let me work."

The councillor held his ground. "I can't."

Thibideaux laughed. "Why not?"

"The provosts have given an ultimatum this time. Your entire career will now balance on this one job. You'll stand review when you're finished here. I'm instructed to maintain an active oversight of your activities throughout this job."

"I don't want anyone looking over my shoulder. I refuse."

"You can't refuse."

Thibideaux looked at the floor and sighed. "Be a nice little boy and stay out of my way. If I'm to stand review at the end of the job, then there's no need for you to keep watch. I'll pass or fail on my own performance."

The councillor folded the paper and shook his head. "I can't."

"Why not? Why are you being such a pain in the ass?"

"There's a second part to the memo." The councillor's shoulders slumped. "If you don't pass the review, you aren't the only one to go."

"Heads will roll, huh?"

"No, not heads. Just mine. My future with the Organization is dependent on your performance, too."

Thibideaux smiled. "And what did you do to deserve this assignment? Have you been a bad little boy, too?"

"You just don't get it, do you? I'm in this situation because I defended you. Time and again. Without me you would've stood review long before now. Because of you, this is my last chance."

"So, you want me to kiss you or something?"

"No. Just try to think of the rules this time. All of them—as they are written. We're in this one together."

Thibideaux turned on his heels and walked over to the fireplace. He poked at the cold ashes with a stick. "You said you'd be brief. You've had your say. Now leave. I have work to do. And try to stay out of my way. If I'm going to be successful in this assignment,

I'll need a free hand."

The councillor shook his head and started to say something, but Thibideaux interrupted. "Leave! Now!"

Thibideaux turned his back. When he turned around, the councillor was gone. He spoke to the chair. "He'll be thanking me on this one. We'll make the target. And we've got a good secondary in the works as well, don't we? Just like the last time we were here. But we won't let the secondary get away this time, will we?"

CHAPTER 16

JOHN JOHNSON HATED funerals for the same reason everyone else in the Tri-counties was drawn to them. Everyone wanted to find out what "really happened." That was his job. Besides, he didn't like being around the locals when they were in the frenzy of inquiry. In this case, the funeral turnout was unusually large since two families were being eulogized together and the buzz of inquisitiveness was hive-deafening due to the nature of the passings.

John looked up at the sky. The weather was beautiful. It remained that way for both the church and cemetery portions of the service, but it suddenly turned nasty when Press' party broke for the Herndon's Edge.

John and Billy rushed in the front door of the Edge as the first raindrops fell. John watched a puddle enlarge in the entryway of the café as the rest of the group filed in. The sudden turn of the weather caught everyone without umbrellas and apparently didn't give Teddy and Deena Lee a chance to pull out the absorbent entry mats.

Teddy had a marvelous table set up with finger sandwiches, potato salad, cheese squares and melon balls. And the staple of all community get-togethers—green jello, with pear pieces this time. Teddy's jello mold was notorious in the Tri-counties. It was huge, more than two feet across, in the shape of a wreath, and Teddy's was the only refrigerator large enough to jell the green syrup. The mold was pressed into service during funerals, for promotions and awards, and following victories in local athletic events. Both fortunately and unfortunately, it wasn't needed very often in the Tri-counties.

John grabbed Billy's arm and steered him over to the far corner booth. He waited until Mac looked in his direction and flicked his head in a sideways "come here" motion. When the new triumvirate was properly sequestered, John put his elbows on the table and lowered his head, leaning toward the other two. They followed suit. John pulled a folded paper from his back pocket, a move that called the meeting to order.

"I been thinking about this situation and I got an idea of what's going on." John's expression bore the confidence of a theory that didn't need to be tested.

All three moved their heads closer together as John unfolded the paper. They were so close a softball would have had trouble falling between them without hitting one or more scalp.

John tapped the paper twice with his right index finger. "This here's a map of the Tri-counties." It was a rough sketch produced by John himself.

With two more taps, he added, "This here's the swamp, and this here's State Route 27. I figure the best route for the freeway shunt is as close to the swamp as possible since it cuts the distance, and making freeways is charged by the mile." He looked up and saw the other two were staring at the map. He removed a stubby pencil from his shirt pocket. "But it can't go too close to the swamp because it always floods a bit in the winter and spring. Also, the winter fogs would be a problem. So, as near as I can figure, the best route is right through here." He traced over a thick line on the drawing with the pencil.

Billy interrupted the moment of silence, his exuberance expressed in decibels. "That's beautiful, John. You should have worked for the highway department."

John and Mac bumped heads before recoiling in their seats. John looked at the crowd in the café and crumpled the map in his lap. "Shut-up, Billy."

When he was sure no one had noticed, John pulled the map back to the table and smoothed it out with his palms. His voice lowered a little as he leaned forward again.

"This route cuts the distance, but it also goes through the fewest number of farms. Look here. If the shunt goes here, it cuts through two extra farms, while taking it down here goes through an extra three." John had the faint outline of the borders of each farm drawn in and with each new pass of his pencil, he traced an alternate, more southerly highway path.

"Holy shit," Mac said, a little too loud.

John crumpled the map into his lap again.

Mac's hands leapt into action and his voice lowered to a whisper. "You suppose Thibideaux knows about this? Maybe we should let him in on it."

"Shut up, Mac," John said between clenched teeth. "This ain't the important stuff. Look here. Here's Press' farm. And here's the one where the house collapsed. Look where they are. Right in the path of the best route."

"Holy shit," Mac said, this time loud enough to turn heads in the Edge. His excitement started a drum solo of muscle twitches.

John had the map between his legs again, and he squeezed his thighs as tightly as if he was about to pee his pants right up on the stage of the Grand Ole Opry.

The three froze.

"Why's this so important?" Billy finally said. "Isn't Thibideaux smart enough to know this is the best way to build the highway?"

"Jesus Christ, Billy," John said. "Can't you see the families that are in the highway path are getting killed off? That's one way to get land cheap in these parts. Kill the whole family and the relatives will sell for a prayer."

Billy frowned. "Who'd want to do that?"

"Think, Billy, think. Who's here to arrange to buy the land? Who's here to find the cheapest path through the Tri-counties?"

Billy's voice climbed an octave. "Thibideaux?"

John's voice went in the opposite direction. "Shut the fuck up, Billy. You trying to bring the whole party over here?"

"Sorry, John, I just—"

"Look," John said. "We got a problem here. We need to go to the sheriff. But if we go with this stuff, he'll throw us out of his office. We need more proof."

Mac leaned forward and frowned. "I don't know, John. Press was killed by lightning hitting a tree, and no one's sure why the house collapsed. How does that go to Thibideaux?"

"I don't know, Mac. But there's just too much coincidence. That's why we can't go to the sheriff yet."

Mac's hands tapped the table in a steady rhythm. "So what do we do?"

John leaned back a little. "I don't know. Maybe we should watch Thibideaux real close. What do the two accidents have in common?"

Billy smiled. "They were both in the line of the new highway."

John rolled his eyes. "We already know that, Billy. Let me and Mac get some thinking done here, okay?"

Billy slumped on the bench.

Mac gazed at the ceiling. "Um . . . I don't know. What do you think they have in common?"

John inched closer to the table so his belly was creased by its edge. "Come on, Mac. Think. What time of day did they occur?"

"At night."

"Right. We're going to have to watch Thibideaux

at night."

"All night?" Billy said.

John frowned. "I'm not sure when the house collapsed, but Press was killed just after dark. Mac, you want to see if the sheriff knows when the house went down? I'll scout out the rectory to see where we can do the best watching."

Billy's forehead creased over a frown. "What if Thibideaux catches you? He might kill you, too."

"Good point." For the first time, John didn't know what to say, so he continued with an ad-lib.

"I know," he said. "Next time Thibideaux comes in here, I'll sneak out and check things out. If he tries to leave, you and Mac will have to stall him."

"How we going to do that?" Billy said.

John leaned back in his seat and brought his hands together behind his neck, interweaving his fingers. "You'll have to figure that out on your own."

Billy looked at Mac and smiled.

"Okay, let's get back to the others before they get suspicious," John said as he folded the map into a neat but edge-frayed rectangle and placed it in his back pocket.

As the three walked toward the others, the sky cleared to reveal a bright sun that glinted off the rain-spotted windshields of the parked cars, causing the patrons to shield their eyes or turn away.

CHAPTER 17

Deena Lee leaned around the half-wall and nodded to Teddy. He returned her smile and walked out to the counter and tapped a spoon on the worn Formica. "Y'all let Deena Lee know if you need anything. She's about to sit down for a spell."

Deena Lee hurried to the far corner booth, slid all the way back on the bench, and stretched both legs flat on the seat. Now in her fifth month, she was feeling the aches and pains of being on her feet the whole day. She looked at Teddy, who worked the griddle like it was an old friend, and smiled. It was his idea to give her five minutes of peace and elevated legs every half hour, and she felt much more than appreciation. She felt lucky. Lucky because, given the choice, Teddy would choose her over the griddle any day.

Deena Lee slid off the bench. As her feet hit the floor, a strong gust of wind blew through the door of the Edge, heralding the appearance of Thibideaux, who headed for his now-customary seat at the bar.

"Afternoon, Mr. Thibideaux. Special again today?" Deena Lee said, cheerful from her recent rest.

"Good afternoon to you, Ms. Murtry. I believe I will try Teddy's special. Do you recommend it?"

"No one's been killed yet." She giggled loud enough for everyone to hear and looked in Teddy's direction. When she looked back at Thibideaux, she thought she saw the hint of a grin.

"The special it is, then. And, you're looking radiant today. The pregnancy seems to be agreeing with you. All is going well with the baby and you?"

"I'm doing all right. Starting to get a bit of the heartburn, and the little tyke's kicking a bit, and my ankles are still swelling. Otherwise, can't complain." Deena Lee smiled at the slight contradiction in her answer.

Thibideaux shook his head. "It must be a wonderful sensation, feeling the baby move. Something no man will ever experience. No wonder the maternal bond is so strong. Have you thought about what you'll do with the child once it is born?"

Deena Lee froze. She only thought about it every spare minute she had, and she hadn't struck on a solution. It created an undercurrent of stress in her happy condition, like a strong undertow that tempers enjoyment of the beautiful waves at the beach. It also put an edge in her voice.

"I'll be able to take care of my child."

Thibideaux straightened on the stool. "I didn't mean to offend you. I was just curious about how you would manage to work and take care of the baby. I presume you'll continue to work here."

Deena Lee skulked behind the half-wall. Almost immediately, she returned to the counter and stopped in front of the little man. "What was it you said you're doing in these parts?"

The Edge went quiet.

"I didn't say, Ms. Murtry. In fact, I can't give details of my job right now. But it is really important, and it will be revealed to some, including you, eventually."

Deena Lee started to turn around, but stopped. "But you are from around New Orleans. Is that right?"

"I have a house just outside the Crescent City, but I don't get to enjoy it as much as I'd like."

Deena Lee put her palms flat on the counter directly in front of Thibideaux and leaned forward to take some of the weight off of her back. "How long do you stay in places like this? You've been here, what, about two months now?"

Thibideaux leaned back and folded his hands in his lap. "That's about right. My jobs are variable. All I can say is that I have to stay on to the end, and I don't know when that is until it's right on top of me."

Deena Lee tried to detect a change in Thibideaux's expression, but it was the usual blank screen.

"So, you have any idea how close you are? How

long can we expect you to come for the specials?" She forced a smile and straightened her back. Staying in one position too long only aggravated her aching knees and ankles. To her surprise, he continued the conversation.

"My guess is I'll be enjoying Teddy's specials for anywhere from six months to nearly a year. I like the country, and your part of it in particular, so I hope it'll be closer to the longer estimate.

"Special up," Teddy said as he leaned over the half wall. "Mr. Thibideaux, I've put together a wailin' dish today. If you like grilled chicken strips in a secret marinade, over wild rice, with a side of assorted greens, you'll be asking for the recipe for the sauce, which you can't have, but thank you."

Thibideaux looked up at Teddy. "Sounds great. Any reason you're in such a good mood today?"

Teddy rounded the kitchen wall and placed a straight arm on the counter. "I just made arrangements to have Teddy Jr. baptized this Sunday. He's able to hold his head up a bit, so I figure Reverend Sather won't give him whiplash when he dunks him."

Deena Lee thought she saw a change in Thibideaux's expression. He swiveled on his chair so he faced directly at Teddy, and his focus seemed to narrow — his eyes seemed more intense. And she thought she saw a slight glint of silver come from his mouth. Kind of like from the braces city kids put on their teeth, but she'd never seen them on a man of Thibideaux's age.

"My sincere congratulations, Teddy," Thibideaux said. "Baptisms are such wonderful events. They offer the hopes of the future and represent such opportunities I can't help but be drawn to them."

Deena Lee noticed that Teddy seemed as startled as she was. She didn't peg Thibideaux as a religious man. He hadn't made an appearance in church. She knew that for sure. Sunday worship was not only for receiving the Word of the Lord, it was also important to be seen receiving the Word. All participants seemed to make mental notes of who was and wasn't in attendance each week because if a regular missed a week, it was likely someone would drop in to see if everything was okay. If two or more weeks were missed, groups of fellow citizens would self-organize to come by to offer assistance.

Teddy stood straight. "Thank you for the good thoughts. You're welcome to drop in to watch the dunking. It'll start around ten, right after the regular service." Teddy's smile nearly reached his ears.

Thibideaux dabbed his mouth with a napkin. "Thank you, Teddy. I may take you up on the offer. I really like baptisms. Now, if you'll excuse me, I have to be going. But before I go, I have to ask for the recipe to your marinade. I don't expect a return—it's just a formality attesting to its great flavor. I'd like to offer a suggestion for a variation that would give it a distinct Cajun twang, though. A healthy dose of cayenne pepper would bring back memories of my home. Good day."

Thibideaux exited through the front door into a swirling gust of dust-laden wind. When the wind died down, he was nowhere to be seen.

Deena Lee turned to Teddy and shook her head. "Dang if I would've thought he'd ever set foot in a church."

Teddy smiled. "I don't know. That's the first time I've jawed with him. Seems nice enough." He walked toward the kitchen but stopped short of the doorway and turned around. "Y'all let Deena Lee know if you need anything. She's about to sit down for a spell.

CHAPTER 18

THE HOT, HUMID day finally surrendered to the dark and Gabe let his head fall into the pillow to form a perfect-fit crater that would cradle him into sleep. He let out a silent chuckle. Hell of a day, he thought, placing a wager he'd wake up in the same exact position.

Before he drifted off, he nudged his mind toward a familiar go-to-sleep scenario. Good night for one of Misty's dances. As soon as he conjured Misty from the narrow gap between wakefulness and sleep, his mind disengaged. There was no dance. Only sleep.

He didn't know how long he'd been away, but it was still night. The room seemed darker than it should have been two nights short of a full moon. Gabe shifted in the bed and stopped. The warmth of another body was close beside him under the covers. This wasn't Misty's way. She would do her dance, engage him on top of the covers and leave. "Sorry to hump and run," she would say with a loud laugh.

He moved again and the body pushed into his side. He felt the warmth from his shoulder to his foot and it triggered an involuntary shudder. Not a big one, and probably noticeable only to him. He struggled to put the sensations into meaningful order. This couldn't be Misty. This was how he imagined it would be with Miz Murtry. No burlesque. Just warmth.

He turned, and through the darkness he thought he saw her smile with half-closed eyes. She exhaled through her nose and the smell of her air was sweet, inviting. He never had that smell with Misty. He'd never had any smell with her.

He put his arm out to surround her and Miz Murtry responded by moving into a tight body hug. He felt skin-on-skin through the entire span of contact, and the hairs on his body rose to her, reached for her. Now he could feel her breathing. It was shallow and fast, with a slight tremolo on each exhalation. He pulled her closer.

A new sensation swept through his body—he wasn't receiving her heat, he was generating his own. It radiated from his body like squiggly distortions rising from distant asphalt on a hot day. His breathing fell into her rhythm.

He pushed his knee between hers and she let it in. He was about to pull her closer when she rolled on her back, pulling him on top of her. It was more a jerk than a pull, and her soft breathing turned to rapid grunts as she positioned herself under him with sharp, jolting twitches.

He straightened his arms and pushed away from her, but she tugged at him, grunting. Something was wrong. He tried to roll off, but she slapped her arms around his back and held tight. She squirmed beneath him. Pushing harder, a grunt parted his lips. Another grunt and he broke her grip. He rolled off, to the side of the bed and then to the floor. His hands shook so badly he nearly upset the light on the nightstand trying to turn it on. The brightness narrowed his eyes. Words flew from his mouth, loud, uncontrolled, like the bark of a dog. All-or-none. For dogs, there is no such thing as a quiet bark—one with some volume held in reserve.

"What the hell are you doing?"

Wanna peeked from under the covers. She smiled.

"I mean it. What the hell are you doing?" He reached for his robe and swung it around his shoulders as he walked to the foot of the bed. "You trying to ruin everything?"

Wanna slid from under the covers and threw her nightgown over her head. She stepped toward the door but Gabe grabbed her arm and pulled her around to face him. The glow of the moon spilled through the east window and illuminated her grin.

"We have to talk about this."

CHAPTER 19

THIBIDEAUX'S EYES OPENED wide. He leaned forward in his chair and mouthed a curse. Each word was exaggerated into a snarl, and with each one his lips parted as much as his paralyzed facial muscles would allow. The miniscule gaps revealed glimpses of silver that reflected the dancing flames of the fireplace, like bursts of razor-thin laser lights flying in radiating directions.

His chair began a slow counterclockwise rotation, through a full circle, and then picked up momentum through the next arc. It stopped before completing the cycle, facing northwest, toward Porter County.

Thibideaux raised his right hand in the air with his forefinger pointed skyward, and began rotating it in elliptical counterclockwise loops. The rotations tightened into small circles as his hand turned faster and faster, until it was a blur. He brought it down, stiff, with a slow shoulder rotation until it was parallel to the ground, pointing a vector in line with the chair. At the end of its swing, he flicked his wrist and released a small vortex of circulating air that exited the rectory through an open window and headed out into the night.

The clouds built up quickly over Porter County in a freak storm that was so localized it was hard to detect on the local weather radar. The twister touched ground for only a couple of minutes and then retracted into the clouds. While on the ground, the swirling tempest scored a direct hit on a single farmhouse, leveling it in a shower of wood fragments and broken lives.

Gabe led the slow trickle of emergency volunteers into the wreckage. He worked through most of the night and found the bodies of three of the six members of the family. This time, there were no muffled cries from the debris. No shouts of joy from the rescuers. He departed when he counted six lumped sheets on the grass under a large oak tree. A tire swing hung motionless over the bodies, tied to a stout limb. It still dripped tears from the brief downpour.

Back at home, Gabe slumped into his recliner and immediately fell into sleep. But it wasn't a restful sleep.

It was perforated by a recurring nightmare that would bring him to the edge of wakefulness, drenched in sweat, and then return him to its depths to repeat the cycle. His world was a never-ending pile of devastated buildings, and while he could hear faint cries for help, he couldn't find a single source of the cries. He sifted through the wreckage, overwhelmed by its volume. He felt minute by comparison, and the pile was growing with each reiteration. Or he was shrinking. All he could do was keep digging. He was developing doubts about his ability to maintain control of his world.

CHAPTER 20

JOHN JOHNSON TAPPED his foot on the floor and kneaded his forehead with his left hand, passing it down over his eyes and then back up his forehead. He pressed the phone against his right ear. "Come on, goddamn it. Come on you dumb sh . . . Billy! You awake? We need to meet at the general store right away."

John paused and tapped his foot on the floor again, this time harder, rhythmically slapping the linoleum. "Tough shit, Billy. We need to meet. In half an hour. Come in your jammies if you have to. Thibideaux's done it again."

John paced in front of the bench on the general store

porch and watched Billy time his passage to the bench, like he was timing a proper entry into the arc of a spinning jump rope. John didn't alter his gait or his expression. Billy was late. And this was as important as life and death.

Billy barely settled on the bench beside Mac when John spun around and verbally lunged at them. "Did you hear what happened out in Porter County last night?" He had his tattered map out of his pocket and smoothed open before the sentence was finished. He slapped it down on the bench between the two men and took a step back. "Look where the farm is." He barely took a breath. "Right in the best path of the new highway." He straightened his back and looked at Billy, then Mac.

Mac's hands began to twitch, and when he raised his eyes to John, the twitches intensified. Billy just stared at the map.

John shouted to get Billy's attention. "Now we got a problem we can take to the sheriff. He'll listen to us this time."

Mac shook his head. "I don't know, John. It was a twister that took that family. How's Thibideaux supposed to make a twister touch down?"

John swung his head from Billy to Mac and his eyes narrowed to slits. His hands balled into fists causing his forearms to expand. He took a deep breath and relaxed his hands. Back on the topic, Mac's challenge didn't cause a ripple in John's glassy smooth lake of intent.

"I don't know how he does it, but I know in my

bones it's him." John looked back at Billy. "Should we wait until he does in the other families to get easy pickings to the whole highway path, or do we do something now to show everyone what he's up to?" My son's got one of them farms in the path, and Gabe's got one. Hell, we know everyone in these parts. Do we just let Thibideaux get them all?"

Mac's facial muscles twitched in four-four time. "I still think the sheriff will throw us out again. We need some proof."

John pointed at the map and bellowed. "How much proof do you need? Maybe we should just knock on Thibideaux's door and ask him if he's killing all the people."

Mac bolted upright on the bench and waved a shaky hand at John. "Shitfire, John. You always get us in trouble with the sheriff. I say we try to get some good evidence. Something the sheriff can't deny. What do you think, Billy? You awake or what?" Mac slumped back on the bench and lowered his eyes. His face contracted in a staccato rhythm and his hands picked up the backbeat.

John snarled but held his tongue. A mutiny of a spastic and an idiot, he thought.

Billy finally looked up. "Why can't we do both? See what we can find out today and tonight and go to the sheriff tomorrow?" He closed his eyes tight, recoiled on the bench, and waited.

John softened his glare. "Good idea, Billy."

Billy's eyes went wide and his mouth gaped. "It is?"

John tapped his right index finger against his lips.

"I got a problem with it, though." He paused, tapped his lips again. "I promised the missus a night out for all the time I been spending at the Herndon's Edge. She's been working her fingers to the bone trying to get some business back. Good thing I got the pension or we'd be selling pencils by now."

Mac sat upright again. His hands circled into blurs. "I got some time tonight. I can sneak around after dark to see what's going on in the rectory. Billy, you want to snoop around a bit today to see what you can find?"

Billy frowned an apology. "I got to get a combine running and I got parts coming in for a couple of mowers."

Mac slapped his hands down and gripped his knees. His hands remained still. "That's all right. Let me check it out tonight and we'll meet back here, same time tomorrow morning, to see if we should go to the sheriff."

"No." John balled his fists and stomped his right foot. He glared at Mac.

Billy and Mac snapped their heads upward.

"Me and the missus will be having a batch of beer tonight and maybe something else, if you know what I mean, so I doubt I'll be able to make it at six thirty." John said. He was the one to call the meetings. "How about seven thirty?"

CHAPTER 21

THE EVENING SHAPED up as a perfect one for clandestine activities. The moon was full, but a dense veil of high clouds subdued its light. Shadows from the one distant streetlight were non-existent if one approached the rectory from the back.

Mac scanned the clothing section of the general store. He had closed early this evening—he hoped he hadn't missed any customers, more for their inconvenience than for his lost profit. He dressed in all black. His mismatched outfit included a long-sleeved sweatshirt with a partially peeling emblem for Harley-Davidson motorcycles. He always dreamed of riding a Harley but he never worked up the nerve. Janice wouldn't have it anyway, he rationalized.

He tugged on his black dress slacks and cinched the belt a little tighter. His gaze fell to his feet. The pants hung a little short, showing black dress socks entering black canvas, high-top Chuck Taylor model Converse sneakers. Mac hadn't slipped them on since the last time he tried to play recreational basketball over twenty years ago. That was before his muscles started working on their own.

He couldn't find a black hat so he broke the motif and slid on a cranium-hugging navy blue stocking hat. Now he needed gloves. Everyone wore gloves when they did this, he thought. Don't want to leave fingerprints.

All he could find was a pair of dark gray rayon-and-wool glove inserts. They would do. He pocketed a small, black Magna-light flashlight—the size that takes two double-A batteries. It was easy to conceal and carry, hands free, without banging around.

Passing the front of the main counter, he paused. The disposable camera display caught his eye, and for an instant his mind embraced the need for documentation of his sortie. A caution flashed like the strobe of one of the cameras. He remembered his days in the National Guard when he learned to fire one of those shoulder-launched surface-to-air, heat-seeking Red Eye missiles at imaginary jets on a strafing run. The Field Operation Manual stated that firing the device required a 100-meter diameter clear space, making the operator as expendable as the disposable launch tube.

Mac took the back way to the rectory, staying away from open spaces. He was halfway across the first of two back yards when his racing pulse and his emotional high returned him to the seventies, and his brief experimentation in mind alteration. Three times. The first two hadn't done much except give him a powerful sore throat, but the third was an experience he would never forget. Everything slowed way down, like a 45 played at 33 1/3. But despite the greater clarity, everything was slightly bent at the edges. He remembered how energized he had felt. Like he held advantage over everyone and everything. But afterward, it had scared him. It was too easy. Easy always had a price and he didn't want to find out what it was.

Now, he had the same feeling—energized, with a sense of clarity. Everything slowed way down. So, when he pressed through a hedgerow separating the two yards, he was keenly aware of the thump coming from the doghouse at the corner of the lot. He took a slow-motion step toward the back of the yard as a Doberman-mix peeked from the darkness and showed two rows of teeth separated by a guttural growl.

Mac's legs felt heavy—gravity was an enemy now. It took three full steps before he shifted into a sprint. Three steps he couldn't afford. The dog didn't move in slow motion. Mac heard its growl build to yipping barks and he felt its foot pats on the ground, coming closer. And something else caught his attention—the tinkling sound of a chain being dragged in the dirt.

At full speed now, the tree line approached, but the growling barks squeezed him. His mind flashed: if a train leaves Chicago going forty five miles an hour, and another leaves an hour later going sixty . . . This was going to be close.

. . . the second train would catch the first at the

tree line . . . Mac dove head-first for the bushes. The dog leapt after him. He felt its hot breath on the back of his neck just before he hit the ground. The force curled him into a ball and spun him around, facing the dog. Everything went back to slow motion. He folded his hands over his head and neck and the airborne dog froze in mid-air. Its growl turned to a loud yip, but it sounded like a slow-speed playback. The chain yanked the dog in a 180-degree head-first spin to the ground where it stayed, motionless.

Mac didn't wait for the dog's confusion to clear. He returned to normal speed and low-crawled through the undergrowth as the lights at the back of the house pushed the blackness of the night all the way back to the tree line.

He didn't know how far he had crawled. It was far enough so the house lights didn't penetrate the brush. Collapsing face-first into the ground, he needed to give his heart rate time to return to human levels. When he leaned up and removed his skullcap, the perspiration of exertion and fright dripped from its edge onto his forehead and ran into his eyes as a stinging punishment for his lack of planning.

He blinked the brine from his eyes and looked around. To his right, the brush thinned to a clearing so he crawled to the edge of his cover. The rectory was silhouetted by the sole streetlight of town. He looked for the usual glow of the fireplace coming from the living room of the rectory, but it wasn't there. That's a first, he thought. He inched his way across the dirt and occasional ragged patches of grass. At least they felt ragged. Halfway to the back of the building, a sharp, high-pitched whine invaded the quiet night. He lowered himself flat on the ground and froze. It took a moment, but the sound registered. It was the singing hinges of the front doors of the rectory. He raised his head enough to see the rectory porch.

Mac tried to control his breathing but it echoed in his ears. Midway through a protracted inhalation, a figure emerged from the rectory porch. The small stature and the shuffling, irregular walk confirmed it was Thibideaux.

Mac watched the little man shuffle down the steps and turn right, toward the two houses Mac had just circled. Thibideaux ambled past the house where a dog had a newly acquired case of whiplash, and on into the night. Mac stayed in place until Thibideaux disappeared into the distance. When he stood up, something wasn't right. His knees felt strange. He looked down and pulled on the legs of his pants. The dive into the brush and the knee-crawl to the rectory produced two large rips in the knees of his dress slacks. He bent over and pulled closer to the rips. Fortunately, his skin hadn't suffered the same fate.

Mac did a mental calculation of Thibideaux's distance and his maximum speed, and then sprinted for the back of the rectory. Better to snoop from the inside than to try to see from black-to-black through the windows. He was comforted by a dense fog that circled the back of the rectory and enveloped the building and surrounding yard.

Mac hurried to the nearest window and pushed

upward. He expected resistance, but it offered none. It slammed open. He paused. No sound from inside. He jumped up but misjudged the height—his center of gravity pulled him past the ledge and he tumbled, head first, into the room. The initial sting singed his forearms, and then his right side as he rolled onto the floor. He waited for a lingering pain to flare somewhere on his body, but only the residual rasp from his initial contact remained. He stayed still. It would take a little while for his eyes to adjust to the abyssal darkness in the rectory.

He reached for his flashlight, but paused. Only if necessary, he thought. Once on, it would have to be left on or his night vision would be reset. The move became moot as the dimensions of the room started to take shape. He released the flashlight and pushed himself upright.

The large bedroom was at the rear of the house. The hall to the left led to the front of the house, past the living room—the main objective of the search. Mac knew the layout well. Two years ago he tried to liberate the toilet from the bathroom halfway down the hall. His plan to sell the used fixture was foiled when the nut on one of the two floor bolts refused to release its rusty grip, even when the largest pipe wrench was enlisted. Hack sawing through the bolt or bringing in a blowtorch was out. In the Tri-counties, it wasn't a crime to claim an unused object as long as two conditions were met. First, there had to be no doubt the object was never going to be of use to the owner. Second, the object had to be removed in such a way that no permanent resident was forced to look, or listen, the other way. It was necessary to avoid the gossip mill.

Mac slipped into the bathroom, partly to see if anyone had managed to free the commode, and partly to see if it was functional, since it was the only refuse receptacle in the building. It was there, in the same non-functional, partly dissembled condition he had left it. He slapped his forehead with his right palm. There, next to the rusted nut, was the crescent wrench he'd been trying to find for ages. He pocketed the wrench and reflected on his good fortune, then on his carelessness.

A sudden chill hit his back and Mac spun on his heels to see nothing. The cold penetrated his clothing like it wasn't there, and an icy cloud puffed from his mouth with each exhalation. He crossed his arms across his chest and slipped out of the bathroom. The next room on the right was the living room, but he stopped short of the opening. A low whirring sound came from the room.

He leaned around the doorway and moved first one eye into the opening, then the other. The hardwood floor complained with a loud creak. The whirring noise increased in tone. He pulled his head back. The whirring stopped.

Mac leaned his head into the doorway again and peered in. He quickly withdrew his head. Only a chair. A big chair. He leaned around again, this time long enough to scan the nearest half of the room. Still only the chair. Another step and the floor groaned again, but this time, there was no whirring sound.

The living room was silent. He leaned his head farther into the room and scanned the other half. As far as he could see in the dark, it was empty. The large chair was the only piece of furniture, and it was placed in the geometric middle of the rectangular room, centered in front of the fireplace. It had a conical pedestal based and a high back of enormous proportions. It faced directly toward him.

He inched closer. His breath came fast, forcing an almost continuous stream of mist. It seemed to get colder the closer he came to the chair. His hand extended, index finger twitching, and touched it. It wasn't cold like he expected, but it wasn't warm either. He put out his palm and the chair turned with his touch. A harder push and it swung halfway around. It moved freely, like there was little friction between base and seat. Harder, and it turned a complete circle. He pushed harder yet, and he had to reach out and stop it when it came back to his position.

The chair was carved in some ornate way, but in the dim light, he couldn't make out the pattern. To get a better look, he walked around in front of the fireplace and swung the chair around to face him. In a single smooth movement, his hands grasped the arms of the chair and he catapulted himself upward, turning 180 degrees to land with his backside on the seat. Good thing I wore my Chucks, he thought. The chair didn't rotate with the leap—it continued to face the fireplace.

Mac wiggled himself back into the seat and rested his back and head against the hardwood seat back.

His legs hung short of the floor by a few inches. He sat motionless and sniffed. An odor rose to him. It smelled like sulfur, but sweet. It was familiar, but he couldn't place it. The smell intensified and Mac's mind clicked. It smelled like the transformer of the electric train he got for Christmas when he was ten. The familiarity of the smell relaxed him, and he slumped into the seat.

Then, he felt the heat. It came from the seat, seat back and arms of the chair. In a matter of seconds, the entire chair seemed to achieve the temperature of his adrenaline-perfused body and hold there.

A crackle sounded below his right arm, then one below his left. He raised his arms and saw the flashes. Electrical arcs jumped between the slats of the chair arms briefly illuminating the sides of the chair. The smell of ozone replaced the transformer odor as Mac pulled his arms together, away from the armrests. He tried to move to the edge of the chair, to dismount, but his body didn't obey his brain's commands. He was frozen in place as miniature lightning bolts surrounded him in the chair.

A low frequency vibration rocked the chair base, then the seat, and then the upper chair. The vibrations spread to the floor, causing a rhythmic groaning that spread along the floor to the junctions of the floor and walls. A non-functional chandelier swayed overhead.

Mac moved his right side, then his left, and this time his body responded. He inched his butt toward the edge of the seat in a right-then-left bun-walk—the only way he could move without touching the electrified arms of the chair.

Before he could get to the edge of the seat and slide down, the chair back heaved forward, launching Mac through the air. He landed near the fireplace hearth with a loud thud, accompanied by a whine as the air was knocked from his lungs. He lay motionless, trying to regain some semblance of a breathing rhythm.

Gasping, Mac looked up at the chair. It was still. No electrical arcs, no vibrations, no smells, and it was cold in the room again. He pulled himself up, favoring his sore right ribcage, and sprinted toward the doorway and the hall. Misjudging the width of the hallway, he smacked his head into the door jam of the bathroom. The angle of the impact stopped the upper part of his body, but allowed the lower part to rotate off the ground until his left hip, leg and both feet slammed into the wall down-hall from the initial contact point. He lay crumpled on the floor facing back toward the living room, dazed.

This time, Mac didn't wait for his breathing to recover. He clamored to hands and knees, then to hands and feet, and monkey walked to the back bedroom and out the open window. The disorienting film of fog triggered a pause while his mind tried to gain hold of landmarks and guideposts. A shadow—his shadow—broke through the confusion. It wasn't much of one, but it was there, showing the direction of the one streetlight in town.

Mac sprinted along the rectory, past the church, and on a diagonal across the vacant lot toward the nearest sanctuary—his General Store. His feet barely touched the ground until they found the porch and the front door. Fumbling in his pocket for the key, he turned the pocket lining inside out. The key clinked on the wooden planks of the porch.

Once inside, he collapsed on the floor, straining with each breath. Then the pain came. With each inhalation, his right side burned. He tried to take short, shallow breaths, but it didn't help. He shifted his position but the pain didn't relent.

Warm sweat dripped from his skullcap onto the floor, so he removed the hat and threw it across the room. He lowered his head. The sweat that fell from his brow stained the floor red. He bolted upright, ignoring the pain in his side. A terrifying thought stopped his breathing—he had left a trail of blood for Thibideaux to follow.

Mac stood and nearly collapsed while he adjusted to the temporary dizziness. He reached in his other pocket and withdrew the flashlight. Flicking it, he opened the door. The thick fog reflected the flashlight beam directly back in his eyes. Squatting down, he duck-walked along the porch to look for a blood path, but he couldn't find a single crimson spot. Back inside, he headed for the first-aid kit under the main counter of the store.

Normally, he would have walked the aisle slowly, admiring his organizational genius in the merchandise displays. The newer, desired items were placed low, in front, and the older merchandise of lesser demand in back, up high. Everything was in rank order. New to old. Front to back. Low to high. The oldest items were out of reach. Mac liked to fetch the ladder to get them down. It highlighted his joy at moving a long ago acquired item so he could celebrate clearing it from his inventory list and recouping his ancient investment. The oldest piece in the store was a wooden-handled de-thatching rake, which was bracketed way up near the rafters.

Mac limped into the garden section and stopped short. The floor vibrated with his weight more than he remembered. He took another step and the vibrations increased in both frequency and intensity. They continued when he stopped. The hanging merchandise swayed with the movements. All around him, items on shelves teetered, and then toppled from the displays. Up near the rafters, the de-thatching rake swayed slowly on its hooks, inching toward the ends of the restraints with each pendulum-like swing.

Mac didn't take another step. The rake reached the limit of the hangers and fell. The weight of the rake-head turned the sharp teeth downward as it descended, and it crashed down on Mac's head before he could react to its approach. The force of the impact created a sickening smack as the tines of the rake dug deep into Mac's scalp and skull. He fell, motionless, in the main aisle of the garden section.

CHAPTER 22

"I'VE BEEN EXPECTING you," Thibideaux said without opening his eyes.

The Councillor moved in front of the chair. "Why do you insist on breaking the rules? Didn't I make myself clear the last time I was here?"

"Crystal."

"Then why do you persist? You know you're not supposed to kill citizens."

Thibideaux opened his eyes. "I didn't."

"What are you talking about? Are you saying the tornado that killed that family wasn't your doing?"

"No, that's not what I'm saying. I'm saying those weren't killings."

The Councillor's brows pressed down, nearly covering his eyes.

Thibideaux scooted forward in his chair and rested

his right elbow on the chair arm. "You just don't get it, do you? They weren't killings, they were just consequences. Acquisitions require set-ups, and set-ups sometimes have consequences. That's all."

The Councillor shook his head and exhaled through his open mouth. "I told you before. The rules are not open to your personal interpretation."

"I can assure you I'm following the rules," Thibideaux said, emphasizing each word. "I can quote the rules right down to the punctuation. 'Never let personal feelings, such as glee, revenge, anger, boastfulness, pride, greed or conceit enter into the business at hand. Completion of the assignment is to be as emotionless as possible. Emotions can be used to set up completion of the assignment as long as setbacks are never dealt with through anger or revenge.' How's that? Or this. 'Recruiters are to blend in with the general population. They are to be an invisible force. They are to avoid any activity or behavior that might make them stand out from the average person. They will take special care to avoid drawing attention to themselves, or to the activities of the Organization.' Then, there's my favorite: 'Most recruiters will fit within an average physical phenotype.'"

The Councillor smiled. "Okay, you can quote from the training manual. How about working in accordance with what you just recited?"

"You mean like the part about blending in? Look at me. I'm afraid I break that one by just being."

"You know what I mean."

Thibideaux slid from the chair and looked up at

the Councillor. "What does the government call it when a military operation results in civilian deaths? Collateral damage? They don't call it killing. That's reserved for the enemy. The civilians are not killed, they're just consequences. Get it?"

"That's still your interpretation."

"Okay, you want to see me following the rules? Go back and pull my file from the last time I was here in Boyston, twenty-five years ago. Read it and think of our conversation today."

"I've seen the file."

"You have to do more than read it. You need to climb into it." Thibideaux paused. He brought his hands up to his mouth, paused again, and then lowered them. "Have you ever wanted to kill someone? I mean really, really wanted to kill someone. To watch their chest rise and fall with the last breath. To watch their eyelids flutter and their eyes defocus to another plane." He shook his head. "No, you wouldn't have, would you? Mid-level officers are never on the front lines when the battle is raging. They never pull triggers."

His eyes went wide. "Try to imagine that feeling—to want to kill that bad, but with rules that say you aren't supposed to. If you obey the rules and don't kill under those circumstances, that's power. And that's following the rules."

He moved a step closer to the Councillor, who backed up an equal step. His voice danced, like that of a child who just struck on a great new idea. "Here's what I think. The do-not-kill rule was written to develop that power, and for no other reason. Why? So we could use that power. When you go back to my file, see how I found a fate much worse than death for that individual. That's power. That's brilliance. That's following the rules. That's using the rules."

The Councillor shifted his weight onto his right leg. "You make a strong point, but I still can't totally agree. I don't think the organization will, either."

Thibideaux turned away. "What's your given name?"

"You know I don't have that information."

"You haven't seen your own file?"

"No. We aren't allowed to see the files of councillors. Only of recruiters."

"Then, what's my given name?"

"I'm not here to play games. I can't give that information."

"Do you know where I was born?"

"Yes."

"Can you tell me?"

"No."

"Well, I know where I was born—in New York City."

The Councillor looked down and shook his head. "Sorry, but you weren't born in New York."

Thibideaux spun around to face the Councillor. "Sorry to say this, young man, but you just broke one of the rules."

The Councillor frowned. "I did no such thing."

"Yes, you did. You're not allowed to tell me where I was born, or any other personal facts. But you just told me where I wasn't born, which is a personal fact that allows me to narrow down my search for my place of birth."

The Councillor started to speak, but Thibideaux held a finger to his face.

"Don't speak. Try to catch my point. If you interpret the rule about divulging personal facts strictly, you broke the rule. But if you interpret it more broadly, by saying you didn't tell me my place of birth, then you're in the clear. So, which is it? Did you break the rule or didn't you? Do you want to take the strict interpretation or the broad one?"

"I understand your point. I'll have to take it under advisement."

Thibideaux jumped back into his chair. "Can you leave me alone to do my work in the meantime?"

"I'll take that under advisement, too."

Thibideaux attempted a smug smile but his mouth maintained its dimensions. The slight tug of the feeble muscles pulled on the scars, giving him the only sensation left in that part of his body. Pain.

CHAPTER 23

GABE LOOKED AT the empty glass in front of the one unoccupied seat at the card table.

"Do you think he'll show?" Teddy said. "You told him it was tonight, right?"

"I told him," Gabe said. "He said he needed to get out with the guys."

The doorknob turned and Dr. Robert Halvorson stepped in and stopped. "This the place?"

"Come on in, Doc," Billy said. "How's Mac doing?"

Teddy stood up and nearly knocked his chair over. "Jesus, Billy. How about a, 'Hi, how are you' first?"

Billy looked at the floor.

Doc walked over and shook Teddy's hand, then Gabe's. He had to reach for Billy's. "Thanks for inviting me to the card game." He pulled a chair to the table and sat down. "Billy, Mac's going to be all right, but he won't be the same as before. He's lost most of his memory, and he has the mind of a twelve year-old. If there's a good thing in it, his hands don't shake any more."

"I want his hands to shake again. I want him back." Billy buried his face in his hands.

"He's in good hands. Janice is a strong woman." Doc rubbed his hand on Billy's shoulder. "Where's John? I thought he played with you guys."

Billy talked from between his hands. "He don't come outside no more. Not since Mac got hurt."

Gabe poured Doc a glass of Jack and tapped the deck of cards on the table. "We'll all chip in. Janice will have help. I don't want to slight Mac, but how about some cards?"

Billy wiped his cheeks and forced a smile. He raised his glass. "This is for Mac."

Two fingers of sour mash was left in the bottle when Teddy got to his first question. "Hey, Doc. You and Misty seem awful close. She as good as they say?"

Doc smiled. "She just works in my clinic."

"Then what goes on in the back room every lunch hour?"

Gabe slapped the table with his right hand. "They do the lab work back there instead of sending it out. It saves us a bundle of money."

Teddy burst into laughter. "Yeah, Gabe. And I suppose you still believe in the tooth fairy?"

Billy giggled. "Doc?"

Doc's smile showed teeth. "She works in my clinic."

Teddy jumped to question number two. "So, what brought you to the Tri-counties? I heard you were some kind of wonder kid up north."

"It's a long story."

Teddy reached for the second bottle of Jack and pushed the deck of cards to Billy.

"We're just warming up here."

Doc leaned back in his chair, lifting the two front legs from the floor. "I guess some people would say I was on the fast track. I graduated number two in my medical school class at Baylor and had a productive internship and residency."

"In what?" Gabe said.

"Internship in obstetrics and gynecology."

Billy giggled.

"Residency in family medicine."

Teddy put his elbows on the table and leaned his chin into his hands. "And you just decided to come to the country?"

"Not exactly. I had two good offers, and not for HMOs either."

Billy turned his chair to face Doc. "What happened?" His eyes were wide, smiling.

"We were in Minneapolis."

"We?" Teddy said.

"I was married, four years. We were trying to have a child, but we couldn't conceive. They had this famous specialist in fertility problems there, so we went. We found out the problem wasn't with her."

"You were shooting blanks?" Teddy said.

Billy giggled again.

"Low sperm count. You sure you want to hear this?"

"Ain't no one around this table within shouting distance of perfect, Doc," Teddy said. "People around here live for problems. You got one, they'll love you for it."

"Anyway, we signed up for the *in vitro* program."

"What?" Billy frowned.

"Test tube babies," Teddy said.

Doc laughed. "Not exactly, but something like that. Part of the way through the preliminary screening, my wife lost interest and cancelled the appointments."

"She chicken out?" Gabe said.

"That's what I thought, but two months later she told me she was leaving me for the famous specialist in fertility problems."

"Damn," Teddy said. "What did you do?"

"Nothing. The jerk told me that if I made trouble for her I wouldn't be able to get a job as janitor in the lowliest HMO in the state."

"You shoulda hit him," Billy said.

Teddy and Gabe looked at Billy and then at each other. Gabe shook his head and smiled. Teddy took a long drink of Jack.

"Didn't have to. He was indicted for not only charging his clients for the *in vitro* procedures, but also billing them to insurance companies, describing them as standard gynecological procedures."

"Bastard," Billy said. "Shoulda hit him."

Teddy laughed. "Okay, Billy. You're cut off for tonight. Can you still deal, or are you done?"

"I'm okay. I just get worked up about that white coat crime."

It was Gabe's turn to laugh. "That's white collar crime, Billy."

"Whatever. I'd get thrown in jail for a long time if I did something like that in my garage, but I bet he just got a slap on the wrist."

Doc leaned forward and the front legs of his chair slapped the floor. "No, he went to prison. But not before he had me blackballed. My two job offers evaporated and no one would give me an interview. And, not just in Minnesota. He had contacts all over the country. I guess he thought I had something to do with busting him."

Teddy took another drink. "What did your wife do?"

"She gave me some song and dance about old Double-Dip not being the man she thought he was, and that she was sorry. She wanted me to give her another chance."

"Shoulda hit her, too."

"Put your guns back in the holster, Billy," Teddy said. He turned to Doc. "What did you tell her?"

"I forgave her by handing her a packet of divorce papers."

"Hit her . . . " Billy said as his head fell onto his arms on the table. He mumbled something and closed his eyes.

"Looks like we're down to three hands," Teddy said. He turned to Doc. "Why here?"

Doc took a long drink of Jack. "I didn't have a long list of possibilities. This was far enough away from both him and her, and the job was in family medicine. I figured he'd never find me here."

"What about your wife?" Gabe said.

"Ex-wife. I don't know, and I don't care. She wasn't what I thought she was. She was pretty, though, and I got caught up in that. She was more concerned about her own appearance than about any aspect of our emotional ties. I can tell you this from experience. A relationship with someone whose primary goal in life is personal glamour is a one-way street. Maintenance of glamour doesn't leave enough time to be concerned about the needs of anyone except the person in the mirror."

"So why you hooked up with Misty?" Teddy said. "She's not exactly the settling down type."

"I'm not looking for anything long term right now, or anytime soon." Doc sipped. "Let's just say Misty's good company."

Teddy slapped the table. "I knew it. She as good as they say?"

Doc belly-laughed. "You guys are pros around here. All I'll say is that she is a very enthusiastic young lady."

Teddy turned serious. "You ever want a settling down type, Gabe's sister's a catch."

Both Gabe and Doc burst into laughter.

"What?" Teddy looked at Doc and then at Gabe.

"We got an arrangement about Wanna," Gabe said.

Teddy frowned. "What kind of arrangement?"

Gabe took a sip of Jack. "Not long after Doc showed up, Wanna went in for a check-up. Doc went to check her girl parts and Wanna went off on him. Busted up the office, wrenched Doc's arm and bloodied his nose."

Doc chuckled. "She accused me of a variety of perversions and threatened a medical malpractice complaint."

"Now, when she gets sick, I get the details and pass them on to Doc," Gabe said. "Anything serious and I just take her to the hospital."

"I still think you should give her another look." Teddy said. "When you're tired of Misty. She'll make one hell of a wife, if you can tame her."

Gabe dropped his cards and walked to the window and looked out into the dark fog. Despite the Jack haze, his mind couldn't leave Mac. And Press. And all the other deaths that seemed suspiciously unrelated. Something bad, he thought. Something bad for sure.

CHAPTER 24

WANNA WAVED AT Janice McKenna and hurried to the food section of the general store. She wanted to offer her regrets about Mac's accident, but she didn't know what to say. Shopping first would give her time to think up the best way to express her feelings before checking out.

A gust of wind slammed the front door into the adjacent wall turning heads throughout the store. Thibideaux closed the door and walked in Wanna's direction.

"Good afternoon, Miss Petersen. We haven't met yet. I'm Jackson Thibibeaux. I've been living in the old rectory for the last few months." He held out a tiny open hand.

Wanna didn't move. Her eyes were riveted on his mouth, his lips. They barely moved when he talked, yet his words were clear. "I can guess who you are, Mr. Thibideaux. Word spreads fast around here. Nice to meet you." She extended her hand and grabbed his with a death grip that would have taken a linebacker to his knees. He didn't react.

"That's what I like about this place," he said. "I'm as observant as your fellow residents, maybe more so. In fact, I have a unique talent along those lines. I've been known to recognize physical problems in others before any of the symptoms are strong enough to be noticed by professionals. So, I may be of some help to you."

Wanna took a half step back and frowned.

"Although I've only observed you from a distance, I've noticed a subtle change in your physical and emotional attitudes that tell me you might be able to use a little medical aid."

Wanna stiffened. Where did the little jerk come off, poking his nose where it didn't belong. She took another half step back and scanned herself. Her eyes shot back to Thibideaux.

"I don't mean to offend you, but you're looking quite pallid compared to how you looked just a month ago," he said. "I thought you'd like to know."

Wanna gritted her teeth and stepped forward again. "Looky here, you little pipsqueek. I don't know you from Adam, and I was taught to never talk one down when making a first meeting. I got nothing wrong with me, and I don't appreciate you saying otherwise." She balled her right hand into a fist. "You a doctor? I got five right here for doctors, and another five just to the south if the first ain't enough." She raised her right fist and sneered at Thibideaux as if he were Doc Halvorson trying to get a free feel of her privates without so much as a little romancing first.

Thibideaux took a small step back and put his hands out, palms up. "I meant no disrespect, Miss Petersen. I'm only suggesting you might want to try some vitamins. This time of year is difficult for most people around here, with the increased workload of the farm. I'll keep my opinions to myself if you'll calm yourself."

"Calm on this," Wanna squeezed through her teeth. She swung her right arm toward, but purposefully above Thibideaux's head.

He didn't flinch. He just stared with that silly grin.

Her bluff called, Wanna paused. The intent wasn't to injure, but to bully a little.

Now she'd have to do one of two things—follow through with a real swing or calm down, all but acknowledging that her act was for show. "I guess if you're looking after my well-being, I can thank you and be off to my place. I still think you should get to know someone before telling them they look bad."

"You are right, Miss Petersen. I just wanted to pass on my observations before anything bad came to you. Please forgive my forwardness. Good day."

Wanna watched the little man amble down the isle and through the front door. She hurried to the toiletries isle and stooped to catch a peek in one of the displayed hand mirrors. There were bags under her eyes.

CHAPTER 25

TEDDY JR.'S BIG day arrived and Teddy Sr. hurried into the church. He had made his weekly trip to the train trestle, and his car had become stuck in the sand. He missed the church service, and he was nearly late for the baptism.

Each week he packed up all of the food items that ran past their usefulness and delivered them to the tracks. The covered space under the trestle was a frequent resting spot for railroad boxcar travelers—they'd make an evening bonfire and get in a day of rest before continuing on their unauthorized journeys. It was such a popular stopping off point someone had erected a sign overhead that read, "The Next Place," in honor of their universal answer when asked where they were heading.

Teddy Sr. paused at the back of the church and

smiled. Looking out at all of his friends, he reflected on his good fortune. Some in attendance made up his regular clientele at the café, and most others came in at least once a week for a bite. He separated the locals into two groups. About half liked the traditional dishes on the menu. For them, he learned how they each liked their food prepared. And he made sure the portions were large enough so no one left without a Styrofoam box in hand.

The others were his challenge, and therefore his favorites. They were the adventurous ones who preferred the daily specials, which were made strictly from leftovers. Teddy was a master at formulating a tasty meal from the most irregular amounts and varieties of food materials, with only an occasional failure. The failures were still palatable and filling, but they paled in comparison to the wonderful tastes he generated in his numerous successes. Besides, the specials were always half the price of the menu items.

Reverend Michael Sather looked splendid in his long white robe, which accentuated his six-foot-two, well-proportioned frame. It was Wes Worthing's words of support that cemented the decision to bring Reverend Sather to the Tri-counties, even though this was his first congregation. From the first wonderful sermon on, the residents couldn't believe their good fortune at landing such a fine minister. They showed their appreciation by packing the church, and the collection baskets, every Sunday.

Teddy was overjoyed to see that nearly everyone remained seated at the end of the service. He scanned the room, trying to make eye contact so he could give a grin to everyone in attendance. When he looked to the back of the hall, he was surprised to see the unmistakable face of Jackson Thibideaux in the very back, next to the doors. Thibideaux stood, but his head barely rose above those of the sitting congregation. Teddy gave Thibideaux a smiling nod, which was returned as a stiff-necked, slight bend of the waist.

Teddy beamed as Teddy Jr. was handed from his wife, Rachel, to the godparents, Wes and Thelma Worthing. Teddy Jr. was dwarfed in Wes' huge hands, and then grew when he was passed to Thelma's petite arms. Teddy Jr. wore a white christening gown that Deena Lee had hand sewn, with an embroidered cross on the chest and "Teddy John Rosewald Jr." on the hemline, all in gold thread.

Teddy's eyes locked on the small man in the back of the church. Thibideaux rubbed his eyes with his fists, then clasped his hands in front of his belt. Teddy watched his wide eyes slowly scan the room as the opening prayers were offered, like he was trying to memorize the layout of every chandelier, crucifix, and decoration. Thibideaux's hands shook as if he were a third grader about to recite the Gettysburg Address, from memory, to an auditorium full of video camera-toting parents.

Reverend Sather took Teddy Jr. from Thelma Worthing and poured water from the baptismal fountain over the baby's forehead, bringing Teddy's attention back to the ceremony. He watched the Reverend hold his thumb and forefinger at right angles as he traced the cross on Teddy Jr.'s forehead with the tip of this thumb. Teddy's eyes brimmed with tears.

At the conclusion of the baptism, Thibideaux waited at the back of the church as all of the well-wishers extended their congratulations to the Rosewalds, and particularly to the newest official member of the congregation. When most of the crowd were gone, Thibideaux came forward, holding out a legal-sized envelope to Teddy Sr.

"I'd like to offer my sincere congratulations to the three of you on this glorious day, and to forward this gift to the man of the hour, Teddy Jr."

Teddy Sr. pulled the envelope sides apart and forced a swallow. By his quick thumb flip, there were ten $100 bills.

"Mr. Thibideaux, this is beyond generous. I don't know what to say. It's a wonderful surprise."

"It's given to the precious Teddy Jr. and only on one condition. The entire amount, not a cent less, must be put away for his future. If it's invested wisely, and added to on a regular basis, he won't be wanting when he reaches adulthood. Can you promise me you'll do that?"

Teddy reached out and shook Thibideaux's hand. "Absolutely. We'll see to it that Teddy Jr. gets a weekly addition. We can't thank you enough. Your kindness brings tears to my eyes."

"It gives me great joy as well. Congratulations again, and good day."

As the church door slammed shut, Teddy thumbed through the bills again. He looked at Teddy Jr. in Rachel's arms. "Your future's going to be bright, little one."

All day, the baptism was the first topic of conversation with each customer, and the constant mention seemed to give Deena Lee some of the energy she had lost in the last couple of weeks.

In honor of Teddy Jr.'s big day, Teddy had offered a free dessert to all who stopped in at the Herndon's Edge the next day. He was up all night baking cakes and pies, and word spread fast making it one of the busiest days since he had bought the café six years ago.

Deena Lee touched her cheeks, which were sore from all the smiling. She was fascinated by the baptism ceremony and the reaction it evoked in the residents. She hadn't been overly religious before moving to the Tri-counties. But lately she was captivated by the weekly sermons of hope and joy offered by Reverend Sather. It seemed like he was talking directly to her every week, like the rest of the worshippers weren't there.

When the afternoon slow-down came, Deena Lee leaned on the half-wall and engaged Teddy's eyes.

"You suppose I could get my young one baptized?"

Teddy smiled. "Of course. Reverend Sather would be honored to do it for him, or her. What is it anyway? It'd be easy to tell by now."

"Don't want to know. I prefer to be surprised." A deep groove cleaved her forehead. "But, I wasn't baptized. Does that matter?"

Teddy rounded the half-wall. "Naw. You could

probably get a two-for-one. Get baptized right along with the tyke."

Deena Lee didn't notice the bright sunny day had given away to a dark, cloudy afternoon, and that it had started to rain. A bright flash of lightning and a near simultaneous clap of thunder both illuminated the café and shook its walls, bringing the weather change to their attention. Deena Lee scrambled for the absorbent entry mat while Teddy checked the fuse box to make sure no fuses had blown.

"How old do they have to be to do the baptism?" Deena Lee called from across the café.

Teddy slapped the fuse box door shut and walked back to the counter, where he half-leaned with his weight supported by his right arm. "Don't really matter that much, but better to do it sooner than later. You never know what's going to happen, so it's better to save their little souls early on."

Deena Lee straightened the mat and returned to her station behind the counter, sliding up next to Teddy.

"I get the best feeling from being in church and listening to Reverend Sather. I want my little one to get the same feeling. I want the child to be like you, Teddy. Would you and Rachel be the godparents?"

Teddy leaned back as an ear-to-ear smile creased his cheeks. He grabbed Deena Lee and gave her a tilting hug. "We'd be proud."

As business started to pick up again, the sky cleared and the sun came out. It shyly peeked around the billowing clouds, then, when the coast was clear, ventured into a clearing and beamed. Following suit, Deena Lee's mind sneaked around in the clouds until finding the clarity to shine brightly about the baptism. There would be no more cloudy days on that matter.

CHAPTER 26

GABE STOMPED OVER to the couch and flopped down next to Wanna. He fumbled with a crease in his overalls, then spun his head in her direction. "You've been under a black cloud lately. What's the matter?"

"Nothing."

"Well." Her squint made him pause. "You got to snap out of it. You ain't been much help around here for the past week, with all the laying around. You sure you're feeling all right?"

She threw her hands in the air and let them smack down on her thighs. "Why's everyone asking if I'm feeling good? Do I look like I've been rolling in doggie doo or something?"

Gabe squeezed back a few inches and smiled. "Geez. Someone had an extra bowl of bitch flakes this morning."

Wanna stared at Gabe. Her eyes watered. "It's that damn Thibideaux."

Gabe leaned away from the couch cushion. "What'd he do?"

"I saw him at the store last week." She wiped her eyes with her sleeve. "He said I didn't look so good."

Gabe rolled his eyes and relaxed into the couch. "Come on, Wanna. You look fine."

"No, I don't. It's worse than the shrimp says. I can see it." She smoothed her hands over her face. "I could get some of the store-bought vitamins, but I think I'm needing some of the strong ones. From Doc. Can you get some for me?" She put her hand on Gabe's thigh. "Tell him I'm so worried I'm thinking of coming in to be examined."

Gabe thought about Wanna's fertile hypochondria and giggled. Then his mind took off. Kill two birds, he thought. "I'll stop by the clinic tomorrow."

"You keep your eyes off Misty's titties when you go there. She'd be with you in an instant if you wanted it. I can see it in the way she looks at you."

Gabe's smile widened.

Gabe pulled a pill from each of the two containers and set them aside. Too bad Misty hadn't been there when he stopped in at Doc's. He poured a large glass of orange juice. One pill was large and he remembered how Wanna had trouble swallowing even average pills, unless she took a full mouthful of fluid before the pill and swallowed both together. The other pill wasn't a problem. It was half the diameter of a pencil eraser, and thin enough to go down easily.

Wanna slumped on the couch, hypnotized by the television. "What's up with the two pills?"

"Just what Doc gave me. He said the big one was to get your energy back and the small one was to put color in your cheeks." Gabe pulled her shoulder away from the couch cushion and peered around at her backside. "Bend over after you take it and let me check to see if it's working."

CHAPTER 27

JOHN JOHNSON DIDN'T move when the doorbell broke the silence of the house. A second ring and he pushed at the armrests of his chair, but to no avail. His mind told him it might be Mac—that he was off the hook. The whole thing was just a nightmare, he thought, hoped. Maybe he hadn't really left Mac hanging when he fabricated a night out with his wife and instead spent it in bed, safe. Was he really that much of a coward?

The doorbell rang again, twice, three times, and John moved to the edge of the chair. Irritation elbowed its way in, doubling his emotional repertoire of the past forty-eight hours. Two more rings and he was at the door, ready to pounce. He yanked open the door. "What the hell's so goddamn important?"

The door-draft startled Billy and his finger pressed

and held the doorbell button for a final double ring. "John . . . I'm scared."

John looked past Billy, to the right, and then he leaned around so he could see to the left. "Come in," he said in a quick burst, like he was welcoming a spy after hearing the proper password.

Billy sat on the edge of the couch and leaned forward with his forearms on his thighs. "We need to go to the sheriff."

John let his weight fall into his chair. He gripped the armrests. "It doesn't make any sense, Billy. Mac lived in town, not in the highway route."

"That don't matter, John. He wasn't killed. Thibideaux didn't hurt Mac to get his property. He did it because Mac was checking him out. Besides—"

"What if we're next?" John looked at his knees.

"Let me finish," Billy said. "I talked with Doc. Something else happened last night. Mac had bruises all over the left side of his body, and his left knee was sprained. He had cuts under his left eye, and a split lip on the left side of his mouth. He needed three stitches for a gash on the left side of his forehead."

John looked up at Billy. "So what?"

Billy moved forward a couple of inches. "The rake hit him in the top of the head, but to the right side. Doc can't figure out how Mac got the other injuries. Come on, John. I can't do this alone."

John pushed his back against the seat cushion. "So, something happened to Mac before the rake hit him?"

"That's what Doc thinks."

"And it had nothing to do with the highway shunt?"

"Yeah."

A smile slowly spread across John's face. "So Thibideaux roughed Mac up for snooping. The sheriff will listen to that."

CHAPTER 28

SHERIFF SAM MERRIWETHER was relatively young to have jurisdiction over a three county area, but in his thirty-one years, he had collected a series of life experiences that set him up for law enforcement. His father had been a police detective in Kansas City, where Sam started going on ride-alongs as soon as he was into puberty. He completed the ROTC program at the University of Kansas and served in the Army after graduation. He chose to get out after Desert Storm, not because of a dislike for the Army, but because he missed the thrill of law enforcement back home.

He breezed through the police academy in Kansas City, and when an opening came up for a sheriff in a rural tri-county area less than a day's drive from home, he had his father pull some strings to get him on the interview list. The rest was his own doing—his personality, dedication and experience came through and Sam was selected.

Sam saw John Johnson heading for the door, followed by Billy Smyth, who stood a full head taller than John. Damn it, he thought. Just what I need today. I'm going to have to charge him with something one of these times or he's going to keep doing the vigilante stuff until he hurts somebody.

John stomped through the door, followed by Billy. "Afternoon, Sam. I got something you need to hear."

Sam didn't let John continue. "I'm kind of busy, John. You haven't been poking your nose in where it doesn't belong again, have you? I'd hate to have to charge you with being a nuisance."

John bumped Sam's desk with his thighs. "Look here, Sam. This is about Mac. And more. We got something that's about to boil over here and we need to do something about it now."

Sam moved against the other side of the desk and looked down at John. "First, you calm down. Tell me what's got your underwear in knots this time." Sam was just short of six feet, and at one hundred eighty-five pounds, he was well endowed with muscle, although it wasn't evident through his uniform. "Sit down, John." It was an order, not an invitation.

John pulled a heavy wooden chair close to the desk. Billy sat back a foot, behind John's shoulder.

"It's about Thibideaux. He's behind it all—"

"Hold on. As far as I know, Mr. Thibideaux has been minding his business since he arrived in Boyston. I haven't had a single call to suggest he's been anything but an upstanding citizen. If you go accusing innocent people again, I'll write you up for false reporting."

"But he ain't innocent, Sam. Just let me explain what I've found and then you be the judge. Hear me out. Please."

The plea caught Sam off guard. He hated John's condescending attitude, which he attributed to John's reaction to his youth and the fact he hadn't grown up in the area. But this was the first time he'd heard John ask instead of demand.

"Okay, okay," Sam said. He pulled his chair across the floor and the wheels squeaked until his weight hit the chair. "What have you got for me?" He looked over John's shoulder at Billy, who returned his look with an eager grin.

Sam drew the left pullout panel of his desk to its limit and raised both of his legs onto it. He crossed them at the ankles and leaned back into his chair. He maintained eye contact as John explained his theory about the divided highway shunt, the best route, the number of farms in that and alternate routes, and the deaths of the families in the best route.

When John spread his tattered map on the desk, Sam pulled his legs down, swiveled them under the desk, and faced John, and the map.

John continued. When he came to Mac's accident, Sam stood up and paced the office, occasionally looking at the two visitors. Every time his eyes locked Billy's, he watched Billy's face smooth into a silly grin.

Sam stood at the west window, looking out at the heavy rain. He paused. His thumbs were hooked in his belt, and his index finger repetitively drummed the thick leather. "I don't know what's up with this strange weather. It changes and then changes back in a matter of minutes."

"What about what we just told you, dammit?" John's voice boomed.

When Sam spun around, John was leaning forward in his chair as if he were about to get up.

Sam extended both hands in a stop gesture. "Keep your pants on, John. I'm thinking about it."

John sat back hard into the chair. He looked at Billy and smiled. He inched forward a little and cleared his throat. "We need to do something right away. My son's farm is in the best route."

"John. Shut up. I didn't say I was buying your story, I just said I was thinking about it."

Sam did two laps around the office while John folded his map and returned it to his pocket. Every time Sam looked, Billy's eyes were riveted to him.

"Your story's interesting, and I have no idea what Mr. Thibideaux is doing in the Tri-counties. It makes some sense, but tying him to lightning, earthquakes and twisters is more far-fetched than anything you've brought in here yet. Maybe it's time to make Mr. Thibideaux's acquaintance and find out just what he's here for. Would that give you some rest?"

"That'd be a good start, Sam," John said. "But I doubt he'll give anything up. He's a clever son-of-a-bitch, as far as I can tell." John leaned back in his chair and grinned.

"I'll go talk to him under one condition. You have

to stop your snooping. And, Billy. Stop staring at me like that. You're giving me the creeps."

Billy's eyes went to the floor and his grin drained to a gape. His shoulders slumped so much they nearly touched.

"I'll lay low, Sam." John's voice filled the office. "But you need to find out what Thibideaux is up to right away. I have a feeling some major bad is coming soon."

"I'll get on it right away. If anything comes of it, I'll get back to you. But don't call me, let me call you." He watched John nearly tip his chair over when he stood. Billy slinked behind him. "And sorry for growling, Billy. I'm just upset by all the accidents lately. Are you up for a ride along one of these nights?" Sam smiled an apology.

Billy's head snapped around to show a wide smile, and he walked right into John's back, who growled a complaint. Billy giggled. Once outside, he jogged to John's car and looked back at Sam, smiling.

CHAPTER 29

GABE AND WANNA were putting up hay in the barn loft and the hot, humid summer day was making it a sweat fest. There wasn't a hint of breeze to help cool them off.

Wanna dropped her bale and wiped her forehead with a bandana. "Tonight's your card game so we better finish this up today. You'll be hung over tomorrow."

Gabe grabbed his lower back in his hands and stretched in a backward arc. "I'll probably stay at Billy's. We're planning to head up to the reservoir for some walleye fishing tomorrow. Should be at it all day if we feel okay. If we're lucky, we'll have Teddy cook up the fish—we'll give you a call. If we don't get any walleye, we'll just have a few more drinks for having to eat Teddy's special." He giggled.

A strong wind whipped up and blew straight through the two open ends of the barn loft. Gabe stripped off his shirt so the sweat would evaporate faster.

"Shit, Gabe. It ain't fair how a man can pull off his shirt and a woman has to keep herself bundled up. It just ain't fair."

Gabe put his hands on his hips. "For Christ sakes. We're up here in the barn and there ain't a soul around but us. If you want to peel off, go ahead." His voice carried a hint of challenge. "It's just us."

"Don't have to be told twice." She had her shirt and bra off in an instant and she waved her hands skyward.

Gabe returned to the bales, but he watched her out of the corners of his eyes. There's something about jiggling breasts that makes it impossible for a man not to look, he thought. And her's are big—puts a sway to the jiggles.

Wanna reached for her bandana again and wiped her forehead. She looked at Gabe and then down at her protruding nipples. She smiled.

After a few more bales, she dropped her bale hook and skipped over to the bucket of drinking water. She bent at her waist so her torso was parallel to the floor, her breasts hanging straight down. She pulled a ladle of water to her mouth, but paused. She straightened up and poured the water down her chest, and flashed an evil grin. "You want some?" She chuckled.

Gabe walked over and exhaled a giggle. "Give me what you got."

Wanna loaded a ladle and gave it a hurl, full force into Gabe's face and chest. She reached for the bucket just before he grabbed it, and in the struggle, most of it spilled on them both. She twisted it away, and his arms wrapped around her. The bucket dropped onto the wooden floor as she turned into him.

It took only seconds for her hands to free him from his trousers. He responded by slipping her jeans from her hips. She kicked the clothing into a pile on the mat of hay that lined the floor and pulled him down. Rolling him on his back in a single quick motion, she straddled him, pinning him down and taking him in at the same time.

Gabe's mind went blank, but only for an instant. Wanna hovered over his face, exhaling in soft grunts. Like a metronome, the vocalizations entrained his movements to hers, their vigor increasing. He heard a second set of sounds, rhythmically entwined with hers, but softer, more like the panting of a dog. The sounds were his.

His right hand pulled from Wanna's back and gripped his head. The left hand stayed on her back. Buck her off like a rodeo horse, he thought, but the urge couldn't compete with what he felt and saw. Her breasts were in a posture no man could resist—hanging straight down—and only inches from his face. Her motion exaggerated their jiggle and sway—he didn't want it to end.

As his excitement built, he grasped for the only out left for him—his secret weapon. He closed his eyes and tried to visualize Miz Murtry. Instead of motivating an escape, this only superimposed Miz Murtry's face on Wanna's body, and within seconds it was all over. He gasped for what little oxygen hadn't exited the barn along with his good intentions.

"Shit, Wanna."

"Don't say a word. Let me enjoy what I'm feeling right now. We'll talk later."

The wind died down in parallel with their excitement, and Gabe rolled on his side, away from her. The mountain of unstacked hay bales seemed small in comparison to the problems he had just created.

Wanna's rhythmic breathing captured his attention, then sent his mind into freewheel. Confession. He needed to confess his sins. But to whom? And where did that come from? He wasn't Catholic.

Thibideaux sat in his chair and grinned, flicking small lightening bolts from his fingertips. They crashed into the walls and extinguished, creating an electric display that would have inspired "oohs and aahs" from an audience, had one existed. His thoughts turned to his job. *Where's the damn councillor when I need him? He missed some of my best handiwork today.*

CHAPTER 30

THE SUN WAS an oversized orange orb on the western horizon as Sam Merriwether drove up to the rectory. His knuckles hit the door once, twice, then hit air as the doors swung inward, serenaded by singing hinges. Thibideaux stood in the center of the double entrance, dwarfed by the rectory atrium.

"Sheriff Merriwether. What a surprise. What can I do for you"?

"Good afternoon, Mr. Thibideaux. I'm here on business." Sam shifted into professional mode. "To be blunt, some of the residents have expressed concerns about the increase in accidents in the area, and a suggestion has surfaced that you might be involved." He paused to watch Thibideaux's expression, but it didn't change. "I know when a person comes into a closed community like this, a state of distrust can make life miserable for the newcomer, so I'll assure you I'm just being thorough by following up on all matters related to these tragedies."

"Fair enough, Sheriff. What can I do for you?"

Sam shifted his weight slightly. "You can start by giving me some information about your business here in the Tri-counties. What's your occupation?" He took a small spiral-bound notebook and pen from his shirt pocket and thumbed to a blank page. Pen touched paper, ready to write.

"I'm not trying to be uncooperative, but I'm afraid I can't divulge my occupation or my business in these parts without compromising the goals of my Organization."

Sam shifted his eyes up to Thibideaux's and a shiver ran up his back. His eyes were black. Sam's eyes returned to the notebook and he tapped the pen tip on the page. "Okay." Not okay. Why would someone refuse such a simple request? "How about this? What if I tell you what's been proposed, and you can tell me if it's off base."

Thibideaux didn't say a word.

Sam shifted his weight to his other leg. "Okay . . . It seems there's a rumor that a new divided highway is going to be constructed between the two interstates. One of the proposed routes runs through the Tri-counties. Is your occupation in any way involved with these plans?" Sam's voice slipped up in volume with the question.

"Once again, with no disrespect intended, I have to decline to discuss any aspect of my business in the

Tri-counties. I hope you will accept that."

Sam dropped both arms to his sides, accidentally drawing a short line on his pants with the pen. His words came loud and fast. "It seems the most economical route through the Tri-counties takes it directly through several farms, including those of the families that have been wiped out recently. Do these occurrences have anything to do with you or your business? Do you have any knowledge of these events?"

"Once again, this time under protest, I will not discuss my work with you. Now, if I may, I have to get back to the very work that interests you." He stepped back and pushed the doors, but Sam stiff-armed them back open.

"Mr. Thibideaux. Some serious complaints have been lodged against you. I'm afraid if you aren't willing to talk here, I'll have to take you in for more formal questioning. Now, once again, would you please tell me . . . do you or your organization have anything to do with the various accidents that have happened over the last few months in the Tri-counties?" Sam bit his lip to keep from expressing the contempt he was developing for the little man.

Thibideaux repetitively balled his hands into tiny fists and released them. "I don't have an obligation to provide that information without a warrant or other formal writ. If you take me in for questioning, I assure you a team of lawyers from my Organization will descend on this town within hours to correct the situation, and to file a complaint against you and your beloved Tri-counties. Now, if I may, I would like to get back to work."

The doors slammed before Sam could react. He stood in place for a full ten seconds, then hurried to his vehicle. His hand slammed against the steering wheel. "What does he have to hide?"

The little jerk was correct about his rights. But why would he avoid such mundane questions? Maybe John and Billy had something this time.

Sam entered his office, welcomed by a ringing phone. The voice of a near hysterical child echoed in the earpiece.

"Calm down and tell me what's wrong," Sam said.

"Help me, please. I'm here alone. He's trying to break into the house."

"Where are you?"

"James Farm. Please. Come quick." The boy began to cry.

"James Farm in Porter County?

"Yes."

"Stay on the line. I'm going to transfer to my cell phone, so there'll be a couple of clicks. I'm on my way. Okay? Hello? Hello? You there?" Sam sprinted for his car, turned onto State Route 27, and headed for Porter County with full siren and lights.

Just over the Boyston-Porter County line, State Route 27 ran through the only non-tillable land in the Tri-counties other than the swamp. A series of small, rocky hills forced the highway into a serpentine path for just over a mile and a half. The curved road slowed Sam's dash, but not as much as the dense fog that shrouded the hills. He rounded a corner made by blasting away half of one of the hills, and he hit his brakes, hard. A partially shrouded figure stood in the road. The car fishtailed to a halt, nearly running into the jagged upright bank of the blasted hill.

Sam trained his floodlight into the fog, focused on the figure and inched his car closer, but most of the light was reflected back in his eyes. He turned it off. Through the mist, he saw the stranger walk toward the car. When about fifty feet separated the two, a wave of recognition gave Sam a hard shake. The small size. The irregular walk. He felt sick. He stopped the car and swung out of the door.

"What are you doing here? I have an emergency to get to at the James farm. Let me pass. Now."

"I'm afraid the only emergency you have tonight is me, Sheriff Merriwether," Thibideaux said as he ambled closer.

Sam drew his service revolver and cocked it, keeping it close to his side. "If you don't allow me to pass, I'll have to arrest you for hindrance. Your lawyers won't be able to get around that one."

"You will do no such thing, my dear Sheriff. You see, you can't even raise your arms from your sides." Thibideaux extended his arms straight out toward Sam, parallel to the ground, fingers extended straight out, palms inward.

Sam tried to raise his arms, but they wouldn't move. He sneered at the little man. "What the hell is going on? I have an emergency to get to. Let me go."

"As I said, you have only one emergency tonight, and that emergency is me," Thibideaux said in the same child's voice Sam heard over the telephone. "Now you see, no one, including you, will interfere with the business I have to conduct for my Organization. I'll go to any length to maintain this situation." He pulled his fingers back to form two fists and the tightness in Sam's arms loosened.

Sam raised his right arm and leveled the revolver directly at Thibideaux's torso. "Now maybe you'll tell me what the hell is going on here."

Thibideaux took a step forward.

Sam put his finger through the trigger guard and onto the trigger. "Freeze! Or I'll shoot!" His voice was pitched high with adrenaline.

Thibideaux took another step.

"Freeze, Thibideaux!"

A slight grin appeared to separate Thibideaux's lips and Sam thought he saw a glint of silver.

"Shoot, Sheriff. I really like this one." He stepped forward again and re-extended his fingers, this time with palms down, parallel to the ground.

Sam pulled the trigger and all motion went slow. There was no sound of discharge, no muzzle flash. The bullet exited the barrel of the gun and began a slow, spinning line toward Thibideaux's chest.

Sam could see it. He could see the bullet move through the air. But as it moved, it dissolved, like a salt crystal dissolves when dropped in a tall glass of water.

Sam's mind spun. Virga, he thought. Like virga, where rain falls from the clouds but evaporates before hitting the ground.

The bullet was a speck when it reached Thibideaux's chest and gone before impact. Sam watched the little man's distorted grin widen to show a double row of silver capped teeth.

"Oh please, Sheriff Merriwether, please shoot me again," Thibideaux said in the little child's voice. "I really love this one." Thibideaux moved his arms out laterally so his body formed a cross.

Sam tried to turn and run but he was frozen in place.

Thibideaux rose on his toes and slowly turned his body toward the jagged hillside. Sam's rigid body levitated a few inches and moved toward the hillside as if Sam were a puppet under control of an invisible puppeteer overhead. The two moved in a one-to-one ballet that would have been graceful in any other context.

When Sam was in reach of the vertical rock wall, Thibideaux lowered from his toes and Sam's feet returned to the road.

The car was only five feet away and the engine was still running. If he lets up, I'll jump in and run the little bastard over, he thought.

"I'm not a bastard," Thibideaux said. "My mother just had no use for my father. After their few minutes were over, of course." He chuckled.

Thibideaux jumped backward on the road and bought his arms over his head in a big sweeping motion. Sam was released from Thibideaux's control, but before he could react, the hillside exploded. Rocks and dirt rained down.

When the dust cleared, the only thing left standing was a partially covered sign that read, "Watch for Falling Rock." Sam was killed outright. It took longer for his car to die.

CHAPTER 31

AT ONE-THIRTY on the nose, Gabe slammed his car door and hurried across the parking lot. His idea looked like a good one—only a few cars meant it was past the noon rush. He'd have most of Miz Murtry's time. Today, he didn't want to flirt. He needed to voice his frustration about Sam's accident. And she was a good listener.

He pushed through the door and immediately lost the bounce in his step. Billy sat at the counter.

"Hey, Billy. You hear about Sam? I was up there last night. Poor guy was killed by a rockslide." Gabe shook his head and sat down next to Billy. "He was a good man."

Billy looked at the counter between his hands. "It wasn't a rockslide."

"What?" Gabe turned his head in Billy's direction.

"It wasn't a rockslide. Me and John went to see Sam yesterday to tell him about Thibideaux, and Sam said he would check him out. Now he's dead. It was Thibideaux who done it." Billy's stare penetrated the counter.

"It was a rockslide, Billy. I went up there."

"It was Thibideaux. Who do you think caused the rockslide?"

Gabe grabbed Billy's shoulder and swung him around on his stool so they were face-to-face. "Look at me, Billy. Tell me what you think's going on."

"Give me a minute. I got to pee." Billy stood up and walked to the bathroom.

Gabe's eyes tracked him until the bathroom door shut. He couldn't remember when he saw Billy so scared.

Teddy rounded the half-wall and leaned an elbow on the counter in front of Gabe. "What's wrong with Billy? He's been here all morning. Had about six or seven cups of coffee. He's been burbling to no one in particular about the sheriff, a highway, accidents that weren't accidents, and Thibideaux.

"I wish I knew. I'll see what I can find out."

On his way back to his stool Billy stopped and said something to Deena Lee, who reached under the counter and gave Billy a piece of paper and a pencil.

Gabe watched as Billy smoothed the paper on the counter and drew several lines. A few more lines and Gabe recognized the sketch as a crude rendition of a map. Billy put the pencil down and turned his head to look at Gabe.

"This here's the Tri-counties," he said.

Over the next fifteen minutes, Gabe sat in silence and listened to Billy's version of John's highway theory, the group decision to investigate Thibideaux, and their theory of Mac McKenna's accident. He let Billy ramble about the meeting with Sam, which was recounted nearly word-for-word, and about Sam's decision to have a talk with Thibideaux yesterday, just hours before his accident. Billy looked directly into Gabe's eyes and then twisted his neck back down toward the counter.

Gabe felt a chill. He was about to speak when Deena Lee walked up.

"You two look like you could use a topper." She tipped her coffee carafe toward Billy's cup.

"Thank you, Miz Murtry," Gabe said. "How are you feeling these days? Getting close to your time?" He didn't intend to smile, and managed to hold it to a slight grin.

"I'm doing all right, I guess. My ankles are swelling more and more, and I'm starting to get a few headaches, but otherwise I'm just trying to rest up as much as I can. I'm just starting my seventh month." She rested her hands on the sides of her abdomen and tapped it with her right hand.

"You're looking the better for it all. Be sure to let me know if you're needing anything. I'm always ready to help."

"Thank you, Gabe. I'll keep that in mind."

Before she turned away, Gabe noticed her smile stretched the limits of her face. He watched her waddle away and entered a daydream of how he would come to her rescue, to get her to the hospital just in time, and of how grateful she would be.

Billy slammed his open hand down on the counter. "Gabe. Get them google eyes back down here and tell me what we should do about Thibideaux and all the bad stuff that's been going on."

Gabe leaned back from Billy a little. His ranting hadn't included a request for instructions. "Tell me again about the highway plan and the accidents." He stared off in the distance, without focus, and tapped his spoon on the counter.

"Gabe. Could you stop banging the spoon?"

His mind came back. It was Miz Murtry's voice, from down the counter. "Sorry. I'm just trying to figure something out." He defocused again but his mind took an unexpected left turn. Miz Murtry's head on Wanna's body, straddling him in the hayloft. He hoped no one was looking at his lap. He was showing his emotions quite clearly.

Billy slammed the counter again. "Why don't you just give her a big kiss and get it over with? We got a serious problem here and all you can do is drool over Deena Lee. And in her condition."

"I don't know what to do, Billy. Let me think about it for awhile."

"Shit," Billy said. "It's like Father Costello all over again, but this time a lot worse." He got up and rushed out the front door of the Edge, into a dense fog.

Gabe watched Billy disappear into the mist and a mental snapshot froze him. He stared at the front door. Father Costello. He knew the lore about the Father's meltdown. How he cut up all those animals and arranged them around the altar for when the people came in to worship. And then he disappeared. Gabe had heard the story a hundred times. But this time something was different. The mention of Father Costello triggered a recollection of fog. And a bicycle. Thoughts he had before, but not all together like this.

He swiveled back around to face the counter, put his clasped hands up to his mouth, and rested his elbows on the formica. He was riding a bicycle through fog. Going to see Father Costello? But what for?

He rocked forward and back on the stool and let his breathing fall into the rhythm. Going to see Father Costello . . . to . . . confess. Confession, in the . . . inhouse. With that final word, a flood of memories swamped his attention, flashed in rapid order. Blood. Parts. Then darkness.

"Thibideaux," Gabe said out loud and snapped the middle finger of his right hand. "He was there."

"You all right, Gabe?"

Miz Murtry's voice again. He looked up. She was coming his way. "Yeah. I'm okay. Just lost in a daydream."

"You scared us half to death. You sure you're all right?"

Gabe stood and slid a bill under his coffee cup, then fished in his pocket for some change to top it off. "I got to go. You let me know if you need any help."

CHAPTER 32

GABE THOUGHT DARKNESS would never come. He wanted to keep the memories coming and the best way to do that was to go back to the scene. To the church. Now, he knew he was there twenty-five years ago. So was Thibideaux. And although the details weren't clear, he knew it wasn't Father Costello who created the carnage that morning. But Father Costello was there, and that confused Gabe.

The first firefly signaled official darkness as Gabe hurried to his truck. The night was clear and warm and the engine roared on the first jolt from the starter. He wanted to get back before Wanna got suspicious.

He decided to let his mind freewheel. Trying to force memories from their hiding places only caused anxiety and he wanted to keep a clear head. Let them come out by themselves. It was like a game of hide-and-seek, but with a casual search. Ollie, Ollie, oxen free.

His thoughts flew to the church. He knew the confessional wasn't there anymore. It was dismantled when the Protestants took over the building. But its place, halfway up the west wall, was still marked by the pews. They survived the remodel, and they were shorter from that point to the back of the church, arranged back then so the confessional wouldn't block anyone's view of the altar. He needed to be there, at the site of the old confessional. Maybe that would bring back the memories.

He parked to the left of the general store and walked the rest of the way to the church. The front door was locked. He hurried around to the back door and another memory surfaced. If the door was locked, Father Costello had told him to lift up on the knob and give a hard shove. It'd push open.

He tried the knob and it resisted his twist. He spun around in the darkness. The only light came from the rectory windows across the street. It was more of a glow, flickering like it was teasing the darkness. Keeping his eyes on the rectory, he lifted up on the doorknob and pushed his shoulder against the door. It didn't move. He took a step back, grabbed the doorknob again, and timed his lift with a harder shoulder lunge. The door opened with a slight pop. The back room was dark but familiar.

The darkness hovered for a full minute, but the shapes in the room gradually appeared, like an image on exposed photographic paper in the developer tray. The door to the worship hall was as he remembered it—he pushed through without hesitation.

It was cold. He had an urge to huddle in the inhouse and a sense of warmth enveloped him. To aid his adapting eyes, he ran his hand on the end support of each pew. When a missing support signaled the indentation of the next pew, he turned to face the wall. The confessional had been right there. He sidestepped two steps. The inhouse, here. He stepped forward and pivoted so his back was against the wall, and froze.

Nothing came. He saw the outline of the altar, and the two steps that led up to it, but that was it. Maybe he was forcing it. Try to relax, he said to himself. Let it come.

He slumped on his haunches, to a crouch, and rubbed his eyes with his fists. When he looked at the center of the altar, the wrought iron railing of the first row pew partially obscured his view. An image flashed. He didn't catch it. He rubbed his eyes again. Just let it come. Another flash lingered for a split second. White robe. But not standing.

He leaned a little to get a better view, and he nearly fell forward. The memory came fast. Father Costello sat on the altar and he wasn't moving. Someone stood in front of him.

Gabe leaned a little to his right for a slightly different angle. The man was one step down from the altar, but his head was level with the sitting priest. The connection was instantaneous. Thibideaux. And he was saying something to Father Costello.

A cramp seized his left thigh and Gabe let out a gasp. He stood and the dizziness of the sudden posture change brought a shrinking darkness like the fade-to-black at the end of a movie scene. The cramp fought through and he staggered forward a step to regain his balance. A few steps to the back of the church and a few retraced paces and the grip on his muscle lessened. He wanted to bring back the memory stream but he couldn't squat right now, so he bent at the waist and leaned forward. His eyes defocused.

It flooded back. Thibideaux placed something on the top step of the altar, but Gabe couldn't see it very well. He leaned left to get a better view and it hit him so quickly he stiffened the just-cramped leg. An extra heartbeat, than another, and another. And then a long pause. This was a bad one. His head went light as darkness fell, and he acted on his one and only impulse. He put out his hands and bent his knees to break his fall.

The first thing to come into focus was the carpet. It registered in all senses. He smelled it, tasted it, felt it pressed against the entire side of his head. He pushed his torso up with his hands. How long was he out? Long enough to break out in a sweat. Long enough to soak through the back of his shirt.

Tightness gripped his chest, and his lungs refused to inflate. He had to get out. Another quick memory. The latch on the front doors was hard to throw in a hurry. He ignored the pain in his leg and scrambled for the back door.

"Shit," he said a little too loud. The back door didn't budge. In his confusion he didn't think to unlock it. Instead, he lifted the knob and gave a firm yank. It came open with a familiar pop.

His breath came easier in the open air. Grasping his upper thighs with his hands, he hunched over until his breathing rate dropped.

A flash of light cut through the clear night air, to his left. He turned his head. Another flash. It was coming from inside the rectory, from the front room. The flashes reminded Gabe of camera flashes. Was someone taking pictures in the rectory?

Part of him wanted to run to his truck, but part wanted to see what Thibideaux was up to. He had the opportunity. Perhaps the sight of the little man would trigger another memory replay. Another flash and he moved, before he made a mental decision to do so. He hurried past the front of the building and rounded the corner.

The windows on the west side of the rectory were high so he walked bent at the waist. The second window up would give a good view of almost the entire room.

He gripped the window ledge with his fingertips and rose on tiptoes. He strained his neck enough to see inside. Thibideaux sat in a huge chair. It was so large he looked like a toddler sitting in a big people's chair. His legs didn't reach the floor. Gabe dropped back onto flat feet.

He re-gripped the window ledge and went back on toe in time to see Thibideaux flick his right arm out to his side with his index and middle fingers pointing at the wall to the right of the fireplace. An electrical arc shot from his two fingers across the room and crashed into the wall with a muffled crackle. The bright flash extinguished to the background flicker of the fireplace.

Gabe lost his grip and slipped below the view line. His heart trotted out a regular rhythm.

He pulled himself up again and watched Thibideaux's left hand flick out like the right had just done. Another electrical arc shot across the room into the wall no more than five feet from Gabe's window. He released his grip and shrunk into the shadow of the window ledge.

His fingers and toes cramped so he looked for another way to get a vantage point. Just down the wall, to the back of the building, sat a galvanized steel garbage can. He lifted the can and hobbled back to the window. From the weight of the can, it was empty or nearly so. He climbed on top, taking care to place his weight near the edges of the lid. When he gained his balance, Thibideaux was in clear view.

Gabe watched Thibideaux flick out two more mini-lightning bolts, thirty seconds apart, then stiffen in his chair. The little man brought both arms to the front, pointing directly at the fireplace and made tiny fists.

Gabe adjusted his weight on the can and leaned forward a little.

Thibideaux slapped his fists together and then opened them. A loud "Ha" escaped his nearly closed lips and a large fireball shot from his hands into the fireplace, launching a shower of sparks that flew half-way across the room.

At impact, Gabe recoiled, and his shifting weight inverted the lid of the garbage can with a loud, metallic pop. He struggled to maintain his balance.

A whirring sound came from inside the rectory. Gabe glanced in as the chair swung in his direction.

He scrambled from the can and it toppled, creating a metal-on-gravel clamor that startled a distant dog to bark. He made a quick dive for an adjacent shrub and tried to cover his body with the foliage. His breathing came loud. Slowing the inhalations only made him feel more out-of-breath. A sweet smell, of Persian lilac, seemed to suck some of the precious oxygen from his hiding place.

The muted light of the evening dimmed even more, and Gabe turned his head up to see a bank of fog circling the corner of the rectory, coming in his direction. He lowered his head into his hands as the chill of the mist penetrated the bush. It felt like he was being probed by dozens of cold, damp hands, like a blind person would feel someone's face to discover the identity. Shivers added to Gabe's breathing problems.

As quickly as the fog appeared, it receded around the corner of the rectory, pulling even more air from Gabe's lungs. He gasped for his next breath.

Run for it, he thought, but his body wasn't ready. He'd have to control his breathing first. Before he could move, the foundation of the rectory groaned, sounding like the complaint of wood joints put under a shear. The ground beneath Gabe seemed to go fluid.

It slumped downward, like the retraction of water prior to the invasion of a large bow wave of an ocean liner. Then the ground heaved upward. He was launched from his hiding place and landed with a thud four feet back from the shrub. Pain shot through his bad knee and extended up into his hip.

Before he could pull himself up on one elbow, another temblor threw him another three feet, this time to his right. The landing shook his bones and pain invaded his left leg—the good one.

One more jolt rolled Gabe onto his back. He stayed there, motionless, waiting for what Thibideaux had for the next round.

The window over the garbage can flew open and banged to a stop hard enough to crack the lower pane. Gabe tried to push his body down into the dirt, to flatten out as much as possible. He heard a "Ha" sound and a large fireball flew through the window in his direction. He closed his eyes as a searing pulse of heat screamed close to his head. It felt like the flash of a grill when a match is thrown onto starter-soaked briquettes.

He turned his head away from the rectory and followed the path of the fireball, which continued on a dead line to Billy Smyth's trailer. Upon impact, the living room of the trailer burst into flames.

Gabe jumped to his feet and ran in the direction of the trailer before the pain in his legs registered. He stumbled, but managed to shuffle the two hundred yards to the burning structure. The door was halfway along the side and the flames hadn't spread that far, so he grabbed the edge of the door with his fingertips, near the bottom, and managed to pop the latch. He crawled low to the back of the trailer, staying below the billowing clouds of smoke.

Billy was in his bedroom in the back of the trailer. The jolt had roused him from a deep sleep but in his confusion he became tangled in his sheets. Gabe freed him and pulled him along the floor to the open door as flames licked walls above them.

He jerked Billy away from the trailer and collapsed in the dirt, cradling Billy across his lap. Molten metal dripped from the wall surrounding the door they just exited.

Gabe strained to breathe, but despite the disaster, he felt a strange sense of relief. Thibideaux had spared him when he could have killed him outright. But why? Gabe thought of John Johnson's highway theory. His own farm was in the best route. But still Thibideaux spared him.

A memory flashed. Thibideaux had spared Father Costello, too. Why? The fire could have, should have, killed Billy, so Billy was expendable. Gabe shook his head. What was so special about him and Father Costello that they both were spared? Maybe Father Costello knew—if he were still alive.

Billy's moans brought Gabe back. He looked down. They were both alive—one by design, one by circumstance.

The engine of the volunteer fire department rounded the corner of Main Street as the flames consumed the far end of Billy's trailer. They might as well go home, Gabe thought. The trailer was a goner. Fortunately, Billy's repair shop was far enough away to be out of danger.

Billy grabbed Gabe's shirt. "What am I going to do now?"

"Don't worry about it, Billy. We've got a bed for you."

Billy looked over Gabe's shoulder. A contrail of dispersing smoke traced the path of the fireball back to the rectory. He looked up at Gabe, rolled off of his lap onto the ground, and jumped to his feet. "Fuck this," he said and made a beeline for his truck. Billy's truck turned east on Main Street and disappeared into the night.

Gabe slumped in the dust, the flames of Billy's former home flickering in parallel with Gabe's mind. He knew what he had to do. He had to find Father Costello.

CHAPTER 33

THIBIDEAUX SAT BACK in his chair but he didn't close his eyes. He was having the first troubled evening of his stay in Boyston. He had to figure out what to do with Gabe Petersen.

"What is it about his place?" he said out loud. He patted the arm of the chair. "Just like last time, I really want to kill a citizen."

He leaned forward in the chair, balled both fists, and punched his thighs. "Not this time. I won't repeat past mistakes. When he's of no more use, I'm going to kill him."

He fell back and took a deep breath. Do as you are trained to do, he thought. Recite the litany. He had the entire text committed to memory. He had to. It was here, twenty-five years ago that his notebook had found its way into the wrong hands. He had to incinerate it on the spot. He was still bitter about the loss, but the sacrifice was in the best interests of the Organization. After all, the notebook was mostly a comforting keepsake. "What is it about this place?"

He slid from the chair and paced in front of the fireplace, but he had trouble keeping his mind on the principles of the Organization. He skipped to the statistics in Section One. Repetition was the key to remembering, so he closed his eyes and pushed the "play" button on his mind's recorder.

"Triple O x Citizen, Training Success Rate = 17.6%. Citizen x Citizen, Training Success Rate = 0.78%. Citizen x Citizen, Absentee, Training Success Rate = 2.6%. Citizen x Citizen, Special Circumstance, Training Success Rate = 6.4%."

Instead of continuing his recitation, he let his mind wander to a familiar time and place. It was when he discovered the magnitude of his special powers. All recruiters had powers. Like the ability to project themselves away from their bodies to observe others, shrouded in a fog, rainstorm, or other meteorological phenomenon. They all could enhance the probability of events, provided the events were initiated without their intervention.

Thibideaux tried to smile. He thought about the physical desires of Gabe and Wanna. It was a good catch—there was an attraction there, but way under the surface.

He reflected on the doctrine again. Recruiters cannot influence citizens to do what they wouldn't ordinarily do, but they can capitalize on inherent weaknesses of individuals to achieve their goals.

"Can't hold a candle to me," he said.

He touched the scars on his cheeks and tried, again, to turn his mouth into a grin, but the paralyzed muscles only allowed a slight gape of his lips. Children can be cruel, he thought. No one knows that better than me.

He jumped up into the chair and settled against its back. It had been his finest hour so he liked to bring the memory back. He was in the barn at the rear of the training compound, a child of six, surrounded by his fellow trainees, mostly older. They teased him about his face, but zeroed in on his inability to smile. I know how to make him smile, one boy had said. He lowered two hooks that were strung over pulleys by stout chains—the pulleys attached to the roof over the hayloft. He slid the hooks into the corners of young Thibideaux's mouth. With the other boys chanting, "Smile . . . Smile . . . Smile," a boy grabbed each chain and began pulling. Thibideaux remembered being lifted off the ground until the skin at the corners of his mouth gave way, releasing him from the hooks.

He touched the scars again, then leaned forward and thrust his fists into the air. That's when the Organization saw the full extent of my powers, he thought. Too bad the boys didn't know what hit them. That's also when the Organization decided to waive the physical stature requirements in my case. He sighed. Probably why I only get assignments in the country.

The victorious memory relaxed him, as it always did, and with relaxation came clarity of thought. The time for achieving his primary objective was coming fast. Since Gabe would be needed in case the secondary objective panned out, he decided to leave Gabe alone. For now. Gabe's knowledge of the Organization was nonexistent. In order to abide by the edict of drawing minimal attention to himself or the Organization's activities, Thibideaux decided to stand pat.

CHAPTER 34

GABE STIRRED. HIS bed shook.

"Gabe, I need a little more help around here."

It was Wanna's voice. He rubbed his eyes and looked for the clock. "What time is it?"

"Time for you to get up and give me some help."

He leaned up on one elbow and waited for the cobwebs to clear from his mind. "It's not even dawn yet. What's so important that I have to get up a whole hour early?"

"I couldn't sleep."

"I know the problem. You got breakfast cooking? I'm really hungry."

Wanna put her left hand to her mouth and her right to her stomach. She turned and ran for the bathroom. Gabe heard her retch, cough, then flush the toilet. A grin creased his cheeks. "I could use a fried pork sandwich. How about you?"

"You son of a . . ." The next word started with a "b" and ended with an explosive regurgitation.

Gabe felt bad until he looked at the clock again. He had noticed the change in Wanna a week after their tryst in the barn. Now, his sympathy was worn as thin as a gossamer thread. Besides, he didn't have time for it all—the morning sickness, the tender breasts, the unreasonable demands, and the hair-trigger mood swings. He knew her too well. And he had something else on his mind—something much more important.

Wanna staggered from the bathroom as Gabe pulled on his overalls.

Her beetle-browed look broke through his armor for an instant. "You all right?" He lifted a shield to cover the breach. He was sure her mind was spinning this all out of proportion. "I have to go out this afternoon. Let me know what you need done and I'll get to what can."

"Don't need nothing. I can do it myself." She burst into tears.

"I'll be at the chores, then. Ring the dinner bell if you need anything."

"Gabe, what are we going to do?"

"Not now, Wanna. I'm not discussing that until you get control of yourself." He closed the door after him, chopping an obscenity in half.

Gabe burst through the doors of the Edge and smiled.

Only two other customers were there. He settled on his stool and smiled at Deena Lee, who filled his cup to the brim.

"Nice to see you, Gabe. What brings you in? To see me, I hope."

He thought he detected an evil tilt to her smile.

Miz Murtry's head, Wanna's body, hay loft . . . His pants tightened. He looked down at his lap and tried to slide forward but the stool was bolted to the floor.

"I always look forward to seeing you," he said. *Ten more degrees of elevation.* He exaggerated a smile to keep her eyes on his face.

"Well, get a good look because in a couple of weeks there won't be so much to look at." She turned to show her profile.

Gabe noticed the swollen abdomen and the arch in her back, apparently necessary to compensate for the change in her center of gravity. The thought of her settling on top of him in the hayloft was unusual enough to break the spell. *Negative twenty-five degrees and falling.* He turned his attention to his mission.

"You or Teddy know anything about Father Costello? You know, the one who killed all the animals in the church years ago." *All calm on the southern front.*

Teddy leaned around the corner of the kitchen. "Before my time here. Sorry."

"Me, too, but you can come in and ask anytime," Deena Lee said with a wink.

Back to battle stations.

Gabe tried to maintain his concentration. "Do either of you know anyone who might know his whereabouts? I need to ask him a few questions."

Teddy walked from the kitchen and centered himself in front of Gabe, forcing Deena Lee to move over a step. "Why? What you got going? You needing some fresh meat?" He laughed.

"Meat's right here, sweetie," Deena Lee said, and exaggerated a hip wiggle timed to her giggles.

Sweat would have appeared on Gabe's forehead if he had any excess fluid in the top half of his body. He slid forward to the very edge of the stool.

Too late. Deena Lee did a double take and let out a loud guffaw. She grabbed a dishtowel and tossed it onto Gabe's lap. "You got a license for that monster?"

It was sauna-hot in the Edge now, but the flow of blood to Gabe's face took his mind away. The towel started to descend.

"I'm really sorry, Miz Murtry." He thought about running out, but that would accentuate his predicament.

"Don't you dare be sorry, Gabe Petersen. It's nice to know I can still do that for a man, and you in particular. Especially as big and round as I am right now."

"You look great to me," he said. It was barely audible, but her smile told him she heard.

"You want anything to eat? Teddy's got a winner of a special today."

"No, thanks. I'm just trying to get some information on Father Costello." He looked down. The towel was flat on his lap. When he looked up, he noticed

Deena Lee watching.

She looked down at the towel with an exaggerated stare. "I bet I can make that towel dance." She wiggled her hips in a mock hula.

Teddy and Deena Lee's laughter was contagious—Gabe let loose with an uzi burst. He grabbed the towel and flung it at Deena Lee, who dodged it, allowing it to fall to the floor. She grabbed a pair of long tongs and picked it up by its extreme edge, holding it at full arm's length.

"My tip's not on here, is it?" With a loud laugh, she flipped the towel into the laundry box.

Gabe wanted to gather her up and take her home. He wondered if she felt the same.

The bell over the front door silenced their laughter and Gabe turned to see a large man in a state police uniform pigeon-toe in. He clomped up to the counter and lowered himself on a stool, two over from Gabe.

"Name's Officer Ralston. I've been assigned to the Tri-counties until you can search for a new sheriff." He offered a hand to Gabe.

"Gabe Petersen." He gave the officer's hand a firm shake.

Deena Lee rounded the kitchen half-wall. "Officer Ralston, I'm Deena Lee. That there's Teddy in the kitchen. This here's his place. He makes the best specials. You hungry?"

"Smells great. I shouldn't, but I believe I'll give the special a try."

Gabe estimated he was around six feet and two-fifty, minimum.

"Seems like you folks have had a streak of bad luck lately," Ralston said. "I knew young Merriwether and his old man. Terrible thing. The old man is really broken up." He drew a deep breath and let it out slowly. "Anything I should know about the Tri-counties that'll help me get adjusted to the place?"

Gabe wasn't tempted to get into what he saw at Thibideaux's.

Deena Lee leaned over the counter. "Just the usual. People coming in here getting excited over a pregnant girl." She smiled at Gabe.

"Ain't against the law, is it?"

Ralston looked at Deena Lee, then at Gabe. He smiled and stroked his chin. "Not that I know of, but I can check the local statutes. Sometimes these small counties have really old laws on the books that cover the dangdest things." He looked at Deena Lee. "You want to file a complaint?"

"Only if he stops."

Gabe looked down at his coffee and smiled. *Battle stations again.*

Ralston cleared this throat. "Anything I can do for you people? I'm here to serve."

Gabe's head turned to the officer. "A long time ago, about twenty-five years, there was a priest in these parts, a Father Costello."

"Yeah. I heard about him. He's the one who cut up a bunch of animals in the church." Ralston swiveled on his stool so he faced Gabe.

"Right. I'm trying to find him. I want to ask him a few questions. Can you find out anything about him?"

"I have some connections at the Capitol. Let me see what I can do. Any other way I can help?" Ralston turned back to the bar as Deena Lee slid a full plate in front of him.

"You can carry this here bundle for awhile," Deena Lee said. "It's paining my back something fierce." She supported her stomach with both hands.

"I've got one of my own," he said. "I can sympathize, but yours will be gone soon. I have to carry this one around for the duration." He patted his midsection and chuckled. The laughter made the rounds.

Gabe rose from his stool and reached for his wallet. "I'd better get back home."

Deena Lee walked through the split in the counter and came close to Gabe's side. Her voice was low. "Thank you for coming in. Come in anytime. And you can bring that monster with you, especially after the baby's out." She pointed at his beltline and giggled.

Battle stations.

Gabe took a deep breath and bent over. He kissed Deena Lee's cheek and ran out the front door, leaving the overhead bell to say his goodbye.

CHAPTER 35

DEENA LEE DIALED the phone and waited for Teddy to pick up. "Teddy, I don't think I can make it in this morning. My head's hurting so bad I can't see straight. I'm going to go to see Doc. Will you be okay at the café?"

"I'll be fine. You take care of yourself. Let me know if you need anything."

One in a million, she thought. She struggled to her feet and with the change in posture, the throbbing in her head intensified. She had to stop and squint her eyes until the pounding let up a little. Driving would be a bitch since the morning sun would be in her eyes most of the way.

✦ ✦ ✦

"Deena Lee. Wake up."

Deena Lee's eyes focused on Misty Rondelunas.

"Doc wants you to wake up now," Misty said. "He wants to talk to you."

"What time is it?"

"Four o'clock."

"I've been asleep the whole day?"

"We didn't want to bother you."

Doc Halvorson stepped into the room and nodded to Misty, who left. "Good afternoon, sleepy head."

"You let me sleep all day?"

"It was probably the best thing for you." He slipped a blood pressure cuff on her arm and pumped on the bulb.

"How's the baby?" she said.

"Shhh." Doc let the air out slowly and frowned at the dial. He slipped the stethoscope from his ears and smiled. "Good. Pressure's down a little. I bet your head feels better, right?"

"Yes. How's the baby?"

"The baby is fine." Doc sat down on a four-wheeled stool next to the bed. "It's you I'm worried about."

"What's wrong with me?" She grabbed his right arm and squeezed. "Am I going to be all right?"

"You'll be fine. You have pregnancy-induced hypertension. What that means is your blood pressure is up a bit." His voice was calm. "It's not serious at this point, but if it goes up much more, we'll have to do something."

She dug her fingernails into his skin. "Do what? Will I lose my baby?"

Doc grabbed her hand and lifted it from his arm, then put it down again, back on his arm. "No. If the situation worsens we'll have to either induce labor or take the baby by Cesarean section."

"That bad?"

"Both are routine medical procedures. I've done them both many times. You're far enough along and your baby is big enough that . . . it . . . should be fine."

Deena Lee's eyes widened. "You know the sex?"

"Yes."

"Don't tell me. It's bad luck." She pulled her hand from his arm and put it to her forehead. "I want to be surprised."

Doc smiled.

Deena Lee leaned up on her elbow. To her surprise, her head didn't pulse with pain. "What should I do now? I can't stay here."

"You need total bed rest, and I mean total. You can get up to go to the bathroom, but that's all. Do you have anyone who can take care of you?" He slid the stool over to the desk in the corner and picked up a laminated card. "If not, I'll have to check you into the hospital."

Deena Lee slumped back into the bed. "I'm alone at my place. I can't ask Teddy—he's too busy. But I can't afford the hospital. I have enough saved to get me through the birth and all, but a stay in the hospital is expensive."

Doc ran his finger down the list of numbers on the card. "Don't you have anyone who can help? It's really important."

She rolled her eyes toward the ceiling. "Can I use your phone?"

Gabe washed his hands—he wanted to get through the paper before supper. He caught the phone on he third ring.

"Gabe, It's Deena Lee. I'm at Doc's—"

"You all right?" Gabe said. It felt like the air was sucked from his lungs. "You need me? I can be there in a shake—"

"Gabe. Calm down. I'm okay. I have a problem but it isn't an emergency. Doc says I have to stay in bed all the time. I can only get up to go to the bathroom. You think you and Wanna can watch over me for a while? I won't be much trouble."

Gabe's pulse picked up. His daydream of coming to Deena Lee's rescue was coming true. "We'd be happy to help. I'll have Wanna make up the extra room. You need a ride over?"

"Just a minute."

Gabe heard Deena Lee's muffled voice, "Doc, can I drive?" He couldn't make out Doc's response.

Deena Lee's voice came back loud. "I'll need a ride, if you don't mind."

"I'll be there in a few minutes." He hung up without saying bye and lifted the sash on the side window. "Wanna. Can you come in here right away?" He hoped she wouldn't object. She was past most of the morning sickness and moodiness.

Wanna rushed into the house. "What's up? You all right?"

"It's not me." He panted. "Miz Murtry needs our help."

"What's wrong?"

"She needs to stay in bed for the rest of her pregnancy. I said she could stay here and we'd look after her. That okay with you?"

"Gabe, you dog." She shook her head and smiled. "You got your heart throb under your roof. She call you?"

"Yup."

"She's sweet on you, too, you dog. I'll be happy to help. I might even put in a good word for you. Tell her what a stud you are." She giggled.

"Don't you dare."

"Relax, big boy. I won't mess it up for you. But we're going to have to think of an excuse if my belly starts to swell before she delivers." She patted her flat stomach.

Gabe straightened a pillow on the couch. "I'm not worried about that. I just want to make sure Miz Murtry and her baby are all right." He gave Wanna a hug. "You don't mind playing maid for her when I'm working the fields?"

"People have been plenty nice to us in these parts, especially when our parents passed. I always have time for our people. And it might get you laid by your dream girl later on." She returned the hug.

Gabe grabbed his truck keys. "I have to go get her."

Wanna hooked his arm and wagged her index

finger in his face. "Stay away from Misty."

Gabe rolled his eyes.

For the first time in his life, he intentionally exceeded the posted speed limit.

CHAPTER 36

THE ROOM WAS cramped but cozy. Gabe liked the feeling of intimacy. Since he moved the portable TV from Wanna's room into Deena Lee's room, the three of them spent the evenings laughing at the comedies, worrying over the dramas, and sharing the appropriate righteous indignation when the investigative journalism programs came on. He smiled. It was Wanna's idea to move the TV.

A lot can be learned by watching a person's reactions to different types of shows, he thought, and he was audience to Deena Lee's behavior as much as he was to the television shows. Without a single reservation, he liked what he saw.

He was particularly proud of Wanna. She was as doting as a future grandmother. For the two weeks of Deena Lee's stay, he watched Wanna ask question after question about the pregnancy. She seemed to revel in the sense of discovery. Deena Lee had told him once that she wished Wanna could experience the joys of impending motherhood. Gabe had nodded and changed the subject.

They had just settled in for a night of sitcoms when the phone rang. Wanna jumped from her chair and sprinted into the front room.

"It's for you, Gabe. Officer Ralson wants to talk to you. You do something wrong?"

Gabe gave Wanna a frown and took the phone.

"Gabe? I have some information on the whereabouts of Father Costello. Can you come in to the office tomorrow morning? The situation is a bit complicated and I got some directions. They'd be hard to give over the phone."

"Be there first thing. Thank you." Gabe felt a rush of excitement sweep his body. It was going to be hard to wait until morning.

Before he could hang up the phone, Wanna was on him. "What's that about?"

He almost said "nothing," but he remembered a delightful passage from one of the short stories by his favorite author, O. Henry, which he committed to memory, word for word, due to the common thread that tied it to his own experience:

"Hearken, brethren. When She-who-has-a-right-to-ask interrogates you concerning a change she finds in your mood answer her thus: Tell her that you, in a sudden rage, have murdered your grandmother; tell her that you have robbed orphans and that remorse has stricken you; tell her your fortune is swept away; that you are beset by enemies, by bunions, by any kind of malevolent fate; but do not, if peace and happiness are worth as much as a grain of mustard seed to you—do not answer her 'Nothing.'"

"I have to go to his office tomorrow morning," he finally said.

"You in trouble?" She poked him in the ribs with her index finger.

"No. I asked for information about Father Costello and he's got some. That's all."

"Why you so fired up to find an old priest? You're not even Catholic."

Ignoring his earlier literary caution, he forwarded a response second worst to 'nothing': "Never mind."

"What do you mean never mind? Gabe Petersen, what's going on here? You in some trouble?"

"For the last time, I'm not in any trouble, dammit." His anger wasn't directed at her. "I'm just checking on some of the strange things that have been going on here lately and Officer Ralston has some information. That's all. So calm yourself." A grin invaded his face. "You swing on me and I'll put you down."

Wanna laughed and gave a wild swing in Gabe's direction. He grabbed her around the waist and pulled her down on the couch. It was the first time they had shared a good laugh together in some time. Before getting up, Wanna whispered in his ear, "Careful. Don't hurt the baby."

Gabe gave her a hug. He felt guilty about what he was doing.

Gabe ambled into the sheriff's office minutes after Officer Ralston arrived.

"Gabe. You're up bright and early this morning." Ralston stretched his arms straight up and yawned.

Gabe didn't catch the yawn—he'd been up for a while. "Yup. What you said sounded interesting so I had trouble sleeping."

"Pull up that chair. You want coffee? Sorry, I don't have any donuts." Ralston chuckled.

"Coffee. Black would be fine. Thanks." Gabe plopped down in the uncomfortable wooden chair.

Ralston sat behind his desk and drew coffee through his lips so it made a loud, twittering slurp. He pulled some notes from his top desk drawer.

"Seems Father Costello did leave a trail, but it wasn't easy to find. Right after his problem here he went to St. Timothy's in St. Louis. The Monsignor there was his mentor when Costello was a novice in the priesthood. He was lucky no one here wanted to press charges for what he did. I couldn't find anything in the books about him or the church around that time. Anyway, he stayed in St. Louis for two weeks, give a day or two. From there he went to Chicago. There's a hospital there that caters to the Catholic Church."

"Hospital? What kind of hospital?" Gabe leaned forward and braced himself by putting his hands on the arms of the chair.

"A mental hospital. It seems the older priests need

a place to go when they lose their wits. What do they call that disease? Alzheimer's? Something like that. Anyway, this hospital gives them the care they need until they pass on. Occasionally they take in a young priest who has problems."

"What kind of problems?"

"Mental problems. It can happen to anyone. Why not priests?" Ralston put his notes flat on the desk. "Father Costello has been in this place for the past twenty-five years now."

"How far is Chicago? Can I drive?"

"Slow down, Gabe. Don't you travel much? It's just under eight hundred miles. You thinking of going there?"

"I really need to talk with the Father."

Ralston pushed away from the desk and stood. He squeezed an exhalation through his lips. "It's not a good idea. There's another problem with Father Costello."

Gabe leaned farther forward. He was on the edge of the seat. "What's the problem?"

Ralston took a long sip of coffee. "He hasn't said a word since he's been there. In twenty-five years. They've had in more than a dozen doctors and none of them could get him to make a peep. He just sits and stares out the windows. He's in his late fifties now, in good shape physically, but he just stares."

"You said you got directions?"

"Gabe. Didn't you hear me? If you're going there to talk with him, he won't talk back. More than a dozen specialists couldn't help him. You think you can do better?"

Gabe frowned. "All I know is I need to try."

Ralston sat down and leaned back in his chair. "When you get something in your head, it stays there. You drive much?"

"No. Had no need of going around." Gabe felt a shortness of breath coming on.

"You better talk to someone who's been to Chicago before going, then. It's a big place. I have directions here, but it'll be easy to get lost." Ralston opened his middle drawer and rifled around in some papers. He pulled out an address book. "Here. Here's the number of an officer I know in Chicago. If you get into trouble, just give him a call." He scribbled the number on a sticky note and stuck it to the page of directions.

Gabe stood and offered his hand to Ralston. "Thank you. I appreciate the trouble you've gone to. If anything comes of the trip, I'll fill you in when I get back."

Ralston returned the handshake. "If it's important to my job, I would appreciate it. If it's personal, there's no need. Be careful driving. People drive really fast on the interstates. And be sure to watch signs. They can be confusing, particularly when you get into big cities."

On the way home, Gabe poured over the directions while driving. He had them memorized by the time he got to the general store. He filled his basket with supplies, including a seven-day pill dispenser designed to help people remember their daily medications. He smiled. It would help Wanna remember to take her vitamins when he was gone.

Back home, he packed an overnight bag.

Wanna burst into his room. "What do you think

you're doing? You going somewhere?"

He didn't look up. "Chicago."

"You know you can't leave the Tri-counties."

"I have to try."

"Chicago? What's there?" Wanna paced in front of the door.

"Officer Ralston found Father Costello. He's in Chicago. Be gone for a few days, no more than a week." He looked in her eyes. "Can you handle everything here?"

"You know I can. You have to go?"

"Yup. I have to talk with him."

She stopped pacing and pushed on his shoulder, turning him to face her. "I don't suppose you're going to tell me what it's about?"

He looked down again. "Nope."

"Well, if you have to—"

"I do. Will you be all right with Miz Murtry? Anything happens, give Doc a call right away." He zipped the bag shut and picked it up.

"When are you leaving?" Wanna followed Gabe into the kitchen.

"First thing after lunch. Would you tell Miz Murtry when she wakes up?"

"Sure. What do you want to eat?"

Gabe felt his stomach growl. He wasn't sure he would be able to hold down any lunch, but he didn't want Wanna to see his nervousness. He ate quickly.

Gabe headed east on State Route 27. He'd get to the Herndon County line before turning north toward Chicago. If he could cross the line.

CHAPTER 37

THE SIGN CAME up fast, even at forty-five miles per hour. Welcome to Franklin County, it said. But the welcome wasn't a warm one. Gabe had to force his foot down just to keep steady pressure on the gas pedal. He wanted to bust through, like it was a finish line with a victory tape stretched across the roadway. But the closer he came, the more the tape looked like a rigid barricade. A roadblock without a detour sign. The speed of the pickup tailed off, the sign fifty yards away.

The tightness hit and he buckled against the steering wheel, causing the pickup to swerve a little. He couldn't catch his breath as the extra large heart contractions rang in his head. Dizziness came fast, and darkness ran a close second. He slammed on the brakes and turned the car to the shoulder. The shower of rocks in the wheel wells created a clamor that faded in parallel with the decreasing light. He was going out this time. He stayed on the brake and stomped the clutch long enough to slide the gearshift into neutral, hoping he could break his momentum before he went down. His last definite sensation was the fishtail of the truck—the rear slid to the left, across the gravel shoulder and into the freshly mowed grass. A horn honked in the distance.

The noise was deafening. The two notes of the horn were purposely out of register—enough to create an irritating cacophony. It was designed to grab attention and it was working. The noise brought the light back, gradually filtering through Gabe's consciousness. He lifted his head and the noise stopped, replaced with a brightness that was visually deafening. It bleached everything. How long had he been out?

Other perceptions came fast. The pain in his forehead led a sensory parade that included bells ringing in his ears, a full marching band of joint aches, and the grand marshal, the irregular thumping in his chest. He gained a focal point, the dashboard, and let his vision clear to the windshield, then beyond.

The front tires of the pickup were on the shoulder of the road, the rear tires in the grass, facing perpendicular to the road. Out the right window, the sign was just fifteen yards away. It went red.

Gabe blinked at the apparition, but it didn't clear.

He brought his fists to his eyes and rubbed hard. A little white light passed through, but his head swirled. He grabbed the steering wheel to help slow the spiral and he noticed his right hand was stained red. A probe of his forehead, and his fingers came away covered with blood. It took a second before it all registered. The horn, the pain, the blood. Must have hit my head on the steering wheel pretty hard, he thought. A drop of red splattered his thigh in agreement.

Gabe reached in his back pocket and yanked his handkerchief up to his forehead in a single movement. Pressure. The first aid course taught him to apply pressure to a cut. He leaned up and looked in the rear view mirror, but the brightness drove him back down. Another wave of extra beats were lining up in his heart and he forced a Valsalva's maneuver to head them off. Instead of dizziness, nausea spread upward from his diaphragm. He barely had time to open the door and lean out before his lunch took a curtain call.

Everything was in focus now. The colors of the day were so sharp they seemed almost artificial. There were no shades, only basic colors. All blues were the same. Greens the same. All reds the same.

He left his truck sideways on the shoulder, walked across the shallow drainage ditch, and collapsed on the grass of the opposite bank. A low guttural growl registered—the truck was still running. At least it wanted to run through the tape. To get past the sign. Gabe looked right. There it was. His mind conjured the right adjective. "Fucking sign." He fought off another bout of extra heartbeats.

To the left the Tri-counties beckoned, like a safe haven in stormy seas. But how safe were they? Ever since Thibideaux showed up Gabe had started having attacks there, too.

A memory struck as he sat up. Then a revelation. It must have started twenty-five years ago. Right there in the church. A flash brought a vision of the altar viewed through the wrought iron railing. Toes. He thought he saw toes. They weren't all four-legged animals.

He retched but managed to hold it in. His breathing was so fast he slumped to push away another bout of extra beats. Thibideaux did it to me twenty-five years ago. He thought. He took away everything outside of the Tri-counties. And now he's taking away the Tri-counties as well. He took Father Costello's life without killing him, and he's doing the same to me. Can't go and can't stay.

A new sensation fought for attention. It battled his fear, gaining ground. It was anger. Thibideaux's after more than just me.

Another thought captured center stage. John Johnson's highway theory. All this for a freeway shunt? Was that what Thibideaux was after? There wasn't a highway plan twenty-five years ago, was there? Even if there was, what would a priest have to do with it? If not for a freeway, then what was Thibideaux back here for? Gabe's mental path turned toward home. Father Costello is the key. He has to know something.

Gabe's anger enlisted an ally and the partnership relaxed him—his heart pounded a steady pattern and slowed to recliner chair levels. Anger led the forward thrust and reason covered the flanks.

He looked up at the sign. It was just a hurdle, and there were no points for style. This kind of barrier had to be breeched, but it didn't matter if it was cleared with room to spare, or if one inched up one side and fell over to the other.

Gabe stood and quick-walked to the truck. He was a little fast with the gearshift and it growled a little before the clutch let it in. The tires threw grass, then rocks, as the truck accelerated onto the road and into a right turn. Toward the sign.

Gabe's heart gave an extra beat, but it seemed a feeble counterattack and he inhaled it into submission. The truck blew past the sign. There was no sonic boom, no band playing, no cheering crowd. It was calm and quiet, just like in the Tri-counties. The truck leveled off at forty-five and headed for the freeway entrance. He was on his way to Chicago.

Gabe navigated the early part of the trip with only an occasional heart acceleration and extra beat. Not enough to establish a beachhead, but a reminder that he was out of his comfort zone. His progress was slow—at fifty miles an hour, the scenery was hardly a blur.

At first, he was surprised at how cars would come up behind him like they were going one hundred miles an hour, and whiz past like he was standing still. But this was different. The eighteen-wheeler snuck up behind him and all Gabe could see were the lines of the grill in his rearview mirror. The behemoth was only inches from his bumper. He had to inhale away a couple of extra beats before the truck swerved into the fast lane and rumbled past. Why was everyone in such a hurry?

He pulled off the highway and into the parking lot of the filling station. He made sure he took frequent breaks—to stretch, get gas, or take care of personal business.

Gabe smiled. He really liked the filling stations with the mini-markets. Kind of like general stores with gasoline pumps. He could buy a sandwich and microwave it right there for a hot meal on the road.

He spotted a wrapped roll that was new to him. Something called a burrito.

He pulled the burrito from the microwave and juggled it up to the counter. He noticed two television sets behind the clerk. One had a picture that focused on him, and the other focused on the front doors of the store. He turned his head right, then left, to verify it was a live feed. Why was the other trained on the front doors? On his way out, he noticed graduations on the edge of each door that indicated feet and inches from the floor.

Gabe didn't know what was in the burrito, but it tasted great. The only problem was it gave him the wind something awful—had to drive with the windows wide open. He made a mental note to buy one on the way back so he could take it in to the Herndon's Edge. Maybe Teddy could whip up something that tasted as good but without the side effects.

Gabe had a knack for inventing time-passing games, honed while working the fields. He found one to pass the time once the sun went down. Some of the eighteen-wheelers going in the opposite direction brightened and then dimmed their lights. With more observation, he noticed they only did it when another truck was passing. Initially he figured it was a greeting since the passing truck would flicker its running lights in response. Eventually, he realized it was a trucker's code indicating that the passing truck's tail end was clear of the front of the other truck—it was safe to merge back into the slow lane. He confirmed it by giving it a try when the next big rig swung around to pass him. Once clear, he brightened and dimmed his lights and the truck immediately merged back in with the running lights "thank you." The new game passed the time until just after midnight.

Fatigue showed its face so Gabe pulled into a rest area and parked between two big trucks—he considered the truckers his brethren now. He curled up in his front seat and drifted off to sleep.

The second day of driving was boring but it went without a hitch. When Gabe hit the outskirts of Chicago he was both surprised and pleased that the signs matched those listed in the directions. Not there yet, though. He needed gas.

The filling station didn't have a market. Instead, a small, narrow building, little more than a booth, stood in the center of three rows of pumps. Thick glass extended from chest height upward on three sides. A pimple-faced man, not more than sixteen years old, sat inside like an astronaut crowded in a space capsule.

Gabe approached the glass as the young man pushed a lever, and a large, silver drawer jutted out at Gabe, nearly smacking him in the chest.

"Thirty-six forty-nine," the young man said through a cheap-sounding microphone.

Gabe looked down at the drawer and then at the man. He put two twenty-dollar bills in the drawer and it retracted into the booth. The young man grabbed the bill, counted out change and threw it in the drawer, then slid it back out. Too bad he didn't slide out a burrito with the change.

Returning to the freeway was a little tricky, but once back, Gabe clicked into search mode. The directions proved accurate and he pulled into the hospital parking lot as the sun's last embers submerged into the horizon.

The lot was nearly deserted so he decided to bed down for the night on the seat of his truck. As he settled into the fabric, he had a strange feeling someone was staring at him through a window on one of the upper floors of the hospital. The thought kept him from sleeping for ten minutes before the fatigue of the drive took over.

CHAPTER 38

IN GABE'S ABSENCE, Deena Lee's headaches had returned. Wanna called Doc Halvorson who came out right away, with Misty Rondelunas in tow. While Doc was tending to Deena Lee, Misty pulled Wanna aside.

"Gabe around?"

Wanna gave Misty a suspicious squint. "No. He's out of town. Why do you ask?" Misty was always effervescent, and now was no exception. Wanna hated her for it.

"I just wanted to talk to him."

"About what?"

Misty leaned close. "I heard he's really big. Huge. Know what I mean? You've probably seen him naked. It true?"

Wanna shoved Misty away. "You hussy. Keep your

hands away from Gabe. He's sweet on someone else and I don't want the likes of you stirring it up. I swear. You'd fuck a horse if it could smile at you. Probably have. Get out of my house before I knock your one-track mind out of your head for good." Wanna cocked her right arm.

Misty ran from the house and jumped in the car, sobbing.

Wanna paced the living room for the next half hour, alternating between worry over Deena Lee and contempt for Misty. At each pass, she sneered out the front window, in the direction of Doc's car.

Doc strode from the bedroom and sat on the sofa, patting the cushion next to him.

Wanna didn't sit. "Is she going to be all right?"

"She'll be fine. I gave her something for the head-ache. Her pressure's still up, but it's not critical. I don't want to take the baby unless I have to. If you can keep her calm, she should be good for another few days or so. The longer we let the baby develop, the better for them both. Is anything upsetting her?"

Wanna tapped her lips with the front of her right index finger while she scanned the ceiling. "Gabe had to go out of town for a few days. Maybe that's eating at her. She's sweet on him."

"In that case, I wish he was here. You said he'd be back in a day or so? Hopefully it will be sooner. I don't want her to get upset." Doc stood.

"Then you keep that whore, Misty, away from here, and away from Gabe." Wanna's eyes were two fireballs.

Doc rolled his. "If the headaches come back, let me know right away. Day or night. I'll check back with you every couple of hours. I'll also notify the hospital so they can be ready, just in case."

Doc fishtailed the car a little as he turned from Gabe's gravel drive onto the paved county road. A huge cloud of dust nearly overtook the car. He looked over at Misty in the passenger seat and saw her eyes were ringed in wet eyeliner.

"What happened in there? Did you say something out of line to Wanna?"

"I just asked about Gabe and she went off on me." Misty sobbed.

Doc looked over again and noticed the wet streaks that led from Misty's eyes to the edges of her jaw were accompanied by more viscous streaks running from her nose to her upper lip. He had been weighing his relationship with her for the last couple of weeks and he was seriously divided on the best path to take. He enjoyed her physical company—there seemed to be no end to her ability and willingness to experiment with the sensory pleasures. But he was in no mood to get into a permanent relationship yet. Even if he was ready, it wouldn't be with Misty. On an existential plane, he longed for a relationship in which he would be the one to dab the tears of his mate, but he didn't want to have to wipe her nose as well.

After a long pause, Doc took a deep breath and

blew it out. "Misty, I've been meaning to tell you. My oldest brother's daughter has just finished a nursing program up north, and she's looking for a job. I've been needing someone with a little more formal training, so I'm going to take her on at the clinic. I'm really sorry, but I can't afford to pay you both. I'm going to have to let you go. I can give you two weeks to find something else and I'll give you some severance pay."

Misty peered at Doc out of the corners of her eyes. "You crazy? I thought you loved me. We've been together for nearly a year. I thought we were going to settle down." Fluids ran tributaries across the lower part of her face.

The situation required a little brutality, he thought. "There's a difference between love and sex. You're good at the second, but that doesn't mean any love has developed between us."

Misty turned her head toward Doc so fast fluids flew from her face to the back of the seat. "You bastard. You're just like all the others. You're fine when you're getting what you want, but if I want something back, then it's over. You bastard." Her head collapsed into her hands and she bawled.

"I'm sorry, Misty, but we discussed this when we first started. I wasn't in the market for a serious relationship then, and I'm not now." He almost said there are lots of men out there who'd love to have her as a partner, but he figured most of them had already.

Misty peeked above her hands. "I think I'm pregnant."

"I doubt that very much, Misty. When we get back

to the clinic, I'll give you a test to make sure." He anticipated this move, so before he initiated his physical liaison with her, he personally checked his own sperm count. It hadn't changed for the better—if anything, it was worse than before. He thought not telling her about his physical problem was unethical, but so was porking her in the clinic lab almost every day. Anyway, he assumed she would be the last person to get upset about it, so he enjoyed the ride and endured the self-disappointment of his ethical slide.

CHAPTER 39

GABE AWAKENED WHEN the first light broke the top of the dashboard. He looked at his watch—six-thirty. The patients would be having breakfast and getting ready for the day, and it made him feel his hunger, and the need to clean up.

A few off-ramps back on the freeway, he'd seen a billboard for a restaurant called "McDonald's." He'd seen advertisements for the chain on the television, and he'd heard they even had one up in Calhoun Township, so he decided to eat there and clean up in their restroom. Hopefully, it wasn't one of those fancy places where everyone had to wear a nice clothes.

The restaurant looked like a cartoon set, with brightly colored chairs and tables. Everything was made of rounded plastic. Cartoon characters adorned the wall displays. He seated himself at a table near the door and sat there drumming his fingers. There wasn't a waitress in sight. After a few minutes a customer walked up to the counter and placed an order, then within a minute or so, he walked away with a full tray of food. As Gabe stood, he thought of a school cafeteria.

The sandwich was wrapped in paper, the orange juice in a paper cup with a plastic lid. He wondered who thought of putting eggs in a sandwich, with cheese and ham, on some kind of biscuit. But it was really good. Another potential addition to Teddy's menu back home?

Gabe pushed through the front doors of the hospital as the clock approached eight o'clock. Sunlight beamed through the windows creating alternating shafts of bright and dim light. He tiptoed to the reception desk. The large McDonald's-like counter, in one of the dim areas, was spot-lighted by two large can lights in the ceiling.

"Can I visit a patient?"

"Which patient would you like to see?" The receptionist was an older woman in a white uniform, grossly overweight, with a kind smile and a patient attitude. The hospital was exceptionally clean, but it looked like only minimal maintenance had been done over the last several years.

"I'd like to see Father Costello, please."

The woman's head snapped up at the mention of the name. "He's not one to have visitors. Are you from the church? Do you have credentials?"

Gabe was stumped. But he hadn't come all this way to be turned back at the reception desk. Tell a half-truth, he thought. Sometimes telling the full truth was as bad as telling an out-and-out lie, but getting half of it right frequently worked like a greased cake pan.

"No, Ma'am. I know all about what happened to the Father. I know about his condition and all. I come from the town where he had his problem—Boyston. If nothing else, it might help him a bit to hear what's come of all of the people there who he used to preach to. Couldn't do any harm, as I see it. Worst could happen, I tell him, and he just stares. If I were in his place, it'd help me to hear. He really cared for us back then."

The receptionist smiled and walked behind a glass wall. She dialed a phone and engaged in a short conversation. Gabe could see that it was neither agitated nor a one-way "yes, sir-no, sir" interaction.

The receptionist waddled back to the counter. "Doctor Lawrence thinks a visit from you might do Father Costello some good. The patients are finishing their breakfast. Then they have to shower and get dressed. Can you come back in an hour?"

"Okay if I wait over there?" He pointed at the small waiting area. "I got nowhere else to go."

"Of course. Here." She handed him a magazine.

The government-issue metal-framed chairs had smooth, green fake-leather seat and back cushions. They were as uncomfortable as they looked. Positioned in a semi-circle under a large window, the light was operating room intense.

Gabe thumbed through the magazine, scanning the pictures—nearly all of smiling men and women. He folded it closed. "People" the cover said in bold white letters. Thumbing through again, he paused at a familiar photo. A woman from one of his favorite TV shows smiled at him. From the caption, her seven-month marriage had just broken up. Why was she smiling?

"Sorry for the delay," the receptionist said, her voice skipping across the room on the slick linoleum. "One of the patients had a little accident and we had to put everyone in their rooms for a while. You can go see Father Costello now. You don't have to worry about being interrupted. All the others will be locked in until we find out where they got the videos. Father Costello is in the Day Room. Number 353. Take the elevator to the third floor and turn right."

"Thank you, Ma'am," Gabe said with a smile. He laid the magazine on the counter like it was a bible.

The only inhabitant in the Day Room was seated in another government-issue chair placed close to one of several windows that ran along the east wall of the room. The man stared out the window like he was in a trance. A table to his right held a few scattered magazines.

Gabe approached the table and looked out the window, over Father Costello's shoulder. It overlooked the parking lot. He took a step closer. From the angle of this window, the entire truck seat, where he had slept, was visible.

He walked around to the opposite side of the table and pulled up a chair. Although the priest was seated, he could tell he was a short man, in his fifties, with white temples blending into jet-black hair peppered with random strands of gray. Small in stature but in good physical shape, he sat erect with his hands folded in his lap. His feet were crossed at the ankles but both were nearly flat on the floor. The traditional suit with collar was impeccably neat and pressed.

Gabe watched him in silence. Not a single subtle movement—even an eye blink.

He leaned over the table. "Father Costello? My name's Gabe Petersen. We knew each other back in Boyston. I was a young man back then, so you probably don't remember me. You remember Boyston?"

The priest stared out of the window.

"Anyhow, some strange things have been happening back there. They remind me of things that happened back when you had your problem. I'm wondering if you could give me some information about what was going on back then."

Nothing.

Gabe leaned farther forward so his chest was on the table. "There's this little man, named Thibideaux. Ever heard of him? He's been doing some strange things—making the earth move, making lightning, throwing fireballs. Ring a bell?"

No change in the priest's expression.

Gabe leaned back. "Pardon me, Father. I'll be

right back."

He took the elevator to the first floor and approached the reception desk. "Can I borrow a pencil and paper?"

The receptionist flashed a knowing smile. "Can't get through to him, can you?"

"Not yet, Ma'am. Still working on it, though." He hurried from the desk. As he entered the elevator, the receptionist's voice rang a sarcastic tone: "Good luck."

Gabe sat down across from Father Costello without saying a word and drew on the paper. Finished, he pushed the paper across the table. "Look familiar?"

Father Costello stared out of the window.

Gabe grabbed the paper and walked around the table. He held the paper between the Father's face and the window and raised his voice. "Look familiar?"

Father Costello's expression went from a blank stare to a slight squint. Then his eyes came alive and focused on the paper.

Gabe had drawn a face with small features, including arching eyebrows and a mouth that was straight. Thick lines turned the mouth upward at the corners.

Father Costello blinked twice and hissed a single hoarse word. "Hughes." He grabbed the paper and slammed it down on the table. "Hughes!" His head swung toward Gabe. He looked scared.

Gabe hurried around the table and sat down. He felt the priest's eyes on him the whole way.

Father Costello spoke in a whiskey-and-cigarettes baritone. "What are you here for? Haven't you people done enough to me already?"

Gabe put his hand up in a stop motion. "Whoa there, Father. I'm not in with Thibideaux, or Hughes, as you call him. I'm here because of things he's doing to people back in Boyston. I need to find out what he's up to. By the way, my name's Gabe Petersen."

The priest turned his head slightly and frowned, scanning Gabe from top to bottom. "My daughter's not really dead. She's living somewhere on the West coast. You can try, but you'll never get out of me where she is."

"The heck you talking about, Father? You got a daughter? I thought you priests weren't supposed to do that kind of stuff."

Father Costello relaxed a little.

Gabe tried to do the same, but he was spooked, like he was talking to a ghost.

"Father, I ain't so interested in what's happened to you unless it has something to do with how we can stop Thibideaux. Hughes. I think he's fixing to do something bad out our way, but I don't know what it is. Can you help?"

A worried look flushed the priest's face as his hands clasped together in front of his mouth. "Is anyone pregnant in Boyston?"

Gabe frowned. "Yeah. A woman named Miz Murtry."

The priest lowered his hands and placed the palms flat on the table. "Is the baby's father around?"

"Naw. He took off as soon as he got the news. Hasn't been seen since. What's that got to do with the price of apples?"

"When is she due?" A deep crease divided the priest's forehead down to the bridge of his nose.

"In about a week or so. You want a birth announcement? Sorry, Father. I don't see what this has to do with my problem."

Father Costello leaned back and let out a loud sigh. The crease in his forehead disappeared. "Hughes wants her baby."

Gabe jerked back in the chair. "He wants her baby? What for?" He leaned across the table.

Father Costello froze. It looked like he was trying to move his lips, but nothing came out.

"Father?"

"What year is this?"

"Two thousand and seven." Gabe drummed his fingers once on the table.

The priest drew a deep breath and held it like he was winding up for something big. "About twenty-five years ago I came across a composition book that belonged to Hughes. It contained notes on his training from when he was a child. It also explained how his organization worked, from top to bottom."

"Organization? What kind of organization?" Gabe rubbed his forehead. "I thought he worked as a land speculator."

"Listen to me. Hughes found out I had the book. I tried to hide it in a Bible, but he made it burst into flames right in the Bible. But I was smart. A few days before that happened, I copied a lot of the information. Anyway, his organization constantly requires new recruits. They get them as babies from people like this friend of yours."

"There are other babies in Boyston. Why Miz Murtry's?"

Father Costello leaned forward and massaged his temples with the thumb and fingers of his right hand. "I just can't remember the details. It was a long time ago. Frankly, it's a time I'd like to forget. I'd give my life just to forget, but that's a mortal sin. That's why I'm here and why I have to withdraw from everyone and everything. From myself."

Get right to it, Gabe thought. "So how can I stop Thibideaux from taking Miz Murtry's baby? I got special feelings for her."

"I'm sorry, Gabe, but I don't have any idea. I just can't remember the details of his organization. I wanted to go through it to see if there was any way to stop him back then, but I never got the chance. Without that information, and a good understanding of his organization, it would be hopeless. I think I remember something in the notes, though."

Gabe sat upright. "You said you made copies? Where did you put them?"

Father Costello looked into Gabe's eyes, through them. "I hid them in the rectory in Boyston, but I'm sure it's been torn down by now, along with the church, after what I did."

"No." Gabe slapped his hand on the desk. "It's still there. Both buildings are, but Thibideaux's living in the rectory. Where'd you hide them?"

A slight smile seemed to elevate Father Costello's cheeks. "I put the papers in an old family Bible, the same one that held the original notes when he burned them. I hid the Bible in the bathroom. The mirrored cabinet on the wall over the sink can be lifted out. It's heavy, but you could handle it. I put the Bible in the wall behind the cabinet. If you could bring it here, I could explain my notes. Maybe something in there would help. You say Thibideaux lives in the rectory?" His grin faded to a frown.

"Yeah. He don't leave very often. And he does strange things. Some families have been killed already."

Father Costello slumped. "Then I wouldn't go in there if I were you. He'll find a way to kill you, too."

Gabe shook his head. "I don't think so. He had a chance once, when I was snooping. He shook me up pretty good, but he didn't kill me."

"He must need you for something. Do you know what that might be?"

Gabe shrugged. "No clue, Father."

"Well, it gives you a chance, anyway. It looks like you have a choice to make. You can go back to Boyston and try to do something to stop Thibideaux or you can try to get the Bible and bring it back here so we can go over the notes. I'd love to get the best of him again, but I can't ask you to put yourself in danger. That will have to be your decision alone." He looked at the table and tapped a foot on the floor. "Is your friend going to have her child baptized?"

"She talks about it all the time."

His eyes defocused. "Time will be getting critical, then."

Gabe leaned forward again. "What does that got

to do with all this?"

The priest appeared to be physically fading. "He takes the babies at baptisms, but I can't go into that now, mostly because I can't remember the details. One thing, though. If you decide to get the notes, it would be best if you didn't open the Bible until you get here. Don't expose the contents to anyone. Not even your family. You never know when Hughes is watching. He could torch the notes, too, and that would be the end of it. You understand all this?"

"No, but I understand what you want me to do. What are you going to do now?"

The priest sighed. "I have to go back to my personal prison. It's my penance for what I've done."

"While you're in there, can you think about his situation?"

Father Costello smiled. "No. I think about one thing, over and over again. And that's what I did. It's my personal hell and I have to live out the rest of my natural life in that hell if my soul will have any chance of being saved after the death of my body."

Gabe didn't know what to say, so he became practical. "So how do I get through to you if you go back inside?"

"Just do what you did today." He pushed the piece of paper across the table. "Save this picture. Put it in front of my face. Hopefully I'll see it, like today."

Father Costello straightened in his chair, put his hands in his lap, and crossed his legs at the ankles. He turned to look out of the window.

"Father? Do you remember a young Lutheran boy

who would come into your church to confess his sins in the inhouse on Sunday mornings?"

Father Costello didn't answer. His eyes defocused, aimed out the window. Gabe stood up and turned to leave, but then he stopped. He looked around at Father Costello. Tears welled in the priest's eyes, then rolled down his cheeks.

CHAPTER 40

THIBIDEAUX FIDGETED IN his chair. He wanted to help the birth of Deena Lee's child along, so he was trying to capitalize on her headache situation by causing the barometric pressure to vacillate wildly. It had little effect. But that was the best he could do.

With all of his powers, he wasn't allowed to bring harm directly to anyone. The Organization's training was clear on that point. If he directly caused the death or discomfort of a citizen, by either using his powers or by using traditional physical force, he could be terminated on the spot.

The lightning couldn't strike Press Cunningham's car directly. It had to strike a tree. He couldn't have taken the sheriff's gun and shoot him with it. The sheriff's death had to be due to an event of nature. And the fireball couldn't incinerate Billy Smyth right off.

It had to light up the trailer to give Billy a chance to get out. Why couldn't the Councillor see that? Why couldn't he understand that all this is aligned with the Organization's rules?

Thibideaux sighed. In his current assignment, he hadn't done anything that could be traced back to him, or the Organization. Everything conformed to the low profile, blend-into-society philosophy of the training.

His mind automatically clicked into recitation mode—he turned trance-like and spewed memorized rules. A recruiter can't cause the death of a priest, minister, or other church leader, including nuns—directly or indirectly. It brings too much attention to the Organization. The same holds for ranking members of State or Federal governments, again for the same reason. The military is to be avoided at all costs. All aspects of life are too regimented there, and the level of record keeping is well in excess of that in public life.

I can't even trigger a headache in Deena Lee Murtry, he thought. He patted the arm of his chair. "Still, it won't be long now," he said out loud.

CHAPTER 41

THE CAR ACCELERATED as it swerved into the fast lane. The roar of its engine registered in Gabe's left ear, to the rear. Then, it was even with the back of the cab. The front fender of the vehicle appeared in his peripheral vision, but he kept his head straight, his attention on the road directly in front of him. The car pulled alongside and seemed to slow. Still, he stared ahead. Movement triggered an involuntary glance, but he did it with his eyes, not his head. The passenger's window slid down. If I slam on the brakes, he'll go past, Gabe thought. His heart gave an extra beat, then another. Why were people like this around the cities?

A larger movement caught his attention. Something extended from the open window, directly at him. He braced himself by stiffening his arms against the steering wheel and hit the brakes—not hard enough to start a skid, but hard enough so the front of the truck dipped downward with the decelerating force. The car flew past and he saw the puff from its exhaust pipe as the driver hit the gas. The car shrunk into the distance.

Gabe was familiar with the middle-finger salute, and its meaning. He'd even used it once when a grain elevator operator tried to cheat him on his vehicle tare weight after he'd offloaded his grain. But the frequency of its use in the Chicago area was incredible—worthy of a call to the Guinness Book of World Records. He had scanned a thick paperback book of their records some time ago and he had been totally unimpressed with the significance of some of the published accomplishments. A category for the frequency of middle finger usage must exist.

A full day's mileage from Chicago brought on a fatigue that lowered its weight on him in parallel with the setting sun. He found the contralateral partner of the rest area he used on his inbound trip and pulled off. Once again, he parked between two eighteen-wheelers and curled up on the front seat of the pickup.

A loud voice broke through his slumber. A shout, and an answer. He looked at his watch. It was quarter to three. He peeked between the steering wheel and the dashboard and saw two men standing face-to-face, backlit by the distant lights of the parking area. He squinted until his eyes adjusted to the muted light. The taller man pushed the other and climbed up into the cab of the truck parked to Gabe's left. The smaller man stumbled and went down on his left hip. His straight left arm prevented a total collapse.

The man propped himself up with both hands on the ground and slowly straightened his back into a hunched stance. He shuffled his feet a few times to gain his balance and stumbled toward Gabe's truck. His clothes were tattered and dirty, his hair plastered to his head and infiltrated with the dulling tint of dust.

He came closer and squinted at the truck. Gabe tried to shrink down below the dash slowly so his movement wouldn't be noticeable.

"Hey," the man shouted and pounded the hood of the truck. He stumbled around to the driver's side window and banged it hard enough to shake the truck. Gabe reached for the window crank, but he wasn't fast enough. The man banged the window again and again.

Gabe didn't want to drive with a broken window so he cranked it down about an inch. "What do you want?"

The man slurred a phrase through yellow teeth. "Knee somebody."

Gabe leaned back away from the window. He wasn't sure if he heard right.

"Knee somebody. Knee somebody."

Gabe still wasn't sure what the man said so he lowered the window another two inches, just enough to prevent the man from pushing his head into the cab.

The man's eyes widened. He brought his mouth to the opening and with a nasal voice, sprayed saliva into Gabe's world. "Need some money."

Gabe fished in his right pants pocket and pulled out a half-fist of coins. He showed it to the man and slid over to the passenger's side window. Cranking it down to the halfway point, he leaned his right arm out of the window. With an elbow flip, he flung the coins backward, past the truck bed and into the night. The money rang on the pavement like metallic chimes. The scavenger stumbled toward the sounds.

Gabe rolled up both windows, started the truck, and pulled out of the parking lot to the freeway entrance. "Might as well drive on through," he said to the steering wheel. "I'm awake now."

He pulled up to the farmhouse in a state of near exhaustion. It was mid-morning, and for half of the time since the sun broke the horizon, it had glared through the driver's side window, high enough to produce a squint but low enough to avoid the rotated visor. It had given him a headache.

He pumped the truck to a stop and hesitated behind the wheel. Something wasn't right. By this time of day the front door should have been open, the doorway protected by the wooden-framed screen door. It was warm enough for most windows to be at least halfway open, but they were all secured.

His eyes returned to the porch and he froze. The porch light was on. The fixture's activity cycle was strictly dusk-to-dawn, and even though it was operated manually, its diurnal rhythm was never altered. Wanna never left it on.

He swung from the pickup and half limped, half

jogged to the front door. It was unlocked. He pushed the door open and hesitated in the doorway. Quiet inside. "Wanna? Miz Murtry?" No answer.

He tiptoed through the front room and peered around the corner into the kitchen. A pot was on the stove. A few steps closer. Soup of some sort was cold but well mixed. A bowl of batter was on the counter next to the stove. He opened the oven. A muffin pan held eight half-cooked muffins. The oven was cold.

"Must have left in a hurry," he said out loud. It took a few more seconds before his road-weary mind clicked. "The hospital. Miz Murtry."

A shower of rocks peppered the porch as he spun the truck around toward the county road. His dream of coming to her rescue, of getting her to the hospital just in time, was gone. Now, he hoped he could get there before the birth, to lend emotional support and words of encouragement. It was little consolation, but it helped him keep the gas pedal down after his speedometer matched the number on the signs.

In the hospital, Gabe heard the answer to his question, but it didn't make much sense. "Dilated to seven centimeters," the nurse had said. It didn't matter. To him, it meant she hadn't delivered yet.

He was ushered into an anteroom and given green paper surgical scrubs to put on over his clothing. The shoe covers didn't fit so he put them on the front of his shoes and walked on this toes. Leaning around the doorway, he saw Wanna trying to feed ice chips to Miz Murtry, who winced with a painful contraction.

"Dammit, Wanna. I don't want ice chips," she

said when the contraction released its grip. "My tummy's hurting something awful and ice ain't going to take the pain away."

Wanna put the cup of ice down. "Sorry. The nurse said it'd make you feel better. I'm trying my best."

"I know. Thank you. But the only thing that'll help me now is to get this young one out of my belly and into the world." She grimaced into another contraction.

Just in time to save the day, Gabe thought. He strode into the room with a triumphant spring. "What are you hassling my Wanna about, little lady? You got something wrong with you, or what?"

Deena Lee slid her eyes toward Gabe then narrowed them to slits as the needle on the chart recorder quivered upward signaling the next contraction. When it let up, she reached a hand toward him. "I knew you'd make it in time. I'm getting close and it's really hurting. I'm needing to tell someone off, particularly a man, since it was one that done this to me. I can't yell at Wanna because she's been so good to me. I need some help to get this critter into daylight. You be my coach now?"

Gabe sat down on the side of the bed. "I'm here to help any way I can. You want some ice chips?" He chuckled.

"I'd like some ice chips to put in your backside and I know Wanna would help me put them there. Right, Wanna?"

Wanna offered a strained grin. "Gabe, I've seen some bad things in my time, but I don't look forward to going through this. I'm mighty frustrated right now, mostly because you ain't been here. So don't you bend over while I got this ice. I'll follow Deena Lee's wishes and give you a shiver you'll never forget." Their laughter was terminated by Deena Lee's next contraction.

Deena Lee hissed through clenched teeth. "Gabe, you turd. You men think you can trot around the country . . . when we're needing your help . . . You look hard at what's happening here . . . and the next time you think women have it so good . . . you think about what this little one's doing to me today."

Gabe squeezed her hand. "Calm yourself. I know they go in easier than they come out so you don't need to get worked up at me. I'm here now. You don't need to get huffy."

The contraction eased. "Huffy's what I need to get. It makes it go easier to yell at someone, you turd."

With the ground rules set, Gabe pushed the hair from Deena Lee's eyes and settled in for a heap of abuse. This wasn't how he imagined his triumphant saving-of-the-day, but if this was how he could help, he wouldn't be a moving target. He leaned close to her ear and whispered a short message.

Deena Lee smiled. Tears filled her eyes. "I love you too, you turd."

After a few more contractions, a nurse came in for the next exam. As she pulled on a latex glove, Gabe got up to leave.

Deena Lee glared. "Where do you think you're going? You sit right on back down. You're in this for the whole show now, you turd."

"I just thought you'd like some privacy." Gabe's

face sweltered.

"Privacy leaves us in the hospital. Besides, you're going to watch this little one come into the world so you can tell me about it later. I'll be a little busy to take it all in."

The nurse pulled the glove from her hand with a snap. "You're ready to go. You can start pushing on the next contraction." She turned to Gabe. "When it comes, you help her sit up. Count off ten seconds for each push. I'll be here to help, but I have to go give Doc a call first."

The next forty-five minutes of pushing made Gabe realize that Deena Lee's privacy comment was an understatement. It was all forgotten when the baby's head crowned. Gabe was so mesmerized, he forgot he was staring at Deena Lee's privates. This was a miracle that immediately and forever changed his views of the functions of these parts.

Doc Halvorson angled the head, then the shoulders from security into uncertainty and Gabe snuffled. He was taught men shouldn't cry in public, but there had to be exceptions. This was at the top of his list.

As the baby's lungs strained to produce their first cries, Doc Halvorson peered over the drapes at Deena Lee. "It's a boy. And a big one, too."

Gabe saw Deena Lee choke with emotion so he leaned close and hugged a hug that committed him to her, on the spot, for the rest of his days.

The baby, cleaned and swaddled, was presented to the new mother. Deena Lee struggled to hold back tears. "What are we going to call you, little one? I had some names picked, but now I'm not so sure. Gabe, you got any ideas?"

He was startled by the question. They had talked about names, but he hadn't given it serious thought. He didn't know what to say. "How about Turd, Jr.?" His was the only laugh.

"I'm serious, Gabe. If what you said to me before was true, you better get used to having this little man in your life. You can start by helping me give him his name. I'm stuck so you look in his eyes and tell me what he looks like." She held the blanketed package out to Gabe.

He took the baby in his huge hands and pulled him close to his chest. His smile faded. How could he keep him safe from Thibideaux? He leaned close and whispered. "I'll make sure nothing happens to you."

"What did you say to him?" Deena Lee said.

He disregarded his literary caution. "Nothing."

Gabe's eyes met those of the little wonder and he blurted the first name that came to him. "Cory Dean. He looks like a Cory. It's a strong name. And Dean is for Deena Lee, his Momma."

Deena Lee smiled. "Cory Dean. Now we just have to come up with a last name."

Gabe smiled at her.

Around nine in the evening, Wanna walked to the window of the nursery and elbowed Gabe in the ribs. "Are you going to spend all night staring at him? We need to get out so everyone can get some rest. Especially you."

He gave a small wave and pivoted as Wanna's hand

hooked his arm.

She stopped him in the parking lot. "You dog. You got to her in a moment of weakness. Now she's hooked on you and you on her. You dog."

"It doesn't bother you, does it?"

"I'm happy for you both. I've been hoping for it to happen for some time. I just don't know where I'll be staying now. I guess I can look for a place of my own, although I don't know what I'll do for it."

Gabe pulled her into a hug. "You're talking garbage. We've always talked about finishing the old playroom in the attic. We can run some plumbing up there and give you a place of your own. I'll still need your help with the farm, particularly with the prices the way they are. We'll just be a big family. You, me, Cory Dean and Deena Lee."

"Since when did you start calling her Deena Lee?"

Gabe shook his head. "After what I saw of her today, Miz Murtry just don't seem appropriate."

CHAPTER 42

JOHN JOHNSON WALKED along Main Street, headed for his wife's café and a bite to eat. He passed a stretch of vacant lots overgrown with intentionally planted shrubs and volunteer weeds, and a gust of wind stirred up a dust devil of road debris that stung his eyes enough to interrupt his gait. With balled fists, he rubbed his eyes until a pyrotechnic display of stars stippled his visual field. It took a full second and a half for his vision to clear and he wished it hadn't. Thibideaux stood in his path, only three feet away.

John let out a loud "Ah" and spun his head to the right, then left to gauge the best path of escape. Despite an overwhelming need to run, none of his muscles cooperated with his brain. Thibideaux broke the silence, but not the tension.

"Good afternoon, Mr. Johnson. I've been looking

for you. Can we talk here or would you prefer to go to you wife's café and talk over a plate of food?"

"What do you want?" John's voice cracked like a teenager's. "I don't want no trouble. I got no beef with you. All the snooping was the others' idea. I had nothing—"

"Relax, Mr. Johnson. I mean you no harm. In fact, I doubt if I could hurt you if I wanted to. I'm just a frail little man." He paused and took a small step closer. "I'm also a businessman and I want to talk to you about my work here. Nothing more."

"What about Press Cunningham and the other families? What about Billy and Mac, and what about the sheriff? Are you telling me you had nothing to do with them?"

Thibideaux shook his head, but with his stiff neck, his entire upper body rotated. "Do I look like the type of person who could do those things? Is there any human on this globe who could do what you're suggesting? Pardon me for saying so, but I suspect you're the type of person who believes in UFOs, voodoo, and mental telepathy. You won't find anything like that in me." He spread his arms out from his sides. "I'm just a physically weak man with a simple job to do here in the Tri-counties and nothing more." He lowered his arms. "I'll admit I'm really good at what I do. There are few better. If you get to know me, you'll see I'm a master of deception. I can make people believe the darndest things. That's the reason I haven't rebutted any of the outrageous accusations some people have directed at me. I've found utility in those rumors. It's helped me go about my work without tipping my hand as to what that work might be." He paused. "Until now, that is."

John inched a half-step closer and put his hands on his hips. "And what might that job be?"

"That's what I came here to talk to you about. It's time for me to reveal my business in the Tri-counties."

John tilted his head and squinted. "Why are you telling me about it?"

"I wanted to tell you first because it seems you've figured it out already. Since you're so perceptive, I wanted to ask your opinion about the best way to announce the results of my work to the citizens."

John stood tall. "So you're working for the highway department on a new freeway shunt?"

"I'm an independent consultant, but I can't tell you who has retained my services. It would be politically unwise." He held out an embossed business card that read, "A. Jackson Thibideaux. Property Consultant." It also had a New Orleans street address and a series of phone numbers.

"What are your results?" John spoke fast. "Is the shunt going through the Tri-counties as I suspected? Have you found the best route? Here, look at what I came up with." John pulled his tattered map from his back pocket. "Here's what I think's the best route. It cuts the distance but stays far enough from the swamp to avoid the flooding. Did you come up with a similar route?"

"Once again, Mr. Johnson, I salute you for your insight. Should a divided highway go through the Tri-counties, that would be the route I'd suggest, for the reasons you've described."

John smiled. Not such a bad guy, he thought.

"But we're getting off the point," Thibideaux said. "I need to know the best way to communicate my information to the citizens."

"You should call a town meeting. I can set it up for you, if you want. I can do it right away. I know the right people."

"That would be very kind."

John shifted his weight onto his left leg. "So what do you think about what people are saying about the families that have been killed? It'd sure make bickering for land easier and cheaper, wouldn't you admit?"

"These are unfortunate incidents—ones that an unscrupulous land speculator could easily use to his advantage. I'll promise you I'm not of that mettle. In fact, my opinion is that negotiations should be initiated with families that are currently in residence in the appropriate corridor of land. I'll even go one step further to prove my integrity. Since your son has a farm in what you call the best route, I'll include in my report that your son should be the one with whom negotiations begin. That way, you can be sure all dealings will be in your son's best interests, and the poor families of the departed will also get fair deals. Would that put your mind at ease?"

The broad smile on John's face answered in the affirmative.

"Okay, Mr. Johnson. Shall we set up a town meeting to bring some good news to the community?"

"There are people around here who think you're up to no good, so a town meeting would be the best way to set them straight."

"And can I count on your support for my proposals?" Thibideaux said.

"You've been up front with me today and I appreciate it." John's eyebrows arched high and he gave a firm nod. "I'll let the others know I stand behind you."

"Thank you, Mr. Johnson. Now, I have a favor to ask of you. Please don't discuss our conversation with anyone else prior to the town meeting. I still have some details to work out and a disclosure could jeopardize the whole plan, including the part that involves your son. Can we keep this between us until the town meeting?"

John's chest expanded with more than an inhalation. "We sure can. My lips are sealed. I swear to God." He drew a cross on his chest.

"Good. Then I won't take any more of your time. I'll be in touch if I need further advice." Thibideaux pivoted and shuffled in the direction of the rectory.

John walked toward the café with a bounce in his step. He couldn't believe how he had misjudged Thibideaux, or Mr. Thibideaux. His mind spun off in a daydream. He was a feudal lord in the Middle Ages who had just formed an alliance with his main competitor to build an insurmountably strong force to dominate all aggressors and thoroughly intimidate all others.

His mind returned to the present and he visualized a business adjacent to the off ramp of a busy freeway. He double-timed his gait.

The first challenge to his pledge of secrecy lay ahead. The fight of ego versus promise was one more people lost than won. The house odds were heavily stacked in favor of the former. For the first time in his life, John Johnson beat the odds.

"You folks know about the town meeting?" John Johnson announced from his perch on the general store bench. "I know what it's about, but I can't tell you. Mr. Thibideaux wants me to keep it quiet for reasons that'll be told at the meeting."

John knew he didn't have to publicize the meeting. Not with the rumor mill and the subject of the meeting. But it didn't hurt to point out his special relationship with Thibideaux to the "common folk."

He was about to command another greeting when a Ford Taurus bearing State Government markings and plates pulled up in front of the general store and came to a jerky halt. Two men in starched white shirts got out and approached John.

"Excuse me, sir. Can you tell me were I can find Wes Worthing?" the taller of the two said.

John flinched. He hated Wes. He doesn't deserve to be so important, he thought. "Wes lives at the southeastern edge of Herndon County. You had to pass the turn-off to get this far. What's your business with Wes? Maybe I can help you. Save you some time and trouble." He stood up and tugged upward on his belt. "Name's John Johnson."

"We've been sent by Senator Ambrose. She's still mourning the loss of Preston Cunningham. Mr. Cunningham came to her a few months ago to inquire about a freeway connection through the Tri-counties. At the time, there weren't any plans, but following his death, the idea grew on the senator, not only as a way to enhance the economy in the area, but also to honor Mr. Cunningham. She wants to prepare a report for consideration by the full legislature. We're here to gauge the feasibility, look for the best route, and estimate the cost. We need to submit a report in the next few months and we need to initiate our research with Wes Worthing's help."

John stepped down from the porch. "Wes ain't the one you need to talk to. Mr. Thibideaux's been putting together the report for the past several months. I'm helping him. You can find him over there in the church rectory." He pointed with his index and pinky fingers extended in parallel. He'd seen some rich guy on an infomercial point that way and he thought it looked authoritative. "I can take you over and give you an introduction."

The shorter man stepped forward. "I'm sorry, Mister . . . Jackson, was it? We don't know anything about this man you're talking about. He isn't working for the State and he certainly hasn't been hired to do any work on a freeway connection in these parts as far as we know."

"It's Johnson. Mr. Thibideaux's an independent consultant. See here. Here's his card." John pulled out his tattered map, one fold of which held Thibideaux's card. He didn't give it to them. He held it at arm's length so they could read it.

The two men looked at each other and the shorter one shrugged. "I'm sorry, but I've never heard of this Mr. Thibideaux. Maybe he's been hired by someone other than the State. If so, we'll have no interest in talking with him. We've been charged to work through Wes Worthing and no one else." He looked down the road in the direction they came. "If you could give us directions to his place, we'd be grateful. And while you're at it, can you suggest a good place to spend the night? We've had other business today and we've been on the road since early morning."

John's gut sent a signal upward that was half nausea and half fear. His voice cracked through the directions.

When the men were gone, he released his weight from a foot above the porch bench and came down on the seat with a thud. His imagination returned to the Middle Ages. His alliance with the feudal lord was really a hoax designed to take his land and people, with or without a fight.

"I wonder what the little bastard is up to," he said out loud. "I'll get him tonight."

He sat on the bench for a half-hour, oblivious to the comings and goings of the town folk, and then jumped to his feet. "I got it. The bastard's got to be working for Rother County. They must be trying to mess with our chances of building the shunt so they can have it."

He paced, mumbling. He could get the little jerk

at the town meeting. This was even better than an alliance with the little bastard. He could expose Thibideaux's plan and save the Tri-counties from a Rother double-cross. In front of all the people. Maybe it was time for Wes to step down as Chairman of the Corporation. Mr. John Johnson would be interested in the post.

On the way home, he envisioned an audience with the King. He revealed the backhanded plan of his former ally, the ruthless feudal lord, and the King dispatched a legion of his best knights to deal with the aggressor. Lord Johnson was knighted for his insight and bravery. As he neared home, the new Sir John Johnson sought the hand, and more, of the damsel, Miss Misty Rondelunas, and the all-too-real daydream went into the gutter, just where Sir John wanted it at that moment.

CHAPTER 43

GABE DIRECTED WANNA as she put Deena Lee's suitcase in Gabe's room.

"Why ain't you going on a honeymoon?" Wanna said. "You made it all the way to Chicago and back. You could take them away for a while. I can take care of things here."

"You've done enough already." Gabe was still amazed. She had pulled everything together so fast—rounded up so many friends there hadn't been enough space in Deena Lee's hospital room. Good thing the hospital had a good-sized chapel. Wanna even had rings. "I still got some business to take care of. We'll celebrate it after things slow down in the fall. How's Doc surviving?"

"What did he expect, coming in there with that new girl on his arm?" Wanna said. "How were we to know it was his niece?"

"How long before word gets around?"

Wanna smiled. "The bad spreads faster than the good. He can expect to be on the shit list for a week or two. He's on my A-list for dumping that Misty, though. He needs a good woman."

Gabe poked her in the side. "I saw you looking at him during the ceremony. You sure did a spin around on him."

"Shut up, Gabe."

"Get him while he's on the rebound—"

Wanna swung and her knuckles dug into his bicep.

"Dang." Gabe grabbed his arm and took a step back. "You gave me a muscle bump." He rubbed the spot like he was trying to erase the pain. "Must be something to it for you to react like that."

"There's more to it, but it don't have to do with Doc." She leaned around and looked down the hall. "Where's Deena Lee and the baby?"

"Both taking a nap in her room."

Wanna grabbed Gabe's shirt and pulled him into the kitchen. "We got to talk about the pregnancy. Now! We can't wait any longer."

Gabe rolled his eyes.

"Dammit, Gabe. I've been putting on weight lately."

"That's because you're eating everything in the kitchen. I'm about to lock up the animals."

"I'm serious. I'm eating for two." She ran her hands over her still-flat stomach. "And any day now, my belly's going to take over and grow without the rest of me. Then it'll be obvious. We need to get a story down."

Gabe walked over to the sink and leaned to look out the window. "Sorry. I've been preoccupied with the Chicago trip and the town meeting. And Thibideaux." He turned and faced her. "You can say what you want and I'll go with it."

"You think this is easy on me? I've been worrying about it something fierce. The least you can do is help with it."

Gabe prepared for the outburst. The freshly stropped edge of a good razor couldn't compare to the cutting edge of her tongue, so he braced himself for a slice or two.

"Please," she said. Her eyes were moist.

This was serious. "Okay. I'm sorry. What have you got for an explanation?"

"I thought I could say I had a man up in Rother who claimed to be in love, but when I got pregnant he took off. Or, I could say that Johnny Robertson was having trouble with his wife and we got our thing going again, but that now he's back with her." She moved a little to cut off his stare. "What do you think?"

He scanned the ceiling, looking for inspiration. "I like the first. Better to leave the man without a name. That way, you won't risk causing problems for Johnny Robertson, although you probably wouldn't mind. The first one's better because you were doing it for love—that's noble. Him running out on you—that gets sympathy. Best leave it at that. If anyone presses you on who it was, just take the high road and refuse to ruin his life."

"What do I put on the birth certificate? What

name do I put down?"

"It'll be a Petersen. Do like I did with Cory Dean."

Wanna put her hand on Gabe's arm, just below his sore spot. "What if the baby has something wrong with it? What would we say then? People will get suspicious and gossipy."

Gabe's hands found the bottoms of his pockets. His eyes went to the ceiling again, then down to the floor. "People have known our family for some time, so maybe it'd be best to say the same problem showed up a few times in your momma's family, and that it usually skipped a few generations. You knew the risk but it happened so rare you didn't think anything of it. That do it?"

"Damn, Gabe. Why'd you wait so long to talk it out?" She threw her arms around his neck and gave him a tight hug. "I'm still a nervous wreck, but at least I'll be able to talk it through."

Gabe returned her hug and then peeled her arms from his shoulders. "Don't get so worked up. Mark my words. You'll see the silly in your reactions when you look back on them. Now, I need to get the barn cleaned. Remember, if anything strange happens, get on the supper bell right away. I'll be here in a shake."

She followed him to the back door. "You know the way you are with Cory Dean? Will you be like that with ours?"

Gabe turned around and stiffened. Her look was intense, but he couldn't place it other than that. Was she jealous about his acceptance of little Cory Dean? He stepped up on the porch and gathered her into a hug. "You know I will." He smiled. "Just quit worrying. Try to relax and enjoy life."

CHAPTER 44

THE NIGHT OF the town meeting was warm—hot in the nearly full auditorium. Gabe looked down at his watch. As usual, no one was on time. They were all there at least five minutes early.

Gabe surveyed the room again. The pre-meeting attitude seemed to be anticipation, which was manifest in several ways among the various individuals. To his left, a group used their nervous energy to catch up with or propagate tidbits of gossip of various denominations. Laughing a few rows to the front sounded forced. Necks craned, presumably to get a good look at Thibideaux, as if a head-to-toe scan would give them a hint about his moral fiber. He thought he saw several people flirting, some directly between two individuals, a form of hand-to-hand flirting. Some, more long range utilizing cruise missile winks and smart bomb smiles. Nearly all female residents took a minute to come over and congratulate Deena Lee on her marriage and to ogle little Cory Dean. As the nervous energy increased, the din in the auditorium built to an all out commotion.

At eight o'clock on the nose, Wes Worthing stood and walked to the podium. He tapped the microphone with the knuckle of his right index finger the required three times and leaned forward, causing the device to squeal. "Can I have your attention?"

Gabe smiled and shook his head. Wes was such an imposing figure, both physically and ethically, he could issue one such statement to accomplish what it would take others three or four tries to pull off.

Everyone turned to face the front and straightened in their seats, and Wes pulled a folded paper from his shirt pocket and opened it a little too close to the active microphone, which objected to the trespass. He leaned forward, but this time not close enough to displease the electronic whiner.

"I'd like to call this meeting to order. I'll start with some announcements. Then, since we don't have any old business, I'll just go right on to the new business and the reason for calling this meeting." Wes adjusted the paper on the podium.

"This Friday'll be the spaghetti feed to benefit the clinic's program for the uninsured. It's potluck, so you'll have to bring either a side dish or a dessert. Doc'll have the clinic parking lot set up early, but he could use some help getting it rolling. See him after if you can lend a hand."

Gabe looked at Doc and smiled. Wanna sat next to him.

"Next Saturday'll be the Women's Relief Society bake sale, but they'll also have some of their quilts up for offering. That'll be in the church side yard. And, don't forget, next Friday night, right here at Boyston High'll be the first football game of the year, against Calhoun . . . Go Badgers!"

The improvisation produced a variety of supportive yells and exclamations, one of which was uttered louder than intended by someone in the back part of the auditorium, and included a somewhat vulgar suggestion about where Calhoun High could go and what it could do when it got there. This created a 40-40 mix of dirty looks and laughs, with the other 20 seconding the motion.

Wes resumed order: "Does anyone have any other announcements?"

Don Monroe, the resident handyman, shot his arm in the air and stood when acknowledged. "As many of you know, Gabe and Deena Lee was married recently and took home a tiny package all at the same time. Gabe is always helping others without wanting notice, and I have it on good word he's fixing to make an apartment out of his attic room for Wanna. As a thank you to Gabe, and congratulations to him and Deena Lee, I'm heading over first thing this Thursday to help him get the plumbing and electrical fixed up for the place. I'd like to invite all others to come and help with the remodeling. Maybe we can get Wanna a place to be proud of in a couple days."

The room reverberated with commitment.

Gabe smiled with one of those stomach-wrenching feelings of happiness that nearly bring men to tears. He turned, mouthed a thank you to Don and the others, looked at the floor, and counted his blessings. For a few moments, he forgot his plan to challenge Thibideaux. When the thought returned, he forced himself to mentally rehearse his diatribe to make sure he wouldn't forget anything.

The plan required that very little information be forwarded that would be meaningful to anyone but Thibideaux, to spare the residents of the details. He didn't know much about Thibideaux's organization, so his inquiry would be a bluff, but Thibideaux wouldn't know that. He silently repeated his opening question one more time. "Mr. Thibideaux, I've just had the pleasure of a long talk with an old friend of yours, Father Costello. He's told me a great deal about you, and about someone you know quite well, Ernest Hughes. I suspect your business in these parts is similar to what the good Father explained, and not what you've given us here tonight. Would you mind giving us your thoughts on that?" He planned to wing it after that.

The goal was to plant a seed of distrust and instill some fear in the minds of the residents. The seed was that Thibideaux was up to something other than whatever he was planning to discuss. The fear was through the linkage of Thibideaux and Father Costello, who was still in the minds and imaginations of the people of the Tri-counties. Father Costello was a tangible evil to the locals, so a linkage would bring suspicion onto

Thibideaux. Best of all, Gabe wouldn't have to reveal any detailed information, which he didn't have yet anyway.

The best outcome of the challenge, in Gabe's mind, would be to scare Thibideaux away from the area without completion of his job. The worst would be no change in the situation, in which case, Gabe would have to follow through with the plan to get the notes and Bible from the rectory bathroom and return to Chicago. Gabe's optimistic glass was three-quarters full.

Wes' voice brought Gabe back to the auditorium. "Are there any other announcements?" With the room silent, Wes continued. "As you may know, this meeting's been called so Mr. A. Jackson Thibideaux of New Orleans can give us some information that's important to us all, and to our future. Since I don't know what this is all about, I'll just turn the meeting over to Mr. Thibideaux. He'll give us a talk first, then he'll be willing to answer questions. Mr. Thibideaux . . ."

The silence in the room allowed a third-row stomach growl to echo throughout the auditorium. Not a single head turned in its direction.

Thibideaux rose to his feet and shuffled toward the podium. To Gabe, his movements presented a contrast in appearances. His short-stepping, stiff-backed ambling projected an image of meekness, even disadvantage, while his erect head and positive countenance portrayed the opposite—a somewhat subtle confidence.

Gabe felt the anticipation in the auditorium settle

like a dense fog, and it was enhanced by Thibideaux's slow-motion navigation of the stage and his deliberate approach to the podium.

Thibideaux reached for the ill-tempered microphone but it was too tall for him. The gooseneck holder twisted in his grasp, but sprung upward before he could grab the mike. He stood on tip-does and grabbed the neck, closer to the mike this time, but once again, it sprung away.

Whispers and giggles pulsed in the squirming audience.

Thibideaux grabbed the contrary appliance and wrestled it out of its holder, and it announced its capture with an ear-piercing scream. He silenced the mike with a tight strangle hold on its neck as he shuffled to the front of the stage. His voice was confident, striking a decisive blow in Gabe's earlier contrast of his appearance.

"Good evening to all residents of the Tri-counties, and thank you for taking your valuable time to hear what I have to say to you on this lovely Fall evening. As you may know, I've been working in your midst for the last several months and I would like to provide the results of this work, and to illuminate the grounds for this effort. If you please, I'd like to ask that you hold all questions until I've finished my entire report, since an early question may be answered later in the presentation. At the conclusion, I'll be happy to answer all questions to the best of my ability. I won't take a great deal of your time, so I won't go into every detail." He scanned the audience.

Gabe looked around the room. All he saw was a sea of attentive faces that was absent riptides or other forms of turbulence.

"For some time now, the State has been considering construction of a divided highway connection between the two north-south interstates that run on either side of your fine state. Several factors are important for the placement of such a connection. The two most important are its position relative to similar shunts to the north and south, and its expense, which is related to the shortest route that avoids all unsuitable terrain. I've been retained to investigate the suitability of a course that would pass through the Tri-counties, and specifically to estimate its cost in both dollars and construction time.

"To summarize what is presented in a rather lengthy report, I'm suggesting that a proposed route that runs through the Tri-counties is a viable option for such a highway. I've determined that a corridor roughly midway between State Route 27 and the southern edge of the swamp has the following attributes that make it an attractive possibility. First, it's nearly equal in distance from the closest shunts to the north and south. Second, the proposed route could be constructed in nearly a straight line between the two interstates without the need to alter its path around geological irregularities. Finally, the terrain along this route is free of obstacles that would require special construction methods." He paused and scanned the audience again.

"This is a good news and bad news situation. However, I think nearly everyone here will agree with me,

SOMETHING BAD • 291

the good greatly outweighs the bad. Please speak up at the conclusion of this presentation if you don't agree.

"The good news is the roadway will have to cut through a number of farms. The State will negotiate for the purchase of the land, and in the past, prices paid for such land have been very generous. It's not my place to participate in these negotiations, although I have included some estimates in my report that are higher than the current net worth of the land. Unfortunately, I won't discuss these estimates today, or any other day, since they must be submitted without input of the local populace. Now for the bad news, which starts exactly the same way as the good. The new highway will cut through a number of farms. This will create logistical challenges for the farmers in terms of working the land. This is not a major problem, as the submitted plan includes ways to deal with these challenges, which we can discuss in the question and answer period."

A few coughs and throat-clearings broke the silence. Gabe noticed the wiggling of a few small children.

"With all of this news thrust upon you at once, I must caution you that my work constitutes a preliminary report only. The highway itself is not a certainty, and it's difficult for me to properly read the collective mind of the State Legislature. For that reason, I must emphasize that it's premature for you to get your hopes up right now. Also, even if the State is serious about constructing a highway shunt, my report doesn't guarantee that the route proposed in the report will be selected. The competition is likely to be fierce, since a shunt will have positive effects on the economy of the selected counties. Also, while the fate of the Tri-county route's position in this competition is dependent upon my report, keep in mind that it is only a preliminary report. In most cases, the State conducts a follow-up investigation after an initial list of finalists is determined. As a final positive note, I will say with confidence, based on my experience in these matters, that the Tri-county route is most certain to make that final list. And, while ultimate State decisions are sometimes capricious, I will stake my reputation on my intuition, which suggests to me that the Tri-counties has an excellent chance to come out on top of the competition.

"Now, if I can have the screen lowered and the lights dimmed, I have some graphics that will help you better conceptualize the route I am forwarding as the best."

Thibideaux half-stepped over to an overhead projector and reached for a manila folder of transparencies. Over the next fifteen minutes, he presented a series of photos, maps, and copies of surveyor land plats that showed, in detail, a corridor of potential highway land and the farms through which it would pass. The polished presentation started with a series of LandSat photos of the area that gradually homed in on the Tricounties, and then gave way to aerial photographs that were coordinated with the maps and plats. He concluded his visual display with a hint of a grin.

Wes Worthing walked to Thibideaux's side, dwarfing him, and took the microphone, which let out a whimper of relief. "I think we should all give a round of applause to Mr. Thibideaux for all the work he's done, and for the report he'll submit."

Gabe thought the response was polite but not quite enthusiastic.

Thibideaux gave a slight nod of his head.

"I'm sure some of you will have questions and Mr. Thibideaux has agreed to answer them up," Wes said. "So please keep order as the questions are asked and answered. If anyone needs to go, do it now before we get going again."

No one moved.

Wes surveyed the group and handed the microphone back to Thibideaux.

"Yes, I will be happy to entertain questions, but I may be limited in what I can say on some subjects. Also, please note that the exact route I've described is not negotiable. It will appear in my report exactly as I have described it, although the State could alter it at a later date. Now, if you have questions, please raise your hand."

Gabe looked around. About a half-dozen hands rose at once, and he raised his to keep pace. He watched Thibideaux scan the hands, and he thought the little man's gaze stopped at his raised paw for an instant before moving on to the next one.

The first question was predictable, from the far right of the auditorium. "For a betting man, what'd you guess are the chances of getting this thing done?"

Thibideaux shuffled along the stage until he was centered above the questioner. "As I said before, I would never bet on the decisions of a State Legislature. However, I feel the route through the Tri-counties should be given odds that are as close to even as any other route that's being considered." He nodded to the next hand.

"I heard the State bought some land in Jefferson County for what they called a 'right-o-way,'" a man in back asked. "From what I heard, they paid a crooked price. You say they'll pay good here. How we know you're right?"

Thibideaux sidestepped on the stage. "I know of the situation you describe, and the land that was purchased was not prime farmland, so it didn't get a top price. In my report, I've included a section on past productivity of the land in question, including this year's crops. With that information as a basis, I've made the case that the land is top quality and should be paid for accordingly." Another nod prompted the next query.

"You mentioned that the farmers will have some problems working their land if the highway is built. What do you mean?"

The question came from the same area, so Thibideaux didn't have to move. "The problem will be accessibility. If the freeway cuts through the middle of a farm, it'll present a challenge to get the farm machinery from one side to the other. Freeways were originally named because they weren't toll roads. Later, the name was used because they allowed free travel without the bother of cross traffic. And that's the problem. I'm proposing a series of underpasses be included in the design to allow easy movement of machinery and livestock under the freeway. They'd be large enough to allow a combine to pass through. While this is a reasonable solution, only a few underpasses can be built because of the cost. Some farmers might find the freeway is more than a small annoyance. If the population of the Tri-counties feels this inconvenience outweighs the financial benefits of the highway, it can be decided at a later date and the information can be conveyed to the State."

Gabe leaned forward in his chair to get his hand higher. The number of raised hands had whittled down to four.

The next inquisitor shouted his question before being called upon. "Who'll do the land negotiating? Will it be you?"

"The actual negotiations will be conducted by members of the State Land Office and the Highway Department. My role will be over soon, when I submit my report."

Three hands left. Thibideaux picked one from the far left of the auditorium.

"How soon do you reckon this will all get going?"

Thibideaux shuffled along the stage. "My best guess, based on the dinosaur-like movements of State Governments, is a final decision will be made within a year. Then, the start of construction will depend on the health of the state budget and the participation of the federal government. My impression is the feds have already shown significant interest, otherwise the project wouldn't have gone this far."

Thibideaux walked back to center stage.

Gabe felt the little man's eyes lock on his, and he watched his tiny right hand move forward a little and ball into a fist. Gabe tried to raise his hand, but it wouldn't move. He tried the other, but it was paralyzed. He tried to make a sound, to complain, but nothing came out. He struggled against the invisible restraints until it felt like his face was on fire.

Thibideaux conducted an exaggerated survey of the room. "I can see there is only one question left, which is good since I still have work to do. You've given me some additional ideas for the report. After this final question, I'll take my leave. I want to thank you for your polite attention." Thibideaux turned John Johnson's way and gave him a nod of his head.

Sir John stood up. "Mr. Thibideaux, I'd like to congratulate you on your fine presentation. I do have a few questions, though. Just this afternoon, I was sitting outside the general store when a state government car pulled up and two men got out to ask me a couple of questions. Seems they was coming to our area to scout out the possibility of a highway shunt running through the Tri-counties. Said it was Senator Ambrose's idea, but it wasn't even put to the legislature yet."

Thibideaux took a step closer to the edge of the stage. He glared at John.

"I told them you was already completing a report on that very thing, and they said they never heard of anyone named Thibideaux, and no way did the state hire anyone to prepare a report on the highway." Sir John paused and looked around the auditorium. "Then they said if you was here studying a highway route, you must be hired by someone other than the state government."

Sir John took a deep breath and let it out slowly. "So, we know that you wasn't hired by the Tri-counties, and now we know you wasn't hired by the government. So I says to myself, who would Thibideaux be working for if not us and the state?" Sir John half-turned and talked to the audience. "What come to my mind on this was Rother County."

Gabed surveyed the room. At the mention of Rother County, a stir in the audience progressed outward from Sir John like a ripple emanating from a pebble thrown in a pond.

"The only other people interested in studying a roadway through the Tri-counties would be Rother County. They'd be trying to get the highway to go along State Route 17, right thorough Calhoun Township."

Sir John whirled back toward Thibideaux and stepped up his voice to a near shout. "So tell us, Mr. Thibideaux. Just who's it you work for if it's not the state or the Tri-counties? Are you working for Rother to certain it that we'll never get the highway?" Sir John remained standing.

Thibideaux stood motionless for ten, fifteen seconds. Gabe thought he looked different, somehow.

"My d-dear Mr. Johnson. Wh-once again y-you have s-surprised me w-with your insight." Thibideaux took a deep breath. "I want to assure you th-that I do not now, a-and have not ever worked for Rother County."

Another deep breath and Gabe saw the old Thibideaux.

"In fact, you are right. I don't work for either the state or the Tri-counties. Unfortunately, I can't tell you who's retained my services. But I can tell you why. In these matters, a number of companies will be encouraged to bid for contracts related to the planning and construction of the highway. These contracts are extremely lucrative. Some businesses hire lobbyists to influence government decisions, and they get advance notice on prospects like this. When this occurs, work like mine is initiated immediately and without knowledge of the government, so a realistic bid can be developed quickly. So you see, I've been retained by an organization that plans to bid on the construction of the highway. The fact that I was retained to prepare my report speaks of the positive position you all occupy in the government's plans for the shunt. I hope this calms your fears, Mr. Johnson."

John sat down, but his bottom barely hit the chair when he sprang back up. "As I see it, you've lied to us all about who you work for already, so how're we to know you're not lying to us again right now? How can we be sure you don't work for Rother?"

"Mr. Johnson, and all good citizens of the Tri-counties. Due to the nature of my work, it was necessary to maintain a curtain of misdirection. It's the nature of the beast. This business is so competitive, organizations will go to great lengths to gain an edge. Some of these actions border on unethical. For this I sincerely apologize. Now, about your concerns. Had I been hired by Rother County, I would have been required to spend much more time in that area preparing a report. It takes very little time to derail a project like this through subterfuge, while it takes a great deal of time to formulate a complete report like the one I presented tonight. It would be totally unnecessary for me to go to all of that work for the Tri-counties if my only aim was to prevent a highway from going through here. It's totally absurd to think I'd be working for Rother County after what you saw tonight."

Thibideaux bent his left arm and slightly raised his hand in the direction of the rear, left quadrant of the room. He curled the fingers of his left hand into the form of a set of claws and an elderly member of the audience let out a whelp and cringed forward, clutching his chest.

As the order in the auditorium disintegrated, Gabe watched Thibideaux grab his manila folder and slip out the back door of the building. Released from his paralysis, Gabe hurried to the back of the room.

CHAPTER 45

THIBIDEAUX PACED IN front of his chair. The town meeting was a calculated risk from the beginning, and the double-cross by John Johnson erased all gains from the presentation. He sensed a significant doubt carried on the wind of the Tri-counties, both about him and his business, and it was more focused than the breeze that wavered prior to the meeting. If he succeeded in one thing, he ratcheted up his presence in the consciousness and emotions of the locals. And that went against the Organization's rule of maintaining a low profile at all times.

He looked around. Where was the councillor? Certainly this warranted a personal visit. And it didn't stop there. He breeched another Organizational precept by directly causing the injury and suffering of a citizen, even though he justified it as a means of extricating himself from a rapidly deteriorating situation.

The Organization had its own rumor mill, and he had heard about similar cases—all involved some form of punishment by the Organization. The cost for the more severe cases didn't require explanation. This case, however, was similar to others that garnered mild rebukes.

He shuffled in long loops around the chair. Leniency was appropriate since the citizen wasn't killed, and the act wasn't born out of anger, jealousy, or revenge.

So, I'm guilty of compromising two separate conventions, each a relatively minor infraction, he thought. But the two together represented uncharted territory of what was covered by Organizational gossip and instruction.

Now he wished the councillor was here, because he wasn't done. He still had one loose end in his ill-fated plan for diversion—in his foray across the borderline of Organizational by-laws.

He stopped in front of the fireplace and spun around to face the chair. "Once one goes into dangerous territory, it's better to cover all bases, even if the maneuver is of questionable value," he said to the chair. "I'm not going to run with my tail between my legs part way through." He jumped into the chair and closed his eyes.

No choice, he thought. I've got to push a little further. He imagined himself crawling out a window, which represented the firm guidelines of the Organization. Since he strayed only slightly across the line, he didn't fall into the precipice on the far side. Instead, he was perched on a narrow ledge, still within reach of the window. The ledge was a necessary construction, since sometimes a slight traverse of the regulations was both necessary and justified.

The white Taurus rounded a slight curve in State Route 27 on its way to Wes Worthing's farm, and was met by a dense, disorienting fog. The headlights blared, but they reflected light back into the eyes of the travelers. The car slowed. On the approach to a right-angle turn in the road, the car's brakes temporarily malfunctioned and the vehicle left the roadway. It lurched as it bounded through a drainage ditch and folded its front end around a tree with a muted crunch. The slow speed of the car and the modest circumference of the tree produced minor injuries to the two occupants, requiring short periods of convalescence.

MEMORANDUM

DATE: August 30, 2005
TO: Councillor USA-4-2143
FROM: Provost Council #21
RE: Recruiter USA-77411

We acknowledge your continued arguments in favor of 77411's activities, and your petition to observe from a distance. Due to the most recent actions of 77411, your petition is denied. You will resume active intervention or both you and 77411 will be pulled from this assignment, without reassignment. We have exercised patience because of the long and productive service of 77411, the impending completion of his assignment, and the development of a secondary target in the area. However, our capacity for patience is now met. We trust you will actively monitor the situation so the actions of 77411 do not come to our attention again.

CC: File of Recruiter USA-77411;   File of Councillor USA-4-2143

CHAPTER 46

GABE RUBBED HIS eyes with his fists, and it took a little longer than usual for his vision to return. He had slept late, but for good reason.

The Tri-counties were abuzz about the Boyston-Calhoun high school football game. The Badgers had pulled off the improbable, tying the score with three seconds left on the clock. The extra point sailed wide-left so the town had to settle for the tie. From the reaction of the citizenry, the sports equivalent of "kissing one's sister" was not that bad in these parts, at least when it came to a Tri-counties-Rother competition. Best of all, Teddy pressed his jello mold into service for the first time in months.

Gabe walked into the kitchen to a plate of eggs and bacon.

"You going to the bonfire tonight?" Wanna said.

"I'll take care of Cory Dean so the two of you can go."

Gabe looked at Deena Lee. She seemed hopeful. "No. I got a problem I have to sort through. It's a small one, but it's like a rock in my shoe—feels ten times as big. Why don't the two of you go? I'll sit with Cory Dean."

He zoned out while the two women discussed the plan. He was torn. Sometimes he wanted time to slow down to delay the unavoidable confrontation with Thibideaux, and at other times he wanted it to speed up to get the clash over with. Time tends to move in inverse proportion to its desired speed, he thought, so the split preference should have produced the accurate clock. He thought about his recent sleepless nights. Alternating on the two sides of relativity produced a rift, each with its own unique anxiety.

"Gabe!" Deena Lee said.

He came back.

"It might be fun for me and Wanna to go to the bonfire. The Tri-counties haven't been so worked up in I don't know how long."

"You be all right with Cory Dean?" Wanna said.

Gabe nodded and forked some eggs. Wanna and Deena Lee were back in conversation so he let his mind go again. Wanna's transformation, really a metamorphosis, was amazing. Ever since Cory Dean came into the house, she donned a mellow attitude—in particular, her temper receded into the background. It was replaced by a patience Gabe hadn't seen in her. The calm seemed to be shared by Cory Dean when he was in Wanna's arms, which is where he could be found every time Wanna had the opportunity.

Gabe circled the front room with Cory Dean in his arms. The little man had fallen asleep minutes after Deena Lee and Wanna had left, but Gabe didn't put him down. His mind overrode his actions—he was on autopilot.

Four problems, he thought. And that's just to get to Chicago. If he rehashed the problems enough, a plan would formalize in their midst.

Have to get Thibideaux out of the rectory long enough to retrieve the Bible. If it's still there. And Thibideaux didn't seem to be leaving the rectory these days. Gabe had asked around at the Herndon's Edge and at church, but no one had seen the little man. Two pieces of evidence suggested he was still in Boyston. The nightly fires in the rectory fireplace continued to burn until dawn, just as they had before the town meeting. Also, Gabe noticed the fogs that occasionally surrounded the Petersen farmhouse had not only continued, they were more frequent, as if his activities were being monitored by Thibideaux more intensely than before.

Gabe had heard others talk about the fogs, with some of the more radical explanations centering on some sort of Rother plot as revenge for the recent football debacle. He found this line of reasoning both humorous and interesting. Every community had its share of doomsayers and mystics, however, meteorological phenomena that would be attributed to supernatural events or UFOs in other places always seemed to be explained as some sort of Rother plot in the Tri-counties. Where fear of the unknown motivated the rumors in the former cases, it was fear of the known that fueled the local conjectures.

Gabe moved on to the second problem. If he did get Thibideaux out of the rectory, he would have to keep him out long enough for the Bible to be found. A safety margin was needed since the bathroom cabinet might not be as easily moved as expected, or the Bible might not be in the exact same location that it was placed twenty-five years ago.

Things seemed to be falling in place. He moved on to problem three.

If he got the Bible out, he would have to keep track of it until he could get back up to Chicago. And he had to keep Thibideaux from knowing anything about it. With the more frequent fog-observations, Gabe knew he would have to be careful about where and how he held onto the book. Father Costello's advice was sound. No one else should know about the book.

A solution came fast. As soon as he verified the Bible contained the notes, he would seal the book without examining a single word. But that was just part of it. How could he keep the Bible's presence from Wanna and Deena Lee? Probably impossible. Then, how could he blunt their curiosity about it? He didn't want to discuss the book with them in case Thibideaux was watching, and listening.

Problem four was one of timing, and there was

nothing he could do but get moving. Deena Lee had made arrangements for Cory Dean's baptism, and it was coming up in just under two weeks. Gabe opened his mental calendar. Have to get Thibideaux out of the rectory, retrieve the Bible, travel to Chicago and back, and then carry out whatever plan he and Father Costello could fabricate in that short time frame. It didn't leave time for dilly-dallying. And how could he justify another trip up north with minimal familial friction? An argument or protracted discussion about it could tip Thibideaux off that something was up.

He looked down and kissed Cory Dean's forehead. The speed of his pacing increased.

"It's about time," Gabe said in a low voice. He looked at the clock—it was two in the morning. Only eleven days left before the baptism. "I think it'll work." His head hit the pillow for the first deep sleep in the last several days and nights.

Cory Dean's cry broke through Gabe's slumber. Light that didn't exist just moments ago spilled into his eyes, bright as noon. He rolled over. "Ten thirty?" he said. He paused, then exhaled in relief. None of his thoughts were lost during his horizontal vacation.

Wanna and Deena Lee sat at the kitchen table, and Cory Dean half-reclined in a sling-chair.

Gabe planted a kiss on Deena Lee's cheek and bent close to Cory Dean. "Good morning, little man. I hope you weren't too much trouble for your momma last night."

Deena Lee smiled.

Wanna slid her chair back and walked to the stove to start a pan of eggs. "Welcome back to the world. I took care of the chores this morning so you owe me big time, Mr. Rip Van Winkle."

Gabe shuffled over to the kitchen window and peered out. A fog billowed toward the house, so it was time to put his plan into action. Back at the table, he pulled a chair next to Deena Lee.

"I been thinking. Maybe it's time you go back to the Herndon's Edge and give it try to see what it's like. Maybe you could go for an afternoon tomorrow or the next day. I know you been feeling cooped up here, and Cory Dean's needs have been taking their toll. Maybe an afternoon just once or twice a week would give you a nice change of pace. Trying it would tell a lot. What do you think?"

Deena Lee threw her arms around Gabe's neck. "Sometimes I think you can read my mind. I'll give Teddy a call after the noon rush. Wanna, you wouldn't mind watching Cory Dean for an afternoon, would you?"

Wanna didn't turn around but her voice reflected the smile on her face. "You know I can't get enough of the little man. You just tell me when and I'll look after him."

Gabe walked back to the window. The fog was

still there. "Try to set it up for tomorrow afternoon. I'll be around for most of the day to help Wanna."

Wanna shot a quick look over her shoulder. "Don't need your help. You'd probably just fall asleep anyway. Besides, you've got work to do around here."

Deena Lee turned her chair to face Gabe. "Why you trying to get me out of the house tomorrow afternoon? You got a hot date you ain't telling us about?"

He returned her smile. "My only hot date's with you. Tonight." He turned in Wanna's direction. "You better put some cotton in your ears tonight. We're going to scare the wildlife."

The raucous laughter brought bright rays of sunshine through the kitchen window.

Wanna turned toward the table with a frying pan full of eggs and potatoes. "After you eat up, you need to get on out and fix the side door of the barn. You been putting it off long enough. And that's not all that's needing fixing. I got a list for you when you get done with the door. This place will fall apart if you keep going like you have the past couple of days."

Gabe sat down to his steaming plate and spoke in its direction. "If I have my way, everything will be fixed up right quick around here."

CHAPTER 47

GABE FOLDED THE phone booth door shut, clinked in coins, and pushed a memorized series of numbers.

"Why'd you have to call now," Teddy laughed into the phone. "I was in a daydream about Teddy Jr. scoring the winning touchdown against the Calhoun Cougars."

Gabe folded an apology into his request.

Teddy stretched the phone cord to the half-wall. "Deena Lee? It's for you."

Deena Lee nearly dropped her coffee decanter. She shoved it into the coffeemaker and it hissed as a little coffee sloshed onto the burner.

"It's Gabe," Teddy said.

She grabbed the phone. "What's wrong? Is Cory Dean all right?" She squeezed all of the words through a half-breath.

"Relax. He's fine. I'm over at the general store, on the pay phone. I had to pick up a few things. He and Wanna were down for a nap when I left. How's it going there?"

A deep breath echoed in the receiver. "I'm doing fine. You should see the crowd here this late in the afternoon. Most of the noon gang are here. They're being really nice to me. I've nearly come to tears more than once."

"Who all's there? Any old boyfriends?"

Deena Lee giggled. "There's the usual group from Boyston. William and Tom from Herndon are here. Wes and Reverend Sather stopped in for a while, and there's even a group out from Porter. I'm real busy, but I love being back. I'd like to keep it up as long as I only have to be here every now and again."

Gabe didn't want to press, but he had to. "Anyone unusual show up to see you? Like Horace Murtry, or Thibideaux, or anyone else from your past?"

"You know Horace wouldn't show his face around here," she said. "I'd have to hurt him if he did."

"Anyone else?"

"Why you so interested in who's here? You writing a book?"

He thought he detected a tease in her voice. "I just want to know who all's nice enough to pay respects so I can thank them when I see them." Come on, dammit, he thought. Tell me.

"Well then, there are three guys in a booth that I don't recognize. Never seen them before. I'll make a point to get their addresses so you can send them a thank-you note. While you're at it, you might want to get an extra card for Thibideaux. He showed up about ten minutes ago. Says he wants to talk to me, but I've been too busy to give him much time. I can't imagine what he wants. He still gives me the creeps. What should I do?"

Gabe slumped against the wall of the phone booth. He had the information he needed. "I'm kind of curious about what the pipsqueak wants to talk about. Why don't you tell him you'll chat a spell when you get a chance? But don't ignore the regulars. Get to him when you can, but only after some of the others take off. You don't want to offend all your favorites. I'm sure Teddy would agree."

"Guess you're right. He'll just have to wait his turn." She paused. "I got to get back to work. But I've got to call Wanna first to make sure everything's all right. See you at supper."

"Don't call. I told you Wanna and Cory Dean were down for a nap. When you called just before I left, he was almost down, but you woke him up. You don't have to call so often. Wanna has it under control."

"You don't understand. You're not a momma."

Gabe turned his pickup onto the gravel road that circumvented the woods behind the rectory, pulled over, and parked in a small thicket so the truck was partially obscured by the brush. The site was a quarter mile from the rectory, on a straight line, but the line ran through the dense stand of woods. The underbrush didn't present a significant challenge to him. These woods had served as his childhood playground.

He stayed a direct course through the woods and approached the back bedroom window of the rectory. He pushed. The window sash moved upward. The emptiness of the bedroom surprised him.

Jumping into the opening, he rolled to the floor. Bright streams of daylight entered uncovered windows, pointing the way through the house. The long hall led from the bedroom to the front of the house, and on the left, halfway down the hall, was the bathroom. A double doorway opened to the right from the hall just four or five feet beyond the bathroom. The front room, he thought. He took the extra steps and peeked around the doorframe—a large fireplace was on the opposite wall, beyond Thibideaux's oversized chair. Other than that, the room was empty.

Gabe turned to go back to the bathroom and the hardwood floor gave a muffled creak. He froze. A sound came from the living room. A whir. Probably just an echo of the squeak, he thought.

On the wall of the bathroom, opposite the door, a toilet sat, obviously non-functional. The seat and lid were in the up position, but their angle relative to the bowl suggested that one of the two mounting bolts was missing and the other was very loose. To the right, a bathtub was stained the color of rust up to two inches short its top edge. To the left, a similarly stained sink was supported by two bolts that entered the wall and two thin, metal legs that extended from the front corners to the floor. There, he thought. Above the sink was a mirrored medicine cabinet, recessed so the mirror was nearly flush with the wall.

Without further inventory, Gabe pulled on the medicine cabinet. It didn't budge. A few harder jerks produced the same result. He opened the door and noticed a wood screw in each side of the cabinet walls, apparently anchoring the cabinet into wall studs. His hand dove into his right front pants pocket and withdrew his Swiss Army knife. It wasn't one of the big ones. They produced too large a lump in his pocket. It was the slim, inexpensive model with two blades, can and bottle openers that had flathead screw drivers on the ends, a Phillips screwdriver, and a hole punch. A toothpick and a flimsy pair of tweezers hid in the red plastic sides.

Gabe hated flathead screws. Knuckle busters, he called them. It was hard to keep the blade from slipping out of the screw head. And with the limited space in the medicine cabinet, he prepared for a couple of scrapes.

The first screw unwound from its anchorage without incident. Inch and a half, he thought. Overkill? With the first few turns, the second screw produced a loud, high-pitched squeak of metal against extremely dry wood. The screw's protest was followed by a low-pitched hum from the living room.

Gabe froze and listened for further noises. There were none. He turned the screw, and another squeal triggered the living room hum again. Just get it out, he thought, and twisted until the screw was free. A push and the cabinet moved, but it was heavy. It wouldn't come out easily. He inched the right side, then the left, with a small stepping walk out of the wall. Nearly free of the wall, he gave it a hard yank and it came free with a loud creak.

The low-pitched sound came again from the living room, but it didn't stop like before. It continued as an intermittent whirring, impossible to ignore.

Gabe lifted the cabinet, lowered it to the floor, and leaned it against one of the metal sink legs. The whirring persisted. He felt the urge to run, but resisted. Too close, he thought, but I better find out what it is. Couldn't be Thibideaux. He'd be in here already. Buoyed, he walked in a crouch to the edge of the living room doorway.

The chair faced in his direction, swaying back and forth as if it were trying to home in on something. The movements produced the whirring sounds.

He pulled his head back but the shift in his weight caused the floorboards to creak under his weight. A more sudden, louder whir came from the room and stopped.

His hand dug in his left pants pocket and withdrew a coin, a penny. He kissed it and rolled it on edge out of the doorway, across the hardwood floor toward the front doors. The sound of its travel started the whirring again, and Gabe leaned around the doorframe in time to see the chair follow the path of the coin across the room. His lean once again angered the floor—its complaint alerted the chair, which swiveled back to the doorway.

Gabe tumbled backward on the floor with a thud. He scrambled to his feet and ran to the bathroom. Just get it out and leave, he said to himself. His pulse pounded in his temples, but it was fast and regular.

Gabe's size fifteen feet gave him trouble more often than benefit, and on his approach to the sink and the gaping hole in the wall above it, his right foot smacked into the medicine cabinet. It fell over his leg, shattering the mirrored glass. Half of the glass stayed in the frame but the other half tinkled onto Gabe's shoe and then onto the floor. The edge of the cabinet dug into his shin and sent a dull ache upward in his leg. He pulled it back out of reflex and the cabinet fell flat on the floor, with more tinkling of glass.

"Damn feet," he said in a whisper.

At the Herndon's Edge, Thibideaux had a fork of Teddy's special half way to his mouth. He stopped, sat straight up on his stool, and opened his eyes wide enough to make them nearly perfect circles. His gaze went beyond anything in the café. Placing his fork on his plate, he stood up and excused himself to no one in particular. A quick pivot and several halting strides, and the bathroom door slammed shut.

Gabe's mind went into overdrive—he needed to fetch the Bible and get out fast. Glass crushed under the weight of his massive work boots, but the external noises were dulled by the sound of his own blood pulsing in his ears. His heart rate was building to a crescendo and the tremors of his nervous hands made his movements clumsy. He thrust his right hand down into the wall before his mind clicked on the number and variety of vermin that might be in there. He pushed downward.

There was nothing. But the sink was in the way. He moved to the left of the sink, so close to the wall his chest was against it. He had to turn his head away from the hole. Straining to force his arm downward, all he felt was a cobweb. He hand swung back and forth and hit studs in both directions, but there wasn't any contact with anything resembling a book.

His right arm was beginning to tingle from the pressure on his armpit, but he bent his knees and crouched down to press harder. The tip of his middle finger brushed against something and it seemed to move with the touch. He shifted his weight and extended his hand farther into the abyss, and his armpit responded with a sharp pain. Better to be numb, he thought. The object moved again. He tried to grasp it between his index and middle fingers, but it was too heavy. It required the force of an opposable thumb. He pushed his arm down harder on the wall opening and the pain retreated. Got to grab fast, he thought, before I lose all feeling.

Gabe felt his thumb touch the object and he clamped hard onto it. With the strength developed from his livelihood, he stabilized it—it responded to his lift. He brought it up slowly. His grip was force-ful but tenuous. Better not bang the thing against a stud. His hand appeared in the opening and then . . . a book.

He transferred the book to his left hand and shook his right arm to regain circulation. He blew the dust of twenty-five years from the book's cover and a surge of excitement blocked the pain in his right armpit. "Holy Bible" appeared in gold print.

He placed the Bible on the edge of the sink and picked up the cabinet, barely pushing it into the hole in the wall. His hands returned to the Bible.

"It's good to see you again, Gabe. What are you doing in here?"

In his startle, Gabe bumped the sink hard and the medicine cabinet released from the wall and crashed into the sink basin, shattering the remainder of the glass. The cabinet knocked the Bible from the sink onto the floor, its pages splayed against the floorboards. The crash produced a second startle and Gabe lost his balance and fell backwards, bumping his back on the side of the bathtub. Pain shot upward to his neck like he'd just been electrocuted. He swung around on all fours and groped for the book. He hoped Thibideaux didn't see it.

Out of the corner of his eye, Gabe saw Thibide-aux raise his right arm, and the medicine cabinet slid off the sink and crashed down on the back of Gabe's neck and head. Pain fought darkness and he struggled to resist the spreading unconsciousness. On the verge of blacking out, he maintained his fix on the Bible and willed himself to stay alert. He scrambled to gain custody of the book as warm streams of blood dripped from the sides of his neck.

Everything turned to slow motion. Even though he was stunned and groggy, one thought broke through the haze. Get the Bible. He grabbed the bound object and slid it into the waistband of his pants. At least he thought that was what he had done, until he bumped the book, which was still on the floor. Had his retreating consciousness played a cruel trick on him? Was he having trouble telling what was real and what was imagined?

The touch of the Bible answered, and he grabbed it, clutching it to his chest with his right hand. He balanced in a three-point stance on the floor.

"What do you have there?" Thibideaux said.

Gabe didn't answer. He turned his head and looked up at Thibideaux, pulling the Bible tighter to his chest. Thibideaux looked large from this angle, and the swirling images in the periphery of Gabe's visual field created a hallucinatory aura around him. Real or artificial?

Thibideaux extended both of his hands toward Gabe, then pulled the left one back toward his body.

Gabe felt a strong tug on the book and tried to resist. The pull was too powerful and yanked the Bible from his grip. He watched it fly into Thibideaux's extended right hand.

Thibideaux rotated the book around, looking at both sides of the outer cover.

Out of the corner of his eyes, Gabe watched Thibideaux open the book near the center, and saw what looked like burned pages. The pages Thibideaux flipped appeared to be burned nearly to the spine, with a progressive burn on the pages closer to the two covers. The book appeared to be partially hollowed out by fire. Real?

"I'll be damned," Thibideaux said. "I know this book." He snapped his head upward and shouted in the high-pitched, twangy voice of Northeasterner. "Where did you get this? What are you doing here?"

Gabe's mind was still slowed by the recent blow to his head and neck. His voice was low. "I was getting the book for someone."

"Who wants this book? Where is this man?"

Gabe tried to think fast. He needed a good lie. One that was believable. Not good at this, he thought. Just say something.

"I don't know who wants it. I just agreed to get it for some man from Rother. Met him at Herndon's Edge. I don't know who he is or who the book belongs to. He just said he wanted it for a friend. I don't know who that friend is." He looked at the floor so he wouldn't be rattled by the surreal image of his tormentor.

"What's your interest?" Thibideaux said. "Why'd you accept this job?"

"Fifty dollars." Gabe studied the floor. "The man gave me fifty dollars and told me to bring him the book."

Thibideaux stepped closer so his right shin was against Gabe's left shoulder. "Was the man a priest?" He seemed to spit out the last word like it tasted bad.

Gabe's mind started to clear so the next lie came easier. "No. He was chawing a big lump of tobacco and he cussed."

Thibideaux nudged Gabe with his shin. "Why does this person want the book?"

Gabe added playing dumb to his lying. "I asked, but he just said, 'None of your business.'"

Gabe heard Thibideaux flip through the Bible again, and then step backwards into the hall. He heard a muffled flip, the sound of a book flying through the air, and then contact with the fireplace grate.

From the hall, he heard Thibideaux's voice, back to that of a southerner.

"Your friend will have to do without this book."

Gabe heard a "Ha" sound and then igniting flames. The smell of burning paper filled the rectory. He slumped on his hand and knees. His increased clarity of thought was accompanied by a parallel increase in his pain, mental as well as physical. With the Bible gone, his thoughts turned to survival. Just get out of the rectory alive. Can't stand yet—dizzy on all fours. He crawled toward the doorway.

From the corner of his eye, he saw Thibideaux make a sweeping motion of his right hand. A large segment of plaster fell from the ceiling and struck Gabe on the head. He collapsed face first on the floor and pieces of broken mirror dug into the skin of his right cheek and forehead.

Once again, he willed the spreading darkness of unconsciousness to back away to the periphery of his mind. The acute pain he felt seconds before was dulled, but throbbed with his pulse. Double time, but regular. Why regular, he thought. This was worse than leaving the Tri-counties. He looked up at Thibideaux and a warm trickle of blood ran into his eyes, clouding his vision.

Thibideaux seemed to hesitate. He must still need me, Gabe thought. It cleared some of the haze from his head. He thought he heard a command: "Stand up," but his attempt to regain his equilibrium was compromised by the blood that clouded his vision. His world spun. He felt like he was going to throw up.

"Stand up!"

The second command registered, and through reflex, he started to his feet. Pushing his upper body off the floor, a wave of dizziness nearly turned the room dark. He grasped his knees with his hands and hunched until the darkness retreated. He pushed again with his hands and staggered backward a half step until he stabilized in an upright position.

Thibideaux's hands slid apart, as if he were calling a baseball player "safe." The floorboards under Gabe's left foot gave way and his left leg fell through the floor. It met no resistance in the crawl space until it contacted dirt, two feet below the floor. The impact put an oblique shear on his left knee, which buckled with a loud pop. Gabe whelped and collapsed sideways on the floor, writhing in pain.

Thibideaux hurled his right arm upward and the sink came loose from the wall and smashed into Gabe's ribs. Pain shot through his torso and seemed to magnify with each breath. He compensated with shallow breaths, but the lack of oxygen brought back the light-headedness. A familiar command startled him. But it was less urgent than before.

"Stand up."

He's not going to kill me, Gabe thought. At least not here.

He pushed himself onto all fours, really threes, and started to crawl into the hall. Each movement amplified the pain in his ribs, and as he dragged his left leg, its pain fought for attention. He found a new focus, an incentive. Cory Dean. He wanted to see Cory Dean.

Thibideaux's New Orleans accent thickened. "It doesn't matter what you do. You won't interfere with my work here." A chuckle, then his voice turned serious. "But take this to heart. You've had two chances now. You won't get a third. Go. Now. And never come near me or the rectory again. Go."

Thibideaux walked into the living room and the chair whirred a welcome.

Gabe crawled to the rear bedroom window and fell out headfirst. He broke his fall with his hands and right shoulder, which set off an electric shock of pain in his chest. He managed to roll onto his right side and come to a stop without further damage to his left knee, and without hesitation, he crawled across the rectory yard and into the woods where he collapsed on his back, still breathing fast, shallow breaths.

Halfway through the woods, the pain in his body and his modified breathing took a toll on his consciousness. He felt lightheaded, disoriented and nauseous.

Visual hallucinations, swirling and flashing lights, added to his fatigue. He wanted to go to sleep.

His subconscious took command—he low-crawled over to the overhang of a vertical rock outcropping, pushed the vegetation aside, and rolled into a shallow concavity he and his friends had called their cave years ago. They had retreated to this hideout whenever they were under siege by imaginary hordes during their games of youth.

He pulled the vegetation back over the opening and rolled flat on his back. The daylight faded, but it wasn't the same as the spreading darkness he felt following the blows to his head. This was a more peaceful fade to black. This was sleep.

Gabe shivered and a contractile jerk punctured his sleep with a stab of pain that radiated throughout his body. Daylight had declined and the air carried a chill. Close to suppertime, he thought. Got to get home or Deena Lee and Wanna will be in a panic. Through the pain, he managed to crawl the rest of the way through the woods, to his truck.

He let out a loud scream when he pushed on the clutch, but the gearshift slid into second. He tried to let the clutch out slowly, but couldn't. It popped, so he hit the gas to compensate and the truck sputtered and lurched, but kept running. Second gear would have to do.

He ran through two stop signs on the way home

and pulled the truck up to the steps of the farmhouse as the sun gave a last call at the horizon. He threw open the door of the truck, slid down on his right leg, and hopped up the two steps onto the porch.

Wanna and Deena Lee met him at the front door. Wanna was first to speak.

"Gabe, where you been? We've been worried sick." In unison, Wanna and Deena Lee let out a loud gasp.

Their exclamations weren't in sync, and they didn't use the exact same words, but the summed expressions came to Gabe as, "My God. What happened to you? Are you all right?"

"I'm okay. I just want to lie down," he said as he hopped through the door.

The women each grabbed an arm and helped Gabe over to the living room couch where he collapsed with a loud groan. He pulled his good leg up and motioned toward the left. "Can you help me get my leg up? The knee's hurting me bad, so take it slow."

Deena Lee nudged Wanna out of the way and lifted Gabe's leg. She paused each time he grimaced, and placed a throw pillow under the injured knee so it was propped at a slight angle.

Wanna was at the phone. "I'm going to call Doc. Should I call the sheriff, too?"

"No! Put the phone down," Gabe said. "I just want to sleep for a while. Doc'll have me going all over the place soon enough. Just let me get some sleep. And don't bother with the sheriff. There's nothing he can do. Put the phone down. Please."

She walked over to the couch and looked him in

the eyes. "I'll do as you want, but first you tell us what happened."

Gabe needed another good lie. He hadn't lied this much in his entire life, but he couldn't worry about that now. He would settle with the One Who Matters later. There was a job to do. Even with a battered intellect, his mind was quick.

"I guess I made the acquaintance of four young fellers from Rother. They were upset about the football game. I rubbed it in a bit and they jumped me. Can't identify them, though. They were all wearing hats with the brims curved, so I couldn't see their faces. One had a beard. That's all. I can't even remember what kind of car they drove. It all happened so fast."

"You can't remember anything else?" Deena Lee said. "What were they wearing? What color were their hats? Anything?"

Gabe closed his eyes like he was trying to picture the attack. It also gave him time to think. "No. First thing they done was club me in the head. With something hard. From then, I was only partially there. No sense calling the sheriff. Nothing he could do."

Wanna went back for the phone. "I've got to call Doc. You look hurt bad."

Gabe raised a hand in her direction and shouted through the pain in his ribs. "Don't. I just want to sleep. You can call Doc first thing in the morning. I'll not argue it then. Please."

Wanna put the phone down.

Deena Lee leaned over Gabe's face. "You have to

let us clean you up a bit."

He was too tired to argue, so he allowed his body to relax into the couch, which seemed to half swallow him. He was on the verge of slumber several times, but each time he was jolted back by the pain of a wet washcloth or a bandage.

Deena Lee left his knee alone. When she pulled his shirttail from his pants to check on his ribs, a large manila envelope projected from his waistband. "What's this?" she said and pulled it out with a tug.

Gabe's mind raced. Memories of the day were garbled into out-of-order snippets. He couldn't remember the envelope or what was in it, or how it got in his pants. But he had a strange feeling that the contents were extremely important, and that it was imperative that no one, including Deena Lee and Wanna, knew what they were.

With the last remaining shred of quick thinking left to him, he forced out a punctate message—a few syllables with each exhalation, more for effect than out of necessity. "It's just . . . some important . . . tax papers. You can . . . take a look . . . but I'd have to . . . explain them to you. Bring them here . . . and I'll explain them."

Wanna grabbed the envelope from Deena Lee and walked over to the roll-top desk on the other side of the room. "I'll just put it in the taxes drawer. No need to explain them. You know how much I hate tax stuff."

"Me, too," Deena Lee said. She placed a hand on Gabe's cheek. "Don't worry about any taxes tonight. You just get some sleep. We'll have Doc out first thing in the morning. If you need anything in the night, one of us'll be sitting here watching over you." She looked at Wanna, who gave a nod of agreement.

"I'll sit up with him," Wanna said. "You need your rest to look after Cory Dean."

Gabe barely heard Wanna's offer. He headed for the peaceful embrace of sleep.

CHAPTER 48

THE NEXT MORNING came too early for Gabe, but his deal was made. Doc was already looking at his knee when the fog inside his head cleared, just as the fog outside of the house rolled in.

Doc's palpitations of Gabe's knee were gentle at first, but Gabe protested, to let Doc know the full workup wouldn't be fun.

"So, Gabe, how'd this all come about anyway? I'm told you were jumped by a group from Rother."

Gabe's mind ran in serpentine thoughts instead of straight lines. "What I told last night was what I know, or at least what I knew then. I can't remember much at all today. I know I was hit over the head and kicked around a bit. Don't know how the knee got hurt."

"Can you tell me anything about the four men who did this to you?"

Gabe put his right hand over his eyes and rubbed his temples with the thumb and fingertips. "I'm not even sure there were four. If I said that last night, it must be so, but I can't remember it so clearly today."

"Do you remember what kind of car they were driving?"

"Sorry, Doc. I got no idea. Maybe something'll come to me later. And tell Wanna I'll be sure to call the sheriff if I remember anything important."

Doc turned around and shook his head at Wanna. She shrugged her shoulders and looked at the floor. Doc turned back to his patient and his injured knee.

"I'm going to bend your knee up part way, like this." He forced Gabe's leg up so it formed a ninety degree angle, with his foot planted on the couch. "Now I'm going to have to pull up on your lower leg. You let me know if it hurts you."

Doc placed his right hand behind Gabe's knee, and his left hand on the top of his leg, near the ankle. When he lifted with his right hand, Gabe let out a muffled yelp. He lowered Gabe's leg back down on the couch and wrote a few notes on a yellow legal pad. He put the pen down and lifted Gabe's shirt.

Deena Lee and Wanna inched closer.

"What's wrong with his knee?" Deena Lee said.

Doc palpated Gabe's ribs and spoke without looking up. "It looks like his anterior cruciate ligament is gone. I can't tell if it's partially torn or if it's totally bisected. We'll have to do an MRI to be sure, which means we'll have to get him over to Regional Hospital in a couple of weeks. If I'm right, he'll need an operation, but we can't do anything until the swelling goes down. In the meantime, I can fit him with a brace so he can get around, although he won't be going much of anywhere for a while. I'm also worried about his ribs." Doc poked Gabe's chest, prompting a subdued cry that came out as a strained grunt. "Hopefully, they're just cracked. We'll need to take some x-rays."

Doc pulled Gabe's shirt back down and wrote on his yellow pad. Finished, he moved up to the top of the couch. "Now, let me have a look at your head. Your face has a few cuts, mostly punctures, but Wanna and Deena Lee, you took good care of them last night. I'm a little worried about the cuts on the back of your head, though. At least one is still oozing a little. Can you turn on your side so I can have a look?"

It took Gabe thirty seconds to shift to his side, and he was unable to subdue his reactions to the pain this time.

Doc probed his scalp around the blood-matted hair and made a "tsk" sound. "It looks like we have three good gashes here. One'll be okay as it is, but two will need a couple of stitches to keep closed." He looked up at Deena Lee and Wanna. "I can do it here, if you don't mind the mess. I'm going to have to cut away some of his hair and he's not going to like the anesthetic shot one bit. What do you think?"

"Go ahead and sew him up," Deena Lee said right away. "If you give him time to think about it, he'll not want it done at all. You'll be lucky to get him in for the x-rays and I won't put odds on the operation. Better do what you can while he's laid up here."

Doc put a butterfly bandage on the smallest cut and closed the next wound with two stitches. The largest one took four. When finished, he helped Gabe turn back over, but cautioned him to keep his weight off the stitched areas. He turned to face Deena Lee.

"I'm concerned about his memory. I want you to watch him closely today. If he goes to sleep, try to rouse him every half hour or so. You don't have to wake him up totally. I just want to see if you can get him to respond to you. And let me know right away if he starts vomiting. He'll have a headache for a while, but it should get better as the day wears on." He turned his head. "Gabe, you tell Deena Lee if it gets worse than it is now. I'm going to give you a prescription for some pain pills."

He looked over at Deena Lee. "Have him take one every four hours today and tonight. Then, have him take one when he needs it."

Doc raised his voice. "Gabe, you have to stay down now. Even if you start to feel better. I don't want you to be moving around much. I'd like you to come in tomorrow for the x-rays. We'll worry about the MRI later." Doc turned back to Deena Lee and Wanna. "I'll swing by later this morning with a knee brace. It'll immobilize it so he doesn't hurt it when he moves around. You have to keep him down for a couple of days, at least."

Doc and Deena Lee helped Gabe to a sitting position. Doc wrapped Gabe's torso with an elastic bandage and re-checked his sutures. When he was done, he packed his bag, stood up, and walked out the door, motioning Deena Lee to follow him.

When they were outside, Deena Lee grabbed his forearm. "Is he going to be all right?"

"Everything but the knee will heal on its own," Doc said with a warm smile. "He'll be mighty sore for a while, and he won't be doing much around the farm in the next few weeks. Good thing it's getting into winter. He'll need surgery, and that'll be followed by a long and difficult recovery, physical therapy. From a physical terrorist." He laughed. "If I'm right, we're looking at around a year to get to where he can move around like before. He'll need a lot of help with the farm come spring. Good thing he has you and Wanna. From what I know of Wanna, the farm work will get done just fine. There's just one thing that's bothering me, though. Do you know anything about what happened to him?"

"Just what he told us last night and today. Why? What's wrong?" Deena Lee chewed her index fingernail.

"He said he was hit over the head, but his wounds are low on the back of his head and neck. Also, the cuts on his face are mostly puncture wounds. That wouldn't happen with a beating like he described. If his memory improves, write down anything he says. Even if he talks in his sleep. I'm not going to bother the sheriff, but I won't rule out the option later. I'm not trying to worry you. I just want to make sure Gabe isn't in any trouble."

"I'll take down what he says and I'll let you know if anything important comes up. Any idea how we can keep him down? You know he'll be wanting to get up, probably before the day's out."

"Sit on him if you have to. He'll just end up hurting himself worse if he moves around too much. I'll be back later with the brace and I'll bring the pain pills."

"Thanks, Doc. We really appreciate you coming out this morning."

Doc's smile widened. "My pleasure. By the way, what's up with Wanna? She seems to have changed, and not just a little."

Deena Lee returned Doc's smile. "I think it's Cory Dean. Ever since he came home, she's been a different person—downright sweet. Little people can do that to big people, particularly the tough ones. I suspect she's feeling the need to be a mother herself, and from what I've seen, she'll be a good one."

"Be sure to tell her goodbye." Doc climbed into his car.

The sun came up in streams of light that struggled against the closed drapes of the living room. Gabe's awakening paralleled the gathering light. As he became aware of his surroundings, and more importantly of his internal condition, he was relieved to find his headache nearly gone. In fact, he felt really good until he tried to move on the couch. Grunting to a sitting position, the pain in his chest told him it was a very bad idea. The grunts brought another sound from the chair to his left.

Wanna stirred. She slouched in the chair with her legs propped up on the coffee table, which was pulled over so her legs were supported from the knees down. She sat up straight and shed her sleep like an unneeded blanket. "Good morning, sleepy head. You been out for a whole day and night. How you feeling? You must be pretty hungry."

"I really need to get to the bathroom. Can you help me get up? You sleep in the chair last night? What day is this, anyway?"

"Slow down on the questions. It's Friday morning, and don't you worry about where I slept. Let's get you to the bathroom before you mess up the couch more than you have already."

She helped Gabe to a sitting position, which took nearly a minute. Helping him stand took a little longer and required three tries to find the best angle for his injured leg. The brace stabilized the knee, but it didn't allow any significant flexion of the joint. When he was standing, Wanna handed him a pair of crutches Doc had dropped off with the knee brace and pain pills.

"Here. You can use these to get to the bathroom. You needing to sit down in there or can you take care of your business standing?"

"I'm needing to stand right now. But if I have to sit later, I'll find a way to do it my own damn self."

"Well, you seem to be feeling better," Wanna said, giggling. "You can bitch all you want, but you're going to get our help whether you like it or not. You're still petty banged up, and Doc says you'll be needing our help for a couple of days."

Deena Lee rounded the hall doorway into the living room with Cory Dean in her arms. "Good morning, Sweetie. Look who's been dying to see you. How you feeling today?"

Gabe pulled a full smile at the sight of Cory Dean and Deena Lee. "I'm feeling a ton better now I get a look at the two of you. But I got to get to the bathroom, so I'll let you know how I'm really feeling after that part of me is feeling better."

Gabe crutched his way out of the room, giving a slight grunt each time his body weight fell on the padded supports in his armpits. The pressure the crutches placed on his ribs made the trip a painful one.

In the time it took Gabe to navigate the house, take care of his business, return to the couch, and lower himself to a sitting position, Deena Lee had a plate of eggs, bacon, and potatoes ready on a lap tray. Although he was famished, Gabe slowly savored each bite. Only a day-and-a-half earlier, he wasn't sure he'd be around to enjoy such a gastronomic delight—or the love of the people who were taking care of his needs. He thought of Wanna sleeping in the chair at his side, and the look of concern on Deena Lee's face. He was the luckiest man on earth, despite his physical wounds.

When he finished his breakfast, Deena Lee again forwarded her query. "How you feeling, Sweetie? You had us plenty scared."

"I'm feeling a whole lot better than yesterday morning." He put on his "I'm fine" look. "My headache's nearly gone, and the knee's stiff but not paining me much. But my chest feels like someone's tightening a vice on it. It hurts to breathe, and moving around gives me some serious pain. The damn crutches do more hurt than good, so I'll just try to get around without them."

"You'll do no such thing," Wanna said, leaning into the conversation. "First of all, you ain't getting around nowhere for the next couple of days. Second, I'd like to see you try to get around without the crutches. Hopping will hurt your ribs more than the crutches, and you better not put any weight on that knee. Doc said the swelling will never go down if you don't stay off it."

Gabe rolled his eyes, even though he knew she was right. He didn't have the luxury of taking a couple of days off—he needed to get up to Chicago right away. That thought took over. How was he going to get up there, particularly without Thibideaux knowing where he was going? He was sure he was being watched very carefully, and would be until the baptism.

The envelope. The memory of it, stuffed in his waistband, returned. What was in it? He'd only presumed it contained the priest's notes. He hadn't looked inside yet. Didn't even know he had it until Deena Lee found it. "Deena Lee, you took an envelope from me when I came in. What'd you do with it?"

Wanna stepped between Gabe and Deena Lee. "Don't you think about that stuff now. You got to rest up without worrying about taxes."

Wanna's response reminded Gabe of his quick-thinking cover. "I won't bother with it now. Just remind me where you put it so I can get to it later."

"I ain't telling." Wanna set her jaw. "You'll just get to it if I do. You lay back and rest up or I'll add to your whipping."

No way to win a battle of stubbornness with Wanna, at least not with the old Wanna. But urgency played in. Sacrifice the sympathy pawn. "I just want to know where you put it so I can get it later. It's really important stuff, so you better tell me or I'll be up after it."

Wanna's hands pinched her hips, elbows out, like she was forming a physical barrier. "I'll tell you under one condition. You promise you won't look at it until tomorrow." She walked over to the couch and picked up the crutches. "And just to make sure you ain't tempted to get it, I'll borrow these for a while." She put the crutches under her arms and effortlessly swung herself across the room.

Gabe was in check, but rather than fight, he tipped over his king. "Okay. You win. I promise. But I have a condition, too. If you bring me the envelope right now, and let me take a quick peek inside, I'll let you put it up for today. I won't take any papers out. I just need to see if I got the right ones. The tax problem came on me fast, so I don't have a lot of time to take care of it. Today, I need to know if I have the right stuff."

Wanna walked over to the roll-top desk, pulled open the left, middle drawer, and withdrew the envelope. "Okay, Mister Tax Man. You take a peek, but I'll keep hold of it. Get your look. I ain't going to keep it here long." She held the envelope by the edges and moved the flap end within Gabe's reach.

The envelope was closed by a string that wound around two raised paper disks. Heart pounding, Gabe unwound the string and lifted the flap. How would he recognize the notes?

Inside were fifteen or twenty age-yellowed pages with hand-written paragraphs and phrases. With a quick flip, he noticed a few graphs and what looked like equations, but with words instead of math symbols. Without time or privacy to read carefully, he had to assume they were written by the priest. The words of Father Costello echoed in his mind as he closed the envelope and re-wound the sealing string. "It's probably better if you don't read the notes either . . . " Gabe released the envelope and Wanna walked it back to the tax drawer.

His mind turned to the problem of timing. The baptism was nine days away and nothing could be done until tomorrow at the earliest. Even if he was physically able to head out to Chicago tomorrow, which was unlikely, it would take him at least one day to get up there. That would get him with Father Costello with seven days left. Then, he would have to drive back, which would make it six days, and all of this ignored the need for sleep. To allow for appropriate rest, he would be within four or five days of the baptism upon his return from Chicago. That wouldn't leave a lot of time to plan the battle with Thibideaux. He thought of all the things that could add delays to his best-case timetable. Wanna interrupted his mental calculations.

"Gabe, I forgot to tell you. Doc wants you to come over this afternoon for them x-rays. I'll drive you over.

He wants you there at two, so we'll have to start getting you out around one-thirty."

Gabe didn't respond. He was back to his calculations. No choice but to give up today entirely, and it was going to be a real challenge getting going on the plan tomorrow. He would have to start a new chess match with Wanna and Deena Lee, and the way he was trounced today was a bad omen. After considering a few more potential hurdles, he relaxed into the couch—the best thing was to rest up. He was going to have to push himself to the limit during the next few days, both mentally and physically. Sleep was his best friend right now.

Deena Lee kneeled by the couch with a glass of water. "Here you go, sweetie. Here's your pain pill. It'll make you a little drowsy. We'll take Cory Dean upstairs so he won't be a bother. You just try to get some sleep."

Gabe swallowed his pill and Deena Lee helped him lay back down. He was asleep within ten minutes, but instead of dreaming about his upcoming adventure, he reflected on his home and happiness. In his dream, Thibideaux was nowhere to be found.

CHAPTER 49

GABE'S X-RAYS DISCLOSED three cracked ribs, and the trip to the clinic and back told him he would need at least a second day of inactivity before heading to Chicago. But he wasn't idle on his second day of rest—a plan had to be set in motion and it would require rather tricky negotiations at home.

First thing in the morning, Gabe called Wes Worthing and set up an appointment to discuss an important county tax matter. He arranged the meeting for eight the next morning, at Wes' house. Next, it was time to grease the skids at home during lunch.

Gabe came into the kitchen and lowered himself onto one of the chairs, determined to eat his lunch without showing any of the pain.

Wanna was on him first.

"What are you doing out here? You should be

resting up on your back. You sure you're okay to be sitting already?"

"I got to get up and move around to get some of the circulation back in my legs. If you'll be kind enough to help me, I'll put my leg up on that chair." He nodded to the one unoccupied chair.

Deena Lee jumped up and pulled the chair over to Gabe's side, and helped lift his leg up onto the seat. "Do you want me to get a pillow for your knee?"

"No. This if fine. Thank you, baby." He smiled through the pain.

"I think I agree with Wanna," Deena Lee said as she sat back down. "You should be on the couch. I'm glad you're feeling better, but you still need your rest."

Gabe followed with a lie, and it bothered him. It wasn't right, deceiving anyone, especially his family, but the phrase "the end justifies the means" made sense. The vacation of truthfulness ripped his emotions. Better not become habit, he thought.

"I'm really feeling good. The pain's nearly gone, and with the pills I hardly notice it." A quick gaze out the kitchen window revealed bright sunshine. It didn't matter on this one. "Besides, I'm needing to do something about that tax stuff. I already called Wes. I'm heading out to his place first thing tomorrow."

Wanna jumped up, her voice an octave above normal. "You're doing what? I don't think so. There ain't no tax stuff this time of year that's so important you have to risk hurting yourself."

Deena Lee nodded.

Gabe turned to face Wanna a little too quickly

and a sharp pain shot through his chest. He paused, hoping the twinge in his facial muscles wasn't noticed. "I'm feeling a lot better. Besides, I have to get out of here before I go crazy. And the tax problem is one we got to get on right away." Another lie, this time carefully rehearsed. "If we don't find a solution, there'll be a need to raise the property taxes. We don't want to do that because some of the local folks are living on the edge, money-wise." On the fly, he thought of a good addition to rally his side. "You can blame it on Rother. They sold us some emergency trucks a few years back and they're calling in the loan. They're trying their best to keep their own taxes down and their idea is to dump it off on us. So, me and Wes need to get together to figure out a plan to come up with the extra money." The proverbial ice underneath Gabe's feet was thick and solid. But still a little slippery.

"I don't like it," Wanna said. She sat back down and blotted her mouth with her napkin. "You should stay in bed for a couple more days. I'll give Doc a call and see what he says."

Deena Lee nodded again.

Gabe counter attacked before Wanna got up again. "I made you a promise about the papers yesterday. Now you have to let me get to them. I'm not going to run out right now. I'll be in bed for the rest of today and tonight. By tomorrow I'll be feeling even better, so I shouldn't have any problems. This is really important. Wes needs my help."

Gabe thought he was off the ice and on solid ground until Wanna made his footing slick again.

"How you going to get over to Wes'? You going to drive? And how do you expect to work the clutch with that bad knee all braced up? Did you think of that, Mister Tax Man?"

He was momentarily stumped. For all of this preparation, he forgot about the clutch. Fortunately, his newfound penchant for fabrication was honed to razor sharpness. Pretending to adjust his knee on the chair gave him more time to think.

"I've been trying to put pressure on the knee to see how it reacts, and it's okay if I keep it straight and put pressure on that way. It only hurts if it's bent and I pressure it, or if the pressure comes from the side. I'll prop myself up in the seat with a pillow so my leg stays straight and I'll be all right." Gabe made direct eye contact with Wanna. She usually dropped hers in response, but not this time. "Tell you what. I'll give it a try after supper tonight. If it pains me, I'll wait another day. Deal?" No matter how much it hurt, he'd hide the pain from Wanna and Deena Lee.

Wanna shook her head. "Why don't you let me drive you? I ain't jawed with Thelma for some time. I'm sure we could pass the time."

"That wouldn't do. The meeting will probably take all morning and go into the afternoon." He turned his head. "Deena Lee, you were planning to go in to the Herndon's Edge tomorrow afternoon, right?"

Deena Lee smiled and nodded.

"See there? You need to watch over Cory Dean tomorrow. It'd be better if I just drove myself over. It's only a few miles. If I have any trouble, I can have Wes drive me back."

"Why don't Wes come over here?" Deena Lee said.

Gabe smiled. He felt a sense of pride over his preparation, until he remembered about the clutch. The dent in his confidence made him lose his train of thought.

"Well . . ." It clicked in. "I mentioned that to Wes, but he said he has all the files out at his place. It'd be easier for me just to go there. He's not sure which files he'll need, so he'd have to carry the whole lot over here. Even though he offered, I thought it would be imposing."

"I'm still going to give Doc a call to see what he thinks." Wanna said.

Gabe put on his best angry face and boomed his voice, scaring Cory Dean into a cry. "Don't you dare. He'll do anything to keep me in bed. He don't understand how important this tax thing is. I won't let him jeopardize money matters for the entire Tri-counties just so he can keep my knee from swelling a little. You call him and I'll go anyway, so I wouldn't bother if I was you."

Wanna backed off while Deena Lee calmed Cory Dean.

Gabe's confidence returned, this time due to good acting. All of the ice was gone and he was free to plot the rest of his plan. "If all that's settled, I need to lay down to get some rest. I have a big day tomorrow."

Gabe pulled his leg from the chair and Deena Lee popped up from hers. "Let me help you."

He held his hand out to her and grimaced through

a hug. "Thank you, baby. I'll be all right."

When no one was looking, Gabe tossed two pain pills into his mouth. Sleep followed.

Gabe awakened before the roosters, cleaned up and dressed before anyone else so the women wouldn't see him struggle with his clothes. He pulled the curtains back. All clear. There was another reason for the early rise. He didn't want them to see him pack his clothes bag.

The "tax" envelope went into the bag first, followed by enough clothing for three days. He grabbed his sleeping bag, then loaded Wanna's pill dispenser with vitamins, leaving them in plain view on the counter. The crutches worked better, but they still hurt his chest and armpits. And carrying the bags out to the pickup was a pain of a different kind. Finished preparing the truck, he went back inside and reclined on the couch.

When the household was up, Gabe came into the kitchen with a huge smile on his face. He planted a kiss on Cory Dean's chubby cheek and did the same for Deena Lee. "I'm feeling really good this morning. I'm looking forward to getting out. How're you all doing?"

Wanna was at the stove with her back turned, but her tone gave away her feelings. "We're not convinced you're doing a good thing. I'm going to call out to Wes' a few times to make sure you're okay. Thelma'll tell me the truth. She gives me a 'no' and I'll be there faster than a firefly flash."

"You didn't even move that fast when you were chasing Johnny Robertson. Maybe I'll tell Thelma to give a bad report just to see you hustling over." Gabe and Deena Lee burst into laughter but Wanna only snickered. A retort was on its way—the wait was short.

"Excuse me for a minute. I have to go out to the dog run and get the sausages to go with your eggs. By the way, that may not be apple juice in your cup. We were a little low, so I whipped something up."

By seven-thirty the dishes were cleared from the table. Gabe made his way to the front door and announced his departure. He returned Deena Lee's hug and kiss, and gave Cory Dean a snuggle. Turning in Wanna's direction, he said. "You got anything for me?"

Wanna passed an evil smile and shook her right fist in the air. "It'll be waiting for you when you get back."

Gabe clamored into the pickup and started it up. He kept the smile on his face as he let the pressure off the clutch, even though the pain was intense. The pickup rumbled down the gravel driveway, winding out first gear nearly to the red line, and turned left onto the county road. The house shrank in the rearview mirror, and then disappeared as a bank of fog surrounded the truck. The mist accompanied it all the way to the edge of Wes Worthing's property.

Gabe steered up the gravel drive, but skidded to a stop and swung his head around. A vertical wall of fog hovered at the edge of Wes's property.

CHAPTER 50

THE MEETING WITH Wes lasted three-quarters of an hour. A curtain of fog waited as the pickup headed back out of Wes's drive. The truck's wheels stirred up a cloud of dust that was dwarfed by the massive fogbank.

Gabe had always commented that his old truck had traveled the roads of the Tri-counties so often it knew its way around without his intervention. In fact, there were two or three times, when he had nights out with his buddies, that he was sure it was the truck that had found its way home, not him.

This trip home was a slow, deliberate one due to the dense fog and the slow shifting of the truck. It was used to being driven around ten miles an hour below the posted speed limit, but today it was more like fifteen.

The truck pulled up to the front of the farmhouse and a surprised Deena Lee and Wanna crowded together in the open front doorway. The pickup door opened as they hustled down the steps. They stopped short of the bumper.

A tall figure stepped out without the aid of crutches or even a hint of knee pain. The figure wore Gabe's coat, and the bill of Gabe's hat was pulled down low over his face.

Wanna registered the startle of surprised recognition. "Wes? Good Lord. What you doing in Gabe's clothes? And his truck?" She peered into the truck cab. "Where's Gabe? What the hell's going on?"

Deena Lee chimed in, "Is Gabe in some kind of trouble?" Her voice wavered.

The dense fog receded so fast it drew the breath out of the three. They gasped in unison and stood in total silence, turning their heads to follow the disappearing mist into the distance.

"Wes, what the hell's going on around here?" Wanna said, scared. "Where's Gabe?"

Wes put his arm on Wanna's shoulder. He looked at Deena Lee and hooked his other arm over her shoulders. He turned the women toward the porch. "Come sit with me on the porch. I'll explain as best I can. Gabe has some instructions for the two of you— he said you need to follow them to a 'T.'"

The three sat on the porch.

"He said it's really important, so he wrote everything down for you. I'll tell you what I know, then you'll have to read the rest. He said you should destroy the letter after you read it. He'll be back in about three days—"

"What?" Wanna shifted away from Wes. "Where'd he go that'll take three days? What the hell's going on, Wes?"

Wes scanned the horizon in the direction of the receded fog. "He went back up to Chicago to see Father Costello again. He explained a little of it to me, but I don't know all the details. Said it had something to do with Thibideaux. He needed to see the priest so he could stop Thibideaux. He didn't explain what it was he was going to stop, though." Wes looked at the horizon. "He told me one other thing to tell you that didn't make any sense until now. He said if there's a fog around the house, don't talk about where he is or what he's there for. If you mention Chicago or Gabe's trip, make sure you check out the windows first. He said Thibideaux snoops on everyone in the fogs. I didn't believe him until now. You saw it. It disappeared in an instant when you all recognized me. If Gabe's right, something really strange is going on around here."

For the first time since she met Wes, Wanna thought she saw an expression of fear in him. He was the one everyone counted on to be steady in any emergency. If he was scared, something must be wrong. She needed some reassurance.

"Wes, is Gabe all right?"

Wes took a deep breath and looked directly into Wanna's eyes. Then into Deena Lee's. "He's fine." He patted Deena Lee's knee. "Fact is, he's probably better than me right now." He looked down at his hands and fumbled with the letter, then handed it to Deena Lee. "Here. Don't read it if there's a fog out, and remember to burn it up when you're finished."

Deena Lee lifted the flap.

"Don't open it now," Wes said. "I'm not supposed to see it either." He took another deep breath. "I'll be off back to my place. Sorry to startle you all."

Deena Lee stopped Wes before he could get in the truck. "If you're driving the truck, how's Gabe getting to Chicago?"

Wes did a three-sixty spin, scanning the horizon. Worry creased his face. "Deena Lee, you got to be careful. Look around before you talk about Gabe's trip. Look for the fog." He looked around again. "He's driving my truck. It's got an automatic transmission so he can drive it without hurting his knee. I'll keep his truck until he gets back. You have something to get around?"

"We got my car," Deena Lee said, pointing to her Volkswagen parked around the side of the house. "And Wanna has another in the shed. We'll be okay, but I'm scared. You sure Gabe's not in any trouble?"

"I don't know what you call what he's doing. You have any problems, you give me a call and I'll be here as fast as this heap of junk can get me here. Gabe told me to tell you to keep a close eye on Cory Dean. Where is he, anyway?"

"Just put him down for a nap," Deena Lee said. "I'd better check on him."

Wes got in the truck and turned it down the gravel

road. There wasn't a vapor of fog around during the entire trip home.

CHAPTER 51

GABE PULLED ONTO the interstate and headed north, astonished at how large Wes' truck was in comparison to his old pickup. It seemed to be as powerful as an eighteen-wheeler. He had seen the new four-door trucks, but he had never been in one. With all the room, both inside and in the truck bed, he decided right then it was time he bought a new truck for the farm, and for the family. Cory Dean would be safe strapped in his infant chair in the back seat of a truck like this, and the vehicle could still be put to work like the old pickup.

The ride was so smooth, it seemed like the truck slipped through the air free of drag. "Holy sh . . . ," he said. "No way I'm going over ninety." Backing off the accelerator, the truck's speed dipped, then settled, nine miles over the posted limit. Keep the excess in single figures and the state troopers won't bother, he thought.

Gabe's mind went as frictionless as the truck. He debated what to say to Father Costello when they met again. A glance at the speedometer. He was getting used to the truck's speed, but he had to squint a little to see the numbers. The light of day was decreasing. But it was too early.

His head jerked upward, his eyes squinting at the rear-view mirror. His heart galloped so hard it hurt his ribs. A bank of fog billowed directly behind the truck, about two hundred yards back, and the distance seemed to be closing. Fast. The wall of mist moved as if by intent, rather than being pushed by prevailing breezes. In a single minute that seemed like an hour, the vapor halved the distance between its leading edge and the truck.

The daylight faded as if it were being sucked into the cloud. Gabe tensed in the seat, bringing his back up away from the upholstery. He stomped on the accelerator so hard it slapped the floorboard, and the truck responded with a downshift and lurch forward that pushed Gabe back into the seat. His heart pumped so hard and fast it seemed to be in his throat—he could hear each beat in his ears. Even though his breathing was fast and shallow, the pain he normally felt with each breath was subdued by the adrenaline coursing through his body. A trickle of sweat ran down his forehead even though it was cold enough to require a light jacket.

His heart gave an extra beat, then another, and

then the long pause. A wave of dizziness spread over his head in slow motion—he tracked its leading edge.

The speedometer crept over the century mark but the fog continued to gain on the truck, although not as fast as before. Another extra beat. "Not now," Gabe shouted.

He needed a point of focus, so he let his mind run to his plan. It included an assumption that Thibideaux's ability to project himself out in the fog had a limited range. Since Thibideaux didn't know Gabe's destination, Gabe expected him to scan the entire perimeter of his snooping area rather than act on a hunch and concentrate on a specific vector. Now, it was obvious Gabe had misjudged Thibideaux's abilities.

He glanced at the speedometer again—over one hundred-ten. Up to the rearview mirror again. The fog was within about fifty yards. Over to the driver's side mirror. Tendrils of mist swirled in the truck's trailing vortex. He pushed harder on the accelerator as if pushing the pedal against the floor with more pressure would send a meaningful signal to the carburetor. His heart gave a series of large beats and the cab nearly went dark.

Gabe shook his head and pounded his chest with his right fist. "Come on, damn it." He looked in the rearview mirror again and leaned forward, closer to the mirror. The leading edge of the fog cut a diagonal across the freeway and sped off toward the west. Gabe squinted at the sudden increase in light intensity. The gas pedal remained on the floor until he could see he was putting distance between himself and the cloud, which was thinning into wisps in the distance. With a release of the accelerator, the speed dropped to just below one hundred. Best to get out of Thibideaux's range for good.

He took a deep breath and leaned up farther. Once again, his pulse was evident in his neck and ears—fast, but regular. Either the effects of the adrenaline were receding or his mind was branching out from its single-minded focus, because the pain in his chest returned with each breath.

He reflected on his good fortune in having Wes' powerful truck, more for its speed than for its comfort. As his heart rate eased downward, he slumped back into the seat and refocused on the drive. He'd be in Chicago sometime after midnight.

Although Gabe didn't have to use his left leg to operate a clutch, the pain in his knee grew with each mile of the trip. His unchanging posture contributed, but mostly it was because he couldn't take his pain pills. They made him too drowsy to drive. There was a positive benefit, however. He would be able to drive straight through to Chicago without worrying about falling asleep. The pain made sure of that.

Nearing Chicago, Gabe contracted a case of the yawns. He let his mind free wheel again. In accordance with his new driving strategy, he hadn't received a single middle finger salute, even though more than a few drivers exceeded his speed enough to allow them to pass and disappear into the distance relatively quickly. What he found interesting was his reaction when he came upon a slower driver in thick traffic. If he happened to get boxed in, so he couldn't pass right away, he felt the distinct sensation of impatience gnaw at him until he could get around the dawdler. He wasn't moved to raise his middle finger, but he understood how some individuals of a different temperament would do so if they were in a hurry, like him, and the traffic wasn't cooperative.

The closer he got to Chicago, the more the countryside reminded him it was running, full bore, into winter. At the start of the trip, only a few kinds of trees had bare branches or leaves in full fall hue. Now, all deciduous trees were totally devoid of leaves. In the Chicago area, the remnants of an early snow were piled low on the roadsides, partly melted into curved mounds of ice that had lost their virgin whiteness to the dinge of road dirt. And there was a change in air temperature—Gabe had to rely on the truck's heating system for comfort. It was a good thing he brought his mummy-style sleeping bag. He planned to sleep away what remained of the night in the hospital parking lot again.

He pulled into the parking lot at ten minutes before two in the morning and found the same space he had used to sleep off his previous trip. This time, he had the luxury of climbing into the back seat, so he could stretch out without competing for space with the steering wheel. Ignoring the pain in his ribs, he kicked off his shoes and wrapped himself in the sleeping bag.

It zipped up so the only exposed part of his body was his face.

Earlier, when he had broken the outskirts of Chicago, he had turned up the heater so the cab of the truck was toasty-hot. A weather report on a local radio station had said the projected low for the area would be in the high thirties to low forties.

In the parking lot, the wind was moderate, and coming in from a direction that was blocked by the hospital building. Since daylight was only a few hours away, it wouldn't be necessary to restart the vehicle to keep warm.

Gabe drifted off to sleep in a matter of minutes, but on the way, he once again had the distinct impression someone was staring at him from an upper floor window of the hospital. Dream or real, he saw the silhouette of a human figure in a third floor window.

The light of day came way too early, and the combination of the restricted room in the truck and the cold made Gabe extremely stiff. Bringing himself to a sitting position brought back the pain in his chest to a level he hadn't experienced in the last two days. He fumbled for his watch, which he had placed in a storage compartment in one of the rear doors. Seven thirty. The more northern latitude brought daylight a little later, and sent it packing a little earlier in the day.

Anxious to see Father Costello, he started the truck, turned the heater to full hot, and drove back to the familiar McDonald's where he freshened up and ate a little breakfast.

Back in the parking lot at nine, he was now comfortable in terms of his basic necessities, although the pain in his chest decreased only slightly, from incendiary to scorching.

Gabe made his way to the front doors of the hospital, the envelope with Father Costello's notes tucked into his waistband. Even with all of his attention devoted to control of the crutches, he was still very awkward in their use. Fortunately, the snow remnants were restricted to the spaces between parking rows—the blacktop was devoid of ice.

Upon entering the foyer, the same overweight receptionist nodded to him with a friendly smile. Gabe had phoned ahead and set up the meeting this time, so he wouldn't have to rely on a surprise phone call to gain admittance.

As he came closer, the smile on the receptionist's face faded. "My Lord. What happened to you? You look terrible. Were you in some kind of accident?"

"It's a long story. Can I go up and see the Father yet?" He didn't slow his forward momentum.

The smile returned to the receptionist's face. "Father Costello is in the same place as when you were here before. In fact, for some reason, he spent the entire night there last night." Her tone turned to a friendly tease. "Do you think you can get through to him this time? If you do, I hope you bought a Lotto ticket. You get him to talk and I'll want your numbers." She chuckled a little too hard for Gabe to appreciate it as a joke.

"Fixing to do my best," he said as he approached the elevator doors. He entered and turned in time to see the receptionist shake her head in what appeared to be a non-verbal form of "what a pity." He imagined her reaching for his commitment papers.

The ancient elevator started its ascent with a sharp jerk that homed in on Gabe's ribs. He let out a muffled grunt. Hopefully, the receptionist didn't hear it through the closed doors.

Father Costello sat in the day room, in the exact same place, and with the same exact posture as when Gabe left him weeks ago. The same magazines were scattered on the table, but in different positions, and the room appeared as if it had been nearly unused in the interim.

Gabe made his way to the table and balanced on one foot as he pulled the envelope from his waistband and withdrew a folded paper from his back pocket. He crutched around the table, up to the priest's left side. The drawing of Thibideaux was smoothed against the window in direct line of Father Costello's blank stare.

The priest didn't respond. Gabe remembered there was no guarantee he would come out of his trance again, even with the picture. For the longest thirty seconds of Gabe's life, Father Costello continued to stare at nothing in this world. Then, a pair of quick eye-blinks started a wave of arousal that gradually brought the priest back to the day room.

Gabe saw him recoil as a look of fear paled his face. He looked up at Gabe and recognition replaced fear. Back at the drawing, he swept his tongue across his lips. A deliberately formed mouth emitted words in such a low tone Gabe had to lean close to hear them.

"How long has it been since you were here?" Before Gabe could answer, the father continued. "What was your name again?"

Gabe was shocked at both questions. Was the priest testing him again, or had he really forgotten the information?

"Name's Gabe. I was here a little over a week ago. You remember much of it?"

Father Costello turned his head to directly address Gabe. "I've been thinking about it on and off. But last night I couldn't keep my mind off of it. I had a strange feeling something was about to happen, and here you are. Did you find the Bible? It's been in my family for three generations."

Gabe ambled back around the table.

"Did Hughes do that to you?"

Gabe lowered himself onto the hard chair and let out a loud sigh. "He caught me when I was getting the Bible. Got hold of it and burned it up. Sorry. He also had some fun with me, but he let me go. Somehow, I managed to get this envelope out of the rectory without him knowing it." He slid the envelope across the table. "These your notes?"

Father Costello unwound the fastener, pulled out the yellowed pages, and thumbed through them without saying a word. When he finished his brief inventory, he held them perpendicular to the table and tapped them into an even stack. At last, he carefully placed them on the table in front of him and looked up at Gabe with a look that seemed gloomy.

"Your trouble did produce positive results. These are my notes. I'm going to ask you to leave now. Could you please come back after lunch?"

"What?" Gabe's voice echoed in the Day Room. "I'm in a bit of a hurry here, Father. Can't we just go through them now?"

Father Costello's expression turned to melancholy.

"Gabe, I'm sorry to put you off, but seeing these notes has brought back a flood of very disturbing memories. I'm afraid I can't go through them without dealing with some strong emotions. It may actually speed up our talk if I have some time to go through the notes by myself. I've suppressed so many of the memories from that time it may take me a while to re-member all of the necessary details. I only hope it all comes back to me and that you didn't take that beating for no good reason."

All of a sudden, Gabe felt tired. He didn't know if it was due to fatigue or frustration. His bed in the back seat of Wes' truck was just below the window, but he worried if he went to sleep, he might not wake up in time. "I'll go down and catch a little nap in the truck. How about I come back around one?"

"Could you make it one-thirty? I want go get some lunch and I want to make sure we won't be dis-turbed in the afternoon. Besides, my appearance in the lunchroom will probably cause a commotion." Father Costello kept his eyes on the stack of notes.

Gabe didn't say a word to the receptionist on the

way out until she forwarded a verbal barb.

"Are you done talking? You didn't drive all this way to give up so soon, did you? Never mind about the Lotto numbers."

"Be back at one-thirty." He didn't look back at her. She'd realize her mistake long before he returned.

Gabe awoke from his nap at twelve-thirty and was afraid to doze back off. A rumbling stomach didn't equate to hunger, but rather to anticipation of the upcoming discussion with Father Costello. The nervous energy had one beneficial side effect—it dulled the pain in his ribs and knee.

Promptly at one-thirty, Gabe crutched through the front doors of the hospital and made his way across the foyer. Before he was halfway to the elevator, the receptionist stood and motioned to two men who were waiting in a small room behind the glass wall. The men hurried around the wall and approached Gabe. The tallest one held out a hand.

"Mr. Petersen, I'm Doctor Ewing, and this is Doctor Freedman. We'd like to talk with you for a minute, please." Dr. Ewing motioned toward the uncomfortable seats in the waiting area and tried to turn Gabe by putting his hand on Gabe's shoulder.

Gabe withdrew his shoulder and stiffened, shifting his weight from the crutches onto his good leg. "You mind telling me what you got in mind? I got an appointment with Father Costello right now." He tried to move toward the elevator but Dr. Freedman blocked his path.

"I'm afraid we must insist. We need to ask you a few questions. That's all." Dr. Ewing put his hand back on Gabe's shoulder.

Gabe once again stiffened, and his voice showed his displeasure at the interference. "I drove all the way up from Boyston and I have some important business with the father. If I don't get it done right away, some major bad will be coming to us down there. Would you please let me talk to Father Costello? Now!"

Dr. Freedman repositioned himself to block Gabe's path while Dr. Ewing put more pressure on Gabe's shoulder. His tone changed. "I'm afraid you don't have a choice in the matter. Either you talk with us or we won't allow you to talk with Father Costello at all. Now, can we please sit down for a few questions?"

Gabe balled his fists, except for the middle fingers, but he resisted the urge to raise them. "If it's the same to you, I'd prefer to do it right here. It pains me to sit down and get up. And if you only have a few questions, like you say, we can get it done right here and now."

"All right." Dr. Ewing's impatient demeanor gave Gabe's irritation a good challenge. "We need to know how you managed to bring Father Costello back. What did you say to him?"

Gabe considered his choices on this one. Tell them the truth and he'd be in for a long line of explanations that wouldn't find solid footing with such learned men. But he'd have to tell them something that would seem somewhat feasible to them. As he did once before, he decided on using a half-truth.

"You know about his problem in Boyston? The one that brought him here?"

Both men nodded.

"Well, there was a man who was very close to the father back then. He was having some problems and Father Costello tried to help him out. Some of the things the father talked about with this man made him worse, and he tried to kill himself. That seemed to really hit the father hard. It was just before the father's big problem, so I suspect it contributed to his breakdown. Anyway, this man has since come around and he's doing really good, although I think he's slipping a little again. He was a very strange looking fellow, so I just showed the father a drawing of his face, and that brought him back."

"That was all you did," Dr. Fredman said. "Just show him a drawing of the man?"

"Yup. That's it." It felt good to give a truthful answer for a change.

Dr. Ewing took over. "Can we see the drawing?"

"Sorry, but that's private. Between me and the father. Since it hit him hard when he saw it, I don't want to share it with anyone else. It would betray his trust in me."

"And if we insist?" An edge returned to Dr. Ewing's voice.

Gabe turned his body to face Dr. Ewing. "Is Father Costello still a priest?"

"Of course he is. Why?"

"As doctors, if I asked you for some confidential

medical information about the father, you could refuse to give it up, right?"

Both doctors furrowed their brows. After a pause, Dr. Ewing spoke. "Yes. We aren't required to violate the doctor-patient privilege. What's that got to do with this?"

Gabe's argument rounded the bend. "I believe priests have the same kind of thing, right?"

Both doctors flashed simultaneous looks of surprise.

"I suppose so, but Father Costello isn't advising you on any personal matter is he?"

"The matter I'm here to discuss with the father is extremely personal, and involves just me, the father, and the man whose face brought the father around." Gabe lifted his chin. "As I see it, I don't have to give you any more information than that. Correct?"

"You do if you want to meet with the father again," Dr. Freedman said.

Gabe spun around so fast he almost fell over one of the crutches. He fixed the doctor with an angry stare and half-growled at him. "Now I don't suppose that if I went to the bishop and told him about the situation, and about our conversation, that he'd agree with your reaction, you think? Besides, it seems I'm the only one who's been able to get Father Costello back home in the last twenty some years. If I go away now, he'll probably never come back again. You want to be responsible for that?"

Dr. Ewing gave Dr. Freedman a cold stare and turned a fake smile to Gabe. "Now, Mr. Petersen. What we all have in mind here is what's best for Father

Costello. Dr. Freedman and I know what's best for him medically, so I'm afraid we must insist that you give us some basic information. We'll need that for his future treatment. Surely, you won't object to that."

Gabe studied the two doctors for a few seconds. They both looked very young, and their protests were a bit too forceful. Probably a couple of entry-level, kiss-ass doctors who wanted to take credit for the father's breakthrough to gain favor with their superiors. Time to test the theory.

He turned to the receptionist. "Excuse me, Ma'am. Who's the doctor in charge of Father Costello's case?"

"That would be Doctor Lawrence."

"He around?" Gabe noticed the two doctors look at one another.

"Sorry, but he's out of town until the day after tomorrow," the receptionist said. "But I can get hold of him on his pager. He has two of them. One's for routine matters and the other's for emergencies. If I use the second one, he'll answer right away. Do you want me to contact him?"

She seemed to be playing into his plan as if she were suddenly an ally. "I don't know," Gabe said. "What do you two think? We need to call Doc Lawrence to get his okay?" Gabe rocked his neck back and forth, glowering at the two young doctors.

"I don't think we need to do that," Doctor Ewing said. He forced another smile. "Maybe we were a little too forward with our intentions. But you have to realize we are only looking after Father Costello's best interests here."

Gabe gave the receptionist a subtle nod. "I'm sure you were."

"Then you wouldn't mind if we gave you a tape recorder so we could enter the information into Father Costello's file," Dr. Ewing said. "We would make sure it was treated with the utmost confidentiality."

"Looks like we'll need to give Doc Lawrence a call," Gabe said in the direction of the receptionist. "Use the emergency line. I don't have a lot of time to waste, so we need to get his thoughts on this right away."

The receptionist picked up the phone and Doctor Ewing held a hand in her direction. "Connie, there's no need to bother Dr. Lawrence." He turned to Gabe. "You can go ahead and talk with Father Costello. At the least, do you mind if we observe from outside the room?"

"Of course I mind." The indignation was an act, but a good one. "What you think I've been talking about all this time? This is personal, and none of your damn business. You doctors seem to be really good at telling people things, but you don't seem to be so good at listening. Let's see if you can hear this. You can't listen in. You can't watch. You can't record us. Far as I'm concerned, I don't even want you on the same floor. Nod your head, or stomp your foot, or do something if you heard that."

The receptionist turned but she couldn't hide her giggles.

Dr. Freedman's face went red as a fire truck. "Now look here, Mr. Petersen. We didn't go through medical school and internships in psychiatry to have our business dictated by people off of the street—"

"Hold that thought," Gabe said, patronizing in return. He raised his right index finger within six inches of Dr. Freedman's face, his voice serious. "Until I give a shit."

All three men swung their heads around as the receptionist exploded into a throaty laugh.

Gabe added, with a chuckle of his own, "Now if you'll excuse me, I'm late for my meeting with Father Costello. If he's zoned back out because I'm late, Doc Lawrence will be called for sure. Nice to meet you both."

The doctors disappeared before Gabe was two crutch lengths toward the elevator. When he pulled even with the reception desk, he stopped and gave the receptionist a large grin. "Thanks for your help. The doc really have two pagers, like you said?"

She laughed her throaty laugh again. "No. Those two drive me nuts. They're just a couple of arrogant residents. They were probably trying to take credit for bringing the father back. They're incredible brown-nosers."

Gabe looked down at her name badge, which said, "Catherine." "Why'd they call you Connie?"

"I don't know," Catherine said with a laugh. "It was the first time they called me anything except, 'Hey, you.' I guess they figure they only have to get the first letter right and I should be happy."

Gabe headed toward the elevator, but turned his head and gave Catherine another warm smile and a chuckle. "Thank you again, Connie."

Catherine returned the smile and giggle. "You're

welcome. And if it's worth anything, what you've done for Father Costello is fantastic. I sure hope he stays with us for a while."

Gabe got in the elevator and braced himself for the jerky take-off. His conversation with the young doctors made his ribs feel much better and he didn't want to bring back the pain.

CHAPTER 52

GABE ENTERED THE day room to find Father Costello sitting alone, facing the door instead of the window. The priest stood and gave Gabe a wide smile. "Gabe. Where have you been? I saw you leave your truck but then you didn't show up. I had a bad thought that maybe Hughes found his way up here and gave you another beating."

Gabe shrugged and one of his crutches fell to the floor. One of Wanna's jokes came to mind. "Naw. I was just talking to a couple of proctologists."

Father Costello bent down and retrieved the fallen crutch. "A couple of who?"

"Never mind." He chuckled. The joke made his mind drift.

Father Costello walked back over to the table and sat down in front of his notes. They were arranged in four stacks, centered in front of him next to a pencil and pad of paper with a full page of scribbled sentences.

"I've been through the notes, and it's all coming back to me, most parts better than I wanted. I'm ready to go over the material with you. I hope it helps. We don't have to worry about being interrupted. I shook everyone up at lunch, and I made sure no one will be coming around until later."

Gabe eased onto the chair opposite the priest and took a pencil and small spiral-bound notepad from his shirt pocket. "So what is it Thibideaux wants again?"

Father Costello looked down at his notes and then a Gabe. "When you came to me last time, you opened up some memories that were hidden deep inside my mind. I told you then that I wouldn't be able to think about it all until you brought these notes, but from the first night after your visit, pieces began to come back to me. I ended up thinking a great deal about everything that happened, but it was only in general terms. I really needed these to put it into a form you'll understand." He tapped the notes with his right palm. "But what I have to say has to stay inside these walls. I don't want you to write any of this down. And, I'll keep these notes when you leave."

"Why? How am I going to remember everything without writing some of it down?"

"It's for your own protection." Father Costello's voice was calm, soothing. "Anyone who has this information is a threat to Hughes' organization. They'll do anything to make sure this information is destroyed. They won't bother me, not here, anyway."

"But Thibideaux had a chance to kill me twice, and he didn't. You say he must need me for something. If he didn't kill me then, why would he do it now?"

Father Costello shook his head. "I don't know. I just have a feeling your usefulness to his organization is only temporary. I'm afraid I'm going to have to insist the notes say with me. Otherwise, I'll stop now and let you go back home."

Gabe nodded and put the pencil and notepad back in his pocket.

"Okay. Now that that's settled, let's get down to business." The priest readjusted the stacks of papers in front of him. "What I have to say comes from a combination of two things. First, the notes you supplied, coupled with my memories, represent the fine detail that supports the general information. Second, the general information comes from a talk I had with Hughes back in Boyston. Parts of it are emblazoned in my mind. Other parts only came out when I read over the notes. You see, Hughes and I had a long night together twenty-five years ago. It was on the night of my horrific sin—a few nights after he caught me with his notebook and destroyed it. He was reveling in my failure, and he decided to rub it in. Do you know what I mean?"

"Yeah. Gabe was mesmerized. "Nowadays they call it talking trash. Like if someone really wants to humiliate another person, they take one of their mistakes and keep harping on it. That what happened?"

"That's similar, but in this case, he did it to send me here." Father Costello's expression sagged. "You'll understand it better when I finish, so let me give you the information. Remember, this will only be a short version of what's contained in the notes. I'll try to get all the general information in, though."

Gabe was so ready he couldn't keep his hands still. A jiggle of his left leg triggered an electric bolt of pain that shot through his knee. His sudden movement startled the father.

"Are you okay?"

Gabe's face reddened. "Yeah. Just had a pain in my knee. Go ahead. I'm dying to hear what you have to say."

"Okay. First, I'll describe Hughes' organization. I'll be giving you some numbers, but don't worry about remembering them. Just remember their approximate value. Hopefully the numbers will answer some of the questions that come up.

"Hughes position in the organization is what they call a Recruiter. His job is to bring babies into the organization for training. But not all babies. They carefully identify them—they call them targets. It's the job of Recruiters to get them away from their parents. To kidnap them."

"That what they want to do with Cory Dean?"

Father Costello looked confused. "Who's Cory Dean?"

"He's my son. He was the baby we talked about last time. He's Deena Lee's baby, and I married her, so now he's my son."

"Just let me go on, Gabe. The specifics of your situation will probably be clear as I explain more. Now, the Recruiters can't just go after any baby. The selection of the babies is done by members of the next higher level in the organization—the Councillors. Do you mind if I use the term 'targets' instead of 'babies?' I find it too disturbing the other way."

Gabe was having trouble with more than that one word. "Fine with me. And could you use some word other than 'kidnap?' It makes my stomach hurt."

"Okay." Father Costello blinked like he was trying to regain his train of thought. "Let's see. The Councillors are also responsible for training the new recruits, which is what the targets become when they're brought into the organization. The Councillors answer to the Provosts. Only a small number of them are rumored to exist. Even Hughes didn't know how many. Anyway, the Provosts make all of the major decisions about the operation and future directions of the organization. They also have to approve all of the acquisitions. So, it's like a pyramid, with only a few Provosts, more Councillors, and lots of Recruiters. Understand?"

Gabe nodded. So far, so good, he thought.

"Good. Once individuals are in the organization, they can't move between the various levels. They're stuck with where their training places them, no matter how good they are."

"Or how bad they are?" Gabe broke in, thinking of the two doctors he met earlier in the day.

Father Costello shook his head. "No, that's not a problem for this organization. If any member doesn't do his or her job satisfactorily, he or she is terminated immediately—no questions asked."

"Terminated? You mean fired?"

"No. I mean terminated, like killed." The priest's expression was serious. "The organization can't afford to have unhappy former employees running around. Besides, they consider it a wonderful motivating tool."

Gabe gasped, but his curiosity took over. "So, who's the boss of this organization?"

"Hughes wasn't clear on that, but his message came across. All he would say is there's no recruiting for the top spot."

Gabe's eyes were as wide as his eyelids would allow.

"Anyway, let me get back to what I know for sure," Father Costello said. "The targets are selected by the Councillors, and the Recruiters go out and 'obtain' them for training. Once in training, only a small percentage of them eventually become Recruiters. Let's see . . ." Father Costello ran his finger across one of the pages of notes in front of him. "Right. Only 17.6% of primary recruits go on to be successfully trained as Recruiters."

"What happens to the rest of them?"

"I'm getting to that," Father Costello said with a hint of impatience. "The ones that don't make it are returned to society, and they're referred to by the organization as 'One of Ours,' although they've shortened it to 'Triple O's.'"

Gabe stroked his chin with his right hand and looked at the ceiling. "Seventeen percent? It's not so good. What kind of organization is happy with only seventeen percent success? If my farm had that percentage, I'd be broke in a year."

"It's worse than that." The priest raised his eyebrows. "They call it the 'Training Success Rate' and shorten it to 'TSR.' Anyway, the seventeen percent TSR is not representative of the total population. It's the TSR for the most carefully selected targets only."

"Who're the best targets?"

"Most targets are children for whom one parent is a Triple O and the other is a regular citizen. You mentioned your son. Do you know his father?" The priest opened his palms to accentuate the question.

"He was a no good chicken. He ran out as soon as he found out Deena Lee was pregnant. He ain't been seen since."

Father Costello bobbed his head. "I'd say he was most definitely a Triple O. Anyway, to move on, if you think the TSR for these targets is bad, for children from a pair of citizens, which is what they call normal members of society, the TSR is . . ." He scanned his notes. ". . . only 0.78%. Less than one percent. During our previous meeting, I believe you asked why Hughes wasn't after another child born in Boyston. Do you remember?"

"Yes. That was Teddy's baby, Teddy Jr."

"Right. The organization won't even bother with most children from a pair of citizens. The TSR is way too low. There are some cases where both parents are citizens, but the father is either not known for sure, or the father leaves before the birth of the child. In these cases, the TSR is still only 2.6%, and that's still not worth the effort. In a few special cases, however, the organization will not only go after the child of a pair of citizens, but do so with significant enthusiasm. These are what they call 'Children of Special Circumstance,' or 'CSCs.' In these cases, the child must be conceived under extremely unusual circumstances, usually something that goes against legal or societal mores. The more immoral, the better for the organization. Although the TSR for these CSCs is only 6.4%, the potential of these individuals being trained into one of the higher echelons of the organizations, like Councillors or Provosts, is extremely high. The organization goes after these children, but usually only as secondary targets. They will almost always require that a primary target be in place so the effort is not totally wasted if the CSC doesn't work out. Do you know anyone who may be a secondary target in Boyston?"

Gabe felt the drip of perspiration on his collar and his face radiated heat like it was on fire. The full impact of his moral slippage with Wanna hit him like an unblocked linebacker. He wanted to tell the priest about it but his mouth wouldn't form the words. He wanted to ask if that was why Thibideaux hadn't killed him before, and to ask for forgiveness, but he couldn't muster the courage. Shame weighed on him like a wall of bricks and all he could do was keep silent. The father's retreat from reality began to make some sense. After a long pause, he answered, "No."

Father Costello fingered the corner of one of the pages in front of him. "The chance of a cross between a citizen and a Triple O reaching either the Councillor or Provost levels of training is virtually nil—let's see . . . it's 0.02 percent—so the organization considers the

CSCs to be worth the effort. If they didn't have the potential of being trained into the higher levels, the organization wouldn't bother with them either." Father Costello stared at Gabe. "Are you okay? Do you want to take a break?"

"I think I need to go to the bathroom for a minute. I'll be right back."

Gabe struggled to his feet. He felt dizzy and nauseous, so he ambled out of the day room and into the adjacent bathroom and splashed water on his face. It seemed the whole Thibideaux situation was centered on him and his family. Replacing his emotional devastation with resolve was proving to be a tough battle. A few laps around the bathroom helped him garner enough control to re-enter the day room.

"Okay, Father. I'm ready to keep going. I just can't get off the seventeen percent success thing. How does the organization keep going with that low success rate?"

"That's the evil beauty of the organization," Father Costello said, a sad smile on his face. "It's not the successful recruits that are important. It's the failures. The Triple O's. They go back into society as liars and cheats and the like. The worst ones are murderers and rapists and thieves, but the majority of them just blend in with all of us. The organization's new emphasis, at least as of twenty-five years ago, was to return Triple O's into what they called 'professional jobs.' These are the bankers, the lawyers, the doctors, the businessmen, things like that. Hughes said they were going to be the invisible crime force of the upcoming century, lying and cheating in subtle ways from inside corporations and businesses."

"Yeah. I think I ran into two of them earlier this afternoon."

"Listen carefully, Gabe. The real beauty of this organization, if it can be called beauty, is that the seventeen percent TSR for Recruiters is just enough to produce an exponential increase in the number of Triple O's. Do you know what I mean by exponential increase?"

"I can draw it." He reached across the table and took the father's pencil. The rough graph had a line that started close to the origin, parallel to the horizontal axis, and arced upward until it was nearly parallel with the vertical axis. He tapped the pencil on the beginning of the line. "Down here, a small increase in the number on the horizontal bar gives a small increase in the number on the vertical bar." He moved the pencil point to the far end of the line. "But out here, a small increase in the horizontal number gives a huge increase in the vertical. How'd I do?"

"Perfect. So, all it takes is a modest increase in the number of recruiters to get a large increase in the number of Triple O's. The low TSR ensures two things: the majority of recruits go back into society as Triple O's, and there will be an ever increasing number of recruiters to bring in more babies. But that's only part of the story. Hughes explained that the Triple O's are the most important people in the plan, and their job is only indirect. Through their lying and cheating, their drug addictions and homelessness, their professional crime, as Hughes called it, and their subtle anti-social behavior, they undermine the confidence of the regular people. Their job is to create a feeling of distrust and fear, so average people have to lock their doors, even when they're home. He predicted that most people would actually put burglar alarms in their houses, like they have at banks. He said people would become more selfish and stick to themselves, that they would live in neighborhoods of houses but never get to know their neighbors because they would be distrustful of anyone but their own family and immediate circle of friends. When this happened, he predicted the divorce rate would go way up and that millions of children would grow up without the influence of two parents. He predicted that these children would not only perpetuate the selfishness and isolation of their parents, but exaggerate it."

The priest wiped his forehead with the back of his hand. "Also, the appearance of violent and sexual acts would increase in the entertainment industry and be accepted by this disjointed public, and this would spill over into everyday life. Using foul language would become acceptable in ordinary speech and behavior, and people would get hardened to seeing violence and sex, not only on television and in movies, but also in real life." Father Costello took a deep breath.

"I can remember his very words. He said evening television shows, like *I Love Lucy*, would have either a violent or sexual story, if you can imagine that. When this happened, average people would become more violent, so a drive down the road would become a dangerous thing. People would be so nervous, a small thing like taking someone's parking space would end in violence."

Gabe covered his mouth with his open left hand and shook his head. Father Costello continued.

"Here's the worst. In business and political worlds, success would be the only measure of value, and no one would care how that success was achieved. Money and power would be the driving force, and much more important than ethics and civility. On his organization's graphs, he showed me how they used measures like a 'citizen fear index,' a 'citizen violence index,' and a 'citizen civility index." Things like that. Tell me, Gabe. Are any of his predictions coming true? I haven't been in touch with the goings on of the world for some time. Please tell me they aren't true."

"Not around Boyston," Gabe said. "People don't lock their doors when they're home, or even when they step out for a spell. If these are the goals of the organization, it's not doing a very good job."

"Well, remember, these are exponential functions." The father's voice was still cautious. "Hughes bragged that in about two or three decades the curve would be at the critical inflection point where it changes from the shallow slope to the steep one. That was twenty-five years ago. This could just be the beginning."

Gabe felt the hesitation of fear, but also the intrigue of curiosity. "What happens then?"

Father Costello sat back in his chair. "Hughes became much more philosophical when he discussed where it would lead. He claimed that when the exponential reached the steep part of the curve, society would begin to implode."

"What'd he mean by that?"

"In a way, he meant it would unravel from the inside. People would stop paying attention to laws, first the little ones, then the big ones. Eventually, the police and legal systems wouldn't be able to keep up with the lawbreakers, so people would start enforcing their own laws. Then, the military would be brought in to help, and that would start riots and other forms of large-scale civil disobedience, and finally the whole system would collapse. The country would become vulnerable to attack by other countries, and warfare would result. He cited the fall of several societies, like the Greeks, Romans, and Mayans, as evidence that his organization's system works. He was so proud of the overall plan, he kept referring to it as 'the logic of evil.' He said people expect evil to be random and emotional—without reason. His organization is exactly the opposite. Everything is based on calm logic and statistics, and emotion is supposed to be totally removed from its actions."

Gabe ran his fingers through his hair and exhaled through pursed lips. "But I still don't see why they'd want to do all this stuff?"

Father Costello shrugged his shoulders. "A lot can be made from chaos, both politically and financially."

"Damn. You think all this is happening now? Seems a bit far fetched to me." A feeling of panic swept Gabe's torso. His mind jumped back to the strange gas station he visited on his first trip to Chicago. The liberal use of the middle finger. The man begging for change and the monitors in the convenience markets.

Recent events from the news came up: a U.S. President who lied about extramarital sex, officials at major corporations who fleeced shareholders and lied about it. More examples flew to the front row of his consciousness, but he stopped the parade by slamming his hand down on the table.

Father Costello jumped. "Something wrong?"

"No. My mind's just playing tricks on me." He rolled his head around, stretching his neck, and he caught movement out of the corner of his eye. The faces of Doctors Ewing and Freedman peered in through the glass pane of the day room door.

"It's them two doctors who kept me from coming up earlier," Gabe said. "I'll go give them a piece of my mind."

"No. Let me handle this." Father Costello pushed his chair back and stood up. "Excuse me."

The priest slipped into the hall and closed the door behind him. Gabe could hear him speak, but he couldn't make out the words. But he could tell it was a one-way conversation. When the door opened again, he saw the two doctors rushing to the elevator. Whatever he said to them sure got their attention.

Father Costello walked to the table, but instead of sitting, he stood next to the window and stared out. Gabe pushed his chair over so he could see as well, and within a short time, the two young doctors rushed out of the building, climbed into a red BMW, and sped away. With their departure, Father Costello sat down.

"Now, where were we?"

"I got a question," Gabe said. "You sure Deena Lee's baby's the one Thibideaux wants, and not some other one, like Teddy's?"

"I don't know this Teddy you refer to. Is he happily married? Is he religious?"

"Yeah. Teddy Jr. was just baptized. Thibideaux was there."

"Like I said before, if a child comes from a stable family, the percentage of successful training by Hughes' organization is too low. They need around seventeen percent to maintain the exponential trajectory of their program. Also, with a stable family background, even for just the first few months of a child's life, the ones that fail in their training don't make good Triple O's. They come back into society as normal citizens and don't cause trouble. Hughes actually showed me another graph that plotted 'individual training success potential' against what he called 'Triple O potential.' The relationship was linear. The greater the training potential, the better Triple O the ones who fail turn out to be. So, Teddy's child would be a total waste of time for the organization. If they invested time in him, the odds are he would fail training. Then he would go out and be useless to them because he wouldn't be a functional Triple O. As far as Deena Lee's child, my guess is that the father of her child was a Triple O. You see, one group of children with both a high success rate for training and a high Triple O potential come from one parent who is a Triple O and one who is not. That's why they are targeted by the organization.

Gabe was angry he couldn't open even a slim possibility that Cory Dean was safe. And he was still disturbed by the baby thing. "Why babies?"

Father Costello looked up from his notes and seemed to stare right through Gabe. "I remember Hughes' explanation really well. He cited specific statistics, but I've given you enough numbers for now. It seems children are most vulnerable to being taken for a brief period in their early lives. They can't be taken while they are totally dependent on their mothers, although to the organization, this includes only the first few weeks or months of life—usually until they are weaned. Even for the organization, the mother-child bond is important to establish or the individual will not acknowledge the authority of the organization, or of any organization for that matter. Taking them too early results in an extremely low TSR. Also, the children must be taken before they are of school age, around five years old."

"Why's that?" Gabe said.

Father Costello continued to stare beyond Gabe. "The way Hughes explained it to me, from birth through the beginning of school, knowledge is gained at an alarming rate. Young children are like sponges. They absorb everything. The organization wants to get them in this period so their training potential is maximized. But this is also the age of innocence. Their experiences are usually limited to those of family and immediate surroundings. As experiences are gained outside of the immediate family circle, there is also loss of innocence. In other words, they become exposed to outside influences that are both good and bad. Through these experiences, the children develop wisdom, but increased wisdom and loss of innocence go hand-in-hand. Hughes said the training potential of children who have reached this trade-off point drops precipitously because the balance between gained wisdom and loss of innocence is too variable, and impossible to predict. Now, if you put all of this together, the best time to take the children is when they are the youngest. That way, the organization will be all they ever know. They will have no memories earlier than those of the organization. It will be their emotional anchor."

A crowd had gathered in the hallway outside the day room, all spectators clad in the white uniforms of nurses and orderlies. One of the men opened the door and entered, carrying a metal meal tray in each hand. He slid a tray in front of Father Costello, watching his reaction. He placed the other in front of Gabe.

"How about a snack?" the orderly said. "We thought you'd be getting hungry since you didn't get much at lunch."

Father Costello smiled. "Thank you."

The orderly's eyes widened and he gave a broad smile. "You're welcome, and welcome back."

"Thank you kindly." Gabe's politeness was ignored.

Father Costello turned to the gathering crowd and gave a backward flip of his right wrist. The observers immediately dispersed from the hallway. Gabe waited until they were all gone before he forwarded his next question.

"What can we do to stop Thibideaux from taking Cory Dean? He and his momma are both special to me."

Father Costello's expression turned pensive. "Hughes inadvertently gave me some hints about that when he was bragging to me. It all centers on baptisms. He can't take the children after they are baptized, no matter how young or old they are. Baptism significantly drops both TSR and Triple O potential of children. So there is a small window of opportunity for Hughes, between the first sign of independence from the child's mother and the baptism. Also, he can't take a child unless one of the parents offers the child voluntarily. That's why having a Triple O for a parent is so important. In a situation like Deena Lee's, the Triple O parent is not around, so the baptism is the prime time to get the child. You see, in most baptism ceremonies, the mother passes the child off to the godparents. At that moment, the mother has intentionally given the child to the care of another, not just the body, but the soul as well. This is different than transferring the care of the child to a babysitter or teacher. Hughes really liked the symbolism of the baptism transfer. Anyway, at the time of transfer, Hughes makes something in the church fall on the mother, to either kill her or cause her to be severely injured. That stops the ceremony, and in all the confusion, he snatches the baby and is off with his prize. He claimed he came up with the technique, and that it was extremely successful."

Gabe pinched the bridge of his nose and closed his eyes tight. "Why don't he just kill the parents straight away and take the baby?" He dropped his hand to the table and opened his eyes.

Father Costello thumbed through one of the stacks of papers in front of him. "They have specific rules about killing people. They have to maintain a low profile in society, so none of their people are allowed to kill a citizen directly. They have to do it indirectly, like causing something to fall on the person. So they always have a chance to escape."

"Or like with lightning, or an earthquake, or falling rocks?"

Father Costello frowned. "Yes, if the recruiter had the power to make those happen. But the rules are specific on a few other points. Let's see . . . oh, yes. Here we are. They're not allowed to kill religious people under any circumstances." He looked up from the papers. "That's why I'm here. And they're not allowed to kill children before they're of school age. To take them during the age of innocence draws too much attention to the recruiters and the organization."

"Wait a minute, Father." Gabe was excited. "That last part. I think I have something there. If I recall correctly, everyone in Press' family was killed except his daughter. She was three or four. They was killed by lightning. And the family that was killed by an earthquake—all killed except a daughter, also three or four. That fit with what you're saying?"

Father Costello nodded. "That would fit."

"Hold on." Gabe's excitement faded as quickly as it had come on. "It's not all good. Another family was killed by a twister. All dead, including a young one under five. That screws up the whole thing."

"Was there anything unusual about that last family? Were they religious?"

Gabe thought for a few seconds. "Now that you mention it, they never came to church. They kept to themselves. People had it they was non-believers. That make a difference?"

"All the difference in the world," Father Costello said with a smile. "The one exception to the under five rule is if the family is atheist or agnostic. They don't bother to spare those children. Kind of ironic, I think. And they're not interested in them as recruits for training. For some reason, their TSR is dismal. I can find the number if you want it."

"That's okay, Father." Gabe held his hands up in a double stop sign. "No more numbers." He slapped his palms flat on the table. "So you're saying Thibideaux's going to snatch Cory Dean when Deena Lee hands him off to Teddy's wife—she's the godmother. And then Thibideaux'll bring harm to Deena Lee? How about if Deena Lee doesn't give Cory Dean up during the ceremony? If she just holds him through it. Thibideaux can't get the baby, right?"

"Sorry, but that won't do it. Even if she doesn't give up the child physically, she does it symbolically. She agrees to give the child's soul to another, and not just to the godparents, but to God—that's the main theme of the ceremony. That's when Hughes steps in—when the child's soul is given, but before the ceremony is complete. That's what excites him about the plan. He said it feels like he's snatching the child from the very hands of God. Besides, if Deena Lee holds the child while Hughes pulls off his trick, there's a chance the child will be hurt as well."

"Maybe we shouldn't have the baby baptized," Gabe said in frustration.

Father Costello straightened in his chair. "No, that would be worse. There are many other ways to get a child before school age. If you can get through the baptism, the child will be protected from apprehension. You need to find some way to prevent Hughes from getting the child at the baptism."

"How can I do that? You got all this information, but no ideas?"

Father Costello's looked down at the notes and shook his head. "I'm afraid I don't have an answer to that one. It's something you'll have to think of. Hughes seemed to think the system was infallible."

"So you can't give me any more help on this?" Gabe said, nearly pleading.

"Sorry Gabe. I didn't come out on top in my experience with Hughes, so I can't give any definitive hints."

Gabe felt sick. All his information, but no solution. On the other hand, there had to be some answer in there. He'd just have to think about it for a while. But another matter edged into his mind.

"While I'm here, Father, I have one more question for you."

"What's that?"

Gabe adjusted his position in his chair so he could comfortably lean forward with his elbows on the table.

"What'd you do to get involved with Thibideaux, or Hughes, and make you keep quiet for all this time?"

The priest seemed to experience a wave of recognition, then resignation. "I guess it's part of my penance to explain it to you. Please don't think less of me. Try to see the higher goals of my actions."

"I'm not sure what you mean, but I'll try to see it your way."

"Thank you." Father Costello looked down at his hands, and his shoulders slumped. He took a long breath and let it out slowly. His eyes stayed on his hands. "I became involved with Hughes because of something I did, which was a moral failure on my part." He paused again. "I became romantically involved with a young girl from Rother County. She was only sixteen at the time and she became pregnant with my child."

Gabe's eyes opened wide and he leaned farther forward. "So you do have a child?"

"Let me finish, Gabe. This is very difficult for me." Father Costello seemed to be getting smaller. He took another long breath. "I wasn't Hughes' primary target. But when he found out about us, he recognized what a great prize my child would be to the organization. You see, the mother wasn't a Triple O. My child became a highly significant secondary target for Hughes and his organization—a CSC with a Priest for a father was a trophy of the highest priority.

Gabe wasn't sure how to react. Priests were human, but they weren't supposed to do that kind of thing. But even that didn't justify Thibideaux trying to swipe the child. He felt a light twinge in his abdomen. He pictured a grown Cory Dean, snatching babies for Thibideaux's organization.

"When the baby was born, and still in the hospital with the mother, Hughes came to me and told me most of the information I have relayed to you today. I guess he couldn't resist rubbing it in. He also gave me a warning. He told me he could detect a baptism from tens of miles, so I wouldn't be able to baptize the child in the hospital and avoid his plan for apprehension of the baby. He also told me that once a baby was born, he could detect its heartbeat, so there was no way I could sneak the baby out of the hospital without him knowing it. He told me I would just have to accept the fact that my daughter would become a high-ranking member of his organization. He viewed it as the ultimate irony." Father Costello took another deep breath, but didn't let it out right away. "I couldn't allow my child to be used that way, so I had to find a way to defeat Hughes regardless of how drastic the method."

The priest paused.

To Gabe, he seemed so emotional he was having trouble getting the words out. With each sentence he slumping more and more into his chair. "You needing some water or something?"

Father Costello put up his hand. "No. Let me continue. I have to explain this." He took in several shallow breaths. "I just couldn't let my child be raised into that situation. I had to do something for my daughter and for our society, so I had to do the unthinkable." A tear ran down his cheek, then one on the other. "I talked the baby's mother into giving her up for adoption one night. I told her I had it all arranged and it would be best if I took her to her new parents right away. I had all the hospital forms signed, although I forged them." The priest wiped his cheeks with his with his fingers. He lowered his face inches from the table. "I took my daughter into a mainte-nance closet and covered her head with a pillow until she was no longer breathing. It was the only way out. I had to do it." Father Costello sobbed. He crossed his arms on the table and his head fell forward onto his forearms.

A feeling of horror and disgust turned outward from Gabe's gut. He was in a state of shock. There wasn't a single reason for ever killing a child, especially one's own. But he wasn't a priest, and he wasn't faced with the situation that faced the father. And, he did agree to try to see it the father's way. He couldn't look straight at the priest.

Father Costello raised his head from his arms, but he still looked down at the table. He cleared his throat. "I took her body to the church so I could give her a proper burial. I had already defeated Hughes, but I had to stand before God and confess. And, I had to do the best I could for my child's poor innocent soul. That's when Hughes caught up to me. When he saw what I'd done, he was furious."

The priest paused and tried to regain some of his composure.

Gabe sat in silence, still in shock.

Father Costello removed a handkerchief from his coat pocket and wiped his eyes and cheeks. It looked like the father's body had just sprung a leak and his life force was slowly seeping from him. He seemed to be dying right there in the chair.

In a quick move, Father Costello looked up, directly into Gabe's eyes, and Gabe recoiled. The father's words came out as a warning.

"You're dealing with an extremely intelligent man. And he's as evil as he is intelligent. He proved it that night." His eyes dropped from Gabe's face and returned to the table. His voice faded. "He proved it that night."

Gabe reached out to place a comforting touch on Father Costello's arm, but he pulled away. Gabe leaned a little closer. "Father, are you all right?"

Father Costello sobbed again. In a voice so quiet Gabe could barely hear it, he uttered single sentences between sobs.

"He made me sit in a chair right there in the church . . . I couldn't move . . . He didn't tie me up, I just couldn't move . . . He had a bag . . . with two lambs, a small dog, and a cat . . . He slaughtered the animals and spread their parts around the church . . . Then he took my daughter's body . . ." His head jerked upward, his eyes wild. His mouth moved in silence, then his voice came, loud. "You were there. In the inhouse. Weren't you?"

Memories swirled in Gabe's head. The inhouse. The little man with the strange smile. Toes . . . he thought he saw toes. Gabe snuffled back a sob and wrung his hands. He didn't know what to do. Was his connection with Thibideaux and Father Costello sealed back then? Twenty-five years ago? He was just a young boy.

Gabe's mind came back to the day room. He wanted to comfort the priest. His shock and horror turned to a nearly overwhelming feeling of sorrow. Standing in the father's shoes, he could see Thibide-aux's evil grin. A lump formed in his throat and his eyes welled with tears. He couldn't hold them back this time. He lowered his head closer to the level of Father Costello's. "Father, you don't have to go on."

Through his sobs, and without raising his head from his arms, the priest said, "Yes, I do. I have to. It's my penance. I knew you had a reason to come here—to bring me out of my prison. But what I didn't realize was I had a reason to come out to talk with you. I have to finish so I can return to my now-strength-ened insanity."

Gabe's sadness was compounded by the news the priest was going back. He sat in silence until Father Costello could speak again.

After a few minutes, the father's sobs faded into occasional whimpers. He raised his head a little and spoke in a whisper.

"After Hughes slaughtered the animals, he took my daughter's body and did the same with it. He made me watch him. I tried to close my eyes, but I couldn't—he wouldn't let me. He cut her little body into such small pieces it was impossible to recognize them as human, and then he mixed them up with all the animal parts. He arranged them all as if there was some sort of ritu-alistic sacrifice—you saw it—and then he covered me with blood. The blood of my daughter. I tried to get up, but I couldn't. I was paralyzed. I couldn't move my legs. He made me sit there until the town people came in to worship. They found me sitting among all the remains, covered with blood." He paused without moving, then raised his head and looked at the ceiling. "Father, forgive me. I'm a sinner in repentance before you. Father, forgive me." His head collapsed back onto his arms and he wept.

Anger pierced Gabe's emotional armor. The shock and disgust were no longer directed at the priest. He tried to place a hand on Father Costello's arm, but the priest pulled away again.

From the cover of his arms, his voice was firm. "Please don't try to comfort me. I don't deserve any comforts in this world." He peered upward. "Gabe, I'd like to ask you two favors before you leave, and before I go back to my prison. First, please don't ever come back here again, and don't send anyone else. I don't want visitors and I don't want to be cured. I've given you all of my information because it has renewed my shame and regret, which I need to continue to suffer through this life I've made so miserable.

"Second, keep the drawing of Hughes. When the situation with Cory Dean has been resolved, one way or the other, send the picture back to me with instructions for a member of the staff to hold it in front of my face, just like you did today. If Hughes wins, send it just as it is now. If you manage to defeat his plan, place a large red X through his face. That way, I'll at least have the satisfaction of knowing he was outsmarted again, or the distaste of knowing he's still at his craft."

Father Costello paused. "Gabe, I want to thank you for coming all this way. I hope I've been of some help. You've given me an opportunity to further pay for my deeds, which I appreciate. Now, I have to return these lucid moments to the past and pay my debt to the future." He turned in his chair and settled his gaze out of the window. And retreated from reality.

Gabe stared. His heart gave an extra beat, then a pause. "Thibideaux," he said out loud. "He took your future and my past on that morning. And now he's trying to take my future."

It was nearly five in the afternoon when Gabe made his way to the elevator. The ride to the ground floor seemed to take forever. As he crutched past the reception desk, a high-pitched voice interrupted his depression. Gabe didn't recognize it.

"Excuse me. Catherine wanted me to congratulate you for bringing Father Costello out of his silence. You've done what no doctor has been able to do for more than twenty years."

Gabe didn't turn his head. "Don't thank me. He was here for only a little bit. Now, he's back where he wants to be. I doubt he'll talk again until he passes." He didn't wait for a reaction. Even if there was one, he wouldn't have heard it. He just ambled out toward the parking lot to head home.

Just outside the front doors, he met Doctors Ewing

and Freedman, who were hurrying into the building, each carrying a heavy box full of something Gabe couldn't see. Doctor Ewing nearly bumped into him on the way past as Doctor Freedman announced his approach, the arrogance thick.

"Get out of the way. We have to get these to Father Costello right away."

Gabe swiveled the crutches toward Wes' truck and let out a loud belly laugh. "A wild goose chase," he said to the row of empty cars. "Good one, Father."

He pulled himself behind the wheel of the truck and his mind turned to the matter at hand. The drive home would allow him time to think about a way to use the father's information. There had to be a plan in there somewhere. If nothing else, the thinking would keep him alert and pass the time.

CHAPTER 53

GABE DIRECTED WES' truck toward the freeway and headed south. Once clear of the crowded roadways of the Chicago area, he welcomed a newfound energy, driven by a mind that was ripe for commanding a solution to the Thibideaux problem. Over and over again, he ran through everything Father Costello had told him. He knew there was a weakness somewhere in Thibideaux's plan. He just had to find it.

With his mind working in overdrive, Gabe had to occasionally redirect his attention to keep his driving speed down. Twice he looked down to see he was gong more than eighty-five miles per hour. Ordinarily, he would have lost his mental edge to fatigue around eight or nine in the evening, but his mind churned over the Father's information at such a rapid rate, time flew by without a single downward head bob.

A road sign with mileage to several cities caught his attention. He wondered how he had managed to drive so far without it registering in his consciousness. Was there such a thing as sleep driving? Everyone drove through a green light and then wondered if it was really green, he thought. Same thing. If there were such a thing, the Guinness Book of World Records would have an entry. Maybe he had advanced the record.

Gabe's mind found a crack and followed it. It led to a fracture, then a chasm—a potential idea for dealing with Thibideaux. He looked at his watch. It was two in the morning. He leaned up in the seat, energized. There would be no nodding off at the wheel for now.

He spent the next two hours in frontal lobe gymnastics, running through all of the various possible outcomes for his putative solution, like a chess player considering all potential scenarios radiating from a single move before advancing a game piece. When his abstract evaluation was complete, he nodded his head and patted the steering wheel. Got an outside chance of success. But I'll need some help.

The elation over his discovery of a possible chink in Thibideaux's armor, together with his repetitive imaginary rehearsal of the plan, held the advancing fatigue at bay until the sky changed from the deep purple of night to a royal blue that signaled the impending breech of the horizon by the sun. It was a little before six and Gabe estimated he was about two hours from home.

The last two hours of the trip were pure agony—a mental back-and-forth tennis match between consciousness and sleep. Unfortunately, the fatigue dulled the pain in Gabe's chest and knee so even his violent head bobs didn't trigger a twitch of pain to help him stay alert. He drove with all of the windows open wide and sang out loud to songs on the radio, whether he knew the words or not. With these tricks and a good bit of luck, he pulled up to the farmhouse a little past eight. He was welcomed by drapes that were opened by a family that was awake for the day, and the smell of bacon, eggs and coffee wafting from an open kitchen window. His fatigue had a worthy competitor in his hunger. A good meal would be a perfect springboard to sleep. He'd return Wes' truck later.

Gabe's welcome was a warm one, at least from the three residents of the farmhouse. In contrast, the welcome forwarded by the fog that enveloped the house carried a distinct chill. Gabe, Deena Lee and Wanna were conscious of the eavesdropping mist, so when Deena Lee inquired about the trip, there was no surprise by Gabe's answer.

"The trip was fine, but I hate going to the Capitol. And having to deal with taxes made it downright painful. The only good thing was Wes letting me use his truck. It really helped my knee not having to work a clutch."

The small talk was a prelude to Gabe's full day of

slumber. He didn't know when the fog dissipated. He only knew that when he awoke, at four-thirty in the afternoon, it was gone.

During his sleep, Gabe was bothered by a nightmare that had visited his pillow before, but only in incomplete snippets. This time, however, he got the full tour.

He was surrounded by a billowing mist so vast he was dwarfed by its volume, and its density was so high only a dim light was available to gauge his surroundings, which seemed bare. But he didn't feel fear. Instead, he had a churning sense of insignificance that made him feel smaller and smaller as the fog billowed around him. That had been the extent of the dreams until today.

In the latest edition, the mist began to clear overhead. He looked up. A vague outline of a face stared down at him. The haze continued to clear, and he saw the outline of a head, although the facial features were still indistinct, shadowy. With time, the features came more into focus, but his brain was slow to recognize them. He expected to see the uniquely distorted features of Thibideaux staring down at him, but they were different, overtly normal. Since the identity of the apparition was unexpected, it took longer than it should have for Gabe to recognize it. It was . . . his own face.

But something wasn't right with it. Instead of the quiet confidence and kind countenance he usually saw in the mirror, the expression on the face above him was decidedly different. The look in its eyes was not one of truthfulness, but lies. The turns at the corners of its mouth didn't speak of responsibility, but shouted deceit.

Gabe felt even more insignificant. The towering face of his recent self pressed his former self into a smaller and smaller corner of his universe. He realized that for the last several months, ever since Thibideaux moved into Boyston, he was seldom totally honest with anyone. He was either telling a half-truth, hiding something, or all-out lying to one or more people. Before Thibideaux's arrival, he was always honest, sometimes brutally so, but now it seemed the lying Gabe was trying to elbow the truthful Gabe into the background.

The feeling of insignificance faded, replaced by a sense of losing control. Unfortunately, the dream was an open ended one. The face never fully cleared in his vision, and the feeling of shrinking in its presence continued unabated. There was no conclusion—no end to the shrinkage, and no way out. There was no death in the dream. It was worse. It was the curse of an eternal sensation of helplessness. Just like Father Costello.

Gabe awoke with a feeling of frustration. Not only did he remember the dream, he sensed the danger posed by the "other" Gabe and its desire to take over his personality. But he had no choice now. He had to continue the lies and deceit a little while longer. To try to defeat Thibideaux, even if the battle turned him to Thibideaux's ways. The end would justify the means. Wouldn't it?

Suppertime was subdued in the Petersen household. The farmhouse was once again shrouded in a thick fog, and little Cory Dean was preoccupied with the pain of colic. Because of his recent lack of sleep, both Deena Lee and Wanna were reduced to the quiet of fatigue, their normally sharp curiosity replaced by what seemed to be apprehension. Probably due to the prospect of yet another rough night.

After eating, Gabe excused himself and headed for the phone in the living room. He parted the drapes. The fog was there. He didn't have the luxury of relaxation—the baptism was only three days away. His first call was to Wes Worthing. He'd return the truck tomorrow morning, around eleven. Wes was glad to hear his truck, and Gabe, had returned safely. Gabe then dialed the number of Reverend Sather. As the Reverend answered, Gabe moved the curtains aside to verify the fog was still surrounding the house.

"Reverend? It's Gabe. I was wondering if I could talk with you about the baptism. I need to know if the ceremony can be changed a bit."

The Reverend's voice didn't carry its usual cheery tone. "Of course. The ceremony is flexible. I can add some things or change some things around, but I can't eliminate any of the basic components of the rite. What do you have in mind?"

Once again, Gabe glanced out the window. "It's kind of complex. I'd like to talk about it in person. Can you meet me at the Herndon's Edge for lunch tomorrow? Around eleven-thirty?"

The Reverend paused. "Eleven thirty will be fine. Is there anything I can do for you in the meantime?" He seemed to be fishing.

"No. Thank you." Gabe hurried off the phone. "I'll see you tomorrow."

Gabe and family spent the early evening watching television sit-coms, but the underlying tension in the room, coming from all corners, reduced their responses to most of the jokes to muffled titters. Deena Lee was first to excuse herself—she had to put Cory Dean down and then head directly to bed. To keep their conversation quiet, Wanna came over and sat down on the couch next to Gabe.

"Gabe, you all right? You're looking really tired. I don't suppose you want to tell me what's been going on?"

Gabe's head snapped around to the window. The fog was still there.

"I'm okay. I just got a lot on my mind right now. Give me a week or so and I'll tell you all about it. I'll know more myself in a few days. Until then, I just need you to be understanding. Can you trust me on that?"

"Does it have anything to do with taxes? We all right with the farm?"

"Yeah. That's part of it. But the farm's fine." He felt the growing insignificance of his dreams. "It should work itself out this weekend."

After Wanna went to bed, Gabe mentally regurgitated every part of his plan, once again measuring all possible outcomes. He needed to be in motion so he paced a circular path around the floor while his mind kept pace, lap for lap. He didn't go to bed until two-thirty—about the same time Cory Dean awoke crying for the third time. Which of the two men in the house was in the most pain was difficult to judge.

There was one other person in the Tri-counties who collected less sleep than Gabe, and that was Reverend Sather. With what Wes had told him, he was desperate to find out what was troubling Gabe.

CHAPTER 54

GABE PULLED INTO the Herndon's Edge parking lot at eleven fifteen. He was glad to have his old, familiar truck back, despite the pain of operating the clutch. The swelling in his knee was coming down, and with it, the discomfort was subsiding. The brace limited his mobility, but stabilized the knee so he could walk with a cane instead of the demon crutches.

Gabe blinked at the bright sky. It was clear in all directions, all the way to the horizon. He pushed through the door of the Edge and scanned the bar and booths. Reverend Sather was seated in a booth by the front window, far from any regulars at the bar. Gabe called out a generic greeting and made his way to the booth and a smiling Reverend Sather.

"Good morning, Gabe. I'm glad to see you're getting around better. I heard about your altercation.

Those people will be dealt with sooner or later." He motioned for Gabe to sit across from him.

"I'm glad about it myself," Gabe said as he lowered himself into the booth. "The crutches were hurting my armpits so bad the knee pain was nothing. You hungry? I'm buying."

Reverend Sather gave a "thank-you" nod. "Don't mind if I do. I'll have the special."

Gabe motioned to the waitress, who was half way to the booth. "Two specials, please." She was nothing like Deena Lee. About ten years older and at least thirty pounds heavier. But she had a friendly smile. Gabe's eyes followed her retreat behind the counter. Reverend Sather brought him back to the booth.

"Gabe, what is it that's bothering you about the baptism ceremony?"

Gabe didn't make eye contact. "How've things been going for you, Reverend? Any strange stuff happening around your place?"

Reverend Sather frowned. "Nothing strange has been happening to me. What kind of things are you talking about?"

Gabe peered out the window. It was still clear. "How's the missus? She still teaching that pre-school Sunday School class before service?"

Reverend Sather leaned forward and put his elbows on the table. "She's fine. Yes, she's got about seven young ones who show up regularly. She really likes the little ones. We've been trying to have one of our own, but we haven't succeeded yet. Because of that, she really dotes on them. Thank you for asking after her." He leaned a little farther forward. "Now, what was it you wanted to do for the baptism?"

Gabe looked outside again. The sun beat in through the window without a hint of fog. "I can't go into all I want to do right now. There are some things I'd like, so I wrote them down." He slid a sealed envelope across the table to the Reverend. "Take a look at this later, when you go home. But I have to ask an important favor." His look turned serious. "If there's a fog outside, don't open the letter until the fog's gone. After you read it, burn it up. And don't discuss it with the Missus if there's a fog. Make sure the sky's clear first. Can you do that?"

Reverend Sather looked out the window, then back at Gabe. "Gabe, is everything all right with you?"

Gabe looked at his watch. The minute hand clicked from eleven twenty-nine to eleven-thirty and he stiffened as a rolling mist surrounded the café— the bright light in the booth dimmed as the sun was eclipsed. Gabe watched Reverend Sather sit hard against the booth back.

Gabe paused as the waitress placed overflowing plates of food in front of the two of them, and he nodded his thanks. And waited for her to leave.

Reverend Sather looked outside again. "Gabe, what's going on here? What's with the fogs? Is there something I should know?"

Gabe noticed a hitch in the Reverend's voice. But he couldn't explain right now. He had a job to do. "Well, Reverend, I was thinking about how Deena Lee hasn't been baptized, and how she really wants to be. You think you can give her a dunking at the same time as Cory Dean? It'd be a real treat to her. I know she's talked to you about it, but I don't think we ever discussed how to do it. Can you do them both at the same time?"

Reverend Sather looked out again at the dim grayness that was a brightly lit day only moments before. He seemed confused. "Umm . . . what?" He shook hid head a little as if he were trying to clear out some thoughts that didn't belong there. "Umm . . . yes. I can do both Deena Lee and Cory Dean at the same time. Is that what you brought me here to ask?"

Gabe remained cheerful. "I wanted to make sure we worked out the change in the ceremony so it was special to both of them. Can you do Cory Dean first? You can read all the scriptures and say all the words together, but I want Cory Dean dunked first. That okay?"

Reverend Sather ignored the fog. "We don't dunk anyone. I thought you knew that. We just pour some water over their foreheads."

"It's just a figure of speech. I was at Teddy Jr.'s baptism, so I know how it goes."

The Reverend dug his fork into the mound of food on his plate, causing some to spill from the edge onto the table. The fork didn't leave the plate. "Well then, yes. I can dunk Cory Dean first. Is there anything else you want said?"

Gabe paused while he swallowed. Teddy was in good form with the special. "Can you say something about how wonderful it is for a normal baptism, but since this one's for a baby and his momma, it makes the ceremony extra special? Makes it an incredibly special day."

The Reverend's grin lasted only a moment. "I can work that thought in almost as you said it. It's really a special day for your family, and for the community. It'll be a beautiful addition. Is there anything else you want changed?"

Gabe slid his hand over toward the Reverend, keeping it on the table. He slowly extended his index finger to point at the envelope the Reverend had shoved into his left jacket pocket. He frowned and gave a slight nod toward the envelope. Without saying a word, he pulled his hand back and dug deep into the food on his plate. When he had a mouthful, he gave a wide grin to the Reverend.

Reverend Sather finished a bite and stared at Gabe. He hesitated, than spoke. "Wes told me you were acting kind of strange lately. Please tell me if there's anything I can do to help. Are you in some kind of trouble?" He looked out at the fog again.

Gabe glanced out the window and then back. "Everything's okay. I got some tax stuff to work out, but it's nothing. I just got a lot on my mind lately, with the baby and all."

Reverend Sather filled his fork. "What kind of tax problems are you having? You in danger of losing your farm? I have some contacts who can help with that sort of thing. And I'm sure our neighbors will help out."

Gabe leaned back. "Naw. The farm's in good shape. No problem there." He reflected on his good fortune with the land. His financial health was second only to Wes Worthing's. "It's more of an aggravation than a threat. It's just come at a bad time for me. It didn't help that I got jumped by those Rother fellows. Thanks for the offer, but I'll get it all cleared up in the next few days." Gabe returned his attention to his plate of food. His next revelation was more for himself than for the Reverend. "I know I ain't been myself lately, but it'll all change soon enough."

For the next fifteen minutes, Gabe and the Reverend engaged in small talk about their families and the Tri-counties as Gabe cleared his plate of any traces of Teddy's special. The Reverend managed to down a few bites, but he mostly redistributed the piles of food on his plate.

Gabe slipped a few bills under his plate and stood to leave. He extended his huge hand to the Reverend, who returned the handshake with vigor. "Thank you for hearing me out on the ceremony. I appreciate your willingness to change it a little." He slid his eyes down to the envelope projecting from the Reverend's coat pocket and then smiled. "I'll be in touch again about it to make sure we're on the same page."

Reverend Sather watched Gabe walk to his truck and start it up. He thought he detected an increase in the light level. As Gabe drove away, the sky cleared to a bright blue, and the Reverend had to squint to follow the pickup down the road. The fog bank moved along with the truck.

The reverend's hand shook as he pulled the envelope from his pocket and laid it flat on the table. He turned it over. There was writing on the sealing flap, so small he had to bend his head close to read it. "Don't open if there's a fog around. Burn this after you read it."

Leaning over so his forehead nearly touched the window, he looked in all directions—no fog. He sat back, slid his finger under the envelope flap, and slowly pulled out the letter. He squinted at the handwritten message.

He re-folded the letter and returned it to the envelope, bent the envelope in the middle, and pushed it into his pocket. He would burn it as soon as he got home. His thoughts turned to Gabe. Must be in some kind of trouble, he thought. But now, he had second thoughts about getting involved.

CHAPTER 55

THE NIGHT BEFORE the baptism, Gabe's dream returned in its entirety. Once again, he sensed the old Gabe, the good Gabe, was being pushed further and further into insignificance by the new Gabe. His inability to change the dream, or end it, triggered a burgeoning panic and he bolted upright in his bed, his bedclothes soaked in sweat. To keep from waking Deena Lee, he deliberately swung out of bed and retired to the living room where he half-reclined on the couch, both waiting for and dreading the break of day. It was Sunday, the day of the greatest battle of his life.

Thibideaux paced in the great room of the rectory. He

found the impending procurement both invigorating and stressful. This time, however, his planning extended beyond the immediate business with Deena Lee's child. He had begun to formulate plans for the acquisition of his secondary target in Boyston, the Child of Special Circumstance—Gabe and Wanna's baby.

This would be his seventy-ninth CSC procurement—he had seventy-seven successes with only one failure. Was that a record for the Organization? He knew he was one of the oldest Recruiters in North America. After all, he was born in 1784 and had begun serving the Organization upon completion of his training and internships in 1801. Long ago, he had lost count of his successful acquisitions of primary targets. How many of his seventy-seven CSCs ended up as Councillors, and how many made it to the Provost level?

He loved the prospect of procuring a CSC, and actually envisioned himself as a former CSC. He rationalized his low level in the Organization as due to his physical appearance, which was well outside of the normal limits of the ideal phenotype. How else could he be allowed to go into the field with such severe physical limitations unless he was a CSC? And, how could his special powers be explained? He knew, early on in his training, that his abilities were well in excess of those of his fellow trainees. On more than one occasion, he was able to shock the Councillors with his powers. He remembered, with pride, how he was allowed to give a demonstration of his abilities to a panel of Provosts on his sixteenth birthday. That led to his early graduation and his first internship. One more time he would repay the Organization with a CSC dividend, for supporting him despite his physical shortcomings.

As the sun topped the horizon to the East, the two generals independently prepared for battle. Both checked and re-checked their plans to make sure no detail was left dangling—no flank was left exposed. Time was now listed among the enemies for the two. For one, it moved way too slow. For the other, it passed much too quickly.

CHAPTER 56

GABE FIDGETED IN the pew. The service passed in an instant and the hymns were sung in double time. He hadn't heard a word of Reverend Sather's sermon—it seemed like the words were strung together in a quickened gibberish.

Before Gabe knew it, Reverend Sather announced to the congregation that the baptism of Cory Dean and Deena Lee Petersen would take place immediately following the benediction, and that all were invited to remain for the special occasion. Gabe's mind searched for comfort.

The organ music brought his full attention back to the church, and a single drop of perspiration released from his forehead and streamed to the bridge of his nose. He yawned, bowed his head, wiped the drip, and looked around to see if anyone noticed. The church was full, everyone's eyes were on Reverend Sather.

Gabe noticed a familiar, small figure slip into the church and stand in the back, along the wall to the right.

Reverend Sather walked to the baptismal fount, on the extreme right of the altar, and invited Gabe, Deena Lee, Cory Dean, and Cory Dean's godparents, Teddy and Rachel Rosewald, to join him. They surrounded the fount in a semi-circle, facing the congregation.

Gabe looked to the back of the church. Thibideaux slowly paced back-and-forth, three shuffling steps in each direction. His hands hung straight at his sides, but his fingers were in constant motion, flexing and extending in unison. His gaze was fixed on the altar and had the intensity of a lioness in the final stalk of prey.

Reverend Sather took out a hymnal and addressed the congregation. "Please turn to hymn number thirty-six in your hymnal and join us in singing, "Jesus Loves Me."

The congregation erupted in song, and Gabe looked back at Thibideaux again. The little man scanned the altar, and Gabe imagined him verifying the layout, planning his abduction.

At the conclusion of the song, Reverend Sather exchanged the hymnal for a Bible, and opened it to a page marked by a red ribbon. "Mark 10: 13-16 says, And they were bringing children to Him so that He might touch them; and the disciples rebuked them. But when Jesus saw this, He was indignant and said to them, 'Permit the children to come to Me; do not hinder them, for the kingdom of God belongs to such as these. Truly I say to you whoever does not receive the kingdom of God like a child shall not enter at all.' And He took them in His arms and began blessing them, laying His hands upon them."

With the reading of the scripture, Gabe felt a sense of clarity sweep over him. He was always uplifted by his worship, but this sensation was different. The feelings of insignificance and hopelessness were easing with the return of self-control. In contrast to the preceding church service, Gabe not only heard every word Reverend Sather said, he focused on them, savoring their meaning. In a way, this was more than a double-baptism. Gabe felt like he was being cleansed and re-dedicated as well.

Reverend Sather placed the Bible down on the fount and bowed his head. "Dearly beloved, the family is a divine institution ordained of God from the beginning of time. Children are a heritage of the Lord committed by Him to their parents for care, protection, and training in His glory. It is important that all parents recognize this sacred obligation and their responsibility to God in this matter."

CHAPTER 57

THIBIDEAUX LISTENED TO the words of the Reverend, and he was struck by how they all made sense, as long as he substituted "the Organization" for every reference to "God" or "family." Then, he broke his concentration on the ceremony and visually homed in on a statuette of John the Baptist placed in a small alcove above the baptismal fount. He mentally rehearsed his plan. He would create a small temblor throughout the church—just enough to steal the attention of the congregation and create a sense of confusion. The statuette would rock with the motion. As Deena Lee presented Cory Dean to Teddy and Rachel, the statuette would fall on Deena Lee, and the procurement would be on. He was ready to unleash the plan as soon as Cory Dean was clear of Deena Lee's arms.

Reverend Sather looked up at the congregation

and smiled. "These parents, recognizing the sacredness of their charge, now bring back to the Lord the treasure which He has entrusted to them. In so doing, they publicly acknowledge their responsibility for the nurture and admonition of this child in the ways of righteousness and godliness."

Thibideaux's hands twitched uncontrollably now, and he slightly hunched at the shoulders. He was pure sinew and muscle, ready to pounce on his prey. He felt the rush of adrenaline, and he relished it. He had memorized every part of the ceremony when he had attended Teddy Jr.'s baptism. It was time for his prize. His focus was jarred when Reverend Sather walked around to the center of the altar and addressed the congregation.

"Gabe and Deena Lee want to add to the joy of this special occasion by inviting members of the congregation to participate."

Thibideaux took two steps toward the altar before he realized what he was doing. Something wasn't right; there was no way he could do anything until he saw what the Reverend was going to do.

Reverend Sather continued. "Since this is a special event for the children, Gabe would like to invite the young children to participate in the ceremony. Would all of the children in the pre-school Sunday School class please come forward?"

Thibideaux felt a wave of panic sweep over his body. What was Gabe up to?

"And I would like to invite some of the older children up as well."

As seven members of Mrs. Sather's Sunday School class and six other children came forward, Gabe directed them to surround the fount, with Deena Lee, Cory Dean, and the Rosewalds within the circle. The three youngest children were positioned close to Deena Lee. As the circle formed, Reverend Sather entered it and proceeded with the ceremony.

Thibideaux's lips curled into a snarl that revealed silver capped teeth. He scanned the altar, trying to salvage an attack that would achieve his goal but spare injury to any of the young children. He was distracted when Gabe instructed Deena Lee to kneel, with Cory Dean in her arms and pulled the children closer around her. As Thibideaux ran through possible modifications of his plan, Reverend Sather continued the ceremony, addressing the adults at the fount.

"As you bring Cory Dean Petersen here today to be baptized, do you solemnly promise before God and these witnesses that you will, with God's help and guidance, undertake to bring this little one up in the sacred and holy faith, making use of all the help God has given you in the family, and in the church?"

Gabe, Deena Lee, Teddy, and Rachel answered in unison, "We do."

Thibideaux pointed at the floor with his right hand and shook it slowly. The floor began to vibrate at a low frequency, below the limits of human hearing. so subtle several people fidgeted in their pews.

As Deena Lee handed Cory Dean to Rachel, who was now kneeling as well, a passage from his training reverberated in Thibideaux's head: "Children under five years of age shall not be harmed." He instinctively withdrew his hand to stop the temblor.

Reverend Sather dipped his hand into the baptismal water, and Thibideaux stomped his right foot on the floor hard enough to cause two people in the last pew to turn around and look. He pivoted on his heels and short-stepped toward the doors of the church. As he approached the doors, Reverend Sather's word rang out loud, painfully, in his ears.

"Cory Dean Petersen, I baptize you in the name of the Father, the Son, and the Holy Spirit, and commend you to God's protection and to His saving and sanctifying grace."

Thibideaux opened one of the doors and turned to look at Gabe. He expected to see a grin of victory. Instead, Gabe looked down at Cory Dean with tears streaming down his cheeks. Thibideaux didn't wait for the duplication of the rite for Deena Lee. He had to remove himself from a potentially difficult situation. Once again, he wanted to kill—really, really wanted to kill. He looked back at Gabe. To kill him right then and there. A hint of a grin tugged at his scars. In time he would, but not right now. When he did, it would be doubly sweet.

Thibideaux was on the rectory porch when Reverend Sather's words again rang in his ears.

"Ladies and gentlemen, it is my joy to introduce to you our newest members of God's family, Cory Dean Petersen and Deena Lee Petersen."

CHAPTER 58

THE RECEPTION AT the Herndon's Edge was well attended, to the point of spilling into the parking lot. The green jello mold surrendered its entire bounty less than halfway through the party, and Teddy had to retreat to the kitchen to restock the food platters three times. It seemed as though all residents of the Tricounties, save one, were in attendance.

Gabe was so overcome with joy he had trouble talking with anyone without getting emotional. He reflected on his happiness and attributed it to three things, in order of importance to him: he was deeply moved by the baptisms, he felt like an emotional weight had been lifted from his shoulders, and he had won the battle with Thibideaux. He had a feeling he would face the little man again, but for now, he had managed the sweetest victory of the war. Cory Dean was saved. All subsequent interactions would seem like minor skirmishes.

It was dark when Gabe, Wanna, Deena Lee and Cory Dean arrived home. Cory Dean was asleep in his car seat, next to Wanna, in the back seat of Deena Lee's Volkswagen, and Gabe was wedged into the front seat. As they went inside, Gabe scanned the horizon. There wasn't a wisp of fog as far as he could see in the dark.

With everyone preparing for bed, Gabe slipped into the kitchen to load the coffee pot for an early morning start-up. As he had done on Sunday evenings for the past several months, he took Wanna's pillbox and reached for the vitamin containers. Out of the corner of his eye, he noticed the familiar churn of a fog-in-motion against the kitchen window. But this fog didn't have the same "feel" as the previous ones. It didn't seem threatening. He couldn't quite place the feeling. It was something like inquisitiveness.

He opened a bottle and placed one large pill in each of the seven chambers of Wanna's weekly pill dispenser. He picked up a disk and started to punch out one of the small pills, but stopped. Have to do it now, he thought, and slipped the circular pill card into his jacket pocket. He closed the seven lids of the pill dispenser and put it next to the coffee machine, where Wanna would see it first thing in the morning.

The evening was the most placid one in weeks in the Petersen household—even Cory Dean seemed to put aside the colic to cuddle up to Deena Lee's chin and coo the evening away.

Gabe was in bed before eight-thirty, and he immediately fell into a deep sleep and into the land of dreams. But this time, his nocturnal fears weren't realized. His dream was of a brightly lit day with Wanna, Deena Lee, and Cory Dean sitting on a large blanket in the middle of a green meadow. Cory Dean was older, walking with outstretched arms and a clumsy, shuffling gait. A lavish picnic spread tempted everyone, including the local ant population. Everyone was happy, especially Gabe. There was only one troubling aspect to this dream. A small individual hoved in the distance. Only its outline was visible, and even that was partially obscured. The small being seemed to be carrying on some form of subliminal communication with Cory Dean, who responded with riffs of toddler giggles.

Gabe tried to move toward the being, but it managed to stay just out of sight—close enough to be noticeable, but far enough to defy contact. Despite the apparition, Gabe subdued any feeling of threat from the being. He decided to let Cory Dean have his fun, but keep an eye on him nonetheless.

His next dream wasn't so pleasing. He was in his truck, but he wasn't in control. It turned when it wanted to turn, ignoring his attempts to steer. All three pedals were locked. He turned the key to the off position, but the truck ran on. And the door handle wouldn't budge. He tried to crank the window down, but the lever turned without engaging the window. The path of the truck was a familiar one. It led to the rectory.

The truck stopped in front of the rectory porch and the driver's side door flew open. Gabe felt a pull on his body. He tried to resist, but he was powerless. Up the steps, through the double doors, and into the great room. He moved effortlessly, but without intent. Thibideaux stood beside his chair, staring at Gabe. And there was someone else there, in the shadows.

He drifted off.

CHAPTER 59

GABE STIRRED AND bright light filtered through his closed eyelids. He was glad it was morning. He turned, but something wasn't right. This wasn't his bed. It was a hard surface, the floor, and he was dressed, with shoes and jacket. Was he still dreaming?

Pushing on the floor, he propped himself up on his left elbow and a clearing image brought a shudder. Immediately in front of him was a fireplace, surrounded by a bare room. The rectory. He pushed harder, to a sitting position, and rubbed his eyes. Pain shot through his left knee. Not a dream. He turned his head and nearly toppled over.

"Good morning, Mr. Petersen. Surprised?" Thibideaux stood, leaning his right arm on the seat of his chair. To his left was a man dressed in a dark pinstripe suit, white shirt, dark tie. "I said you wouldn't get another chance."

"How did I get here?" Gabe said.

"You drove. Look out front. There's your truck." Thibideaux pointed out one of the front windows.

Gabe tried to scramble to his feet, but Thibideaux extended his left hand and Gabe's feet went out from under him. He came down on his left side, stirring the pain in his knee and ribs.

"Don't move," Thibideaux said. He turned to face the Councillor. "I suppose you're going to stop me, or did you come here to remind me of my recent failure? Both, right?"

"I'm here because the Organization wants me here. You may want to re-think your plans."

"I know I failed," Thibideaux said with an air of impatience. "I under-estimated this simian." He pointed in Gabe's direction. "It won't happen again, particularly since my secondary target is his child. Now I know who I'm dealing with, so I'll get him out of the way before he can interfere again."

The councillor stepped forward. "That's not the Organization's way. You know that."

"But it's the way in the field. You'd know that if you ever had to work out here." Thibideaux shouted, but his voice came out as a high-pitched northeasterner. "I have to make sure I get this secondary. I can't take any chances."

The councillor remained calm. "How much do you know about this secondary? Have you researched it?"

Thibideaux spun around to face the councillor. "I looked into it."

Gabe leaned up so his vision was vertical instead of horizontal. The two men were only a foot-and-a-half apart. The suited man towered over Thibideaux.

"Then you know this man and Ms. Wanna Petersen aren't brother and sister?" the councillor said, pointing Gabe's way. "Ms. Petersen's father was Mr. Gabe Petersen's uncle Raymond. He and his wife were killed in an automobile accident on the way home from the hospital after Ms. Petersen's birth. Gabe Petersen's parents took in their infant niece and raised her as their own."

Thibideaux's hands balled into fists and he stared at the councillor. He didn't say anything for what seemed like a century to Gabe. Thibideaux leaned against the chair again.

"Children of first cousins still make excellent CSCs. It's a high priority. I have all the paperwork. It'll probably become a provost."

Gabe squeezed his trunk muscles but his voice came out weak. "Not my cousin."

Both men turned to face Gabe. Thibideaux raised his left arm but the councillor caught it with his hand.

"What did you say?" the councillor said. "Speak."

Gabe pushed up on his elbow again and took a deep breath. "Neither of you did your research. Wanna's not my cousin. Her momma was pregnant before Uncle Ray married her. She wasn't Uncle Ray's. Her daddy's last name was Wanna." He leaned back down—his chest hurt when he leaned up.

"So the pregnancy isn't from siblings, or even

cousins? You're not related?" the councillor said. He lightened his grip on Thibideaux's arm.

"No pregnancy, either," Gabe said.

Thibideaux took a step toward Gabe. The councillor stayed at the little man's side, but his eyes were on Gabe, not Thibideaux.

Thibideaux's voice was almost as high-pitched as a child. "What do you mean there isn't a pregnancy?" His voice rocketed into a scream. "I made it happen in the hayloft. I was there."

Gabe reached in his jacket pocket and pulled out a circular disk. He slid it on the floor, over to the men. "Birth control pills," he said. "Been giving them to her since before the hayloft. One every day. She thinks they're vitamins." He looked up at Thibideaux. "The vitamins you told her to take." He expected an explosion, but instead he heard a child-like giggle. He looked up. It was the councillor whose face projected hate.

Thibideaux turned to the councillor. "You're feeling it, aren't you? Now, you know what it's like. You want to kill him? Be my guest. Now you know what it's like to be in the field. How does it feel? How do you like it?"

The councillor shook his head and turned away.

"Come on," Thibideaux said, his voice back to southern drawl. "We can do him together."

"No," the councillor said. He turned back to face Gabe. "The Organization doesn't allow it."

Thibideaux huffed and gave his left hand a backward flip.

Gabe slid backward across the floor. His head

stopped his momentum as it crashed into the wall with a thud. Darkness came fast and complete.

"Stop," the councillor said. "Our work is done in Area Four." He reached in his pocket and pulled out a cellular phone and punched numbers. Before the fourth beep, Thibideaux raised his left hand toward the councillor, who fell back, nearly losing his balance. The phone fell from his hand. Thibideaux closed the fist and the councillor's legs seemed to go limp.

The councillor put both hands out straight and pushed in Thibideaux's direction. Movement in his legs returned. He swung his head to the right and uttered a "Fizzzz" sound. The chair swung around to face Thibideaux. It vibrated, and with a crackling sound, it emitted small arcs of electricity between the arms and the seat.

Thibideaux struggled against the councillor's invisible force. He seemed to gain strength. The councillor shouted, "Haaah," and the chair threw a bolt of electricity that landed squarely in the front of Thibideaux's torso. The oscillating arcs maintained contact with his chest and slowly lifted him so his feet were held six inches off the floor. With the forced levitation, Thibideaux lowered his hands.

"I thought the chair was mine," he said in the whiny northeastern voice.

"The chair belongs to the Organization, as do you," the councillor said. "Now let me do what I have to do. We're through here."

Thibideaux spoke through gritted teeth. "What do you mean we? I'm the one who's going to be terminated."

The councillor kept his hands outstretched toward Thibideaux. "Don't you remember? Our fates are tied together on this one." He issued a muffled chuckle. "You shouldn't complain. You'll get the quick termination reserved for councillors, not the slow, painful one used on recruiters."

Thibideaux's expression changed from a sneer to its usual blank screen and his voice returned to that of a southerner. "If you have to do it, can I ask a question or two first? There's something I need to know before I go."

The councillor kept his grip, but softened his expression. "I guess there's no harm. But get on with it. If I don't call in the next few minutes, the whole rectory will be demolished and our demise will be on the painful side."

Thibideaux arched his eyebrows higher than usual. "Was I a CSC?"

The councillor frowned. "I'm familiar with your file. Are you sure you want this information? You may not like it once you hear it."

"Does it matter now?"

"I guess not," the councillor said. "Pardon my bluntness. You were the son of a Pennsylvania congressman, a citizen, and a Philadelphia prostitute, a Triple O. In other words, you were a normal primary target. Although normal isn't a good word for your procurement."

"What do you mean?"

The councillor turned serious. "Your mother hosted a suite of venereal diseases throughout her pregnancy. You were born almost two months early, at just over three pounds. If it weren't for the fast action of the Organization, you would have died. My guess is you can thank your mother for your appearance, but maybe for your powers as well."

Thibideaux paused to digest the information, then he became pensive. He noticed the councillor beginning to relax. "I have another question. Does the Organization appreciate what I've done? Have I served the Organization well?"

"Your longevity speaks to that question. You don't know it, but you're the oldest of all North American recruiters, past and present. There are some who are older in other parts of the world, but you're number one in these parts. You wouldn't be here if you didn't serve the Organization well." His expression brightened. "Although I shouldn't tell you this, I guess it doesn't matter now." He paused as if he expected to be struck down before he could forward his revelation. "Your technique for procurement at baptisms—it was so successful, and it increased the success rate in rural areas so much it was adopted as a normal part of the training regimen. It's named after you."

Thibideaux flashed a look of calm and stared into the councillor's eyes. He wanted to prolong the conversation a little longer. "Why have you been arguing on my behalf?"

"I've admired your work for some time. I thought you were still of value to the Organization."

"And that's it? You thought I was still of value, so you put your life on the line?"

The councillor looked at his watch. "There's more to it than that. It has to do with my own situation." He paused. "Obviously, I was a CSC—sixty-four years ago, in the State of Montana." He paused again. "Was I one of yours? I have a strange feeling I was."

Thibideaux's expression brightened. He enjoyed mentally out-dueling a foe more than he enjoyed bringing a foe to his knees with his powers. "If it was Billings, I believe I'm your man." He had never knowingly encountered one of his own procurements, particularly one of his CSCs.

"Then, can you tell me about my parents? Who were they? Why was I a CSC?"

Thibideaux was excited by the request, for more than one reason. His memory was keen on all of his CSCs. "If you're the one, your mother was also your sister." The twinkle in his eye remained long enough for the councillor to figure out the puzzle. "Your father molested your sister, who was also his biological daughter, and she became pregnant with you. What made it even more special—both were citizens. In most cases of incest, the molester is a Triple O. It's rare to find one that's a citizen, and even more rare for a pregnancy to result. You were a very high priority for the Organization back then." Thibideaux became serious. "I thought you'd go higher. A provost for sure."

The councillor looked down, his face reddened.

He reached for his phone.

"I have a final question," Thibideaux said. "Why did you stop a few minutes ago? You felt the hate, the desire to kill? Why didn't you finish him?" He pointed at Gabe, who stirred.

The councillor became business-like again. "You know as well as I do that power is only effectively used if it is controlled by logic and reason. It becomes dangerous if it's controlled by emotion, particularly anger or revenge. This is true of any organization, not just ours. Even though we'll be departing soon, we still have to think of the Organization to the last second. We owe it our lives. Now, if you don't mind, I have to check in or we'll not like the outcome."

CHAPTER 60

GABE STIRRED. HE felt pain. It was dull at first, but it came on stronger and stronger. And the light— it was turning up as if controlled by a rheostat. He blinked, and a regular, red pattern appeared. He tried to lift his head, but it throbbed with pain, and dizziness made the room swirl. Focus on the pattern. His mind was slow, but steady. Bricks? It clicked again. The rectory. The floor of the rectory, at the side of the fireplace. He looked beyond the hearth and saw two men standing face-to-face. One was Thibideaux, but he seemed taller than usual. He could only see them from the knees up, but Thibideaux was only a few inches shorter than the suited man.

The suited man held what appeared to be a phone. He lowered his right arm and Thibideaux shrank back to his normal height. The suited man pushed buttons on the phone, and Thibideaux pointed his right hand at the fireplace and then swung it around to point at the man. With a grinding sound, three bricks came loose from the fireplace, next to Gabe's head, and flew toward the man.

Gabe watched the first brick tear into the suited man's left knee, causing his leg to buckle. The second brick crashed into the man's left hand, removing three fingers and knocking the cellular phone to the floor. The third brick hit the man's head just above the right ear, indenting the skull with a loud pop. The impact toppled the already wavering man, and he fell to the floor, conscious but disoriented.

Gabe's head cleared like he'd just jumped into icy water.

"You and all the other councillors are no match for this lowly recruiter," Thibideaux said, and he extended both hands. A fireball flew toward the suited man, who rolled on his back and put out his right hand. The fireball stopped, mid-way between the two men, but inched toward the prostrate man. He put up his left hand, minus three fingers, and the fireball hovered again.

Gabe leaned up on his right elbow, then went to all fours. He wanted to run, but he was way too dizzy and nauseous. His head pounded with his pulse.

Thibideaux appeared to be straining against the power of the suited man. Gabe could see it in his face. It was like they were in some sort of surreal tug-of-war or arm wrestling match. The advantage was going to the suited man.

Thibideaux uttered a "Ha" and the chair whirred

around to face the suited man. It held its position, whirring slowly, its back-and-forth movement barely perceptible. It reminded Gabe of a cobra, ready to strike. With the chair homed in on the suited man, the fireball started to move in his direction. Thibideaux was winning.

Gabe raised his right foot to the floor, like he was preparing to run the 100-yard dash. His mind floated. He was back on the Boyston High football team, and he had the Calhoun quarterback in his sights. He pushed off with his right leg and flung his body forward, arms outstretched. He made contact with the chair, and it gave with his weight, toppling to the floor. The pain of the hardwood tore into his ribs, and he careened across the floor and into the opposite wall. His head hit again and his vision faded. On the way to black, he thought he heard the beep of cell phone buttons.

CHAPTER 61

PAIN, LIGHT, COLD. Gabe rolled on the hardwood floor and tried to recognize his surroundings. Not dead. He wondered why he expected death. He rolled onto his left side. The pain in his ribs squeezed a groan through his closed lips, again when he raised his head and looked around. A large room. Empty. "The rectory," he said out loud and tried to get up, but the pain from all corners of his body wouldn't let him. He rolled to his other side. The chair. Where is the chair? The room was empty. There was no chair. He tried to rise up to his right elbow, and succeeded, although it cost him pain-wise. The room was empty.

He inched across the floor toward the front doors but a shiny glint in front of the fireplace caught his attention. He turned and saw several reflecting sparks. Part of him said, crawl away fast, but from somewhere in the deep recesses of his memory, a voice told him to look closer. The latter won—he crawled to the fireplace and found two piles of what appeared to be ashes. The bright spots came from the far pile. He pulled himself over to it.

In the ash were several shiny metal blobs. He reached in his pocket and withdrew his Swiss Army knife, opened the large blade, and stirred the ashes. By his count, there were about twenty of the metal pieces—each was irregular in shape, but rounded. He stirred again, and one piece caught his attention. It was more squared than the others, but with the same rounded edges. Turning it over with the knife blade, the air left his lungs. It was the cap for a tooth.

Gabe collapsed onto his back and fought for breath, but it took a while to stabilize. His heart beat was fast, but regular. He rolled over and turned toward the door. As he pulled himself along the floor toward the front doors, he spoke to the room.

"Something bad."

CHAPTER 62

CATHERINE, THE RECEPTIONIST, entered the day room and walked over to the statue-like figure of Father Costello, who was seated in front of the window.

"I got some mail today from that man who came to visit you," she said. "It was addressed to me. He told me to hold this picture in front of your eyes and you would know what to do." She paused but there was no change in the father's expression. "Okay . . . here goes."

Catherine held the tattered piece of paper against the window, as instructed, in the direct sight line of Father Costello's blank stare. The letter said to hold it there for as long as necessary, whatever that meant. The picture was a freehand sketch of a strange looking face that Catherine didn't recognize. There was a large red "X" drawn through the face, and the word

"DEAD" was scrawled in red ink just below the face.

Catherine held the picture in place for a little over a minute, until her arms tired. She was just about to take it down when she noticed a change in the pupils of Father Costello's eyes. He didn't move or change his expression, but his eyes welled with tears. Fluid released and spilled down his cheeks.

"Father Costello. Are you here? Are you all right?"

A tear fell from the priest's jaw and landed on his left hand, which was folded with the right one on his lap. His eyes defocused again.

CHAPTER 63

TEDDY SHUFFLED THE cards, put them down, and filled his glass with Jack. "Glad to have you back, Billy. How's it going up in Rother, you traitor?" He chuckled as he picked up the cards and resumed shuffling.

"The shop's doing good. I hardly have time to myself. May have to hire somebody."

"I heard the women are pretty nice in Rother," Gabe said. "Anything on the line?"

"Strange thing. Misty showed up a few weeks ago. Said she wanted to go out."

Teddy leaned forward, his elbows on the table. "How was she?"

"She seemed fine. Same as always."

"No. I mean how was she?"

"Oh, that." Billy looked at Doc, then back at Teddy. "I didn't go with her. I've got my eye on a cutie. She's the mail lady. Always brings my mail at lunchtime, so we have a bite together."

"A bite?" Teddy said.

"Does your mind go anywhere else?" Gabe said. He flicked a popcorn kernel at Teddy.

Teddy let loose a belly laugh. "Billy's the only one left without it. We got to live the moment through him."

Gabe leaned toward Teddy. "I think those are shuffled enough. And it's my turn to deal." He reached across the table and his shirtsleeve rose up his arm.

"Whoa. Where'd you get that?" Doc said, touching a finger to Gabe's bruised bicep. "You run into some more kids from Rother?"

"Wanna got me."

"What'd you do, tell her she couldn't see Doc anymore?" Teddy said.

Doc laughed. And blushed.

Gabe bit his lip. "Naw. I played a trick on her and she just found out. She didn't think it was funny. I'm lucky this is all I have to show for it."

All three men leaned in.

"What'd you do?" Billy said.

"If I tell, she'll make this look like a love tap. So get off it. I ain't telling."

"Does it have anything to do with the new pickup?" Billy said.

Teddy grabbed a fist of popcorn. "That's a nice one. You rob a bank?" He stuffed the popcorn into his mouth.

"It was time," Gabe said. "Four doors and a back seat are good for the family."

"And plenty timely," Doc said. "Tell Deena Lee the test came back positive. She's definitely pregnant."

Gabe dropped the cards. "What?"

"You don't know?"

"Deena Lee's pregnant?" Gabe said. His rounded mouth twisted into a grin.

"Oh, hell," Doc said. "I thought you knew about it. God. Don't tell Deena Lee that I told you. She'll give me an arm to match yours."

Gabe settled back in his chair and put his hand over his mouth. His eyes couldn't hide his smile. "I won't tell her. I'll let her surprise me." His mind went to his recent dream and the vague being off in the distance.

"Looks like we have something to celebrate to-night," Teddy said. "Here's to the newest Petersen."

Gabe touched his bottle of Pepsi to the three glasses of Jack.

<u>EPILOGUE</u>

<u>MEMORANDUM</u>

DATE: November 12, 2005
TO: Councillor USA-4-3778
FROM: Provost Council # 21
RE: Approval for Procurement of Infant Recruit

Father: Johnathan Robinson, Citizen.
      Calhoun Township
Mother: Misty Lee Rondelunas, Triple O.
      Calhoun Township
Approximate time of birth: June 2006
Priority: Moderate
Assignment: Recruiter USA-427301025

Notes: (1) The above-referenced Recruiter is a trained mechanic. A position will be advertised at Billy Smyth's Mechanical Shop in Calhoun Township. (2) It is recommended that 427301025 receive refresher training in technique 77411 for rural procurements since his previous experience has been in mid-sized cities.
Ms. Rondelunas' file will be forwarded.

Don't miss Richard Satterlie's next novel
from Medallion Press:

Agnes Hahn

August, 2008

ISBN: 9781933836454
Mass Market Paperback
US $7.95 / CDN $9.95
www.medallionpress.com

For more information
about other great titles from
Medallion Press, visit

www.medallionpress.com